Dreamkill

by

Michael Davies

Dreamkill

This is a work of fiction.
All characters and events portrayed in the book are
fictional.
Any resemblance to real persons or events is purely
coincidental.

For information address: mickiedaltonbooks@lycos.com

First Published in 1996 in the USA
Second Edition Published in Australia November 2008

ISBN: 978-0-9923422-0-3

Published by The Mickie Dalton Foundation
NSW
Australia

To my two sisters, Shula and Deborah

Nobody could be more fortunate with siblings than I was

Other Books by Michael Davies

The Nightmares of God
The Janus Conspiracy
Accounts of a Killing
A Friendly Killing
Ready, Steady, KILL!
Helix Dreams

For the Young Adults (12-18)
The Many Worlds of Mickie Dalton
The Many Galaxies of Mickie Dalton
The Many Universes of Mickie Dalton

For the 8-12 age group
The Julie Malloy Gang and the Smugglers
The Quest for the Locket
The Secret of Yuri Kirilenko
The Secret of Charlotte's Cello
The United Nations and the Extra-Terrestrial
The Star of the Yshan Kings
The War of the Yshan Empire
The Star of the New Yshan Empire
The Red Fog of Time
The Mysterious Recorder and the Door to Elsewhere
Prisoners of the Picture
The Strange World of Mark and Anna
A Step Into the Past
What Can't Be Seen Can Exist

For the Little Ones (3-5)
Mary's World

And in non-fiction
The Business School Approach to Writing Your Novel

Chapter 1

Dan Bailey died on a Thursday afternoon at five o'clock. The process was intensely uncomfortable, accompanied by vomiting, a headache like Vesuvius erupting, and a cramping of every muscle he had.

His death was watched impassively by a middle-aged man of stocky build, bald head and a flat, peasant face. As Dan went through the dreadful business, huddled up and retching in the corner of the office, all he could see of his executioner were his argyle socks above black, wingtip shoes. When it was over, the middle-aged killer called the building janitor to come and clean up the mess, pulled Dan back to his seat and gave him a drink of water from the carafe on the shelf behind the expansive executive desk. Dan sipped the water tentatively, grimacing at the acrid taste of vomit in his throat. When he had finished, when his world stopped shaking, when the cramps in his gut subsided, and when the janitor had completed his distasteful task, the man who had once been Dan Bailey stared across the desk and croaked through the pain in his temples, "Jesus Christ, Carson, just what the hell am I? And who in God's name are you?"

* * *

The day was much like any other day, no indications that the end of Dan Bailey's life was just a few weeks away. Soon after eight in the morning, he entered the marble-walled lobby of the office block across from the

First Bank of Chicago. The elevator took him to the twenty-second floor, and he walked past the empty reception desk to his office down one corridor. As always, he felt a streak of pleasure on entering his working place.

The room was big enough to hold a large desk, two filing cabinets, and a circular conference table with four chairs around it. A calendar from the Royal Air Force Museum in Hendon, England showed a painting of a World War II Lancaster Bomber flying through stormy clouds escorted by a Hurricane Fighter. A personal computer on the desk had a laser printer attached to it, and one window looked out onto the square in front of the city administrative offices. The opposite wall was a glass panel from floor to ceiling.

On the other side of the panel, the untended oblong shapes of a series of computer racks and other boxes stood silently, no indication of the many millions of electronic instructions that were being followed every second inside them. Dan slid into the comfortable seat behind his desk. Almost as he did, the telephone rang, and the day launched itself into the standard busy, interesting, sometimes frustrating series of activities that kept Dan at work as the Director of Information Systems.

He spent an hour preparing job evaluation sheets for the salary and performance reviews that he would be conducting with his analysts and programmers next month. That task completed, he keyed in the instructions on his desk top personal computer that let him log into the nation-wide network of systems and checked the status of all the computers around the country, read the electronic mail messages that had been sent to him, responded to them, and wrote a few more of his own.

The rest of the day passed at the usual furious rate. He interviewed a number of young men and women for a vacant position as a programmer, and decided to offer jobs to two of them who seemed to have enough sense of humor to match their technical skills. He spent an hour with the Financial Controller polishing up the data processing budgets for the next quarter, and eventually returned to contemplation of a problem he had been wrestling with for some days, whether to use existing Chicago staff on a new system in Kansas City, or plan for a permanent installation there. He switched on the personal computer, called up the electronic spreadsheet software and began to crunch some cash flow numbers to compare relative personnel costs.

Lunch was a rapid sandwich and a cup of coffee at his desk, working with the Personnel Officer on a new salary structure for the Systems Department. In the afternoon, he met with a variety of salesmen, technicians, some of his systems analysts and network engineers and the accounting supervisor on a problem in the General Ledger system.

Finally, he returned to his desk and the complex cash flow model he had built for analyzing comparative costs of the Kansas City project. The number crunching went on till seven in the evening when Dan finally stretched the cramps out of his shoulders and arms and left the blue screen and white numbers for another day.

Emily met him at the door with a warm smile and a tulip glass of champagne, an endearing routine that for Dan had improved the process of homecoming immeasurably. He dropped his briefcase on the floor, put one arm around her slender waist, and made a major dent in the quantity of Veuve Cliquot. It fizzled on his tongue as good champagne should, then he kissed her firmly, pushing the door closed behind him with a backward shove of his heel.

"Mmm," she said appreciatively. "That stuff's better than Listerine any time!"

They repeated the process to make sure, and Dan squeezed her waist a little tighter. The firm line of her hip under his hand felt erotically smooth.

"You make it difficult to work late, dear lady," he said, taking another sip of the champagne, and handing the glass back to her. A delicious smell of roasting chicken reached him, and competed with her perfume without rancor.

"That's my function," she said gravely. "I make you withstand temptation and learn self discipline!"

With a laugh, Dan finally let her go, and they walked to the main bedroom of his apartment on the north side of Chicago's lakeside. After only two weeks of living together, they had already developed some routines, and easy conversation in the bedroom while Dan changed was a simple but pleasant one. He sat on the white bedspread of the emperor-size platform bed while he removed his shoes, then stood up and gratefully took off the expensive, European-cut suit, sighing with relief as the air conditioning reached his skin. He hung the suit away in the walk-in closet, wondering as always what Emily saw in him.

Barely five-foot-nine if he took a deep breath, dark brown hair, reasonable complexion, hazel eyes that he thought were perhaps his best feature, and lips that she had always told him were sensuous, but failed to impress him as anything other than a device to stop the mouth from fraying at the edges. He had a body of average shape, he thought, a body that had always served him well in sporting activities, but would never let him challenge a real athlete. True, there was little fat, and the chest and shoulders had definite muscularity, but he hardly felt like Michelangelo's David. In contrast, Emily had the loveliness that radiated from models on the covers of the sort of exotic fashion magazines that caused men to linger over their purchase of the *Wall Street Journal* at the news rack so that they could indulge in small fantasies. Dan was baffled by the thought that this woman who could have had her pick of men, had chosen him.

He stopped worrying about the mystery and returned to the bedroom carrying the jeans and sloppy shirt he intended to wear. She was sipping the champagne, sitting in the silk covered Italian chair she had brought to the apartment when she had moved in.

"The red Jockeys again, I see," she murmured in the deliberately sensual style of a Mae West. "Are you trying to get me all stirred up, Bailey?"

Dan laughed at her deadpan expression and drew up the jeans pretending a false modesty. "Control yourself, woman," he said reprovingly. "This man has had a busy day. I need a hot meal and more of that bubbly stuff before rompies."

She chuckled and passed him the glass. He took another draught and returned it to her, pulling on the blue cotton shirt he had selected. It hardly matched her perfectly white silk slacks and bright red blouse, but Dan was comfortable leaving the task of being gorgeous to those best qualified.

Emily James was a regular freelance contributor to the business columns of the Chicago newspapers, usually writing on technical matters of computers and telecommunications, and her name was familiar to Dan the first time he heard her voice on his telephone. She was calling, she said, to ask about Dan's plans to implement a decentralised control system of warehouse systems on the company's network of tiny, sophisticated microcomputers.

"It's a highly interesting course of action, Mister Bailey," said the musical voice in his telephone.

Oof! thought Dan. *If she's even half as beautiful as she sounds, I'm in love.* She spoke with perfect diction, he thought, and a lilt that suggested musical training. The laughter was not quite suppressed by the polite tones she was using. He took a breath. "It's a highly cost-effective course of action, Miss James. We did some pretty hefty number-crunching on the data."

"Emily, please." The politely formal note had eased, and the warmth in her tones was distracting Dan from the point of the conversation. He was glad there was nobody else sitting in his office. "I will probably want to write an article on the subject if you approve," she continued. "Could I discuss the whole thing with you, maybe see the analysis you did to justify it?"

Dan swallowed and tried to make his voice sound calm, confident, and senior executive-like. "I'm sure that will be okay," he said. "Would you like to start with lunch?"

"I'd like that," she replied.

"Then why don't you come to my office at noon on Thursday?"

"Thursday, twelve o'clock it is," she said, and Dan hung up, feeling as if he had just made a date with the winner of a national beauty competition.

Two days later, she walked into Dan's office, a slim, elegant woman in a blue business suit, dark hair down to the shoulders, bright, intelligent eyes, and a smile that curved the sexiest mouth since Audrey Hepburn. Dan fell in love immediately. There was almost a crashing sense of homecoming, of familiarity, of knowledge that somehow he had been waiting for her for years. Lunch lasted till three, and she seemed no more eager than Dan to end it. Dinner followed lunch that day, dinner followed the next day, and bed followed the day after that. Within a week she had moved in. Dan soon found it hard to remember a life before Emily, certainly not anything of importance.

His clothing changed, they strolled from the bedroom to the blue-carpeted living room, the empty champagne glass still in her hand.

"We're rich again!" she said cheerfully as they reached the luxurious expanse that for Dan had been the chief reason for buying this condominium.

"I hadn't realized we'd been poor," he laughed.

"Destitute!" she said. "We're down to our last six cases of champagne."

"But now we can buy some more?" He watched the laughter chase across her face and felt his blood pound a little harder in his veins. *She's just so damn beautiful*, he thought.

"Crane's have offered me three thousand to do an article on electronic commerce through the internet," she said. "And there's a couple of other series they're planning for me."

"Wonderful! Another three thousand dollars will help the family finances nicely," he said. "That certainly means we can afford another drink of this bubbly stuff!"

He opened the fridge door, extracted the heavy bottle, and poured refills. They drank her health, arms around each other's waists and again tested the breath-cleansing qualities of the champagne with a lengthy kiss.

"Maybe we should brush our teeth with it?" suggested Dan, his breathing a little heavy. She chuckled, and slipped away from him before things got too steamy, bending down to the oven from where the smell of roast chicken was reminding Dan strongly that lunch had been a quick sandwich at his desk.

"About ten minutes," Emily said, looking up at him. "Just time to finish off my last article. To the study, sir!"

In the third bedroom that they had converted to a home office, he watched her transmit her latest article from her laptop computer to the newspaper's computer on Michigan Avenue. She switched off the machine, closed the lid, took a sip from her glass, and came into his arms. The shock of delight never seemed to fade, he thought. Her voice was slightly muffled under his right ear and her perfume issued subtle signals to his libido.

"So what about your day?" she murmured into the side of Dan's neck.

"Not much really," he said softly into her fine brown hair as it floated around his face. "Just your average grind. The usual problems, alligators in the washrooms, couple of suicides in the executive lounge, nuclear devices in the elevators, you know, that sort of thing."

She chuckled and clung a little tighter. Dan carefully put his glass on the desk between their two computers and wrapped his arms more firmly around her. They stood like that for a few minutes, Dan experiencing as always the wonder at her presence and his bewilderment at her choice of him.

She pulled away from him and her eyes opened wide. "The chicken!" she gasped, and raced for the kitchen. Dan followed and prepared the table. They had dinner, chatting comfortably in their usual manner, a gentle air of comfort and happiness wrapping Dan as it had for three months. They watched the local news, a movie on one of the cable TV channels, and went to bed at eleven. It had been the sort of evening that had become the happiest part of Dan's existence, and which he hoped would be a permanent feature for the rest of his life. The nightmare that hit him some time after midnight was the first indication that things were not that predictable.

The wind shrieked with a personal hatred and attacked me with vicious, lethally sharp claws. Despite the heavy sheepskin coat and thick boots, the cold hurt my arms, legs and chest, and chiselled with a sculptor's delicate slice at the small areas of my face that it could find exposed. I leaned into the pitiless force and followed the large, bear-like man in front of me, his rifle slung over his left shoulder, the massive fur coat making him like some prehistoric beast. He walked in front of me, keeping some of the force of the gale from me, stamping out a path through the snow that was already a foot deep. Even with his help, the passage was mercilessly hard, a nightmare of perpetually walking uphill with aching, trembling legs.

Under the agony of walking in this blizzard lay the fear of the next three days. The anxiety worried at my bowels, made the cold work outwards from my guts to meet the pain of the ice from the wind. I was going to meet the old man with the bright blue eyes again and I was afraid of the meeting.

The black, windowless building materialized out of the streaking snow, flashes of lights from the compound sentry posts marking out strands of racing flakes from the dark of the howling storm. The wind curled around it and struck us from both sides instead of from directly ahead, but no lessening in the cold could be felt. Snowflakes spun around us in the miniature whirlwinds and seemed to concentrate around the lights on the building's corners like insane moths that performed their mating dance in the depths of a hellish winter. The fear of the building, of the old man and what he would do to me bit deeper into my insides, but I had nowhere to run.

The huge man tramped round one side of the building, and we came to the heavy door. It was the only door to the building, and it was blank, formless, nothing but a solid metal monolith. The man unslung his rifle, and used the stock to bang three times on the metal slab. The sound was a dull thud, no echo from inside, the sound outside almost drowned by the shrieking wind. The man then moved behind me, as if in fear of what awaited us inside, but knowing that whatever it was, it waited for me alone. He had every right to be afraid, but only for me, not for him. The old man had no interest in him.

We waited in silence for nearly a minute, standing motionless in the dark and the cold and the insane winter moths of snow. My feet were numb, and the pain in my elbows had become a dulled, persistent ache. Almost, I would welcome the opening of that door. But when it did finally slide open, the fear in me rose to a crescendo, and I nearly broke and ran. But I knew there was nowhere I could go, and the crippling cold made even that building a better place to be.

The door slid fully open, and a dim light revealed a gloomy corridor, plain wooden floor and dirty, whitewashed walls. The old man with blue eyes was waiting for me.

Dan shouted in despair and woke up. Gasping and weeping, he fumbled for the light switch, and turned it, covering his eyes and feeling beads of perspiration on his face. Beside him, Emily came sharply awake. She sat upright, slid over to his side of the bed, and put her arm round his shoulder.

"Bad dream, my love?" she said. "I've never known you to have a nightmare before."

"Nor me," replied Dan, breathing easier, the lump of grief in his throat subsiding. "Not since I was a kid in England, anyway."

"What was it about?" she asked. "Can you remember?"

"Snow and ice," said Dan, struggling with fast-fading images. "Something about struggling through a blizzard to a building. You know those dreams where you're always trying to get uphill? It was like that."

"Yes, I've had those myself," she said, and kissed his cheek. "I think they're supposed to mean you're having some stress at work, or something like that."

"Hell, if that's all it means, I'd have them every day," Dan replied and tried to laugh. The images had almost gone, leaving only a sense of fear and helplessness. He stood up. "Go back to sleep, sweetheart," he said. "I'll make myself a hot drink, and join you again in a few minutes."

He looked at her, and for a moment saw an expression of serious worry. He bent down and kissed her. "I'm okay," he said, and touched her cheek. She turned her head and kissed the palm of his hand. "Go to sleep," he said again, and turned the light off. As he moved to the door, she slipped under the sheet and slid over to her own side of the bed.

Dan went to the kitchen, made a hot cocoa drink, and stood thoughtfully by the refrigerator for a few moments as he drank it, but the dream had faded completely. He went back to bed, and was asleep in a few minutes.

Later that night, Dan awoke again with a sense of being called from a great distance. He turned over and found Emily's half of the bed empty. Coming awake rapidly, he heard the quiet weeping in the next room. Worried, he slipped on the light robe Emily had given him the day she had moved into his apartment, and padded into the living room. She was curled up in the red wing-back chair, dressed in one of his old business shirts.

Dan kneeled in front of her and took her hands. "This is not like you at all, my love," he said, trying to make his tone light.

She mumbled something, swung her feet on the floor, put her arms around his neck and leaned forward to rest her head on his shoulder. A wisp of smooth dark hair floated over Dan's nose and mouth and he blew it away. He felt the dampness of tears against his neck.

"I've never been so frightened about losing anyone before," she whispered.

"You have the weirdest way of paying a man a compliment," replied Dan, stroking the back of her head.

He was rewarded by the faintest of chuckles and her grip tightened on his neck. "Why should you be losing me anyway?" he continued, feeling happy with her closeness. "You'll have to work a damn sight harder than this to get rid of me!"

She rubbed her face against his cheek. "I'm just being silly, I know," she said. "Maybe I'm pre-menstrual or something."

"Or something," he agreed. He changed his grip and swung her onto his lap. "Now if I can just stand up under all this load..." He tried and failed ignominiously to sweep her up and instead collapsed all over the floor with both of them giggling like children. It broke the mood and she smiled as Dan slipped his right arm under her and held her tight. She smiled even more when he pulled back his arm, gently unbuttoned the top of the old shirt she was wearing and touched the nipple of her left breast. It rose up against his hand, and her breathing came a little harder. He began to stroke her breast and somehow the rest of the shirt was unfastened and they were both breathing hard, and his robe had vanished, and they lost themselves in the heat and passion that they had always generated.

As she cried out at some point, and he hugged her close as he gasped his own release, he was thinking again how incredible it was that she should be with him, almost as if dictated by some outside force. Then he lost that strange thought in the wonderment of the peace and loveliness of holding her close as she trembled slightly and hid her face in his neck, and their sweat mingled as closely as their bodies had just done.

Chapter 2

A few days later, Dan took a break from the daily grind of running the computer facilities at MidWestern, and went on a one-day conference at the Marriott Hotel. These were regular events, useful not just for gathering information, but meeting many of the business heavyweights in the USA.

The morning was the usual format. Crowds of men in business suits and a respectable leavening of the mix with smartly-dressed women of all ages gathered for the coffee and danish cakes laid out in the lobby of the fifth floor while registration took place. Groups who knew each other clustered in protective huddles, the unfortunates who knew nobody stood alone and drank their coffee, trying to look cool and unconcerned, looking carefully for a familiar face to break their isolation.

As always, a number of computer types were present, and Dan found himself chatting easily with a sales executive from Sun Systems, a communications specialist from Oracle, and the branch manager from a software house based in Oakbrook. All three of them knew Emily personally, having read her material and sometimes contributed to her research, and Dan had met them all on other professional occasions, so they talked as friends.

At nine, the bells rang to summon everyone into the main conference where they received an almost evangelical greeting from a one-time Super Bowl quarterback who now ran a public relations firm out of Baltimore. A pair of papers on business communications and organizational strategy started the real business of the day, one from an English professor of business administration at Harvard who spoke with an accent that was, for Dan, a pleasantly familiar Manchester sound. A presentation from a Californian consultant who ran her own computer industry analysis business rounded out the morning, and it was time for lunch.

The dining room was divided into a number of circular tables, each seating ten. Dan took a gap in one and found himself sitting next to a man about his own age. He was tall with jet black hair, extraordinarily brilliant eyes, and he greeted Dan with a pleasant smile. "Hello, I'm Kevin Fitzpatrick," he said. That agreed with his nametag on the left side of his chest, Dan saw. "Caradoc Metals," said the second line.

"Dan Bailey," Dan replied and they shook hands.

Fitzpatrick peered at Dan's nametag. "MidWestern?" he said. "I've heard of you."

"I would hope so!" Dan said with a grin. "We're pretty big! And we're one of your larger customers too."

Fitzpatrick laughed pleasantly. "That much I know! But I was talking about your firm to one of my Vice-Presidents the other day. He'd read about the warehouse management system you'd implemented."

Dan laughed. "He approved, I hope?"

Fitzpatrick laughed. "Very much so. He's talking to the suppliers as we speak!"

They paused while a waiter placed the standard conference lunch plate of chicken, broccoli and mashed potatoes on the table. While Dan poured a glass of wine and unwrapped his knife and fork from the table napkin, he suddenly remembered who Kevin Fitzpatrick was; not just a senior executive of Caradoc Metals, a metal-working plant of some considerable size based in Bloomington, about a hundred miles south of Chicago, Fitzpatrick was the president. The firm had a reputation for being an excellent corporate citizen, funding a number of successful programs for retraining workers, and providing remedial education for the kids who so badly needed it.

"What's your position at MidWestern, Dan?" Fitzpatrick asked, as he broke a slice of bread off the loaf in the middle of the table.

"I'm not sure I dare admit it," said Dan. "But I'm the director of information systems."

"Really?" Fitzpatrick looked sharply at him. "So it was you that put the system in?"

They were ignoring the rest of the table, which was impolite, Dan worried, but two or three of the others were listening in on their conversation.

"In that case, we need to talk," said Fitzpatrick. "We've got some tricky problems with our stock control systems in Bloomington."

"I'd be delighted," said Dan. "Why don't we finish lunch and go and grab a corner in the lobby somewhere?"

"Great!" said Fitzpatrick and bent to tackle the chicken. Dan did the same, and they finished the half hour talking lightly with others around the table while Dan tried to remember what he could about Kevin Fitzpatrick.

His wife was a practising pediatrician, he recalled, a one-time Miss Illinois. Despite the almost too perfect image of classic Mr. and Mrs. Successful Corporate America, they had the reputation of being truly nice people. Caradoc was an excellent employer with some advanced practices that resulted in a high employee loyalty, always a good business practice.

After leaving the coffee and cookies, Dan and Fitzpatrick strolled into the lounge area and by mutual agreement decided to miss the next presentation, something on distributed warehousing systems. Instead, they found a corner of the lounge, took a pair of armchairs, and talked data processing for an hour, and they both clearly enjoyed the discussion. When they had finished, they shook hands with genuine friendship and returned to the conference.

That evening, Dan had a lot of pleasure telling Emily about the meeting. Curiously, she seemed to turn the discussion away from the topic of Kevin Fitzpatrick, and poured two glasses of champagne. She pulled Dan into the lounge and pushed him into the settee, snuggling up to him. Dan forgot about the subject of the day's encounter and Emily's seeming reluctance to discuss it, and relaxed in the pleasure of the contact.

"You're a fascinating mixture, Dan Bailey," she said. "And I get a bit confused about your history sometimes. After all, we've only been living together a couple of weeks and we seem to have spent all our time doing other stuff!"

Dan chuckled. "And I've enjoyed every second," he said. "I always thought we could get round to our histories later."

Emily laughed and took a sip of the champagne. "I know you were born in England," she said. "But I don't know much of your beginnings."

Dan copied her action with the contents of the tulip champagne glass. "Yes, I was born near Birmingham," he said. "At least, I think so, that's where I was found."

"Found? You never told me that." Emily raised her head from Dan's shoulder and looked at him.

"The police found me wrapped in newspapers by the library when I was about three days old," said Dan. "My mother had obviously left me there, but we never found out who she was."

"How terrible!" Emily touched his cheek softly.

"Not really. I was adopted by a young couple and was brought up by them as if I had been their own child."

"Any brothers and sisters?"

"No," said Dan. "I used to regret that, but my parents had never seemed to want another kid, and poured all their love onto me."

"And you grew up in.. where did you say?.. Birmingham?" She leaned back against his shoulder.

"No," replied Dan. "When I was ten, my father got a job as an electrician with the Granada television network in Manchester, and we moved up there."

"And you went to school there?"

"Yes, at the Central Grammar School."

"Then university?"

"Not at first," said Dan. "I spent a year travelling around Europe on my motorbike, then managed to get to Australia for a year doing anything I could, driving vans, working in a supermarket, all that sort of stuff, then I came back to England. I'd done okay in school, so I was able to get into Birmingham University, got a degree in Economics."

Emily got up from the settee and took their glasses, which were almost empty. She walked to the kitchen and refilled them from the bottle in the fridge. When she returned, she curled up on the floor at Dan's knee and passed him the refilled glass. He smiled, stroked her hair, and took a drink.

"Any more of my history you need?" he asked with a smile. For some reason that disturbed him, she didn't return the smile.

"How did you end up in the States?" she asked.

Trying to ease the tiny undercurrent of concern that ran through him at her coolness, Dan answered. "When I graduated from Birmingham," he said, "I went through the usual round of applications for a job, but a small computer company in London head-hunted me and offered me a position as a programmer."

"Unusual," said Emily thoughtfully. "Why would they do that for a totally inexperienced person?" She looked up from her position on the floor.

"I had often wondered the same thing myself," replied Dan. "The company almost picked me out of a crowd as if they actually knew me. It was quite strange."

"I'd say so," said Emily. She seemed preoccupied by something. "Could they have heard about you in some way?"

"Don't know," said Dan. "I'd got pretty good programming aptitude test results at university, so maybe they saw them."

"That must have been it," said Emily, and took a deep gulp of the champagne. She burped slightly, and giggled. It broke the minute tension that her thoughtfulness was causing in Dan. "Then what happened?" she continued.

"They were a subsidiary of an American software house," said Dan. "After three years they offered me a transfer to Cleveland, and I took it. I like travel, and I'd always wanted to come to the USA. They arranged my green card and I spent six years with them as systems manager. They gave me some assignments in Europe and Australia, and also one in Singapore, so I got a great chance to see some of the world. They were pretty good to me, because when I was ready to move on, they found me my present position."

"Do you plan on staying?" Emily's voice was a little muffled, and Dan touched her cheek.

"Dearest Emily," he said. "How could I live anywhere else if you're here?" She turned to look up at him, and he smiled, thankful that the odd tension was over. "I like England," he continued, "and I want to do the whole tourist thing with you some day soon. I want to show you my favourite places, visit some great pubs, and show off how brilliantly I can drive on the left with a manual gearshift. But considering the life we have here, how could I possibly want to go back to England?"

She snuggled up to his knees and curled her arms round his legs. "Good," she said. "I think it's time to go to bed!"

"A splendid idea," laughed Dan. He bent down and kissed the top of her head. She reached up and wrapped her arms round his neck, and it took quite a time before they finally reached the bedroom. An hour later, they fell into a happily exhausted sleep, and Dan's last coherent thought as he drifted into the deepest of sleeps, was the one he had so often. Why had this incredible woman chosen him?

* * *

His dreams were happier that night. The discussion with Emily must have triggered them, and when the extra champagne he had drunk made its pressures felt some time in the middle of the night, he reflected back on the dream of childhood he had been having when he woke up.

Oh, Les and Freda, how I miss you! The stocky, happy, so alike people who took such delight in their child that I returned their happiness with my own. The house was my heaven, I always ran the last mile home from school and would hang on the arms of my mother until my father got home some time later, then I would rush to him for more of the same. His wine-making hobby filled the house with strange smells, and I would wake in the night to the gloop-gloop-gloop of the wine fermenting in the huge glass carboys in the basement, the attic, or any spare spot, feeling safe, secure and wanted. Mother would get regular passions for baking, and then the smells of hot cakes and pies drove out the odors of fermenting wine for a few days, and the house would later fill up with neighbors coming for an impromptu party to eat the massive excess of food she had prepared.

I loved you both and will always love you, even if you died over ten years ago.

As dawn lightened the walls round the edges of the dove-grey blinds, Dan experienced some more sweet memories of childhood.

Christmas was wonderful at home. All the neighbors came in and sampled Father's range of home-made wines. He wore a paper hat and kept walking around with several bottles begging people to sample the different flavors. He made wine of flowers, of vegetables, of odd fruits. There was rose wine, dandelion wine, orange wine, apple wine, everything he could find. He was a popular man in Walsall, President of the Wine Society, and his wine was only equaled by Mother's home-baked pies. Our house was so much fun, so much laughter. On Christmas Eve, I went to bed but couldn't sleep for the excitement of wondering what Father Christmas would bring me, and I was convinced I could stay up all night and wait for him. I woke up in the morning, and the pillowcase stuffed with parcels was hanging from the end of the bed.

Christmas Day was full of excitement, of people coming in to see us, of presents being opened, of toys to play with, and eventually collapsing in front of the television to watch the Queen's Christmas Message. I liked to sit between both parents to watch, alternately leaning up against each of them. Mother smelled of fresh soap, and sometimes she would pick me up and cuddle me on her lap. Other times, I saw them watching me when I played with my toys, and they seemed to be happy. I loved Christmas. When we moved to Manchester, it didn't seem to take long before the neighbors called in just as they had in Walsall. Les and Freda were that sort of couple.

I passed my school exams well, and when I was just eleven years old, I went to the Central Grammar School on Whitworth Street, almost in the center of Manchester. Classes were held all over the building, and we seemed to be constantly racing from the gymnasium in the basement to the chemistry classrooms six floors up or to levels in between. The girls' school was next door, actually the same building, but separated by locked doors. A lot of time was spent surreptitiously looking through the keyholes, or leaning out of the windows to watch the girls in their school-yard.

At lunchtime, we could leave the grounds, and often, I walked with friends up to the railway station, or over the canal to the little food shops in the area and bought a pork pie and a drink. Sometimes, we would sit in the little park next to the school and watch the girls, who were not allowed out, but sat on benches in their own garden next to the park, or walked around and looked out at the boys. My friend John, who was twelve, was utterly obsessed by one girl of about fourteen who had enormous breasts. He would talk about her, gasping for breath as we raced between classes on the many floors of the building. But he was too shy about his spotty face and protruding teeth ever to try and talk to her. I secretly longed to meet the slim one with the graceful walk and long black hair. She had a nice smile. But I never talked to her, either.

The news on the radio at six-thirty broke the warm memories, and Dan and Emily rose to meet another day.

Chapter 3

Three weeks later, Dan was again at home in the evening, enjoying a quiet relaxed time with Emily. Business pressures were still high, but basically routine, so he was able to switch off the tension at home. They had finished dinner, loaded the dishwasher, and carried their champagne glasses into the lounge.

Dan leaned back in the sofa, and Emily snuggled up against his shoulder while he switched on the television with the remote control. The nine o'clock news had just started. They sat through the usual round of political stupidities, Chicago violence and the sports roundup, then got to the business news.

"Nice to have you back, love," Dan said softly to the mass of dark hair on his left shoulder. She kissed his cheek in response, and they took another sip of shooting stars from the tall tulip glasses. Emily had been away on a short trip to Minneapolis for two days to research some technical material, and this was her first evening back, so it was an extra pleasure for both of them to relax together again.

"The take-over campaign by the Hanfield Group for Caradoc Metals is heating up," said the thin-faced man on the television screen. "By all accounts, it's a hostile take-over which Caradoc is resisting strongly."

Dan felt a sharp shock go through him. Somebody was taking over Caradoc? He could not see Kevin Fitzpatrick allowing that at all. The discussion with Fitzpatrick some weeks before had left Dan with the impression of a man who gave in to nobody. Beside him, Emily stirred. She too, was looking at the screen intently, and her expression was almost of anger.

"Oh, God, I hope not," she said, her voice scratchy with the tension.

"Me too," Dan answered. He looked down at Emily. She was sitting forward, staring at the screen where the reporter was reading off some financial data on the battle. She seemed more affected by the news than Dan would have expected.

"Emily?" he said. "Are you okay?"

"What? Oh..." She looked round at him then tried to smile. "Yes, I'm fine," she said. "It's just that I think taking over Caradoc would be a disaster for the people in Bloomington."

"Then let's hope Fitzpatrick can fight it off," Dan murmured, pulling her head back onto his shoulder.

The sports commentator came back on to chat endlessly about the Cubs' game with the Giants, and Dan forgot about the Caradoc takeover for a while.

Over the next three weeks, he followed the battle with interest. The company trying to take over Caradoc was the Hanfield Group, a huge conglomerate in Chicago. Despite the massive financial resources of the Hanfield Group, the battle was a stalemate. Caradoc's shareholders were showing exceptional loyalty and rejecting the offers made by the Hanfield Group. By the end of August, the *Wall Street Journal* was writing off the takeover attempt as a failure. But then...

An evening at home again. Dan had worked late the previous night, not returning home until nearly two in the morning, a rare but not unknown requirement of the job, and he was feeling weary. They had dinner, some easy chatter, more champagne, then snuggled on the sofa to catch the television news.

"Police are totally unable to understand the motives behind the murder late last night of Kevin Fitzpatrick, the president of the Caradoc Metals Company in Bloomington," said the middle-aged announcer with the authoritative look of a senior business executive. The scene shifted to a stretch of highway.

"Mister Fitzpatrick was shot sometime after eleven on this stretch of Route 51, just south of Bloomington. He was returning home from a business banquet in Decatur, when, police believe, the rear tires of his car were shot out, probably by a shotgun. They think that when he got out to investigate, somebody shot him through the head with a heavy-caliber handgun."

"Oh my God!" exclaimed Dan. An inexplicable wave of horror ran through him. Beside him, Emily was rigid. She slowly put her glass down on the coffee table.

"Police have no motive for the killing," continued the newsreader. "The body was found lying by the side of the car at three in the morning, a wallet containing cash and credit cards was still in his jacket. No clues have been found so far..."

Emily burst into tears and buried her head in Dan's shoulder. It took twenty minutes before she was calm enough to talk, but she could not give any reasons for her distress. Not that Dan's own horror was any less. He had met the man and liked him. He wondered what effect this would have on the take-over battle.

Two days later, they knew. The Caradoc shareholders collapsed and the take-over was complete. Vincent Carson, the president of the Hanfield Group was interviewed by the journalists, and he expressed his own shock and horror at the events.

Dan watched the broadcast on the ten o'clock news on NBC a few days later. The flat, immobile face of Vincent Carson looked more like a hillbilly farmer than the chief of a multi-billion dollar business, thought Dan, and something in him felt a startling hostility to the man. Dan didn't quite join in the few rumblings of conspiracy that were heard, but certainly felt some resentment at Carson's fortune in the battle that clearly he had been losing.

The rumblings and the hostility did nothing to prevent the takeover, however, and within a few weeks, Caradoc had vanished into the capacious maw of the Hanfield Group, and the sound and fury faded. Like most others, Dan eventually shrugged it off under the pressure of day-to-day living.

Life was sweet. Emily and Dan grew closer as the weeks of living with each other stretched into months. Occasionally, they both experienced some tensions over their jobs, but it was always forgotten in the daily delight of meeting at home, of the giggles and cuddles, and of the breathless, startling passion of their lovemaking.

Until September.

* * *

They spent a beautiful Sunday driving around the lake into Michigan and up to Benton Harbor looking at the first glorious colours of fall. By six, they had returned home, slightly sleepy from the sunshine and the walking, and Emily prepared dinner of fresh fish and salads. Dan opened another case of Veuve Cliquot and carried a couple of bottles from the den to the refrigerator to replace the chilled one he opened for dinner. By ten, they were barely holding their eyes open, and by mutual agreement weaved their way to the bedroom. Neither of them was up to making love, and after a few sleepy chuckles fell heavily asleep.

The dream that night was worse than anything Dan had ever experienced before, so vivid it was almost life-like.

The phone rang in the darkness. I groped for it, nearly dropped it, and mumbled something, vaguely noting the time was three o'clock, as displayed by the red digits on the clock radio. At the other end, the female voice was sharp, aggressive.

"Misha, listen to me," said the voice. "Consider doing something special for the Party." The words were Russian, but I knew them and woke up totally.

"I'm listening," I said, clearly. I got clear instructions on the mission, and the telephone at the other end was gently replaced.

The early evening of the next day, I took the train instead of the regular bus and got off at Argyle Street, several stops north of my Lake Shore Drive home. I walked through the Vietnamese enclave that flourished there, for the first time ever failing to be tempted by the smells of the local restaurants, carried on the few yards to Broadway, turned south and entered the car rental office. I produced the forged driver's licence and American Express card, signed the name Alan J. Killian to the forms and took the Ford Taurus from the side street where they pointed it out to me. I drove in the heavy evening traffic on Lake Shore Drive, turned onto Interstate 55 and carried on south. At Bloomington, I turned onto Route 51 and after only a few hundred yards, drove off the main route into a side road and parked under the trees. The time was ten o'clock. I sat in the dark and waited.

I stirred when a whisper from the radio lying on the passenger seat called me. I started the car and returned to within a hundred yards of Route 51. The rest of the way I walked, carrying the Remington 870 shotgun and the Smith & Wesson .38 pistol I had taken from the trunk. The moon was almost new, the light was limited.

"The next car," the small voice said from the radio in my breast pocket. The car whispered along the road

towards me, only the headlights seen. I turned my head away to protect my night vision, and as the car passed me, I pointed the shotgun at the rear tires and pulled the trigger. The explosion seemed to rock the world, and the light from the barrel illuminated the rear end of the car and the road for several yards. The car swerved, swung into the middle of the road, then lurched onto the shoulder and stopped. A man got out. I walked up to him. He turned.

I shot him in the head.

Dan woke up, gagging on the pool of blood in his mouth. He thrashed violently, as if struggling to break free of the confining bonds of the bedclothes. Still not fully aware, he threw himself from the bed, banged against the wall nearest to him, and ended up crouched against the window, bent over double, every muscle locked rigid, his teeth clenching the bottom of the curtain and his throat burning and raw from the suppressed screams.

Gradually, he recovered enough awareness to realize that Emily was holding him tightly, calling his name over and over again until her voice cut through the horrors in his head. The images of death slowly faded, leaving a hideous sense of foreboding and despair. Emily was kneeling alongside him, her arms wrapped around one shoulder and his neck. Torrents of sweat soaked through the pyjama trousers, dampening the carpet under his knees, seeping into the old shirt she wore to sleep. Dan was shaking like a man with malaria.

Over a period of a few minutes, the trembling eased.

"Oh Daniel," she murmured. "That was dreadful. Try and relax."

Her gentle voice worked its magic on him, and he recovered some composure. His head was on her shoulder, his face against her warm neck. A whiff of Chanel reached him and helped him to concentrate on Emily rather than on the nightmare.

"What on earth was that all about?" said her soft tones.

Dan no longer had any memory of the dream, just the fear of the nightmare laying sour on his brain. "God knows," he murmured into her neck, the words causing a rasp in his throat. "Something scared the absolute hell out of me." Blood from his bitten tongue fell to her neck and dribbled eagerly down her right breast. Dan followed its path and shifted slightly to see it veer downwards before meeting her nipple and soak into the shirt. *If I can notice that,* he thought, *I'm getting better.*

"Did it ever!" she said. "Never known such a shock as waking up to find you making like a vampire on the hunt!"

He was able to smile and eased away from the shelter of her embrace. Damp clothes weakly resisted parting and another drop of blood was shaken onto her shirt. On the patch of heavy moisture, it spread slowly, like a rose opening in the sun.

"You're all covered in sweat, my love!" Dan mumbled past his sore tongue.

"You and me both! You need a long, hot shower."

"Join me!"

She shook her head firmly. Only then did Dan notice that tears were sliding down her face.

"No way!" she said, and stroked his cheek. "I'll go and make you a cup of cocoa and maybe slip you a small something to make you sleep. I think the bed needs changing, too."

"How terribly domesticated." Dan was grasping at normality, and a small joke seemed to help.

She laughed softly. "Domesticated is what's needed right now. Don't forget to wash your hair. You're a mess."

For a moment longer, Dan clung to her, unwilling to let go of the sweetness and safety she gave him. His arms tightened about her slender waist and he put his face back in the warm space of her neck. More blood smudged her skin and he flinched a little from the pain of his tongue.

She felt the movement and it broke the gathering sexual tension. "Not a good idea," she said, the smile obvious in her voice. "All that action on top of what you've gone through already could give you heart problems. Maybe you should have a cold shower!"

His feelings lightening by the second, Dan did as she ordered, and rose unsteadily to his feet, threw off the sodden pyjamas, and found his way to the shower. By the time he had returned, she had made the promised drink, extracted a small white pill from her private store in the closet of the second bedroom, and supervised him as he swallowed both. The fresh sheets she had spread on the bed suddenly looked inviting, and he stretched out on the cool cotton, prepared to wait until she returned from her own shower. But his next memory was the radio switching itself on for the six-thirty news, and no more interruptions occurred that night.

* * *

The next day, Dan found it hard to concentrate on the problems of Kansas City, Denver and other locations. He sat at his desk, terrible depression numbing his capacity to concentrate. When Ginnie came in to see him to discuss her new position and duties, Dan was unable to be his normal, friendly self, and he snapped at her, the first time he had ever done so. Apologizing quickly, he tried to smile.

"I'm sorry, Ginnie," he said. "I slept badly last night, and I'm a bit jumpy."

"That's okay, Dan," she replied, though her face reflected her uncertainty at this new aspect of her boss. "But I have to get clear about what you want me to do on the Kansas City project."

Dan slumped in his chair and took a deep breath, trying to clear the fog and unhappiness from his mind. After a moment, he was able to concentrate better, and spent the next thirty minutes defining what had to be done with the new systems being developed. When Ginnie left, she seemed more comfortable, but she gave Dan a final curious glance as she closed the door behind her.

Dan's sleep began to suffer. Not that he had any more nightmares to fling him out of bed, crying in horror, but he stopped sleeping his normal sweet, sound nights.

About a week after the awful awakening that had flung him from the bed, he woke in the dark, feeling his heart pounding, and a sense of despair and fear. He looked over at the radio and saw the red digits glowing at just after two in the morning. That was supposed to be the time of the human body's lowest ebb, he had once read somewhere. It certainly felt like it now.

Emily was curled up against his side, and he tried to relax his panic by concentrating on that, but it didn't work. After nearly fifteen minutes, he got up carefully, put on his robe, went into the kitchen, made a cup of cocoa and sat with the previous day's *Chicago Tribune*. He felt that his brain was almost trying to jump out of his head, and his hands twitched occasionally, but after nearly an hour, his system calmed down, and his eyes began to feel heavy again.

The shock on the man's face had been obvious as I suddenly materialized out of the dark. "What..? Dan! What are you...?" he said, then froze as he saw the pistol. I pointed and fired in one smooth movement and the bullet took him between the eyes as I had been taught. His head simply dissolved, and a fine spray caught the thin moonlight...

JESUS! What was that? The tiny flicker of a memory had exploded in Dan's mind with the brilliance of a Jackson Pollock painting then vanished again. But a trace of memory, a tall man in a business suit, gun exploding... His heart was pounding again, but after a minute or two, it subsided. It must have been a memory of something seen on the television, he thought, maybe a thriller series, something out of *'Spooks'* or *'CSI'* perhaps. But God! it had been vivid. Feeling his pulse thumping a little harder than normal, he tried to relax, sat back in his armchair and took several deep breaths. After a few minutes he felt better.

"You've been watching too much television, Bailey," he muttered to himself.

He returned to the bedroom, hung the robe away, and crept back into bed. Emily stirred slightly, turned over, murmured something incoherent and cuddled back up to him like a sleepy kitten. Smiling a little, Dan put his arms around her and cradled one beautiful breast in each hand, their regular final cuddle before falling asleep. She gave a small sound in her throat and wriggled against him, but didn't wake up. He finally fell asleep.

In the morning, Dan woke feeling doped, sluggish and lethargic.

"Honey?" said Emily, nudging his shoulder. "Hey, it's morning! Shift your bod!"

Dan groaned.

"Dan?" she said, sounding alarmed. "Are you okay?"

"I will be," he slurred through the fog in his head. "Couldn't sleep last night for some reason. Why don't you go first?"

"You sure you'll be okay?"

"Have to be. Got a heavy day."

She climbed out of her side and walked around to the bathroom. The sight of her long, slender legs under his old business shirt gave him a reasonably effective wake-up call, and finally he made it up and into work. The fatigue stayed with him all day.

The next night, it was worse. At the same time as before, Dan woke up, wasted no time lying there and got out of bed at once. He finished the *Tribune,* and was into the latest edition of *Time* before he was ready to return to bed.

In the morning, the sluggishness was more pronounced. Emily's look of anxiety over breakfast was intense. "Maybe you should see a doctor?" she suggested.

"Hell, no! I think it's just nerves about work. Should be okay in a few days. I'll try one of your magic knock-out pills tonight."

"Okay. But if this persists, to the doctor, young man!"

He kissed her gently and left for work.

Her magic pill didn't function properly. Dan woke up again, just after two, and the sluggishness was more pronounced, despite his pounding heart and feeling of panic. This time, he was still awake as dawn crept up over the park, and he got only another hour of sleep before the radio came on. It began to slow him down at work. He grew moody and anxious.

After another three nights of disturbed sleep, Emily leaned over him at the breakfast table and put her head on his shoulder. The wetness on her cheeks ran down into his collar.

"We need to get this cleared up," she said, the tightness of tears in her throat. He put his hand on her arm, unable to say anything sensible, fearful of what was hurting them like this.

"This has never happened to me before," said Dan, struggling to control his voice. "I'm terrified of what it's doing to us."

"Are you getting any more nightmares?" she asked, brushing her hand over his cheek.

Dan shook his head. "Just one, though I was awake, really. It happened a couple of nights ago, when I was about to get back into bed. But I think it was really a memory of something I'd seen on television."

"What was it? Can you remember?" she asked. Dan looked up at her, aware of tension in her voice and puzzled by it. She had her eyes closed and didn't see the look.

"It's not clear any more," he said, looking down at his hands and pushing his mind for the memory. "Just firing a Smith & Wesson .38 at some man, and..."

He stopped. *A Smith & Wesson .38?* Why did he say that? Dan had no experience with hand guns, and couldn't have told a Smith & Wesson from a Colt or a Browning or any other weapon. But the words had flowed from him without any doubts.

"And what?" she asked. She moved a little away from him and was looking hard into his eyes.

"And..." He looked back at her, and felt the grief and bewilderment welling up inside him. "And... *I killed him."*

The tears took him over, and Dan put his hands over his face. "God, Emily, what's happening to me?" he gasped through the pain. She moved back to him and took his head in her arms.

"Dan, sweetheart, it'll be fine, it was only a dream. Just try and relax... hush now," she murmured into his ears and stroked him gently.

After ten minutes, Dan recovered his control and stood up. "I'll go and wash up," he said and tried to smile. He could see the same pain and bewilderment in her as he was feeling, but there also seemed to be some anger. Confused by that, he shook away the idea, telling himself he was already confused, and couldn't see straight through the tears anyway. He spent some time in the bathroom, trying to cool his face and subdue the redness in his eyes, and eventually decided he had to leave for work. When he put on his jacket and walked out, the tears still gleamed on her cheeks like tiny sequins.

Dan had no idea what to do. And it got worse.

* * *

Tuesday morning, and Dan had a meeting with the software company that had supplied the package Dan's team had installed in the Denver plant. He was considering an additional module to tie in the warehouse management needs, and the conversation was amiable.

"Suppose we decide to use radio-frequency terminals on the fork-lift trucks?" Dan asked the account representative. She was a sophisticated, highly intelligent woman in her twenties, who seemed to know her system inside out. "Can your software support any of them or are you restricted to specific models?"

"Not a problem, Dan," she began. Her voice was East Coast, a slight Boston flavor still evident. "We have it structured so that you just enter the model type, and our package selects the correct driver...."

Driver..... *driver*.... Her voice faded in Dan's ears, and he felt his body go numb, as if lightly anaesthetized.....

Just before the bridge over the Des Plaines River, I took a side road from the I-55 and drove through the pale moonlight to a landing stage. I took the two guns and the radio and threw them far out into the water. Then I extracted the credit card and driver's license from my wallet, burned them into black treacle with a series of matches, dropped the remains into the water also. With some difficulty, I reversed the car ...

"... so you can choose whatever system you like."

Dan jolted back to awareness of where he was. His shirt felt clammy. There was something about that image that had crashed into his mind that seemed horribly familiar. It tied in with something that had happened a few days ago....

He put it down to the poor night's sleep, and concentrated on what she was saying. Somehow he got through the discussion, and she left, happily clutching the signed contract for the new modules of her system. Dan went to the kitchen, next to the computer room, and made himself a cup of lemon tea.

He had never felt this distressed before. Even those awful days when he had first arrived in Sydney, was looking for work and feeling dreadfully lonely, and the telegram came with the news of his parents' death, even that time was not as bad as now. Then he had grieved, but it was the normal grief of a man facing the same loss that happens to most people. This present situation was tearing him apart with pain and confusion, complete helplessness about what to do.

The worst part, he felt, was the vividness of the dreams, or nightmares, and the tiny, explosive images that rammed into his head like a meteorite strike. Nothing like those had ever happened to him.

Dan finished his tea, returned to his desk and concentrated on his computer screen, and no more weird images interrupted his work that day.

The next day, he hit rock bottom. At least, that's how it seemed at the time.

* * *

"Morning, Dan!"

Dan looked up as David and Ginnie walked into his office. He felt slightly fuzzy from the concentration of the last hour of close examination of the fine detail of the network diagram of the Kansas City installation of linked minicomputers.

"Hi Ginnie, David," he said with a smile. "Make yourselves comfortable while I clean up this mess!"

The other two took seats across from Dan and continued peacefully sipping from their coffee cups while Dan rolled up the blueprint and cleared a space on the working surface of his desk. Both of the project leaders had come in for a scheduled review meeting of their assignments, and Dan had looked forward to the meeting. Ginnie had been in her new job for a month now and was displaying all the technical and professional competence Dan had expected. She had raised the performance of her team of analysts and programmers and cut the project time by several days. David was a heavy-set, red-bearded man, an avuncular type who gave confidence to anyone working with him. He never panicked, raved or threatened, but regarded the world as a generally funny place where everything worked out well in the end. He had been a colleague, subordinate and friend of Dan's for some years.

"Okay guys, shoot!" said Dan, closing the drawer of his desk. "Ginnie, what's happening?"

"Me?" Ginnie frowned delicately at him.

"You."

"I'm not a guy!"

"We had noticed," said Dan. "The term was strictly generic."

"I'm glad to hear it!" Ginnie said with a straight face. "In that case, it's all right."

The two men grinned at each other and sat back. Ginnie opened her file and began reading. "All the file maintenance routines are complete and tested with bulk data. The transmission routines from the factory terminals are in beta testing this week, three weeks ahead of schedule after we had done an express conversion..."

Express... *express...* Dan felt as if a sound-deadening blanket had just dropped over the room. Ginnie's voice faded into a darkling distance, and...

The brown envelope had lain on the table with the rest of the day's mail. I opened it, shook out the green American Express card and Illinois driver's license and checked the photograph and signatures. Alan J. Killian. I put both in...

"Dan? Dan!"

Startled, Dan looked up to see David's hard stare. "Dan, you're white as a sheet!" said David. "Are you okay?"

His voice seemed to come from miles away. A heavy banging in Dan's ears was shrouding the sounds of the office, and his heart was pounding erratically. Sweat lay heavily in his armpits and made his shirt clammy. Dan felt numb, unable to speak.

"Dan, please! Say something!" Ginnie's voice was urgent and cut through the fog. "David, maybe we should call the nurse?"

Dan felt his mind snap back into the room, the blanketing sensation fading away like steam in a fresh wind. "Sorry!" he said, trying to smile at the others. "I don't know what came over me! I think I may have a touch of flu or something." He took a deep breath. *Where had my mind been?* he thought. The other two were watching him with concern on their faces.

"Ginnie," said Dan, trying to sound confident and in control. "What was that last part?"

Ginnie exchanged a glance with David, gave Dan another anxious look and returned to her file that had nearly fallen from her knees. She gathered some loose papers and began reading again. "The hardware was delivered on time, but the protocol converter was two days late so we had to delay the connectivity tests. Garry Porter was away for a couple of days when his wife had their kid, but we switched....."

... a plain white envelope lying in my mail box. When I got upstairs, the phone was already ringing. "Misha, listen to me," said a voice and I was somehow frozen in obedience. I opened the envelope on the whispered order. The woman was pretty, high cheek bones, wide, generous mouth, luxurious hair. Her eyes smiled at me. "Her name is Emily James," said the small voice in my ear. "She is everything you dreamed of in a woman. She is beautiful, intelligent, sexy. You will love her always...."

"Dan, maybe we should put this off till tomorrow?" David's voice called from a far canyon. "DAN! For God's sake, what's the matter with you?"

Dan's hands were shaking so hard that sweat drops fell from his palms to the table in a fine spray. He could feel the wetness in his armpits and back and a trembling ran up his body.

"Wha.. what?" he mumbled. "Oh!" He came back to reality and realized they were staring at him. David had half risen from his seat, Ginnie had her hands in front of her mouth and her eyes were almost circular. "Hell, sorry people," mumbled Dan. "I really must be coming down with something."

Whatever it is, thought Dan through a rising sense of panic, *it's scaring the hell out of me.* He wiped his palms with his handkerchief. David and Ginnie were looking at him with considerable worry. They had become accustomed to short, incisive meetings with him, where things got done, decisions were made and problems were solved. This was not what they were used to.

"I'm really sorry, both of you," said Dan, trying to smile with no success. "I think I've been sleeping badly, and perhaps I need a break. Let's try and finish this thing and maybe I'll go home."

"You really should." Ginnie looked distressed. Dan had always known she regarded him with a sort of heroic admiration, and he knew this could not be comfortable for her.

"No maybe about it, Dan!" snapped David. He was a good enough friend to tell Dan the truth when it mattered. "You're in a bloody awful state, I think you should go right down to the doctor's office this instant!"

"David, I'll be okay," said Dan. "Let's try and finish this session, eh? Ginnie, you are what, about three weeks ahead of schedule?"

"Just under," she said, a slight tremble in her voice. She dragged her eyes down to her file again. "Fourteen working days to be exact, and we'll lose another two days because the electricians have put back the wiring of the computer room until...."

For a second or two, the headless body had stood still, leaning backward a little from the force of the bullet that had exploded the face into a luminous cloud of blood. Then it collapsed with astonishing speed, as if the strings had been cut from a marionette and the ground was seizing its new prize....

"... and the final systems test should be started the first week of November."

Dan returned to the world of his office, his jaw clenched tight in fear and his hands slippery with a slick of oily dread. The trembling in his body was threatening to shake the table, but Ginnie and David were studying their bar charts and graphs and not looking at him. For some moments, Dan fought furiously for self-control until the trembling eased, but the cold sweat in his armpits and on his back remained, clammy and evil.

"... the programmers will finish the file maintenance programs by Friday and we'll begin testing on Monday."

"Huh?" *What in God's name is going on with me?* he thought, almost overwhelmed by the helpless sensation.

"Dan, this is no bloody use at all! You're as much use today as ice-skates in the desert." David looked irritable and concerned at the same time, while Ginnie was almost in tears.

Dan stood up and tried to ease the cramps in his arms and legs, walked around the desk and stretched, looking through the glass wall at the computer room where the engineers were connecting a new communications link. "You're right," he said, turning back to his colleagues at his desk. "Look, I'm sorry, both of you, you're quite right. This is wasting your time. Why don't you just get on with the projects? I know you're on top of things, let's just leave the review until next week. I think I'll go home to bed."

David and Ginnie stood and began packing up their folders. Dan walked around the office for a few more moments to try to get feeling back in his legs and arms, and finally returned to his desk.

"Need a ride home, pal?" David was closing his briefcase and he looked carefully at Dan. "I don't think you should rely on public transport."

"No thanks, David, but you're right." replied Dan. "I'll get a cab."

David looked hard at his boss, and his glance lingered on the sweat-soaked patches under Dan's arms and on his back. Dan felt his face slick with perspiration.

"Dan, it looks like flu!" said David. "How about you call in at the doctor's office before you go? Maybe a shot of antibiotics will help?"

"Sure, David, stop playing mother hen with me!" said Dan. "Go on, bugger off, before I have to act the heavy boss with you!"

David looked relieved that at least Dan was showing something of a spark again, and followed Ginnie out of the office. In the next room the lights went out as the engineers left, their task complete. Dan sat down to call the department's secretary and tell her he was going to be out the rest of the day. He liked the secretary. She was a countrywoman of Dan's, whose Manchester accent was delightfully familiar to him and a source of affectionate amusement to the Americans in the office. Reaching for the handset....

"... a broader sound, Misha, broader, move the tongue further forward and open the lips wider... that's better, now again... say after me... good! That's how a Manchester man speaks..."

Dan was staring at the polished surface of his desk top, feeling as if he were looking at a shadowy scene from a play being performed just for him. Insanely, he felt as though he knew the players. He sat at his desk, shaking, his arm still reaching out for the telephone, the shadowy figures fading from his sight. What in Hell's name was that memory of? he asked himself.

Georgii Vilnikov, that's who.

WHAT?

His chest hurt so that he couldn't breathe.

WHAT IS THIS? WHAT AM I SEEING? he shouted inside his head. The vision had been perfect, despite the shadows. A wood-lined room, tea in silver-framed glasses, a small fire burning. Georgii sitting up against the table, his scarf tucked into his jacket, steel-capped teeth gleaming in the dim light.

He was my only friend, said a tiny voice, a child's voice in Dan's head.

A wave of pain drew sudden tears, and Dan gasped with the shock. Then he broke into a full, deep-throated weeping, helpless with the weight of the sadness and loneliness, but completely unable to understand what was causing it. Twenty minutes passed before he was able to take control again, and he was thankful that nobody came into his office or into the computer room the other side of the full-length window. At last, Dan was able to compose himself enough to walk out to the washroom and repair some of the damage, but he was still shaking from the severity of the inexplicable sadness that had overwhelmed him for a while.

He sat back in his leather chair behind his desk and took several deep breaths to try and calm down. Enough crazy, inexplicable shocks to his system had occurred for any one day, he decided. He tried to remember when things had started to go wrong.

The first time he had woken up, shivering with visions of blinding snow and soul-killing cold. The second time, waking with a scream and blood from a bitten tongue making him choke, awful memories of a terrifying nightmare causing him to throw himself from the bed and grovel in fear by the wall. That seemed to be the beginning of the problem, he decided. He tried to remember details of the nightmares, remembered only confusion and the aching sensation of toiling endlessly through shrieking winds and murderous cold.....

... Once I walked through the blizzard alone on my way back from the black building and missed the fork to the living quarters. I was leaning into the wind when I was stopped by a loud yell. Four armed guards were standing by the steel barred gate, and the wind was shrieking triumphant fury through the girders. The guards didn't unsling their weapons, but they were menacing, for all that.....

Dan stood up violently, flinging his chair backward on its rollers and it crashed against the back wall. He held his head and tried to stop the pounding that was thundering through his eyes and brain... NO! he screamed inside himself. He scrabbled furiously for self-control, found just a coat-tail of it and hung on tight. STOP IT! he shouted at the demons that were roaring in triumph into his head. He took a deep breath, held it, concentrated on forcing the world to be normal.

His breathing eased from the harsh snorts from flared, fearful nostrils, his pulse slowed from the frenetic drumbeat, clammy sweat remained on his neck and back. *This is unbearable, my God...* His knees buckled and he sank to the carpet, feeling as if his brain was spinning completely off its gimbals ...

"DAN! Good grief, Dan, what the bloody hell is happening to you..?" Strong arms hauling him off the floor, putting him in his chair, loosening his collar... "Ginnie! Call the sick room, get the nurse up here... Bailey, you lousy bastard, why didn't you say you were sick?... drink this... you stupid...! What the hell's the matter...?" Frightened eyes of a close friend... comfort of supporting shoulder... *no need to be ashamed of tears,* thought Dan through the mists, *not with David...*

Hazy memories of the nurse taking his pulse, his temperature, murmuring something about both being high, being carried downstairs to the office of a doctor's group in the same building. Valium, something liquid, sleep....

* * *

Sometime in the early afternoon, Dan returned to a semblance of reality. He was lying on a leather couch, a light blanket over him. The room was small, with just a single window letting in dusty light. An unidentifiable steel contraption stood in the corner regarding him with metallic inscrutability. Sweat had dried on his legs and chest, and in his unawareness of what had brought him there, Dan felt a twinge of irritation that his suit had been dry-cleaned only a day or two before and now would need it again. He sat upright and tried to remember why he was here. Only snatches of fear and confusion came back. Beyond that, nothing. Standing upright seemed to have no ill effects, walking to the door of the small room was a breeze. Outside sat a receptionist, typing notes. A handful of people sat in the cool, well-lit waiting area waiting for attention, reading magazines, talking in low tones, being bored.

"Mister Bailey, you had us worried back there!" Dan turned to see a youngish woman in a white coat approaching him from a door across the waiting room. He assumed it was the doctor who had treated him. He smiled, still feeling weakness in his legs.

"I had *you* worried?" Dan replied. "I felt a minor twinge of concern myself!"

The woman grinned. "No need for it!" she said. "We got your temperature and everything else down to where they should be, no obvious cause for the whole thing. Probably just a bit tensed up, maybe your diet has been a little unhealthy lately. Why not take a day or two off?"

I really don't think that's it, thought Dan to himself, but hid his doubts. "Seeing as my insurance company has just incurred outrageous fees for that bit of advice," he replied, "I might as well take it."

The doctor smiled, and turned to walk back through the door from which she had emerged. Dan returned to his office, finally told his secretary he was going home, and did just that.

The apartment was empty when he got in, and Dan assumed that Emily was out on an interview or researching some topic. He removed his suit and took a shower, later dressing in his customary jeans and light shirt, and tried not to think about the day's happenings. He sat in his wing chair, looked out on the balcony and the pigeons flying in the park, and tried to order his thoughts, failing miserably. He felt the tension building again as he relived the confusion, without any memory of what had caused the panic. There had been fear and sadness but no reason why.

The afternoon passed round him, like an uncaring pedestrian ignoring an accident.

* * *

Sometime between five and six, the front door rattled and swung open as Emily came in. She hummed gently to herself as she hung her coat away in the closet, dropped her shoes on the floor and switched on the hall light to repel the gathering evening gloom. Dan sat unmoving, listening to the sounds of her homecoming, a feeling of helpless misery washing over him. She walked to the bedroom, and the closet door creaked slightly as she opened it to hang away her work clothes, and there was a clash of coat hangers as she selected something casual to wear. Dan knew that he should have gone to meet her, called out to her, behaved like they were still the same people they had been for the last few months. But he was numb, weak, unable to get up. The combined shocks of the day and the overwhelming fear he was feeling for what the recent events might mean for him were paralyzing him.

The sounds of Emily were painfully intimate and his hearing was acutely attuned to her. Gentle sliding of jeans over her legs, tearing sound of zipper closing, swish of brush over long hair, he heard them all with almost supernatural clarity. *How can I tell her about these horrors?* he said to himself. *Could they mean my sanity is leaving me, is some awful disease striking my nervous system? What will she do?* The fear that she might leave him was almost worse than the fear of what was wrong.

He heard her cough gently, then the sound of the bedside telephone being picked up. The soft tones of the buttons as she pushed them were echoed by the telephone in the lounge, just a few feet from where he sat.

"I want you to stop," she said. Somebody had presumably answered the telephone. Emily was silent for a few seconds as the other person spoke.

"You must," said Emily. "It's not working properly."

A few seconds passed and then she spoke again. "Some memories are returning."

Dan felt a crawling sensation of dismay. This conversation with an unknown correspondent held dreadful implications. Dan knew that his world was changing for the worse. Emily was still speaking, and the tension in her voice was filling the room and shouting across the space to Dan.

"He had a dream of his early training," she was saying. "It was in the compound. And I think he's getting some recall of the Fitzpatrick event."

Fitzpatrick! Dear God! Dan jerked in his seat. Was she talking about Kevin Fitzpatrick? The company executive shot next to his car on an Illinois roadside?

"You know I never wanted you to use him," she was saying, and her voice was pleading with the other speaker. "The whole thing is a mistake, and I wanted out a long time ago."

The other speaker took a lengthy interval to speak. Dan could hear Emily try and break in several times, but was clearly over-ridden by the man or woman at the other end.

"No, you can't," Emily finally said. The weariness and despair in her voice struck Dan with force. "You know what happened to the others. And I'm not going to help you any more with this insanity. It's a new world now."

For a second, Dan could hear an incoherent blast of sound from the telephone as the other speaker shouted furiously.

"I told you!" said Emily, speaking into the noise. "For the last time, I won't do it! For God's sake, give it up."

She slammed the phone back on its stand, and Dan could hear her heavy breathing for several seconds. A few moments later, she walked into the lounge, switched on the television and was about to turn on the light when she saw Dan in the armchair.

"Dan!" she exclaimed. "Good grief, honey, you scared me to death! What are you doing home at this time?" She moved over to him and stooped to kiss him. Long brown hair fell over his eyes and stroked his face. "Are you all right?"

She left her hand on his cheek and peered closely into his eyes. Behind her, coloured scenes from the television threw frenetic shadows around the room and a murmured cacophony of voices and music washed gently over the furniture, the walls and themselves. The shadows did not completely hide the anxiety in her eyes.

"Sweetheart, you look terrible!" Her tone was sharp, edgy, almost anticipatory.

"Emily...?" Dan wanted to say something, but couldn't form the words. His mouth felt numb as if he had just come from a dentist's chair. The shock of the morning's events coupled with the growing horror at the implications of what he had just heard in her telephone conversation were driving him beyond his control. The nightmares of killing he had been having, the dreadful, bloody vividness of the dream, the death of Kevin Fitzpatrick, the insane and inexplicable visions of a bleak, snow-swept landscape, and the child's memory of a man called Georgii, somehow they were linked, and somehow Emily was involved. It was all too much to take in a rational world.

"Dan, what is it?" Her tone was softer, almost despairing.

He felt her hand touching his face. Dampness on his cheeks told him that his control was going and tears were starting to ooze.

"Emily, I think I'm going insane," he mumbled. "I keep getting horrible memories of things, I don't know what they are, they frighten me silly..."

She dropped down suddenly at his feet and held both his hands. For a moment, Dan remembered a night a few weeks ago when their positions were reversed and she was sitting in the chair, weeping quietly as he knelt in front of her, holding her hands. How far we've come, he thought through the distress he was feeling. Her eyes stared into his, one side of her face illuminated by the glow of the television, the other reclusive in the shadows of the darkened walls. Her voice was urgent.

"Dan! What memories? Please, try and tell me, what are you seeing?"

He looked at her, feeling a distance grow between them. Too many questions had arisen for the love and trust he had held. His bitterness rising like poisoned water in a well, he thought about the telephone conversation he had just heard.

"Why?" he asked, his voice tight. "You were telling somebody just now that you know what I'm seeing."

She sat back on her heels, shoulders slumping in sorrow. "Oh God," she whispered. "You heard all that?"

"Who was it, Emily?" he demanded. He couldn't show any of the old love and delight in his voice. Something was grotesquely wrong, she was part of it, and for a time, he couldn't love her. "What the hell is happening? Whoever that was you were talking to, you both know what this is all about. Tell me!" The last words were almost a shout, so painful and desperate was his need and bewilderment.

Emily shook her head, tears starting to slide down her cheeks. "I can't Dan, believe me, I can't. I wish you could understand that whatever it was, it's something well and truly over. It needn't bother us again."

He felt rage at her, and at the same time, horrified that he could feel such a thing about Emily. It made the rage even worse, at her, at himself, at his helplessness.

"God damn you, Emily!" he roared, and she flinched, hiding her face in her hands. At the sight, he choked on his own tears, calmed down, and leaned forward to try and take her hand. She jerked away from him, and this first ever sign of the loss of love ripped through him.

"Emily, please!" he said, more quietly now. "How can I let this alone? Terrible things are happening to us, and it's obvious you know something about it. What was all that about Fitzpatrick? What did you mean about my early training and the compound? Please, sweetheart, what the hell is going on?"

Her head shook in violent denial, then she flung herself forward, wrapped her arms around his neck and clung to him. Her trembling communicated itself to him, and her face was drenched against his neck.

"Daniel, this is horrible," she whispered. "I wish I could tell you some of the things I've done in the past, but I can't. But believe me, my love, it's over, and we're okay. Can't you just leave it at that?"

Dan shook his head. The pain of her grief and of his own confusion was overwhelming him, and he knew that even if it meant losing her, he couldn't let this go.

"I can't," he said. He pulled her arms from his neck and pushed her away a little, staring hard at her. Her cheeks were red and stained with tears, and her eyes still brimmed over.

"Emily," he said. "That bit about Fitzpatrick. Was it Kevin Fitzpatrick?"

She shook her head, but her lack of conviction was obvious.

"Did you have something to do with his murder?" he asked, hating himself as he spoke and feeling the horror of what he was asking eat into his insides.

She shook her head again. "No," she said, so softly he could hardly hear her.

He tried another tack. "What were you talking about when you mentioned the compound and my early training? What compound? What early training?"

Her voice was toneless, as if she had given up the fight and was merely answering with simple statements, like a prisoner of war being interrogated by his captors.

"I can't tell you any more, Dan. Please stop asking."

"Who were you talking to on the phone?"

She shook her head and sat back on her heels again, her face empty of emotion or life.

For a moment longer, he looked at her, seeing the emptiness, the grief much like his own, and wondered if this could be the end, after only four or five months of such happiness. He stood up and walked past her into the bedroom. He picked up two pillows from his side of the bed and walked across the corridor into the second bedroom, closing the door behind him. As he did so, he heard the muffled sob from Emily, and it almost made him break into tears himself. But he lay down on the bed, and stared at the ceiling.

Some time later, he heard the door of the other bedroom close gently, and this time he did let the tears flow.

Dan felt that it was the longest night of his life. He lay on his back, unable to sleep, staring into a blackness that was as impenetrable as his misery. This was not like a marital fight. It was not about differences in philosophy, or a spat about a behavioral misunderstanding. Emily knew something about him that indicated appalling mysteries about himself. She was somehow involved in a terrible, senseless murder of a businessman. She had some mysterious relationship, though obviously not a friendly, co-operative one, with someone she refused to identify to Dan. How could a loving, wonderful life together be sustained in the face of these factors? he asked himself, and saw no answer in the silent darkness.

He looked sideways at the clock radio on the bedside table. It was two in the morning, and he had never felt less like sleeping. Yet when he looked again, it was after eight, it was morning, and the apartment was empty.

He spent the day in silence. He didn't turn on the radio, didn't speak aloud to himself, made no telephone calls. He left the answering system on, feeling himself incapable of talking to anyone. He paced around the spacious lounge room, hands in pockets, shoulders hunched as if against some psychic cold wind.

Something was bouncing around in his mind, some clue, some link between the things that had been happening. But the unknown thing eluded his grasp, like a small animal that hopped always a foot away from his hands.

At eleven, he stopped the pacing and made a pot of coffee. He watched the steam rising slowly from the kettle as the water came to the boil, and his mind roamed free for a while, forgetting the bleakness and the misery. On mental autopilot, he opened the jar of coffee, spooned some into the large mug with the crest of the Apollo XI Moon Shot, poured the hot water and added sweetener. Holding the mug, he resumed his pacing. He stopped opposite the bookcase that held so many of his favourite novels, smiling as he remembered an early attempt to write a mystery thriller along the lines of Dick Francis. He had managed fifty or so pages, then thrown the work away in disgust, so inept did it seem. As a child in England, he had read the complete works of Sir Arthur Conan Doyle and followed the artistic analysis of Holmes and Watson with the delight he later experienced designing a clever computer system.

Who benefits?

He choked on the mouthful of hot coffee as the thought roared into his mind like a train racing through a country station.

Who benefits? The voice in his mind was the dry, sardonic tone of Sherlock Holmes as portrayed by an English actor on a television series he had been watching recently.

He walked into the kitchen for a damp towel, wiped his mouth and dampened the stain on his sleeve where some random drops of coffee had landed.

Who benefits from what? he asked himself, confused by the power with which the words had come to him. He puzzled at the matter until the answer came. In any good crime mystery, the detective always asks that question, he remembered. The motive will usually lead to the criminal. But what crime was he thinking about?

"The human mind is totally astounding," he muttered, the first words he had spoken all day, and sat in his favourite wing chair. He was just like a computer, performing some tasks in the foreground, and some in the background. Something had obviously been going on in his head in background mode, he decided. Who benefits from what? He stared out of the window at the park.

What benefit was coming to Emily? Hell, he thought, how could I work that out when I don't know what she's done? Who benefitted from.... what? He took another sip of the coffee, now cooling in its mug.

WHO BENEFITTED FROM THE DEATH OF KEVIN FITZPATRICK?

This time, he spilled the coffee on his trousers.

He had the answer.

As he took his trousers off, flung them into the washing machine and added detergent power, he worked through the flash that had come to him. Kevin Fitzpatrick had been fighting a take-over bid by the Hanfield Group, a huge conglomerate of industrial companies. He had been winning, the bid had been faltering, and Wall Street had concluded the Hanfield Group would pull back within days. But the death of Fitzpatrick had ruined all that, and the Hanfield Group had grabbed Caradoc Metals and swallowed it whole.

Vincent Carson had benefitted. Dan felt the same wave of anger and hostility run through his body at the mention of the name as he had when Carson had appeared on the television news after the takeover had been concluded. However crazy the whole thing was, Dan concluded, Vincent Carson was somehow involved. Involved with the murder of Kevin Fitzpatrick, with whatever Emily was doing or had done, and with whatever maniacal things were happening to him.

"Vincent Carson," muttered Dan. "You and I have a date."

Just how he was going to manage it, Dan was without suggestions at this stage. But he was certain of two things. He was very bright and he was a good salesman. Somehow he was going to use those factors to get to see Vincent Carson, alone.

Meanwhile, he had the painful problem of Emily. Their loving, trusting and happy relationship had shattered like a wineglass falling on to a concrete floor.

Dan couldn't see how his intelligence and sales ability were going to help with that one.

* * *

When she returned to the apartment soon after six that evening, Dan was feeling tense and angry. He stood up as he heard the key in the lock, and was standing by the wing chair as she came in. She looked hard at him for a second, then closed the door behind her and walked up the short hallway into the living room. Her face was white, drawn, somehow thinner than Dan remembered it.

"We need to discuss this thing," said Dan.

"I suppose so," she answered. Her voice was subdued. She walked past him into the kitchen and extracted a glass from the cabinet. It was a heavy crystal scotch glass, one that had been unused since her arrival and the start of the ritual of champagne as the evening drink. She took ice from the fridge and walked over to the drinks cabinet, opened it and took a bottle of Smirnoff vodka, poured a generous helping into the glass, then returned to the lounge room and sat down on the couch. She didn't look at Dan. The loneliness and misery in her face nearly made him choke, but he forced self-control.

"Are you going to tell me the truth about what's going on?" he asked, sitting opposite her in the wing-back chair.

She took a gulp of the vodka without showing any effect, and shook her head. "I can't," she said. "I wish you could believe me when I tell you that whatever happened in the past is over. If I told you about it, we could both be badly hurt. If we can let it go, we'll be okay."

"Let it go?" he echoed. "You know something about me I don't know myself. Somehow you're involved in the killing of Kevin Fitzpatrick. How can I ever trust you? I don't even know who you are, anymore."

She flinched at that, and took another drink. The first tears were shining in her eyes. "I'm Emily James," she said curtly, and looked at him. "Dan," she said, "I love you.

I don't want anything else but to live with you and forget the last few days. I need you very much."

Dan almost shook from the pain her words caused him. "I love you too, Emily," he said. "But how can I cope with what's happened? How can we live without being able to trust each other?"

The silence in the room lasted several minutes. Dan tried to consider a life without Emily, and the distress he felt at the idea was unbearable. Tears were dangerously close to his eyes, too.

"Will you give me a little time?" she asked.

"Time for what?"

"To try and work something out."

"Any idea how long?" he asked, curious at her words.

She shook her head. "Maybe a week or two."

He looked at her for a moment or two, thought about how much he loved her, and needed her, and missed the happiness that had become so integral a part of his life during the last few months.

"We can try," he said, and felt an enormous weight lift from him. A tiny smile appeared on he mouth, and she stood up.

"Good," she said, and walked out to the kitchen with the glass of vodka. A few moments later she returned, carrying two glasses of champagne. She passed him one.

"Can we drink to that?" she asked. Her voice was almost a child's, with tension still evident in it. She sounded uncertain, begging for reassurance. Dan touched his glass to hers.

"We can drink to it," he said, and smiled at her. They took a sip then he bent down and kissed her. He could taste the tears on her lips.

Some time later they went to bed, but didn't make love. It was too soon for that, but they held each other for a few minutes before Dan finally moved away. Things were not yet back to normal and might never be again. And he still had the problem of Vincent Carson. He didn't feel comfortable asking Emily about Carson. It might trigger worse problems if Carson really was the unseen player in the game. And he still had to figure out how to force a meeting.

In the end, that problem was solved for him.

Chapter 4

"Yes, this is Dan Bailey," said Dan. The phone had rung within minutes of Dan's entering his office soon after eight in the morning. He felt irritated. One of his favourite routines was to read the paper for fifteen minutes in peace, with a cup of fresh coffee and a danish purchased from the bakery near the subway station. Today it was denied him. And added to that was the fact that Emily was away. She had told him two days ago of her plans to travel to Boston for a few days of computer research. Though their relationship was still strained as they worked out how to solve their problems, he still missed her badly.

The voice at the other end of the telephone was cultured, well educated and confident. It could have been a top computer salesman or business executive.

"Dan, good morning," said the voice. "My name is Brandon Shelby. I'm a head-hunter with Shelby, Lake and Associates."

"Yes," said Dan. "I've heard of you, and I've seen your advertisements. How can I help you?"

He unfolded the *Tribune* on his desk and looked casually at the headlines, taking a sip of his hot coffee. These sorts of calls were not uncommon. Dan estimated he received an average of one a month, and since taking his current job had found no reason to consider a change. He pulled the sports section out of the rest of the *Tribune*.

"We've been given a particularly exciting assignment, Dan," said Shelby. "A large, international conglomerate is seeking a vice president of information systems for their entire operations."

"Aha," said Dan, keeping his voice cool. The Chicago Bears were playing at home that weekend, and Dan checked the betting data. The Bears were underdogs? Dan felt slightly irritated by that.

"We have some data on you, Dan, and we feel you would be highly suited for the position." Shelby was putting on the best salesman's persuasive manner.

"What sort of salary are we talking?" asked Dan. At least he could see if the job was at the right level.

"Upward of three hundred thousand," replied Shelby.

Whoops! thought Dan, and slid the paper away. This was a serious discussion, after all. "All right, Brandon," he said. "You have my interest."

"Thought that might get you," replied Shelby. Dan could hear the amusement in the other man's voice.

"And the head office is here?" asked Dan. A move from Chicago was impossible, as Emily's main customer base was here.

"Yes, it is," said the other man. "Though of course, a lot of travel would be involved."

"Where are their other locations?" asked Dan. He had always loved to travel, and this sounded almost like the perfect job.

"South America, Europe, Singapore, Indonesia and Australia," answered Shelby. "Plus several locations in the USA."

"And how did you hear about me?" asked Dan. His interest had grown, though he knew that the competition for such a dream job would be immense.

"Well, I have to tell you, Dan," said Shelby. "The company specifically asked us to contact you."

"Really?" Dan felt flattered. As the systems director for a large company like MidWestern, he knew he had a high profile in the computer industry, but to be specifically targeted for a job like this! He felt good.

"Really," agreed Shelby. "In fact, the instruction to call you came directly from the president."

Under the pleasurable glow, a small warning light came on in Dan's mind. Presidents of multi-billion-dollar organizations did not make requests like that. Even for a senior position like this one, the protocols of head-hunting would have insisted that Dan first be screened by several other corporate heavies before the president became involved.

"That's very unusual," said Dan. "Can you tell me which company this is?"

"Let's be clear first on whether you're interested," said Shelby. "I can't reveal my client's name until you commit to an interview."

"Oh, I'm interested, of course," said Dan. "Who wouldn't be for a job like that?"

"Good," replied Shelby. "Would you be free to go for an interview this afternoon?"

"This afternoon? That's very short notice," replied Dan, turning to his desk calendar. "Just let me check."

He opened up the calendar, found the day, and inspected it. He had an appointment with the communications specialist from the computer supplier at two, a meeting with Human Resources at three to go through the salary levels for the next year, but nothing after that.

"I could go at four," he said into the phone. "I assume the office is in the city?"

"Very close to you, about ten minutes walk," replied Shelby. "Four is okay with my client. I'll call him and confirm it, then?"

"Do that," said Dan. "Who do I see?"

"You see the president," replied Shelby.

"The president? For the first interview?" More warning lights went on in Dan's mind. "Brandon, that's most unusual! Aren't you going to do a first screening interview before that?"

"Not in this case, Dan," said Shelby. "Apparently he's heard about you from direct sources, and he's keen to meet with you immediately."

"Well, okay," replied Dan. "I can't imagine how anyone at that level has heard enough about me to want this, but if you say so, I suppose it's okay. Who is this guy?"

"Vincent Carson," said the voice in his ear.

Dan felt cold water fill his insides. A slight tremble broke out in his left hand holding the telephone.

"Vincent Carson?" he asked. His voice sounded like a small croak to him.

"That's right," said Shelby, cheerfully. "The Hanfield Group. You've heard of him?"

"Yes," replied Dan. "I've heard of him." His hand was trembling worse, and his skin prickled. The back of his neck felt slimy so that he wanted to go into the washroom and rinse his face.

"Great!" replied Shelby, seeming not to notice the subdued tones of Dan's voice. "Their offices are on Madison. Thirty-second floor."

"Yes. I know," said Dan. "I'll be there at four."

He replaced the phone and watched the hair rise on the back of his hands.

According to the vast information board in the cathedral-like lobby of the glass tower on Madison, the Hanfield Group occupied three floors, the reception desk being on the top one, the thirty-second. Dan walked past the circular security desk, receiving a programmed inspection by the three uniformed guards sitting within their walled fortress, and found the express elevator servicing the top ten floors. The doors closed as he pressed the button, letting him inspect his image in the shiny metal surface. The elevator's synthetic voice told off the floor numbers as it ascended, speaking gently in a nasal twang that Dan found irritating. With relief, he walked out into the reception area as the doors opened with an electronic beep.

The floor was black and white marble. Three enormous sofas covered in dark green upholstery sat in the waiting area and the panoramic windows looked out onto the waters of Lake Michigan where a cruise vessel was sailing along the shoreline, giving the passengers a superb view of what Dan had always felt was one of the best skylines in the world.

A wide, sweeping circular staircase gave access to the lower floors, and to one side of the ornately carved handrail, a woman sat at a simple desk equipped only with a telephone console. *She was astonishingly beautiful,* thought Dan, with immaculate make-up, blonde hair painstakingly prepared in the style of "I just got out of bed," and eyes of a violet shade that would outdo Elizabeth Taylor. She gave Dan a smile, evidently accustomed to the effect she had on the male visitors to her domain. Dan swallowed, took a deep breath and announced himself.

"Yes, Mister Bailey, Mister Carson is expecting you," the vision at the desk said. Her husky voice matched the rest of her highly idealized image. "Please take a seat, and I'll call his assistant."

Instead, Dan stood by the window, and looked out past the Planetarium, the Shedd Aquarium and the lake up to Navy Pier. *The passengers in the cruiser would be getting a great view,* thought Dan, trying to calm his nerves.

"Mister Bailey?"

Dan turned at the sound of the female voice, to see a middle-aged woman of stick-like thinness. Her hair was set in a fashion he had not seen outside of pictures of models in the fifties, a roll across the front over her forehead, the rest falling to her neck in a forced curl. But the dress was modern enough and looked expensive, as did the heavy gold band on her wrist. Dan nodded, feeling curls of anxiety knotting at his bowels.

"Would you follow me, please? Mister Carson is in his office."

Dan walked behind the bony frame, past the oak doors of private offices, most of them open to show elderly men behind heavy desks. In one of the offices, a group of young men gathered round a computer terminal, talking in subdued tones, most of them with their arms folded in defensive positions. One of them was pointing to the screen and holding his other hand to his mouth as if fearing the effects of his words. *They look almost as scared as I feel,* thought Dan and swallowed the acid taste of fear.

At the end of the corridor was one more door. The woman tapped gently on the gleaming wood and opened it with a slight swoosh of air resistance. Dan walked through, and the woman followed him in.

The president occupied the corner office, a standard perk if the view merited it, and this view certainly did. Two walls of glass scintillated with the sunshine and reflections off the lake. To the south, the complete spread of the lake-front park was open to inspection, and Dan could see down to the Gothic pillars of the Field Museum and over the single runway of Meigs Field airport built out into the water. The coloured rows of seats of Soldier Field football stadium looked like a child's board game from this elevation, and the massive structure of the McCormick Convention Centre sat solidly beyond it. The white sun-blinds built into the window frames would be essential in the morning to block out the early direct glare, but they had been drawn back to permit an unblocked view for the afternoon.

In all this brightness, the office was in no need of any decoration, Dan thought, the views were splendour enough. Despite that, two paintings hung side by side on the wall adjoining the door through which he had just entered. In the glance he was able to give them, they seemed to be Victorian battle scenes, all horses, cannon, soldiers with white bandaged heads, and flags flying bravely.

Tacky, thought Dan, whose tastes went to Picasso, the Impressionists and Rembrandt.

"Mister Bailey," announced the thin woman. Vincent Carson was on his feet and already advancing on him as Dan was announced.

"Dan!" he said with enthusiasm, extending his hand. Unable to resist the energetic force, Dan took it and nearly had his wrist broken as Carson shook it with gusto. He was a short, stocky man, completely bald, the face Slavic in the flatness and coarse features, but bright blue eyes glittered at Dan, alleviating the peasant face. His suit was an elegant grey, cut with a style that looked European and pricy.

"Mister Carson," said Dan formally, feeling the hostility rise in him again as it had when he had first seen Carson on television. It swamped the fear for a few seconds.

"Vincent, please." Carson gave him an expansive smile, displaying a healthy set of bright teeth. The smile seemed not to reach the eyes, which were examining Dan with cool interest.

"Thank you," said Dan cautiously, and took a seat across from the large black desk, watching Carson carefully as he returned to his own.

"Coffee or tea?" asked Carson as he sat in his dark leather executive chair and swung himself to face Dan. Dan examined Carson's face for a few moments, looking for the truth behind this meeting, but the impassive features merely stared back at him.

"Tea, please." Dan decided to go along with whatever game this was.

Carson nodded at the woman waiting silently by the door and she left, closing the heavy oak behind her with another slight swish.

"I appreciate you taking the time to come and see me," said Carson, opening the conversation with a conventional gambit.

"Not at all," said Dan. What the hell is going on here? he asked himself. Could there really be a job here after all? "I'm honoured that you asked specifically to see me. I'm curious how you knew about my work."

"I read the article Emily James wrote on you in Crane's."

"I see." Dan felt a jolt run through him. There was no job of international systems director. Here was the link with Emily. The man across the desk was playing games.

"And I play golf with your president," added Carson.

"Ah!" said Dan. His boss was someone he admired enormously, and it worried him that Carson would be an acquaintance of his. Carson seemed intent on continuing his game of conducting a formal interview. Dan could see no alternative but to play along for a while longer.

"He said you had more than halved his computer costs and certainly provided vastly more effective systems," continued Carson. "How did you do it?"

Dan shrugged. If the man was genuinely interested in developments in information technology, Dan had no objection to enlightening him. “Just common sense,” he said. “I simply used modern technology to provide the people who do the actual work with what they needed.”

The expression on Carson’s face was cold. The small smile was almost predatory, and a small gleam of satisfaction seemed to peep out. Dan was feeling extremely uncomfortable with everything he had seen so far, apart from the worries of the reality behind the meeting. *If I had really come for a job interview*, he thought, *this would have turned me off by now*. The layout of the area reflected a conventional, autocratic organizational hierarchy, with high expenses lavished on the head office. Marble floors, mythically beautiful receptionists, heavy oak doors and spiral staircases, Dan didn’t believe in any of that stuff at all. Businesses that ran this way had been collapsing at a great rate after the spendthrift silliness of the last decade, and Dan had wasted no tears on them. He had always felt that money should be spent on the business of doing business, on operating equipment, computers and communications, not creature comforts for corporate giants. The sort of lavishness that surrounded him reflected a selfishness and meanness of spirit that he had always distrusted. For a few seconds, he forgot the worry of just why he was here, and what to do. This was not the sort of place in which he could ever work.

The moment of unease was interrupted by the door opening and Carson’s assistant entered, walked softly up to the ebony desk and deposited a silver tray on the empty surface. More lavish expenditure, thought Dan. The tray contained a large silver teapot off which the bright sunlight reflected patterns on the wall. The pot was matched by a tiny filigree silver platter of lemon slices and a small silver basin filled with sugar cubes. Instead of cups and saucers, tall glasses were held in patterned silver holders with handles. Some painful memory twitched at the sight of the glass holders, and Dan found himself staring at the silver items, almost hypnotized, until his head swam and his heart pounded so hard he could have sworn Carson could hear it.

The woman left, and the sound of the door opening and closing shook Dan out of the helplessness that held him. Carson poured the tea into the glasses, took a slice of lemon and dropped it into one glass, followed by two cubes of sugar and used a long slender spoon to stir the mixture. He waved in a general sort of way at the silverware.

"Please help yourself," he said.

Dan followed his example warily. He had never had tea this way before. As a child of working-class parents in England, tea was a strong brew served in earthenware cups with milk and sugar, not this fancy fiddling with lemon and silver spoons. He sipped the liquid and found it utterly delightful. But again, under the treat given to his taste buds, he felt a small twinge of tension. Maybe I'm coming down with a cold, he thought.

"So, Dan," said Carson. "Let's get started. Can we talk about your early life for few moments?"

Dan stared at him. This was the same request Emily had made a few weeks ago, and he remembered then that he had felt some uncertainty at the way she had questioned him. It was time to take the offensive, he decided.

"Mister Carson," he said, feeling his heart fluttering as he leapt off into the void. "I don't believe any of this. There's no systems director's job. You wanted to see me, probably for exactly the same reasons I wanted to see you. Let's stop playing games."

Carson blinked and sat back in his seat. He folded his hands in front of his jaw and studied Dan like a butterfly in a collection.

"Games?" he said. "Dan, I fail to understand you."

For just a second or two, Dan's conviction wavered. Was he making a complete fool of himself? Then he saw the coldness in Carson's eyes, and the hostility, and he knew that he was in no error.

"Somehow you and Emily James are linked," he said. "The link includes the recent murder of Kevin Fitzpatrick which allowed your organization to win a battle you were otherwise losing. You appear to know things about me that I don't know myself. So, let's stop playing the game, and let's get down to the truth."

The silence rang in the office like a gong. Carson leaned forward in his chair, reached for his glass of tea and sipped it. For a few seconds, Dan felt sure he saw worry in the other man's face. Carson lifted his eyes from his tea and stared directly at Dan. The blank, impervious face was icy. Then the horror started.

"Misha," he said. *"Slooshaiche mnye."*

Dan could not move. He couldn't even look away from Carson's stare.

"Muy nadsmotrchiki," Carson said. *"Muy tvoi nozhki, tron."*

Dan's heart began to pound. His head throbbed.

Dan Bailey began to die.

Death began as a numbing blow in his stomach, like a punch from a heavy fist. It paralyzed him, stole the breath from him, and all he could do was stare blankly at the flat, watchful face before him. A jangling began in his ears, grew so loud that it vibrated his ear drums with pain. His hands were sweating, clenched so tightly on the chair that his forearms were cramped. Only his knees moved, with a rapid jiggling completely out of his control. The din in his ears became a scream so intense that it lost clarity and grew into a roaring like a cyclone. Cramps began in his legs, his guts and his shoulders, and he vomited straight in front of himself, covering his knees and splashing the front of Carson's immaculate desk. All he could focus on was that dreadful, impassive face that watched him die.

The cramps got worse, every limb was shaking, and the immobility vanished as he flung himself forward, his knees rose and he clamped his arms around them, falling off the chair in fetal rigidity. He rolled hard against the wall, choking for breath, seeing the other man's eyes still on him, the unmoving figure in the leather chair, argyle socks over perfectly polished black shoes. Dan stared at those socks, grasping for something normal in the insanity all around him until the winds of horror blacked out the room and replaced it with something worse.

He saw through an insane blizzard, a miserable landscape. Flat, endless plains, dirty brown in the grip of winter. Faces moved before him, dulled with hopelessness and hunger. One turned to him, frightened, looking around for hateful ears. "MISHA!" she screamed, and the echoes of his name, his name, *oh God, my name,* slammed around the void of his skull. The faces, the landscape vanished, a bleak, empty, undecorated room took its place. There were others around him but he knew he dare not look at them, only at the thin man before them. Earphones clamped on his head removed all sound from space but the sibilant voice.

"Dan Bailey Dan Bailey Dan Bailey Dan Bailey...." On and on the voice went, no pause, no intonation, no life, just his name. His name? *Where was Misha...?* The agony took his breath away as it ripped through his body. There is no Misha until... until they say... until they say... *Misha, slooshaiche mnye. Muy nadsmotrchiki, muy tvoi nozhki, tron...* Dan Bailey Dan Bailey Dan Bailey....

Another room. Dark. A movie screen on one wall. Pictures of England. Of Birmingham. Manchester. Places he had never visited but knew as his home. Familiarity born from coloured flickers on a wall. Days and days and days into endless days, watching these pictures. The red brick of the Central Grammar School on Whitworth Street... it was a women's college now.. they had moved to Longsight to a new building when he was a junior.. *he had never been there...* the bus station in Piccadilly, multiple floors of Lewis' Department Store, the huge dome of the Central Library where he had spent days reading in the echoing silence, the Town Hall where, at Christmas they draped a massive Santa Claus in his sleigh, engulfing the structure like King Kong on the Empire State Building, all these sights were completely familiar, never seen. His house with the stained-glass leaded windows in the quiet cul-de-sac in Victoria Park, his parents with the nasal Birmingham whine at odds with the broad Manchester accent he had picked up so quickly... *he had never known them, they had never existed...* He saw scenes that he knew intimately from growing up among them, but knew also that not one of them was true.

Dan had no idea how long it had lasted, but slowly the madness faded. As his mind cleared, Dan found himself still huddled in a corner of Vincent Carson's office. A janitor, armed with a bucket and mop was standing over him. Carson stirred and leaned forward to help him. Dan shook off the hand and staggered to his feet, somehow made it to his chair from which he had collapsed (how long ago? he wondered), and fell into it. Carson poured a glass of water from the carafe behind his chair and passed it to Dan. Dan sipped it cautiously, grimacing at the acrid taste of vomit in his throat, then sipped some more.

"My visitor was taken ill, Ed," said Carson. "Sorry to have to ask you to clean this mess up."

Frozen in his chair, Dan watched as the janitor mopped hot water over the stains on the carpet, scrubbed at the revolting mess then dried it off with a heavy cloth. The janitor finally sprayed the afflicted areas with an odour-killing scent, then packed up his equipment and left. It helped a little, but the awful stench remained on Dan's clothes and his breath. All he wanted to do was get to a shower and clean up. He took another drink of water and finally managed to get some words out. It was more a tortured croak than a coherent speech.

"Jesus Christ, Carson, just what the hell am I? And who in God's name are you?"

Carson's smile had no warmth in it. "You are my completely faithful and reliable servant," he said. "That's who you are."

"I don't understand." Carson's words had flown over Dan's head like a flight of migrating geese.

"No doubt," said Carson, the smile as cold as last week's ashes in the fireplace. "But you will."

"Please, Carson," Dan begged. "For God's sake, tell me what's going on!"

"God, Misha? God has no place in this!"

Dan shook his head in frustration and pain.

"TELL ME!!" cried Dan. "Why Misha?" Though he already knew why. Misha, nickname form of Mikhail, a Russian form of Michael. That much he had picked up over the years. And it was truly Dan's name, not Daniel, not any English name, he already understood that much, knew it like any person knows his own name. "Why any of this?" he asked, feeling the pain.

Carson shook his head. "Not yet," he said. "You smell too much. There's a private washroom across from here. Go and clean up."

Dan badly wanted explanations, but just as badly he wanted to remove some of the damage from himself. Feeling as if his legs were working to the pull of a puppet-master, he walked out of the office into the empty corridor, crossed to the unmarked door opposite the office entrance, and found himself in a small, but luxurious washroom. He took his trousers off and spent half an hour doing as much as he could to clean up the awful mess with hot water and soap. While he scrubbed, dampened, wiped and rinsed, his mind went blank. When he had finished, it seemed as if only a few seconds had passed when he weaved an unsteady path back to the office. Everywhere was silence. Somehow the time had flashed to after five, and a ringing emptiness covered the floor.

Carson seemed not to have moved when Dan opened the door. Only some papers had appeared on his desk, and he was reading them with bifocal spectacles which he removed as Dan slipped nervously through the doorway.

"Ah, Misha, I'm glad you could clean up a little," he said with a small smile. "Sit down again."

Dan returned to the seat across from Carson as meekly obedient as a small puppy. Puppets moved like this, he thought vacantly.

"They did say the first time would be violent," said Carson, more to himself than as a conversational piece.

"The first...?"

"It's been eighteen years since that trigger was placed in your mind. They said the first time it was used, your mind would have difficulties breaking out of the moulds."

Dan shook his head in incomprehension.

Carson nodded. "Your name is Mikhail Vorosov," he said. "You were born in Kharborovsk in August, 1956." He gazed absently out of window at Lake Michigan and spoke as if the words were learned by heart. "Your father died when you were five and we took you away when you were eight," he said.

"We?" croaked Dan. "Who's we?"

"The Party."

"The Communist Party?"

Carson's blue eyes swung back to him from the Lake. "Of course!" he snapped. "What else?" The contempt and arrogance in his voice were knife-edged.

Dan wanted to bolt from his chair, but his muscles wouldn't respond. He seemed to have no control over his body at all.

"We put you in a training school next to the naval base in Murmansk," continued Carson, "and made you into an English schoolboy."

His eyes studied the bowed head of Dan in the opposite chair. Dan saw a brief glimpse in his mind of the Siberian landscape, the miserable huts, the training room.

"There was a Dan Bailey, of course," Carson said. "He was an abandoned child, just as you remember, and he really was adopted by a couple in Walsall. But he died of meningitis when he was five. Our people in England got his birth certificate and had a valid passport issued for him with your photograph. It's not difficult."

Dan made no sound.

"Your last three years of training were under deep mental conditioning," said Carson. "Amazingly accurate the way some people had forecast that capability. We had been trying for years to achieve it and yours was the first class to graduate under the technique."

He was talking in a gentle, friendly fashion now, like an elderly uncle helping out a nephew with some good advice. "You forgot everything about your past life except for the triggers planted deep in your mind. We smuggled you into Finland with a BMW motorcycle just as you remember, for a European vacation. We let you go on to Australia and then back to England from there. You had been provided with perfectly forged graduation certificates from high school with grades good enough to get you into University and we left you alone for a time to get your degree."

Dan couldn't speak. He had such clear memories of the excitement of preparing for the European trip, loading the BMW and crossing the Channel on the Hovercraft. He had headed south after reaching Calais and spent three months roaming around before he got to Finland... *None of it had happened,* said his mind. *All of the travelling before Finland was a dream.. How could the girl in Milan be a dream? The astonishing legs astride a Lambretta scooter had drawn alongside as we rounded the cathedral, she had waved at me, I waved back, and drove to a halt in a small parking spot. I took off my helmet and was delighted by her soft voice and delicious accent, and we spent the day together seeing her city as a local would. Three days later I left, with memories that made me smile many times in the years since. How could that memory not be real?*

I had stopped by Munich Cathedral, and an old man had stared at me, finally approaching with hesitation. A conversation started, and the old man told me of the days when the British bombers had hit this town, and he had hidden in the cellar with his mother and three sisters. Warmed by the old man's friendliness, and feeling some guilt for the event, I followed him to a pavement cafe, and we had sat for an hour talking about the war and how it should never happen again. Had that old man ever really existed?

On a bridge in a tiny, beautiful village near Florence, I had parked the BMW and sat on the wall, enjoying the warm sunshine and the clear water chattering underneath. A crowd of small children gathered round me, and eventually a few of their parents followed. I spent the afternoon giving rides on my bike to the small children and the whole village had finally turned out to watch, laughing and having themselves a ball. It turned into an impromptu picnic on the bridge that lasted till nightfall, and I had difficulty finding a spot to pitch my tent. That delightful, enchanted afternoon was a fiction? That will break my heart.

The crowd of New Zealanders having a barbecue by the roadside near Geneva who had waved me into the party, were they all phantoms moving to the choreography of a dream-master somewhere in Russia? There had been six of them, travelling in an old Ford Transit van. Three men with beards, three girls with long hair, all speaking in that curious accent that had lost the vowels into a generalized neutral sound that was characteristic of Kiwis, they said. Wonderful sense of humor in all of them, all so delighted to be seeing Europe, so natural in their friendship to me. A dream? A lie? It couldn't be.

"The software house in England that recruited you, they were our people of course." Carson had paused, seeing Dan reflect back on old, false memories. "We put the reins back on as you graduated. The opening for a legend was spotted by Moscow and you were perfect for it."

"A... legend..?" Dan threw off the implanted memories of a holiday he had never had and fought to concentrate on what was being said. Despite the agony and despair, he knew he had to learn everything he could about this dreadful thing that had happened to him. In the knowledge there might be a way out.

Carson nodded in an agreeable manner. "The technical term," he said, as if conducting a classroom seminar. "A complete myth, but a perfect cover, all the details documented and forged to perfection. A real live person with a verifiable background but nobody to dispute it. Notice how you went back to England several times in the last few years but never went to Manchester or Birmingham?"

That hit Dan hard. Carson was right. Dan had returned to England six times since coming to the USA, but each time he had thought of a trip down memory lane to his old "childhood" haunts, something had stopped him, some reluctance, some fear he had rationalized as unwillingness to go back after his parents had died. He had not looked up old friends, nor visited his old school, just stayed in the London region and done the tourist things, feeling like an Englishman, sneering at the visitors.

"We put that block in just to make sure," said Carson. "Then we arranged the transfer to the US. I'd been here for ten years already, establishing myself as a businessman when Moscow sent you to me. I've been watching you ever since, waiting for the next step."

He looked hard at Dan, studied him for few seconds. "So now we are here," he smiled gently, "and I want your help."

"You won't get it."

"Oh, but I will," said Carson softly. "You really have no choice in the matter, I'm sure you can see that. After all, you're a loyal Russian and a Communist. How can you not serve your country?"

"NO!" The words came out weakly, but Dan felt his anger. "I'm not a Russian! I'm Dan Bailey, I'm English! I like living here, and I like this country. I won't help you damage it."

Carson was unmoved. "As I said, Misha, you have no choice. Triggers remain in your mind, I know how to pull them, and when I do, you will obey me. It really doesn't matter at all if you want to or not. *You will obey me."*

Dan struggled with a need to argue. "This is crazy," he said. "You can't hypnotize people like that. You can't make people do things they don't want to do."

Carson let out a laugh. “Misha,” he said, glee lighting up his face. “Hypnotism has as much to with what we did as a haircut has to do with brain surgery.”

He tapped his fingers on his desk as if considering how much to say. “We had you for twelve years,” he continued. “We had the finest skills in the world working on you. We had chemicals the Americans have only dreamed of. We had so many things, Misha. Hypnotism had very little to do with it.”

Dan still felt rebellion. “I could tell the authorities.” His defiant words were stronger than he was, but he had to fight back somehow.

Carson’s smile widened. “And just whom would you tell, Misha?”

Dan found it difficult to meet Carson’s eyes. The force of his personality easily rode over Dan’s weakened spirits, but he kept trying. “The FBI,” he said. “Maybe the CIA.”

Carson laughed outright. “And naturally they’d believe you!” he said. “Can you imagine it? They’d show you to the door or insist on a psychiatric examination! Anyway, you can’t tell anyone.”

“Why not?”

“Because that’s one of the blocks, Misha,” replied Carson. “Please, try it, tell anyone you want, you’ll see.”

He was right, Dan knew. He could feel the blockages as he tried to form the words in his mind. The nausea rose in his throat, the sweat formed again on his forehead and in his armpits, and his breathing became tortured. He could see the satisfied look on Carson’s face.

“I have several ideas of how to use you, Misha,” said Carson. “I’ll think about the best one and call you later.”

Dan shook his head violently in anger and frustration. “For Christ’s sake, WHY, Carson? The Cold War has been over for years. What earthly bloody use is there in starting that garbage up again?”

Carson's laugh was straight out, open, totally amused. "Of course it's over, Misha, that's the glorious point!" He leaned back in his leather armchair and waved his arm expansively. A gleam of light reflected off the gold cufflink in his perfect French-cuffed shirt and raced around the walls. "Your training school in Murmansk was closed many years ago, the department that ran you and the other legends was disbanded. I have nobody to report to, nobody knows we're here or who we are. Don't you see, I have you all to myself!"

"To do what, for God's sake?"

"To take full advantage of this wonderful free-market, capitalist system, that's what!"

Dan was bewildered. "I don't understand," he said.

Carson chuckled again and leaned forward on his desk, looking confidingly at Dan. *How horrible it is,* thought Dan, *that he could look so friendly, but speak such terrifying words.*

"I'm a pretty good businessman for a loyal Communist," Carson said with a smile. "But do you think I got to be President of the Hanfield Group just on ability? Of course not, there were several men better qualified. They just got removed, that's all."

Dan stared blankly at the silver teapot, easier to do than watch Carson's face and the evil that sat there. The curve of the pot showed a miniature version of Carson gesticulating, his arms distorted to many times the length of his body.

"A traffic accident," continued Carson. "An air crash, a drug misadventure, a couple of scandals with well-placed ladies operating under orders, it's amazing how easily the competition can be removed if you have the right tools!" The pride and amusement in his face were evident, like a middle-aged salesman talking about some of his successes in the marketplace.

"You mean you have more like me?" The idea had not struck Dan before, but now it did with an awful sensation of fear. And under the fear, some memory...

"I used to have several," Carson said, snapping Dan back from the shadowy memories of other children, weeping at the pain of Gemorov's whiplashes *(Gemorov? The thin man who lashed out at us with his cane. I remember his name!)*. "Most have been damaged in one way or another. But I don't need many now. Just a controller, a couple of assistants and you. That will do fine for the future."

"Controller?" Dan heard the word 'damaged' too, and wanted to ask about it, but Carson gave him no chance.

"Of course!" he said. "I can't keep my eyes on you all by myself." For the first time since the initial meeting, Carson rose from his desk and moved to the wall where the awful pictures hung. He took a handkerchief from his pocket and carefully dusted the frames, peering closely at the ornate gold surrounds. "Several of us came over with me in the beginning," he continued. "Not conditioned like you, but well trained to take over the life of some American who had vanished somewhere. Just a few of my team remain. You will meet them eventually."

"What happens then?" Dan had to ask, but feared the answer.

"Then you'll help me expand the business," replied Carson.

"Like hell I will!"

"But Misha," countered Carson. "You already have! And most professionally, I may add."

Dan's mouth was dry. "How?" he croaked, dreading the answer, but already knowing what it was.

"You removed Kevin Fitzpatrick for me," was the reply.

Dan sat motionless. He remembered now, how he had obeyed the instructions placed in his head by the night-time telephone caller. He had located the forged credit cards and driver's license from a secret cache in the apartment, and that evening, hired the car and driven to Bloomington. He had no memory of how the guns had been placed in the trunk. When he woke the following morning, his memories had told him that he had worked late at the office.

Dan looked up at his tormentor with agony in his face. "Carson, you're a bastard!" he grated. "One way or the other, I'll get out of this. And when I do, I'll be coming to kill you."

Carson walked back to his desk and leaned against the front of it, folding his arms, looking down at Dan like a parent patiently correcting a naughty child. "Misha, we've already covered this. You don't have a choice."

"I won't help you!"

"Misha, I told you..."

"NO! I don't give a damn what you say, somehow I'll fight you!"

Carson shook his head wearily and looked straight into Dan's defiant face. Anticipation gleamed in his blue eyes. *"Misha, slooshaiche mnye,"* he murmured. *"Nad toboyoo mstryahshchooyoo rookoo, ee bezzhalostno palyetz vneez."*

The scream of pain Dan let out would have been heard over the whole floor if anyone had been there. Fire consumed his whole head and every nerve in his body jammed wide open to let the pain pass through. A thought moved feebly behind his eyes that this was how death in the electric chair must feel, then he blacked out.

* * *

"You see, Misha, you really don't have a choice."

The words reached Dan across a vast plain of silence. They murmured gently in his ear as the waves of pain receded down towards his right foot and finally faded with a last regretful tingle. He felt as if he had been drowned in a flood of pain, until a drain hole had been opened and the pain had run away, leaving him alone on the bottom of a vanished ocean. He became conscious of aches and creaks across his back and shoulders. He was lying flat out on the ground by the seat he had occupied many years ago when Carson had spoken some simple phrase...

'I raise my avenging hand and, showing no mercy, turn my thumb down?' Was that all it took, a few key words spoken in Russian? A line or two from a poem by Yevtoshenko? Dan was not surprised any more that he had understood the phrase or its origins, just as he now understood the first trigger phrase *'We are the overseers, we are your legs, oh throne'* that had tied ropes of slavery around him and forced him to sit motionless while Carson told him of his real identity. More Yevtoshenko. How odd that a communist agent would use the words of a dissident Russian poet to enslave him, he thought.

The first words had been an order to listen to Carson. The second had been a punishment trigger. So simple, but worse than a nuclear bomb to the one programmed to hear it. Dan shivered at the recollection of the agony and wondered if permanent damage had been caused.

"You will be able to go home soon, Misha," the gentle voice continued. "But please do believe me, whatever I ask of you, you will do."

Dan hauled himself to his feet with care and difficulty, and managed to stand upright, trembling with the shock of the events of the afternoon. Carson was sitting back in his seat, but some time must have passed, because he had made fresh tea and was sipping it thoughtfully from his silver-handled glass. Steam was rising from the silver pot, and the sun no longer glinted off the shining surfaces.

The Russian style of drinking was now familiar to Dan. That was how the guards at the compound had drunk, he remembered. That was how Georgii had prepared it in his room across from his... *What was that memory?* He now recognized the "Soviet Realism" school of painting on the wall. Not Victorian at all, but some scene of a post-revolution Russian battle with the traditional heroes in head bandages, so beloved of the Stalinist-era bureaucrats who dictated what was acceptable and what was not. Carson flaunted his Russian origins at the world and nobody had noticed.

Carson continued to sip his tea calmly and watched Dan. Dan felt weak and shattered, as if he had completed a marathon run for which he had not trained properly.

"What do you want of me, Carson?" His voice was faltering, uncertain.

"Here are some instructions, Misha," said Carson. "You will think no more about Kevin Fitzpatrick. You will forget your suspicions of Emily. Now you will go home to her and wait for me to call for you." Carson placed his glass on the desk and stood up. "Go back to your job at MidWestern, we will tell the head-hunter that you were not interested in the position here. Put today's conversation out of your mind. One day I will call, and you will come."

Oh God, of course! Emily! thought Dan in despair. *How closely have I been watched all these years, and even more so since Emily moved in?*

"I will let you go now, Misha," said Carson. Dan felt his muscles return to his control, felt the power of movement again. He pulled himself to his feet from the chair, walked from the beautiful office with the ugly paintings, took the elevator to the street level and caught a cab home.

* * *

Dan stood in the shower confused and disorientated and let the hot water thunder over his head. He remembered walking in through his doorway, grateful that he had met no other occupants of the building on the way in, then flung his suit into a pile on the floor of the bedroom. He was almost frantic to reach the cleansing torrent of hot water.

But I didn't normally get home this way, he thought as the water poured over his head. *What was the problem?* Normally, he reached his apartment in a mixture of eagerness to see Emily and with a healthy hunger for dinner. Why this distress and sense of defilement?

Vague pictures floated through his mind. He had left his office early in the afternoon, that he remembered. *An interview, that's right, I'd had an interview,* he thought. But the details were hazy. And for some strange reason, he felt uninterested in exploring why. He was far more concerned with the memo he wanted to write to his boss, the company president about an idea he'd had for linking other systems into the network.

He turned off the hot water, climbed out of the shower and dried off in the pleasant warmth of his bedroom. He dressed in light jeans and a tee-shirt, selected a steak from the freezer and began grilling it with care. Lost in the friendly hissing of the meat, he worked out details of the memo to the president.

A meeting with Vincent Carson, he thought, idly. A real industrial heavy. *Couldn't have been too interesting,* he thought, *I can hardly remember a thing about it. Odd looking little bugger, bald head, served tea in a strange fashion....*

He tested the steak, it seemed about right. He lifted it out to a plate, poured some canned corn to join it, and extracted yesterday's half-finished bottle of champagne to accompany the meal. *Not a bad way to live,* he mused contentedly. *That memo, I'll prepare it tonight on my computer, take it to work on a diskette tomorrow, have it on the boss' desk by nine...*

The phone buzzed. Swallowing the mouthful of champagne he had just taken, he lifted it.

"This is me!"

Her voice was the most beautiful thing Dan had ever heard.

"So how is my favourite technical writer?" he said. *I miss you terribly,* he thought. *Emily, please come home.*

"Pooped!" she said. "I've talked to four separate companies today, taken a ton of notes and I'm trying to type them up in my hotel room." Her voice had the crystal-clear diction and lilt that he loved so much, but another note was there, one he could not identify.

"Keeps you out of the bar and all those skirt-chasing salesmen, at least!" For some reason, Dan didn't want to let her know how lonely and confused he was feeling. *Why am I feeling this way?* he wondered. *This is silly, Dan.*

"Just make sure you're not bringing any strange women to that apartment while I'm away!" Her voice was warm.

"They're not strange!" he said, feeling better by the moment. "I know every one of them!"

"So, what happened today?" she asked. Suddenly the tension was evident in her voice. Dan realized it always had been, but he hadn't recognized what it was until now.

"Not a lot," he answered, puzzled by her tone. "Though I got called for an interview for a job."

A short silence rang down the line.

"Who from?" she asked. There was an edge to her voice.

"It was..." He had to search his mind for the company's name. It seemed to be receding rapidly. "It was with the Hanfield Group," he finally said.

The silence from Emily was longer. "And how did it go?" she asked after a few seconds.

"Can't really remember," said Dan. "It didn't seem to last all that long." Something puzzled him about his answer, but he couldn't place it. *Why was I so late getting home?*

"Daniel my love, please be careful." It seemed an odd thing to say, thought Dan, but he disregarded it as part of the general confusion he was experiencing.

"I will," he said. "When are you coming home? I miss you."

Her voice was gentle again, and still had the power to send shivers through him. "I'm arriving on United's 471 at six tomorrow," she said. "Will you meet me at O'Hare?"

"Try keeping me away! I'll be there by lunchtime, waiting! I love you."

"I love you too." Her voice was so sweet, he thought. He badly needed her here to keep the demons away from his mind. "Throw those other women out!" she added.

"Okay, just for you. They're gone."

"I should hope so!" The smile was back in her voice. "'Bye, love!"

"See you tomorrow," he said. "Don't work too hard!"

He hung up the phone and finished the steak and the champagne feeling on top of the world, then returned to the computer to complete his memo to the president. At nine, he switched on the television to watch something mindless for a while and went to bed early, feeling totally at peace with the universe. The interview with Carson seemed distant and irrelevant. He thought about Emily again and fell asleep.

* * *

He was waiting at the airline gate when she came out, and the sight of her drove everything else from his mind. Any strain that might have existed between them vanished, indeed he could no longer remember that anything had ever been wrong. She walked straight into his arms and hugged him, ignoring the lines of travellers and greeters flowing around them.

"Let's go home," he said, and watched the smile grow in her eyes.

"A great idea," she replied. He picked up her small suitcase, she linked her arm in his and they walked the endless corridors of O'Hare Field to the car park.

On the drive home, she told him about the companies she had visited, the research she had covered, and Dan didn't see the occasional anxious glances she directed at him.

They reached home, entered the apartment, and Emily went to unpack while Dan poured champagne. She walked back into the lounge as he was switching on the television, took the glass he offered her, kissed him, and then took a mouthful of champagne. She drew a deep breath.

"God!" she said. "I needed that!"

"God?" he echoed, without thinking. "God has no place in this."

"In what?" she asked, looking curiously at him.

"I don't know," he replied, puzzled. "It just..." He stopped. "The words just popped into my head. Maybe it was something I saw on television."

"You're weird, Bailey," she said with a grin, and took another drink. He followed her example, and tried to ignore the slight trembling in his hand and the inexplicable feeling of anger he felt.

She studied him carefully, and for a second he felt cold, almost as if her gaze were coolly analytical. Then the tiny spell broke as she moved towards the kitchen.

"Just a light snack?" she asked. "I got a sandwich on the plane. How about you?"

"Something light sounds good," he called back, sweeping away the tiny discomfort he had felt. He followed her into the kitchen, refilled the champagne glass then laughed as she made sweeping gestures at him to get back to the living room. He obeyed her, sat in the sofa and turned up the television sound a little. A few minutes later, she joined him carrying a tray of cold cuts of meat, a small slab of brie cheese and some biscuits, and they settled down to watch an old classic on the American Movie Channel.

At ten, Dan switched back to the news channel, and they listened to the international news, the latest developments out of Washington, and the local Chicago regional events. Dan leaned forward to take the last olive from its bowl, and pour the remainder of the champagne. The television was burbling quietly, the American standard blonde with big jaws and a plastic smile reciting the day's news, sharing the lines with a vapidly handsome male in rimless spectacles.

Dan jerked upright with a wail of distress. The house on the screen was familiar to him, dreadfully familiar. *I know it!* he cried inside. *Oh God, it's happening again!*

"... and this news just in. In Wilmette, a bizarre murder was discovered this morning when police noticed a pile of newspapers on the lawn and decided to investigate. Inside, they found the body of Paul Jackson, aged fifty....."

Dan was standing, staring at the screen, rigid. Dimly, he could hear Emily calling his name, trying to turn him away... *... the knife in my hand was bloody. Some of the blood stained the edges of my shirt cuff and hazed the gleam of the gold cuff link. His body sprawled across the armchair, the dazed expression still on his face...*

"NO!" The voice was his own, rasping oddly in his throat. "No, oh please God, no, no, no..."

"… he had been dead for several days and appeared to have been stabbed to death…"

Dan was wailing incoherently, the pain and fear tearing at his chest, tears falling in splashes, no words, no thoughts, just pictures in his head of blood on a brocade armchair, ripped hands, screams. Emily was pulling at him, shouting his name, and then she moved directly between him and the television. For a brief moment, she looked hard into his eyes, then slapped him, a full-blooded, flat-handed blow on his right cheek. Dan barely felt the sting of the strike, as if his face was already numbed. Blankly, he looked down at her, her action, not the pain shocking him out of the uncontrollable dread. Her face was full of love, gentle and caring. She looked deeply into his eyes and touched his cheek where he could feel the sting.

"Misha, slooshaiche mnye" she said. *"Muy nadsmotrchiki, muy tvoi nozhki, tron."*

Chapter 5

No sickness.

That was all Dan could think of for a few seconds. The memory of the first time that phrase had been spoken returned to his mind like a tornado, and for a moment he tensed himself for a repeat of that awful time. But there was no sickness. Just an enervating fatigue, almost pleasant, the sort of weariness felt after finishing a long drive home.

He stared at her. He could say nothing. Muscles hung slackly in his body like becalmed sails. He remembered the entire meeting with Vincent Carson, and understood now why he had lost all memories of the stress that had arisen with Emily.

"Sit down, Misha," she said. Obediently, Dan walked back to his favourite chair and carefully lowered himself into the red surrounds. He couldn't take his eyes off her. She turned to the television, switched it off and turned back to face him. Her arms were folded across her chest, placing even more distance between them.

"I had to do that, Misha. It was the only way to stop you going crazy."

"That is not my name." Dan felt cold in her betrayal.

She shook her head, irritated. "When you're under control, it would be risky to call you anything but Misha. The conditioning is very deep."

"And I'm under control now?" He didn't know why he asked. He knew he couldn't move, but he wanted to hear it from her own lips.

"Yes," she said, sadness in her eyes. "That trigger phrase was designed for initial control. Until I release you, you'll stay this way. You can ask questions, remember your Russian life, but you can't move. There are other phrases, too, depending on what's needed."

Dan shivered with the memory of the pain Carson had inflicted on him and a warning tingle flickered behind his eyes. "Yes, I know," he said hoarsely.

"You know?" She stared at him, moving her face closer to his. "What else has been said?"

"Carson nearly killed me with one." He felt a tiny tweak of pain behind his eyeballs, remembering the agony he had undergone on the carpet of Carson's luxurious office.

"Oh Jesus, the bastard used the punishment trigger on you?"

"If that's what it was, he used it."

"He's a worse pig than I thought."

How could you know what he is? thought Dan. As much as he could move his head, he looked at her, standing motionless a few feet away.

"Have you been part of this thing all along?" he asked.

"Yes," she said. "I came over about fifteen years ago to join Carson's team."

Depression flooded his whole body. Any lingering energy was submerged beneath the dark wave and he felt barely able to sit upright. His arms lay flat on his thighs.

"You mean all this, our relationship, loving you, living together, that was all play acting, was it?" The most beautiful thing in his life had turned to rank, rotting garbage in seconds. He wanted to hate her, but could do nothing but grieve. The first warning prickle of tears made her image blur a little.

She dropped her arms from across her chest and moved to him, knelt down at his knees just as they had been only a little while ago. The tracks of the dried tears were dim lines on her face. Her fine eyes reflected the warm yellow glow of the light from the hallway.

"That's how it was supposed to be," she said softly. "Carson gave me your name three years ago, and I've been watching you since. When he told me to, I made contact with you. The developments you had carried out at work gave me a perfect excuse. Things went wrong at that point."

"How?"

She got to her feet and began to walk around the room.

"Misha, I need to tell you something and try and explain what's happened. Please try to understand."

"Do I have a choice?" Her hands fluttered around her face in distress. *God, how I want to get up,* thought Dan, *to hold her, put things back to where they had been.* He loved her, hated her, feared her, loved her.

"I began my training twenty years ago, when I was just fifteen," she continued. "Both my parents had been in the military. I was just a child, growing up in a time when the Cold War was really intense. I got all the propaganda, all the bullshit about what an evil place America was. I swallowed it all, I really believed that America was out to destroy the world and take over everything, including us! That's what I'd been *taught,* dammit!"

Her pacing on the blue carpet was agitated, deep indents appeared in her tracks where she whirled and turned. Dan could only watch and hurt.

"Then my mother died and I was given a place with the Intelligence Service. They offered to make me an agent, put me over here and work with the espionage teams. It seemed like a good thing to do, and I took it."

"So who was Emily James?"

She shrugged. "Similar story to yours. She was an orphan from South Carolina, died when she was three.

Our teams here are adept at getting the documents and creating genuine histories. I just took over a ready-made life here."

"Poor Emily James. I really loved her."

"Dan, please..." She gasped, realizing her error in using his other name. For a second, Dan felt oddly twisted inside, the feeling of looking at one of those clever pictures where the perspective can make several different patterns, and the mind has just clicked into a different viewpoint.

"I think it's okay," he said. "No effect."

"Thank God!"

"God, Emily? God has no place in this." Dan had no weapons at all, just silly, sarcastic comments. This time, he remembered who had first used that phrase on him. Carson!

"For eight years I did what I believed was good for Russia, and for everybody else, Dan. I did it well, too," she continued. "Then everything changed. I made friends, got into the work I do and realized how happy I could be, just being an ordinary person." She paused for a moment, her face in shadows, lost in some private memories. Despite the numbed feelings, Dan felt a flash of jealousy wondering who she had loved that caused that momentary reflection. She stopped her pacing in front of him.

"After I while, I realized that all the stuff they had taught me was garbage! I could see that America had problems, but it wasn't the vicious, inhuman place the KGB had told me. And then Gorbachev came along and the whole rotten business fell apart. Carson's team was suddenly on its own, no mission, no goals. We didn't even know who to contact back in Moscow. I thought we'd be called home, but nothing happened. I think the whole program of deep-cover agents had been cancelled, and in the confusion, they must have forgotten about us. Dan, you can't believe how happy I was! I thought I had a real chance just to live the life I had and forget all the past stuff."

Dan felt as a quadriplegic must feel, tied immobile to a chair while his mind was free to feel anger, hurt, frustration. "But you kept on working as an agent," he said harshly. "What did you do, put poison in wells?"

She shook her head, ignoring the petty sarcasm. "I've done nothing for many years, not since everything fell apart. My work was mainly obtaining military technical data and providing false data for double agents. When Carson made me contact you, I assumed it was to make sure your conditioning was still sound. I did what he asked, but we forgot to allow for one thing."

"What, that I might fall in love with you and complicate the issue?"

She came back to the chair and knelt at his feet again, taking his hands. Her fingers were cool. He wanted to hold them, pull her to him, but the blackness in his mind left him unmoving.

"No, Dan," she said gently, looking into his face. There was a small smile curving her lips. "Falling in love with me was totally predictable. You had been set up to do that for the last ten years. You won't remember any of it, but three or four times you've been called with trigger phrases, then sent photographs of me. I was always going to be your controller eventually."

He looked down at her face, and for a weird moment, her features seemed fuzzy, seen through a wave of distorting hot air. She was still beautiful, but the face was not quite the flawless loveliness that he first had seen. He stared, and her face returned to normal. *So that was the reason for the violently wonderful way in which I had fallen in love,* he thought. *Even my passions were dictated by somebody else.* She sensed the hurt in him.

"The problem was a lot worse than that," she whispered. "I really did fall in love with you."

"Like hell you did!"

She flinched at the violence in his voice, but kept hold of his hands. "Dan, do you really think I could play-act the way we have lived together for six months? Do you think I could pretend the way we've been in bed?"

"The KGB obviously trained you well."

It hurt her, he could tell. He felt a flash of triumph that one of his small weapons had worked. *Oh Emily, I had loved you so much,* he wept inside.

She looked down at her lap, hiding her face as if to avoid the hatred he was hurling at her. "Then Carson called you, and I realized he was up to something. I knew he was using you somehow, but I didn't know for what."

"Now you know! I've been killing people for him." Oh GOD how that hurt! he cried. At least two innocent people had died at his hands, how could he ever live with that?

... he had opened the door when I had called out that I had a parcel for him from the Hanfield Group. "Ah yes," he said, "Mister Carson had told me to expect documents in connection with the credit line we were discussing." I followed him into the living room and waited while he ripped open the heavy brown envelope. Inside was blank paper. "What's this?" he said, turning to me, and gasped in shock as he saw the heavy knife in my hand...

Had there been more, would he remember them in time, also?

"Yes," she said. "Now I know. And I also know that your conditioning was not as strong as it was supposed to be. These memory flashbacks, the dreams, they were never supposed to happen."

"Are there more like me?"

She shook her head. "You're the only one that seemed to work. Lots of others were trained, but something always went wrong. They think that you were a success because you were already pre-conditioned as a child, and they had twelve years to work on you."

"Pre-conditioned?" Dan had to think hard to remember what she had been saying. A loud buzzing was hurting his ears.

"You were a single child of a widowed mother," she said, sitting back on her heels but still keeping a gentle hold of his hands. He stared down at the entwined fingers, hating the touch, but terrified she would let go. "You had spent four years in the Young Communists before they took you away, so they had all the time in the world to soak you with their ideas. You were tested for your reaction to hypnosis many times and they found that you were a good subject. And when they took you to the compound, they had another twelve years of uninterrupted freedom to keep working on you. It seemed to be successful."

"What a bloody evil thing to do to people!" Even in the grip of her control, Dan could feel rage at what had been done to a small child and his mother. *It was you, Misha!* he shouted inside his mind. *You and your mother that you haven't seen for twenty-five years.* "Maybe we should have blasted the Soviets out of existence," he continued. "Just like all the hawks wanted to, back in the sixties."

She stood up, angry, whirled around and stamped back to the hallway, away from him. "Don't be stupid, Dan! Do you think we were the only people to try it? Don't you think the CIA was trying for years to achieve the same thing?"

"Were they?" He hardly cared what her answer was. It had nothing to do with him, he felt.

"Of course they were!" she snapped. "They started in the late fifties with a thing called Project Bluebird. Then it became Project Artichoke, Project MKultra, a whole series of experiments. They tried all sorts of stuff, putting LSD in people's drink in bars, hypnosis, everything! We had our agents in those project teams, just as the CIA probably had agents in ours. The effect they were trying for was to produce somebody just like you!"

"Did they succeed?" Even under the misery, Dan found himself wanting to know.

"Maybe they did, I don't know," she said, her arms dropping to her sides in depression and weariness. "The CIA Director, Helms said he closed the whole sordid business down, but who knows? There may a whole bunch of people right now thinking they're Russians until the Pentagon gives them a call."

The whole thing was just too sick for words, thought Dan. A few weeks ago, he had been happy with his life, an Englishman living in Chicago, in love with the most wonderful woman he had ever met, successful in his career, affluent. Now he was a puppet on a string, dominated by a megalomaniac, a killer for rent. Hatred and despair had replaced love and optimism. All he wanted to do was go to sleep, wake up and find none of it had ever happened. Inside of himself, he knew that it could not happen that way.

He looked up at her. "Emily, or whatever the hell your name is," he said, feeling rage at her, at Carson, everything she stood for, "get out of my life! I'll fight Carson somehow, and I'll fight you. Just let me free of this thing now, and go!"

Her face was white. She squeezed his arm urgently and her voice cracked with tension. "Haven't you understood a word I've said to you? Dan, I want you free of this whole thing too. I'll help you, I know how to."

"I don't believe you."

"Dan, I love you! If we can break this thing, we can go back to what we had before and be free of it, free of Carson, the whole damn thing. It's obvious your conditioning is not as successful as they thought it was. Don't you see, there must be a way to break it down!"

"Crap! I've killed people! That sounds pretty successful to me! I want you out of here. If you loved me, why would you have done what you did already? How could you continue to obey Carson?"

She turned away and put her head in her hands. Her reply was muffled.

"He's my father," she said.

* * *

One in the morning. She had left hours ago, taking just a small bag, saying nothing about where she was going. While she moved softly around the bedroom, gathering her things, Dan continued to sit in his armchair, overwhelmed with what had happened. Even without the control mechanism working in his head, he wasn't certain he could stand up. Once or twice, he heard a muffled sob coming from the room, but it was unable to break through the icy weariness he felt.

At the end, she said "I will let you go now, Misha," and stood rigidly at the door, maybe frightened that he would attack her once he was free. For several moments she watched him, but he didn't look back at her, just stayed seated in his envelope of despair. Finally, she opened the door and walked out, the small clunk of the closing door behind her sounding dismal.

She had gone. For a long while, that was the only coherent thought in his mind. He forgot the dreadful events of today, forgot the unbelievable story both she and Carson had told him, and totally ignored the frightening possibilities of what might happen next. He sat and looked at the night outside, so much brighter than the darkness within him.

She had gone.

With her had gone six months of delight, laughter, loving. The apartment had absorbed the scent of her, the colour, her warmth and become more of a home and a shelter for him than any of the many places around the world he had ever lived before. Now it was just an apartment again. Only incidentally did he wonder how he could return to a normal life, his work, a career. Memories stayed with him this time, unlike the time he had left the meeting with Carson. Interesting that now I can remember the fateful meeting with Carson, he mused. Once Emily had spoken the trigger words to him, most of the details had been gradually returning to his mind.

His daughter! My God, had there been even a second in the last six months when he was not under the Carson microscope? Had she told him everything? Even the most intimate details of the loving times together? Had Carson sat like an evil toad while she told him about the first time she had spent the night at Dan's apartment, just two days after meeting him? Had she laughingly regaled him with the details of that weekend when they had hardly put clothes on at all, and kept falling back into the huge bed? Had he gloated over the story of how they had made love in Dan's office one night when she had called to collect him after a late meeting? The idea made Dan nauseous.

Nowhere could Dan see a sign of the blood-line. Maybe the high, classical cheek-bones had a certain Slavic look? But her gold-flecked, hazel eyes were nothing like the cold blue of Carson's. The wide, generous mouth with the sensual lower lip was not the thin-lipped Carson. Small elfin ears had nothing of his heavy-lobed attachments. Maybe she was more her mother's daughter. He was able to bring both father and daughter's faces to his mind quite easily, and examine the differences. Somehow he knew, however, that by the time he had gone to bed, the conditioning would take over again, and by morning, nothing would remain. He wondered how he would handle the situation if he could remember nothing of this evening.

She had gone, but memories of two killings stayed. Or were there more that he had yet to remember?

Jackson backed away from me, mouth working frantically but making no noise. I advanced carefully, trying to make sure as little damage was done as possible. My first slash caught his hands raised uselessly to protect his body, the blade sliced a neat, curved line of crimson from his wrist to his fingertips and he squealed like small child, staring in disbelief at the wound. I took advantage of the immobility to move in and caught him in an uppercut sweep just below the bottom rib. The knife handle jarred solidly against bone...

He had killed two men, wrecked two families. What else had he done that he could not yet remember? The killing, the agony, all to enhance the wealth and power of Vincent Carson? *How could I live with that?* he wondered.

He got out of the armchair, his first movement for over seven hours, and stretched intensely. He needed something to kick his body into gear, and he poured a tumbler of Japanese sake, placed it in the microwave oven and watched abstractedly as it heated. He filled a tiny bowl with the clear liquid, looked lovingly at the black and gold painting on the side of it then swallowed the contents. The hot fragrance burned its way to his guts and partially loosened the frozen misery. He stood by the window and looked out, not really thinking about anything, letting his mind roam un-tethered.

He was pretty certain he couldn't live with this situation, and that stopping Carson was more important than his already-wrecked life. He no longer cared what happened to him, everything seemed so pointless. He finished the jar of sake, heated up another one, stood for more long, empty moments by the window. Finally, he came to the only decision possible and walked to the telephone, picked it up and dialled 911.

Only two rings.

"Emergency. What service?"

"Police."

"This is the police. State your name."

"I am..." A wave of panic swept over Dan, freezing his voice as if somebody had clamped mechanical fingers on his throat. He shuddered and doubled over as if to protect himself against a killing blow that he felt certain was coming. Tight cramps seized his stomach. Fever rose and burned his head, a heavy pounding started behind his eyes. He drew on every ounce of strength and tried again. "I want to..." and his vision went red with pain. Dimly, he heard the call of the female operator, calmly but loudly trying to get his attention. He clutched the phone and tried to speak, emitted only a tortured rasp.

"... you can't tell anyone."

"Why not?"

"Because that's one of the blocks, Misha! Please, try it..."

Faint echoes of his tortured words to the flat, cold face in front of him. He remembered his defiance, and how easily Carson had struck it down. Damn you Carson, he thought. I will still try it, and try and try...

"... stay where you are, caller. Stay where..."

His breathing was a loud whooping in frantic efforts to get air. His legs had failed completely, he had no feeling in them or any control. He was sinking to his knees and a similar numbness was creeping into his arms. The heat of his face was radiating like a sunburn and the buttons on the phone multiplied in front of his eyes like pictures simulating the vision of a housefly. The dizziness increased like an accelerating merry-go-round, the room began to dance a violent polka around him, his eyes seemed to swell in their sockets and try to jump out to join the fun, and he passed out.

* * *

Chicago must have implemented its emergency call tracking system, thought Dan through the haze. He woke, wishing he hadn't, feeling so ill that every breath was a payment to the Devil. A paramedic and a policeman were crouched over him, an oxygen mask pressed to his face. The building superintendent was fluttering anxiously in the background, Dan could just hear his panicky voice, but unable to make out the words. A random thought ambled along his brain's bruised pathways that he was heartily sick of waking up lying on floors. *(Why? When had I last woken this way? What a crazy...)*

"Just relax, son." The cop was lean, dark, seemed about fifty. Without his cap over thinning grey hair he looked gentle, concerned, a friendly uncle.

The clean oxygen swept the fog away from Dan's mind, and he felt strength returning to him in great surges, like the surf sweeping in on his favourite beach in Sydney, bringing cool power from the blue waters further out and dropping on the radiating sand, soaking it with vigour.

"Holy cow, man!" The paramedic had his fingers on Dan's pulse and turned an astonished stare at him. Over the man's green jacket, a youthful, fresh face with round dark eyes looked like a teenager. "You just dropped from over a hundred to seventy!" he said, with the sort of enthusiasm he probably normally reserved for a winning Cubs' game at Wrigley Field. "Let's have a look at the rest of you." He slid the metal disk of a stethoscope inside Dan's shirt and looked intently into the distance. The cop watched the paramedic's face and the room went silent for a few moments. Dan became aware of the hard floor underneath him, worm's eye view of furniture and lighting, it reminded him sharply of a similar situation.... *damn, it had gone!* The memory had been on the edge of his mind, then slipped away, scuttling into the darkness like a cockroach.

"Heart's okay, too! That's one hell of a recovery, Mister Bailey. Doesn't seem to be a thing wrong with you now!"

"Ever had anything like this before?" The cop was friendly enough but a lifetime of Chicago's streets had made him constitutionally suspicious.

"No," said Dan. Perhaps his own uncertainty on that subject showed through, for the cop was not reassured.

"Then I suggest you head over to the hospital later today and ask for a scan. You may have something hidden fairly deep."

The paramedic nodded agreement and began tucking his stethoscope into the bag by his knees. He looked barely old enough to vote.

"Could be something there, Mister Bailey," he said. "Better get it checked out. These things can be pretty well hidden."

"I'll do that," murmured Dan, feeling weaker than a starved kitten. "Help me up, will you?"

He received an enthusiastic lift upwards from the cop's muscular arms, and staggered as he reached an upright position. Dizziness swept over him like a small surf for a few seconds, and the cop held his shoulders while it lasted.

Dan looked round the room. It was only the number of strangers in the place that indicated that something unusual had happened. Nothing else seemed out of the ordinary.

"Anything else we can do?" The paramedic was cleaning away the last of his equipment and preparing to leave.

"No, really," replied Dan. "Thank you very much. You'll send me the bill, of course?"

"Of course," the young man said dryly. "The office never forgets things like that!"

Dan wanted the place to himself so that he could go to sleep in a more normal fashion. It was after two in the morning, and the fatigue of an exceptionally full day was getting to him... What do you mean, Dan, a full day? he asked himself. What's been going on? What the hell was I doing lying on the carpet?....

Within ten minutes the others had packed away the equipment and left, the superintendent still looking frightened, but saying nothing directly to Dan. Dan walked around the apartment for nearly half an hour, trying to understand what had happened, what had caused the crisis, why his depression was so deep, why Emily wasn't there. Finally, he turned off the clock radio alarm and fell asleep, blacking out almost before he reached the bed.

* * *

The morning was a horror. It was even worse than he had anticipated the night before, because Dan remembered.

He remembered the meeting with Vincent Carson, and how Carson had ordered him to forget. He remembered the casual way in which Carson had thrown a net over his mind and controlled him with just the utterance of a few words written by a Russian poet. He remembered the killing of Kevin Fitzpatrick, how he had been woken in the middle of the night, been given clear instructions by a female voice over the telephone, and had followed them with precision and the absence of thought.

Dan's rage rose in him as he remembered that Emily was part of this evil, that she had played a role in the killing, that she had manipulated him like a fish on a line.

He knew he loved her still, but that his love was implanted in him, just as the memories of twenty years of a life in England had also been implanted in him by magicians of the mind somewhere in Siberia. He thought of her claim that she really did love him in return, and that she would help him break free of Carson. With a rush of pain, he discarded her words as being as big a lie as his life with her.

Not even the few cubic inches within his head was a private place for him. Even within that tiny sanctuary, men had trodden and left their filth behind. He wondered if he would ever be able to remember the truth about his first twenty years.

Emily's bottles of perfume, cleansing lotions and skin creams sat isolated on the marble of the bathroom, mute reminders of her presence. In the kitchen, he had to reach past her favourite cereal to get his own, ignore her decaffeinated coffee to extract his jar of roasted blend, and ate breakfast standing tensely by the counter top instead of sitting companionably with her at the kitchen table.

The snow and the slush outside darkened his mood even further when he waited for the bus on Lake Shore Drive and the excessive delay caused by the first flurries of winter helped not at all. But by the time he had reached his office and was standing with six other silent people in the elevator, watching the numbers climb on the display panel, he had come to a firm decision that he would apply every effort he could to breaking free of Carson. And if he couldn't do that, he would somehow stop Carson doing any more damage. Until then, he would live as normal a life as possible.

The elevator let out three of the travellers at the fifteenth floor and the remaining four of them automatically spread out to adjust their body territories.

Dan stared at the image of himself and the others in the shiny metal surface of the elevator doors.

To hell with Emily. He tried hard to believe in himself when he said that, and he may have succeeded.

Twentieth floor, the other unknown travellers departed on their mysterious ventures, and Dan was left alone with the muzak and Mantovani. The thin tones from the undersized loudspeaker above his head sounded like depressed cats on a rainy night.

To hell with Carson.

He reached his office. He had little time to think of any real plans, as the phone rang with the first corporate problem of the day, and there was no time to think about anything personal for the next nine hours.

Luckily, he had no appointments that day, and he managed to put off any meetings with other workers in the place. He left at the unusually early hour of five, and joined the throngs pouring out of the building.

When he got home, the apartment was no more cheerful than when he had left. The dove-grey walls, blue carpet and collection of pictures on the wall, each with its personal story for him failed to provide the normal welcome. Unable to think about making a meal in the echoing vastness of the kitchen, he walked out and found a small Italian restaurant on Belmont, spent a joyless hour watching the couples and groups seeming so happy in each other's company. The seafood marinara tasted like dry chalk, the Chardonnay like flushings from a radiator. Finally, he returned to the apartment.

He sat in front of the television and switched to one of the cable movie channels, could make no sense of what he was seeing, and aimlessly roamed the dial with the remote control. David Attenborough waving a fossil rock... British warships bombarding the coast of France... kangaroos racing before hunters in a Landrover... Humphrey Bogart in naval uniform pouring a drink... the Cubs in the fourth inning against Houston...

The apartment faded from his awareness.

Chapter 6

Mother bought me a dog when I was six. I called her Krasiva, Beauty, because she was red and sleek. I walked her around the grey streets of Kharbarovsk and into the park to throw sticks for her. My friends joined us and we ran wild. All of us wore the red neck scarves of the Komsomolski Youth. My dog lived for those walks, and when I got home from school and opened the door, she would leap at me and smother me with excitement. Mother didn't get home till two hours later, so she had the neighbor's Babushka come in and feed us both, and then I would take Krasiva to the park. I loved my dog so much, and when the soldiers took me away, I wept as much for Krasiva as for my mother.

Every summer, the Komsomolski Youth went away to camp. It was always fun. We lived in wooden huts by the lake and spent the days swimming, sailing, or taking long walks through the woods. The Party officials who came with us also seemed to like it, because they were much more friendly with us than in the meetings in town. Once, I found two of them, Alexei and Sasha hiding in the bushes. They had no clothes on, so they must have been swimming, and they seemed angry at me for walking up to them. But the next day, all the leaders laughed at them, and gave me hugs as if I had done something very clever.

On my first camp, when I was five, the doctors took each of us in turn into the main hut, but it wasn't for the usual sort of examination. I remember I just sat in front of the doctor, and he touched my forehead with his finger. The next thing I knew, it was time for dinner, and I couldn't remember what I had been doing. The doctor seemed very interested in me, and I had to go back and see him again two days later, instead of going sailing with the others. Two more doctors came and saw me some days later, and when I got back home, I saw the same doctors again.

I had to see them each month for a long time, and Mother was always nervous when she took me there. But they never did anything like normal doctors, they just touched me on the forehead and I went to sleep.

The heavy banging on the door scared me terribly... I ran into the bedroom of the miserable, dull apartment of a miserable, dull block, hiding as Mother straightened and seemed to draw on inner reserves. She opened the door, and I heard loud male voices speaking over her hysterical shouts... gigantic boots hammered on the naked floors. The soldiers found me crunched inside the wardrobe and pulled me out with an odd gentleness. "Come, Misha," one said, towering above me, his head made huge by the army hat with the red star on the front. "We have wonderful things to show you..."

I tried to run to Mother but the soldier held me firmly against his coat where the smell of damp snow on rough cloth almost stifled me. He pulled me across the patches of ice and snow left on the floor by intruding feet, to the front door, to the balcony where the sub-zero wind howled vindictively. Mother stood, frozen in fear as I was taken out... I called, panic-stricken, and they pulled me down the stairs to the roadside and to the black car that waited, the engine running. Suddenly she broke away and ran to the balcony...

"MISHA!" she screamed, but the neighbors pulled her hurriedly away and the car door closed on any other sound she may have uttered...

It was exciting being put on a plane, and I spent the entire flight staring out of the window at the snow-covered plains and craggy mountains. The soldiers seemed amused, but one or two of them I remember were kind to me. I heard one of them saying to another that only the Devil would do this to an eight-year-old kid. I didn't understand him.

When the plane landed, we drove in a big car again and reached huge iron gates. Inside, it was almost like being in camp again with the Komsomolski Youth, lines of wooden huts. But there were lots of soldiers here, not friendly youth leaders. And the scenery was not like the lakeside of my old camp. It was harsh, bleak, empty of trees or water or grassy hills.

They said "You will become an English gentleman, Misha," but I didn't know what that meant. When I met the man called Gemorov, I was afraid. He seemed so tall, and he was thin, and his eyes were very cold. He carried a stick with him everywhere he went. The first time I saw him I was taken into one of the larger huts, and placed in a hard wooden chair. Somebody put earphones on my head, and told me to watch the pictures on the wall. The pictures were of some streets, and buildings, and I didn't understand what was happening. My earphones began to hurt, and I pulled them off, but suddenly Gemorov was there, and he swished his cane across my legs and it hurt even more, so I put the earphones back on.

The earphones only said one thing.

"Dan Bailey.. Dan Bailey... Dan Bailey..." they said, and I didn't know what that meant.

I was eight years old when they took me to the camp and the first four years had been miserable, lonely and homesick. I cried for my mother, and even though there were other children in the camp, we rarely saw each other because they were being conditioned for other cultures, other languages. I yearned for friends of my own age, feared the cold, unfeeling discipline of the military base. After two years, I grew accustomed to these things, almost learned to enjoy them as I sensed new skills, new abilities and new horizons develop within me. Certainly I enjoyed the pleasures of being an English schoolboy, the bicycle, the books I could read, Dickens, Shakespeare, Jules Verne in the classes, while on my own I could stay for hours in the library and absorb children's adventure stories, science fiction and Agatha Christie. Gemorov approved of Agatha Christie. He said it gave me an excellent picture of the British class structure. Gemorov had never been outside Russia.

By the time I was eleven, they weaned me off the Russian diet and introduced me to meals of strange English foods, bacon and eggs, bread and butter pudding, pork pies, apple crumble and custard, things no Russian would experience. I liked most of them, but some tastes I could never accept. There was something called parkin, an acrid, ginger cake that they told me was a traditional delicacy on Guy Fawkes Night, when the children burned an effigy on a bonfire and let off fireworks. I couldn't get to like tripe and onions either, and that bothered Gemorov, because he said it was a traditional Lancashire dish.

The good times were rare in the compound, but there were some. Reading books that no Russian child would ever see was one of them. Not only science fiction and thrillers, but also American and British history, the geography of the whole world, tales of King Arthur and the Round Table, dreams in which a child could lose himself... There was special wonder in the mythologies of the Ancient Greeks, the Romans and the Norse people of Scandinavia. I spent hundreds of hours reading about those strange gods that displayed the lusts and rages of mortals and fought battles that swamped the world with blood and death.

I found books about the two great wars. They must have been western books, because they referred to The Great Patriotic War as World War One, which I had never heard before. The Fascist War was called World War Two, and I discovered wonderful stories of the aeroplanes of that time. I read about the Battle of Britain, about Spitfires and Hurricanes, and how they fought off the Luftwaffe's Messerschmidt fighters and the Stuka and Heinkel bombers. I dreamed of being like those gallant men of the Royal Air Force.

The other good times were the days when I was allowed to take my Raleigh bicycle like any British schoolboy and ride for hours in the specially built housing estate on the south quadrant of the compound, made to look like a typical middle-class English suburb and used for many training purposes.

People lived in some of the houses, and neat English hedges separated the front gardens from the road and from each other. The cars parked in the driveways were Austin Cambridges, Sunbeam Talbots, MG Midgets, Ford Cortinas, and I had to learn the forms that the registration plates took. I leaned that the second two letters were the indicators that the car had been registered in towns like Stoke-on-Trent, or counties like Berkshire and I learned to tell where the car came from according to those letters.

The corner shop sold the *Times,* the *Guardian* and the *Daily Telegraph,* pork pies and thick sausages, and a genial, middle-aged man served his customers from behind a counter, talking amiably about the weather, the cricket season, or the chances for various soccer teams in the cup final. Payment was in pounds and pence and they would give me a collection of the notes and coins at regular intervals to use.

Every day, from the time I was twelve, I had to go to the shop, buy a newspaper, usually the *Daily Telegraph,* and study the news, sports and political commentary so that I became immersed in Britain's daily events. I became addicted to the crosswords, the convoluted logic and obscure references to literature and history that required a broad education to follow. After about a year, I was usually able to do about three-quarters of the puzzle, and twice, in my last year at the compound, I finished it. I went to the pub and drank two pints of Newcastle Brown Ale those nights and got very sick.

When I was about fifteen, I was also required to watch hours of the television that showed *Benny Hill,* the *Avengers* and Patrick McGoohan in *The Prisoner*. I loved that one, Georgii and I had been the only ones who really could follow the weird story of Number Six's adventures in The Village. It was terribly English in its subtlety and low key humor. Privately, when we were sure nobody could hear us, Georgii and I called the training camp "The Village" and Sergei Arbatskii was Number Two. But we never joked about who was Number One. We were also the only ones who truly understood *Monty Python's Flying Circus.* Sometimes we had to explain the jokes to the other watchers, and we didn't always succeed in getting the point across.

The worst days were the ones spent cooped up in the gloomy, windowless training room where Alexei Gemorov watched as I sat in the hard chair with the headphones that bruised my ears as I watched pictures of England on the screen for hours on end. There were others in that room, I remembered, children like myself, some younger, some older. There was a girl, a little older than I was, she used to cry with the pain of the earphones. In my head, only a name... *Dan Bailey Dan Bailey Dan Bailey..* endlessly until it became *my* name. If I moved, if I eased the pain by moving the phones, if I turned my head from the screen, Gemorov would whip my bare knees with a small bamboo cane. Just like in an English school, he said. He whipped everybody like that, and the sounds of England and the repetition of my name in the earphones often had a background noise of sniffling and crying of other children...

Later on, I learned to drive with the steering wheel on the right. I got behind the wheel of the swift little red MG Midget sports car and roared around the housing estate doing lightning-fast double-declutches with a bellow of the tiny one-litre engine and a squeal of the Michelin tires. Soon after that, they delivered the BMW motorcycle with the British registration plates from Manchester, and I learned how to ride the wind with fear and passion.

And there was beer. The British Village had a pub that somehow kept a supply of McKewen's, Newcastle Brown, Double Diamond and Flowers' Keg. I learned to ask for peculiar but delicious mixtures like lager and lime, rum and blackcurrant, Old and Mild, to take my glass back to the bar for refills, not to expect a new one, to eat pork pies with mustard and pungent white pickled onions, scotch eggs, ham sandwiches. I learned to be an Englishman, and looked forward to the day when they would put me into England and let me live the life properly.

My very best friend and really my only true companion was Georgii Vilnikov. At first, I had been nervous about him, and had hated the initial attempts to learn to speak English when I was eight. But like all children, languages came easily to me, and by the time I was ten, I could speak English fairly well. Georgii's job then moved to a higher plane of intensity. The thin, bespectacled language teacher had liked me and talked to me for hours until the Lancashire dialect of the north-west of England was natural to me. He had spent fifteen years in England as a chauffeur for the Soviet Embassy, his musical ear soaking up the numerous dialects and speech patterns of the British Isles until he could pass as a native almost everywhere.

"Only the eastern counties defeated me, Misha," he told me over tea one morning. "Never could get that flatness of the Lincolnshire tone. But Wales, north or south, Scotland from the Isles to Edinburgh, Geordie, Scouse, Brummie, you name it, I can talk like it!" He challenged me to listen to the hundreds of tapes he had of English people from all over the country, and Scots, Welsh and Irish, and I absorbed them like a sponge.

Sometimes we played games, switching dialects and challenging the other with obscure variations. I could speak with a Welsh accent of the southern mining regions that Georgii said could never be told from the real thing, even by a local. He had mastered the Scottish Highland dialects, even the subtle differences of the Shetlands, which I couldn't do.

* * *

The tramping of many boots in the corridor outside shattered the gentle calm in the room. Georgii had been telling me about the county of Lancashire, how the city of Manchester was such a culturally sophisticated place. He was telling me how he used to join the crowds lining up in that courteous English way to buy tickets for concerts by the Hallé Orchestra. The conductor, Sir John Barbarolli was regarded as a personal friend by almost the whole city, and people would cram the concert hall and sit on the floor, the stairs, even the edge of the stage and converse with him between pieces. Georgii said he had once been one of those on the stage, and in his best Lancashire accent, had asked Sir John to play a Tchaikovsky piece.

But the door slamming inwards decapitated the conversation and three soldiers suddenly filled the small room.

"Georgii Vilnikov, you will come with us." The officer had a hand on his pistol at his waist. His young face under the peaked cap with the light blue band around it was expressionless. The red cap badge reflected the dim light from the window as a rosy patch on the wall. Georgii's face was white as he stood up from the table where he had been about to pour more tea from the silver samovar into the glasses in their filigreed silver holders, but he held himself firmly, putting a gentle hand on my shoulder.

"Look after yourself, Misha," he whispered. "Study hard and make me proud of you." Then one of the soldiers seized his arm and pulled him almost off his feet, to the door. Moments later I watched through the window as his tiny, thin frame, dwarfed by the soldiers, walked across the yard to the confinement quarters...

They shot Georgii Vilnikov the day after arresting him. Crimes against the State, they said in the official notices, but no more details were given. Later, one of the other language teachers whispered to me that he had heard that a bureaucrat in Moscow had been suspicious that Georgii had learned his foreign languages too well, he had become an Anglophile and was no longer considered reliable. The teacher was frightened that the same might be thought of him.

I missed Georgii. My hours spent with him honing my Lancashire speech patterns were some of the most pleasant times in Murmansk.

Sometimes I got to leave the compound. In the later years, these events became more and more frequent, and I always enjoyed those days because I was treated like a young officer when I visited the naval base a few miles away. Those were the weapons and unarmed-combat training days when the guard would wake me at four in the morning and wait patiently while I dressed and carried my bag, packed the night before to the big old Zim automobile. Then he would drive me from the compound, along the straight concrete road for twenty minutes to the huge gates. The guard never spoke on this duty, and when I had been passed over to the sentries at the gate, he would turn the car round and head back to the compound. The sea air smelled stronger here, and the enormous shipyard cranes stood in serried ranks like watchful storks waiting for fish.

The sentry would talk to someone on the telephone, and ten minutes later, a non-commissioned officer would drive up in a military jeep. I would be taken to the gymnasium and left alone to change into my warm-up suit, then escorted to the shooting range by five-thirty.

I would spend two hours first on the gun ranges, practising, practising, practising, with revolvers, automatic pistols, rifles and light machine guns. I was given an enormous range of weapons from different countries. From the old Colt .45s, to the newer .38 calibres, to the massive power of the Smith & Wesson .357 revolvers, I shot hundreds of rounds into the cut-out shapes in the target ranges. Then I would move to the automatics, and would let off equal numbers of cartridges from Beretta nine-millimetres, Finnish Lahti L35s, British Brownings and German Walthers and Heckler & Koch HK4s.

At seven-thirty I would be released to change back to civilian clothes and taken to breakfast with the naval officers. Hot pans of food would be laid out for the men and women to select their own and take their plates to the tables. Only tea and coffee would be served by uniformed waiters. Those officers whom I was able to meet said the scene was exactly the same in nearly all the armed forces anywhere in the world.

After breakfast, more gunnery. First, I would be equipped with rifles, and would spend two hours shooting at different distances. I shot with the French snipers' FR-F2 bolt-action weapon, Britain's Lee-Enfield, and German Mauser SP66 rifles. Then the machine guns, everything from light Uzis from Israel to the heavy Brens from Britain. Our own Kalashnikov AK-47s were also used, and I had to be able to strip down and reassemble every weapon I fired. Sometimes I had to do it blindfolded, and the young sergeant who supervised me on these occasions was merciless, making me repeat until I had the art perfected.

A quick lunch of cold cuts, black bread and sweet tea, and I was taken back to the gymnasium for the hardest part of the day, unarmed-combat. My instructor, Sergeant Kutchinski, was barely five-foot-five, all muscle, string and bone. He called me Mister Bailey, the way non-commissioned officers addressed officer cadets in Western military academies, he said. He was polite, courteous, though hardly respectful, sarcasm dripping from his voice with every syllable. Nobody could call a man "Mister" while grinding him into the dust the way a military sergeant could do, said one of the recently graduated naval officers to me with a sympathetic grin over breakfast one morning.

In the beginning, when I just fourteen, Sergeant Kutchinski had not raised a sweat or drawn a deep breath while he proceeded to beat me to a pulp and throw me around the room. After two years of his tutelage, there came a day when I was able to stay upright, and even got a solid blow in to his body. On that well-remembered day, he smiled gently, said “Excellent, Mister Bailey” then smashed me to the floor with a hit that I never saw coming.

After three years, I had become hard for him to hit, and we both sweated heavily with much ducking, dancing and swinging at each other before any blows were struck. Then, one morning, I knocked him unconscious and broke a pair of his ribs. Five minutes later, he woke up and got slowly to his feet, looking hard at me. Tensely I waited, terrified of the revenge he would take. But he bowed gently.

“That was very well done, sir!” he said, and left the gymnasium.

From that point on, he called me sir, and there was never any sarcasm in his voice. For the remaining year of his training, he spoke to me the way he spoke to other officers. He hurt me a lot in that last year, but he also taught me how to kill without weapons and without thinking.

When I was sixteen, the Blank Days began. I called them that because all I knew was that a Sunday would be followed by a Tuesday, or a Monday by a Thursday. They would call me from my room late in the evening and a guard would take me to the dark, windowless building in the northern corner of the compound. In the brief summer, the walk would be a pleasure, the smell of the grass luxuriant, the insects whirring a rhythmic pattern of courtship. In the winter it took a long time to dress to go outside, and the walk would be a battle against deep snow and heavy ice, the wind a screaming harpy with sharp claws.

I would have to wait a few moments outside that forbidding building before the door opened and I would be led down a narrow corridor, placed in a wooden chair in an empty room with dirty green walls and an unpolished wooden floor. A single naked light hung from the ceiling and the guard would stand motionless behind me, the damp smell of snow on his coat reminding me of that day seven or eight years ago when I had been taken from my mother. The guard would sniff noisily until the old man came in. The stooped, fragile man would look at me, scratch his heavy white moustache and remove the wire-framed spectacles from brilliant blue eyes. Then he would place his hand on my right shoulder, always my right shoulder, and say "Now Misha, it is time to sleep..." Then I would wake up in my bed and it would be Tuesday. Or Thursday. My hands would be wrinkled, as if I had stayed too long in the bath, and I would be drained, lethargic for days after. After six months, nobody called me Misha any more. I had become Dan Bailey, and everything that had gone before became misty, and finally vanished. The time of the Blank Days had lasted three years. I never learned the old man's name.

When I was twenty, they took me away without ceremony. I remember how the old man with the blue eyes had given me one last and very lengthy session in the tank, and I had only woken up when I was already on an aircraft flying toward Helsinki. Even though I was awake, everything was very hazy and muffled. As we flew, two soldiers made me enter the large crate and they nailed the sides closed. I could smell the oil of my BMW motorbike in the crate with me. I must have slept again, because the next thing I saw was the skyline of Helsinki, and I was on the BMW, riding smoothly into the city.

I know that I forgot everything then, but what had been placed in my head. I became Dan Bailey, and I was a young Englishman who had travelled around Europe on his motorbike, and after Helsinki I would go to Australia for a year, then return home to England and go to University.

Dear God, I remember it all!

Dan returned to the present with dull shock running through his limbs. He felt as if he had just had a narrow miss from a collision with a car, trembling, breathless, thin beads of sweat running down his nose. The memories did not scuttle away and hide, the way the tiny flashbacks had done before, they remained, harsh, vivid, painful.

I AM MIKHAIL VOROSOV.

He did not dare move, as frightened now as he had ever been under the gaze of Alexei Gemorov. Something incredible was happening in his head and he both feared it and wanted it. Outside in the hallway, a group walked past, laughing about something. A door opened, closed, and the voices faded.

"... the words 'Misha, listen to me' will trigger your immediate attention and make you listen for the command phrase.." The dry, reedy tones were Gemorov's. He had lectured little Misha on his role, responsibilities and training that he would receive during the years in the compound. Later, the old man with blue eyes had slipped those instructions deep inside Misha's head as he slept in the tank.

The compressor of the refrigerator cut in with a slight rattle of the metal base and whined up into the inaudible range.

"... the words from Yevtoshenko's poem 'The Song of the Overseer,' 'We are the overseers, we are your legs, oh throne' place you under the control of the speaker and while you are in this state, you must obey all instructions and you cannot move without permission. You can remember your Russian life, ask questions, be angry, sad or happy, but you cannot move..."

A police siren howled along Lake Shore Drive and dopplered into the distance. The blue flashes of light reflected off the pictures on the wall. Dan felt a million miles away.

"... the phrase 'I will let you go now, Misha' releases you. Everything that happened while under control is forgotten after you have slept..."

Captain Furillo was delivering a lecture to Andy Renko and Bobby Hill... Dan had forgotten the TV was still on. He grabbed the remote device and switched it off, fearful of losing track of the astounding developments that were unfolding like a flower inside his head.

"... there is a punishment trigger. It will cause intense pain."

A second police car howled along the Drive, this time chased by the harsh, rasping bellows of a fire engine, like a gigantic prehistoric predator hunting down a smaller prey which signalled its panic with high-pitched shrieks.

"Your body has been taught to feel great fear and then sickness if you try to tell any other person the truth of what you are... The words 'Consider doing something special for the party' prepare you to receive detailed instructions for an assignment..."

Dan had slipped down to the floor and was sitting cross-legged on the carpet, his head bowed over his knees, in almost a Zen-like state of concentration, listening to the echoes of that long-gone voice. A stereo set in another apartment boomed as it was turned on, then faded as the volume was lowered.

"I am Mikhail Vorosov," he said, aloud. "I am a Russian."

The telephone screamed an abusive assault, shattering the clear pictures in his mind. He jerked his head violently, snapped from the bleakness of a Siberian winter to his luxurious Chicago living room. It rang only once, the answering system switching in rapidly, the way he always left it in the evenings to screen out the telephone marketers. The machine was silent for a few seconds as it played his words to the caller and Dan waited for the system to reset itself when the frustrated seller of magazine contributions or seekers of charity donations hung up. But a thin, female voice rattled through the loudspeaker, as if she knew Dan was at home and would hear her. The words were Russian, the accent Georgian.

"Misha, listen to me," she said. "Consider doing something special for the party."

* * *

The orders over the phone were simple. The female voice spoke a short instruction in that Georgian-accented Russian.

"You will come to Mister Carson's office tomorrow morning at eight o'clock, Misha. Now pick up the phone if you are there."

Dan leaned over to his coffee table, his guts crawling with fear but unable to disobey. He picked up the cordless phone.

"I'm here," he said, also in Russian. He heard his own voice echoing from the speaker of the answering system in the kitchen.

"Good. Now go to bed," said the thin voice, and the clatter of the telephone being replaced at the other end was the only social amenity Dan got. He put down his own phone, got to his feet and walked around the apartment turning off lights. Then he went to bed.

* * *

The next morning, Dan rose with fear in his mind. Knowing that he had no choice, he still struggled to refuse the order he had received the previous night. He was able to think about it, remember the words, remember the shattering revelations of the evening as he sat on the floor in front of his television. But he could not go his own way.

He took the usual bus, and got off at his usual stop. But when he tried to walk to his own office block, his legs refused to obey him. Instead, he continued walking and reached the building that housed the Hanfield Group's offices.

Raging internally at his inability to act for himself, he gave his name to the beautiful woman at the desk and waited, dividing his time between looking at the lake, now shrouded in a cold morning mist and carefully eyeing the receptionist whose form-fitting dress displayed a body of Playboy centrefold standard. Even with the horrors circulating through him, he could not ignore that body. The lobby was too warm. A smell of fresh-brewing coffee floated from the kitchen behind the reception desk.

The bony, skinny woman with the fifties hair-style atop a rat-like face with shadowed eyes spoke his name behind his back, just like before, and led him to the corner office. He followed the expensively-cut woollen dress of autumnal colours slung gracelessly on the fleshless frame and was shown into the bright office. He walked in, feeling his heart beating with mixed fear and rage, dreading the encounter. Carson did not rise to greet him, the way he had on their first meeting. His blue glare was full of enmity, anger seemed to make him hyperactive, and patterns of light and shade explored his dark grey suit.

Apprehension churned Dan's stomach and made his hands damp as he sat in front of the huge black desk.

Carson's office was exactly as it had been the last time Dan visited, except that now the blinds were drawn to block out the wintry morning sun. The same ugly paintings of glamorized battle scenes hung on the white walls, the same silver tea set sat on the black desk while Carson sipped delicately from the tall glass held in the patterned silver holder. He did not offer Dan any tea, and his secretary had not left when she had shown Dan in, but had taken a chair next to Carson and stared at Dan in prim disapproval from under the dark roll of tight-wound hair.

"Misha, slooshaiche mnye. Muy nadsmotrchiki, muy tvoi nozhki, tron." The words were recited rapidly by the secretary as she closed the door behind Dan, no intonation, just a muttered incantation, spoken for some forgotten ritual. But the effect was the same. Dan felt a curious flicker in his head, as one set of controls was replaced by another. Despite the fear and the turmoil, he thought about that flicker, and decided that his mission imposed on him last night by one control phrase was complete as soon as he walked into the office. At that stage, he presumed that his mind was programmed to release him. So a new control had to be imposed, just as the woman had done with the trigger phrase she had just spoken.

Dan walked over to the same chair in which he had sat on that remote summer's day when the nightmare had started, sat down and felt the heavy weights of long-ago orders settle on his limbs, making him immobile. So this insubstantial, colourless woman was the caller last night and other nights, giving him instructions, sending him off to kill for her master. Dan stared back at her, radiating his hatred, and her eyes dropped, confused, and she played with the heavy gold band on her wrist under the rust brown sleeve.

"So, Misha. You are trying to become free of us?"

"Meaning?" Dan might be under Carson's control, but his fury at the two Russians could not be suppressed. Carson shifted a little in his seat, showing discomfort.

"You ordered Emily out of the house, tried to call the police," said Carson. "I gave you no such permission for these things."

"I told you I'd fight you."

"Yes you did, and I told you, you couldn't win. Remember how I can punish you, Misha?"

"I remember." Dan stared hard at him, suppressing his fear of that dreadful pain. Carson's discomfort showed again in a small sideways look to his left, away from Dan and at the lake, where the mist was rising into the frigid air.

"Then don't make me do it again," he said, still looking out of the window.

Dan said nothing. Carson turned back to him and glared for a moment, then smiled gently, as if he had forgiven Dan for some minor transgression. He raised his glass of tea and took a small sip. The lemon smell mingled with the fresh scent of polish and gently floated past Dan's nose.

"Our plans go well, Misha," he said with another smile. "The integration of Caradoc Metals has been most profitable, and we have expanded our market share significantly. I am pleased with your assistance, it was most professionally done."

The woman smiled and looked respectfully at Carson, then picked up the silver teapot and refilled his glass. He took it without looking at her and she subsided back in her chair with a hurt expression. *Like a puppy*, thought Dan. She would not meet his eye.

"Why did I kill Paul Jackson?" snapped Dan. He was aware of his freedom to speak, despite the control, and threw a sharp challenge at his tormentor.

Carson waved his hand as if to dismiss Dan's question as irrelevant. "He got in my way," he said. "I wanted a line of credit at his bank and he refused it. It made me angry."

"I killed him for that?" Dan's breathing got faster in his outrage

"Why not?" Carson seemed surprised at the question. "I wanted to test you again, anyway."

Jackson had stared at me, both hands weakly pulling at the knife handle rammed so firmly against his ribs. Then his weight settled on my wrist, and I let him drop back onto his armchair, holding the knife firmly so that it slid jerkily out of his body, releasing a gush of bright red blood over the golden cover of the chair. He was still staring when the light faded from the eyes fixed rigidly on a spot on the wall behind me...

The inhumanity froze Dan. A man had died in a dreadfully painful and bloody manner because he had annoyed Carson? It had the same casual viciousness as the killings for athletic shoes and ball club jackets on Chicago's streets.

"Why?" Dan forced the question through stiff lips, despairing at his inability to clear the dreadful picture from his mind.

"That's no business of yours..."

"WHY?"

Carson sat back in his seat. The woman was looking almost frightened. Carson was tense, then suddenly relaxed, as if he finally remembered that the control was with him. He smiled at Dan in a conspiratorial way.

"I told you, Misha," he said. "I needed another test of your abilities."

Dan felt the breath slammed out of his body. There was such mindless brutality in those few words. He took a few seconds and struggled for whatever control was left to him.

"Why am I here, Carson?"

His defiance seemed to disturb them again, and Carson exchanged glances with his assistant. They looked worried. He turned his face back to Dan.

"To be warned, Misha," he said. "I have more work for you and I will not tolerate this independence. Your entire reason for existence is to serve me, not yourself!" He stared at Dan as if to underline what he was saying. "You will allow Miss James back in your house and she will give you your orders and ensure full obedience. Remember how I hurt you last time. I can do it again and even worse."

He picked up his glass to drink, not meeting Dan's eye.

Dan took a deep breath and launched his own assault. "Your daughter does you proud, Carson," he said, looking him directly in the eyes and suppressing his bitterness.

"WHAT?"

Dan felt sure their combined voices could be heard back at the reception desk. Both of them jumped to their feet, shock radiating from their faces. To Dan's delight, Carson spilled his tea and it ran along the black expanse of desk, over some papers and down onto his trousers. The woman began to fuss over him with a napkin and he shoved her away, brutally. She cowered back against the wall and looked about to weep. Dan enjoyed every second of the byplay.

"Who told you that?" Carson was still shouting, and his face was red.

"She did," Dan said calmly, revelling in the sight of Carson's dismay.

"You lying little bastard!"

Drops of spittle shot from his furious mouth and left a thin track between them on the polished surface of the desk.

"Me?" said Dan, managing a small smile. "How can I be lying, Carson? I'm under control, am I not?"

"... while you are in this state, you must obey all instructions and you cannot move without permission. You can remember your Russian life, ask question, be angry, sad or happy, but you cannot move." Gemorov, you KGB dogturd, you were right, but you forgot to tell me I couldn't be insolent! thought Dan. Despite the anguish of his entrapment, he felt a wave of exhilaration at this small, unexpected freedom. One small step for Mikhail Vorosov/Dan Bailey.

Carson's rage was washed out by the realization of what Dan was saying. The conditioning was so strong that Dan could not be lying. Carson sat down and stared sightlessly at the wall, gathering his self-control. Then he stood up and walked round the desk to the hideous battle paintings, brushing past Dan as he went but ignoring him. Dan was able to shift his head a little to watch him *(that's interesting,* he thought. *I can actually move a bit! What could this foretell?)* as Carson took out his handkerchief and began delicately wiping the ornate, gold painted framework of one of the pictures. The silence lasted for several moments.

When he spoke, Carson's voice was tense, sharp. "It makes no difference," he said. "You would have learned some time. In two or three days, I will have another assignment for you. I will release you shortly and you will go back to work. Before you leave, Sasha Greshtyenka here will take you to our sick room and you will sleep for twenty minutes to ensure you forget this meeting. We will call you soon. I will let you go now, Misha."

Dan felt the heavy drapes fall away from him and he stood up, shaking the stiffness from his limbs. He looked firmly at Carson, taking confidence and sustenance from his tiny discoveries that he could lash at him with his tongue even when Carson had control over him, and that the law of no movement had developed a tiny bug.

Carson nodded at the woman, and she led Dan from the office to a smaller room next to it. As Dan subsided into a deep sleep, he couldn't help but smile at the woman as she watched him. *Just wait, you bitch*, he said to himself. *Your time will come. The system has another bug in it. I don't forget any more after I sleep.*

She seemed nervous as Dan's eyes closed, and his last thought was simple pleasure at that fact.

* * *

The bug in the system was not entirely operational, Dan discovered, because he had no memory of leaving Carson's building and returning to his office. His next conscious moment was as he sat at his desk, looking blindly at his computer screen.

David provided the break in the void of Dan's mind, waltzing into his office with a smile a yard wide on his face.

"It works!" he called. "Sound the tocsin and raise the flags! Oh my people, rejoice, the damn thing works!"

"What works, you crazy bugger?" Dan snapped wide awake. *Oh thank God for you David,* he said to himself. *I wonder how long I would have sat there if you hadn't come in.*

"The control system in Denver," shouted David. "That's what bloody works! The plant manager just called to say the acceptance tests have been finished!" He waltzed out again, humming happily, not noticing the lack of any obvious response from Dan.

But Dan was not as inactive internally as he looked. The memories of the morning's meeting had just returned to him, and he sat, fighting the rage and hatred he felt for Carson and the woman who served him. The fury expanded to encompass Emily, her betrayal of him and the lies she told him as she left. He so desperately wished he could believe her when she said she loved him and would help him break free. Even if all the controls were broken, he knew he would still love her, regardless of how he had been conditioned to be enslaved by her.

Trembling from the power of the hatred and despair, he went into the washroom and washed his face. When he returned, he applied all his considerable discipline to tackling the problems of the office. He called in all his staff for review meetings, and in the debates, arguments and planning, he forgot the other miseries. The day passed in a relatively up-beat style.

He reached the front door of his apartment block at a little before eight. Despite the productive day, depression began to creep over him, slowing his thinking, dulling his mind. Yet a strange excitement was nibbling at him too. A feeling of expectation ran through him, of anticipation, new grounds to be broken.

Enough of the astounding revelations of the previous night remained in his mind, but he was aware that the memories had become fuzzy. He wanted time to recapture them, break down the remaining elements of the conditioning that were trying to clear the pictures from his head, to fix the memories permanently.

He picked out a couple of bread rolls from the freezer, made dinner of roast beef, mustard and a can of beer poured into an ornate, hand made ceramic beer mug picked up at the Evanston Arts Fair a couple of summers ago. He sat before the television and felt the rush of expectation again. This had happened last night... what had he been doing? Out to dinner, he remembered that... Depressing meal, watching happier people.... Home to an empty apartment... switched on the television.. that's right... let's do it again and see what happens... He picked up the remote controller. He remembered he had been rambling through the channels, not able to concentrate... He switched on the set, started at Channel 2.....

Some sitcom, grotesquely fat man on small chair... an English soccer match on the sports channel... Larry King talking to an unrecognized middle-aged woman with an extraordinary cleavage displayed in a red silk dress... Gregory Peck, a *young* Gregory Peck in a Biblical epic... dark, grainy film of tanks in the desert flying the swastika...

MY NAME IS MIKHAIL VOROSOV. I am a Russian.

His breathing coming faster and the pounding of his pulse echoing in his ears, Dan made the same shattering rediscovery of truth that had occurred the previous night. And no trigger phrases had been spoken...

"I am Mikhail Vorosov," he said, and laughed out loud.

Over the next hour he drew the veils away from the lost years of his life. Georgii Vilnikov, small, thin, fragile, with steel-rimmed spectacles, his language teacher at Murmansk, looking more like a college professor than a KGB agent, who had taught him to speak English like a Lancashire schoolboy. The thin, tall, cold Alexei Gemorov, totally bald and skin of old lizard, cane in hand, who used fear and pain to force the mind of Misha Vorosov into believing and remembering that he was Dan Bailey. Sergei Arbatskii, Camp Commandant, seen rarely, always dressed in full military regalia on a stocky, muscular form.

And the old man with white moustache and blue eyes, who put teen-aged Misha under hypnosis and then supervised his hours in the sensory deprivation tank while whispered words slithered programmed instructions deep,

deep, deep into his mind where nobody could ever find them again.

The strange thing was that while these memories of what Dan knew to be his real life grew stronger, the implanted memories of his English life did not fade. They remained in peaceful coexistence, letting him keep his happy memories of a childhood that never was, of loving parents who had never existed, and an English upbringing that he never had. For a time in that weird, exciting, terrifying, mind-unfolding evening, Dan was happier than he had been since the whole dreadful business began.

"I am Mikhail Vorosov. I am a Russian." Spoken aloud, the words coursed through his body like fresh spring water. He knew who he was.

But the peace of mind was only transient. What was he going to do? His hypnotic conditioning was still too powerful to resist. Trying to tell anyone of the situation caused sickness that nearly killed him, perhaps *would* kill him if he tried any harder. Trigger phrases still made him do hideous things, acts he could never have contemplated himself. When will I get the next call? he wondered in agony. Something niggled in his mind that he had little time to wait before his next assignment, though he was not clear where the idea came from. Something said at that morning's meeting with Vincent Carson?

This morning, how Carson and that awful bony woman had lectured him with such disapproval and yet had clearly been uncomfortable with his unexpected defiance of them.

The killings. God, the killings! Ferociously the pictures erupted again in Dan's head. Fitzpatrick, lying on the gravel by his car, his head a bloody stump after a soft-nosed bullet had taken him between the eyes. Jackson, lying dazed on his gold brocade armchair, blood over his body, blood on the floor, blood staining the gold, blood on Dan's sleeve. Blood dripping silently from the knife to the carpet, the first horrible smell of the evisceration that would soon stench out the whole house.

Dan heard a groan of agony and grief, and recognized it as his own. This morning... *"... in two or three days I will have another assignment for you..."* Dan remembered the words he was supposed to have forgotten. He had slept, and his conditioning was supposed to make him forget. But it hadn't. The conditioning had been breaking down as his capacity to remember was growing stronger every hour. But the power of the trigger phrases had not shown any weakening at all. Dan was still under the mastery of Vincent Carson.

Only one way existed to stop Carson, Dan realized, and the sadness he felt as he saw the path nearly overwhelmed him. Emily had said Dan was the only one that had been fully trained this way, the others had not worked... well, maybe this one hadn't, either.

He got up from his armchair and went to the kitchen. On the top shelf of the cabinet was the bottle of Laphroaig single malt scotch that he had bought in the duty-free shop at Heathrow Airport on his last trip to England. He had been reserving it for any special occasion that seemed to merit it, and nothing yet had come to mind. Too much Veuve Cliquot perhaps, since Emily had moved in... *Oh Emily... I had never thought that this night would be the suitable moment.*

He left the bottle on the small table by the armchair and collected a crystal glass from the kitchen to place by it. He walked into the study and stood silently for a moment, looking at the pair of computers sitting side by side, remembering the many evenings they had worked together, long periods punctuated only by the rattle of the keyboards and the wheezing and sighing of the laser printer as it slid pages into the tray. Sometimes she leaned over to him, stroked his neck and asked for help with a software routine on her machine. Sometimes he needed to get up to collect a file, or more paper from the shelf of stores and he kissed the back of her neck as he passed. She wriggled appreciatively and their productivity suffered for a few moments.

He shook himself from that tiny flash of a long-gone memory, took a single sheet of paper from the table, picked up a pen and returned to the armchair. He poured a generous helping of Laphroaig, smelt the smoky tang of burned peat and took a first sip, letting the sensation work its way down to his stomach. He sat back to write a short note. At least he could leave a pointer to Carson's activities and hope somebody would treat it seriously.

He couldn't. As soon as the words formed in his mind, that terrible sense of overwhelming fear made his hair stand on end and froze his hands in tight, frightened cramps. A dangerous heat on his forehead told him that path was not open. He sat back again, taking deep breaths and tried to settle his system. Another mouthful of scotch was despatched to meet the first and that helped a little. He took a firm grip on his pen, but even before he could touch the paper, his heart felt as if somebody had seized it in a powerful grasp. He gasped with the pain and dropped both pen and paper. Carson was protecting himself even at this distance.

Only one thing was left. He reached down to his feet and picked up the pen and paper again and wrote as carefully as he could, just the simple words.. *"Emily, I loved you."* He stood up, took the paper to the dining room table and placed it carefully in the middle of the polished wood. His reflection stared back at him and he stopped for a second, fascinated by the mysterious person on the other side of the brown shimmering curtain. *What does he think of what I'm about to do?* he thought and got no answer.

What do I think of it myself? he asked. Even in the depression, he spent a few minutes on that subject. The compound had made one mistake, it occurred to him. Tied within the straitjackets of their own culture and politics, nobody had thought about any religious training for little Misha or Dan Bailey. There were no books on the subject in the library either, so Dan had begun his life as an Englishman without any of the bigotries, preconceptions or guilt that most people in the west seemed to suffer.

When he got to Birmingham as an undergraduate, the academic freedom triggered something off in his mind, and he went on a rampage of religious discovery, much to the amusement and some confusion of his friends. After a year or so of attending different church services, reading everything he could find, and talking to priests and rabbis, he came to the conclusion that the Buddhists were the only ones with any idea at all. The others all seemed to him laughably off the wall. He stopped the rampage about then, but was left with a firm conviction of the rationality of reincarnation.

Are you chickening out, Misha? he asked himself, sitting back in his armchair. Will this cause a karmic string that makes you come back again as something diminished? No! he told himself with vigour. I want to live! This was the only way he could think of to prevent the greater evil of Carson running rampant and uncontrolled.

In the sadness, he took some comfort from that thought.

He rose and walked slowly to the second bedroom and opened the wardrobe where Emily kept the clothes she wore only on occasions or for different seasons. Her summer dresses were arrayed in silent rainbow rows, a bright yellow raincoat, two suit-bags, one white, one royal blue, containing her formal dresses. She had planned to wear the blue gown at the company's Christmas Ball in a few weeks. A row of shoes stood at attention on the floor, pointing mute noses at him in contempt. He ignored them and looked to the shelf above, reached down the old shoebox. The small bottle was what he wanted, the bottle from which she had taken an aid to sleep a million years ago when he had first woken, howling to images of death. It was nearly full.

Back in his armchair, he felt almost at peace. He had used his considerable intelligence to find another path and couldn't. The need to stop Carson was paramount, Dan was the only one who could do it, and this was the only way for him. All other regrets had to be forgotten, all sadness ignored, all losses written off. This was the only way. By relieving himself of the responsibility, some of the pain was reduced.

No point in messing around, he thought. He shook out the contents of the bottle, took several of the smooth, white, oval-shaped pills at a time with a mouthful of fine scotch, repeated the dose, and sat back to wait for peace. He thought of old lives, his mother, Georgii, the wonderful trip in Europe on his motorbike. He relived the three days with the girl in Milan, the barbecue by the roadside with the bunch of rambunctious Kiwis, the peaceful talk with the old man in Munich and the spiritual peace he had found in Finland's lake lands. He didn't bother trying to work out what was reality and what had been given to him in the tank at Murmansk by the old man with blue eyes. All the memories were alive, fresh, wonderful.

The crystal glass dropped from his hand and bounced without a sound on the carpet. A small stain spread onto the blue pile. He watched it for a thousand years as the darkness spread like a field of flowers over the blue. He hoped the next owner would clean it up. The door rattled behind him as somebody put a key in the lock, undid the dead bolt and opened the latch. The sounds were muffled, coming from a hundred miles away or inside Dan's head. His eyelids were heavy and he could not have lifted his arms however hard he might have tried. Somewhere through a dense pile of cotton wool a voice rumbled, words unknown.. he thought it was "Dan?" It sounded almost like Emily, but that was impossible... she had gone... Dan fell asleep.

Chapter 7

Jane Fonda and Queen Elizabeth were rotating round his head as if he were standing in the middle of a carousel at a circus. Jane Fonda was wearing a space suit that somehow managed to display her legs in white boots, and the Queen was dressed in a long ball gown, holding the massively-jewelled mace in one hand, waving it slowly. They were shouting at him.

"Wake up, Dan! Wake up, Dan! Wake up, Dan!..." Alternately they called in perfect rhythm, racing from left to right and reappearing on the left like some maniacal solar system.

"Oh shut up!" Dan said.

"Oh shut up! Oh shut up! Oh shut....," they echoed.

"You know, Jane, you really give me the shits!" said Dan, plaintively. ""I just want to sleep!" He knew he couldn't address the Queen that way. He was English, after all.

"He said something! He said something! He said..." Jane and Her Majesty picked up the lunatic refrain and kept squawking around Dan's head. *There's no way out of this,* he thought, *unless I open my eyes and tell them to piss off directly.* It was quite a struggle.

The wildly orbiting faces and insane voices faded, and bright lights shouted into his eyes like the crowd at a ball game.

"Thank God for that!"

A young and powerfully-built man was looming over him. His dark, hairy arms strained the seams of the short-sleeved green gown. A searing pain burned in Dan's throat and stomach. He felt as if he had been coughing up fresh coral.

"We nearly lost you." The doctor tucked the stethoscope into his ears and placed the metal disk on Dan's chest. Dan stared at the ceiling, completely unable to fathom out why he was there.

"Okay, you'll do." The young man tucked away the instrument into a large pocket on his side and stood up. "You were goddamn lucky, Dan," he said. "I think you did actually die for a few seconds."

"Sore throat," rasped Dan, feeling a desperate need for a hot drink to tackle his throat, knowing that he would have time to think later about what the doctor had told him. The doctor smiled in sympathy.

"I'm not surprised, the way we had to pump you out. Like draining Boston Harbour!"

Pump me out? thought Dan in bewilderment. Then he remembered, slipping into sleep in his red armchair, whiskey glass dropping onto the floor, somebody coming in... Emily?

"Who?" said the doctor. *I must have mumbled her name out aloud,* thought Dan. The doctor grinned. "Oh, the lady who came in with you," he said. "She's been here all night."

Dan tried to work out what he meant by 'all night' and gave up. He had the same sense of lost time as if he had just woken from more of the Blank Days, the same lethargy and weakness holding his limbs to the bed like a wrestler's grip.

"Need a drink." Dan's voice sounded like shoes on loose gravel. The doctor reached the door and looked back.

"I'll see to it," he said and walked out.

Dan fell asleep again, because almost instantly, it seemed to him, he was sitting up, leaning against a huge collection of pillows, and Whoopi Goldberg was holding something with a lemon flavour against his mouth. *No,* thought Dan in confusion, *she just looks like her.* The same black face with laughter falling out of every pore of her skin, glorious black eyes.

"Back with us, Mister Bailey? Here, let me swab that throat a little." Her voice was like an organ being played quietly.

Mikhail Vorosov, he said to himself.

"Pardon?" Bright black eyes snapped in his direction.

Whoops! Must be careful, he thought and opened his mouth. The soothing lemon stuff started to work some effect on his bruised throat. A few more seconds and he fell asleep again.

She was stroking his cheek.

"Hello," said Dan. *You're here!* he cried to himself. *Thank God you're here!*

"Hi!" Her fingers touched his cheek and caressed his forehead.

"I missed you," he whispered. *I'm so glad you're here.*

"Me too."

He smiled at her and returned to the comforting, dreamless dark. She was here.

Some unknown time later. She was still holding his hand, sitting on a chair by the bed, but she had leaned forward and her head was on the blanket by her shoulder. Her breathing was slow, she was heavily asleep. Dan pulled his hand from hers and gently stroked the fine brown hair over the back of her neck. After a while she stirred slightly, and he eased his hand away.

"Put it back," she said clearly. He laughed, but the pain in his throat stopped that immediately. He began to stroke her neck again. She shifted her head and sat up, stiffly stretched and moved her shoulders around. Her face was pale, fatigue showing in the puffy eyes and hollow cheeks. A trolley rattled past the door to the room, two women talking loudly about somebody's sister in Oak Park, that terrible dress she had worn at the wedding in Schaumburg and how rude...

"How long have you been here?" he asked, forcing the words through the shards of glass in his throat.

"Three days. Same as you."

"Three days? Haven't you had a proper night's sleep since then?"

"The nurses let me sack out in their lounge. I'm okay."

They looked at each other for a long time. A telephone rang in the distance then stopped.

"You sound like a small frog," she said, lips twitching slightly.

"You know what they say about frogs!"

"It's worth a try, I suppose," she smiled and leaned over and kissed him gently. Her familiar perfume was just a ghost, but it was beautiful anyway. When she moved back, her eyes were sparkling.

"It didn't work!" she said, her wonderful mouth curving the way he always thought of it.

"Nobody ever said it was easy," he complained. "Remember how many the princess had to work through!"

"Okay, one more go. How about some input from you, eh?"

She leaned forward and kissed him again, and this time they concentrated on it, and before too long, Dan felt a little more prince-like.

She put her head back on the bed side and they stayed like that for a few moments. Dan studied the graceful lines of her neck and shoulders. Two men stopped outside the door, one of them leaning against the frosted glass. His coat made a huge white Rorschach blob, topped by red hair. The men spoke softly, their words a gentle murmur, then the white blob moved away as they parted and went in opposite directions.

"Emily?" Dan felt the pressure building in him to tell her what had happened to him. Somehow, with her return, all barriers had collapsed. She was part of him now.

"Yes, Dan?" Her voice was sleepy, and for a second or two he wondered whether this was the right time. He decided it was.

"I remember everything," he said.

"About what?" She was muffled, speaking into the bedspread.

"Everything. The training camp in Murmansk, killing Fitzpatrick and Jackson, how Carson controls me. You being his daughter. Everything. It's all come back in the last few days."

For a moment she stayed face down, as if unwilling to admit the reality of what he was saying. Then she sat up and looked at him. Her hair was in a mess, and she had no make-up on. She was beautiful, but she was not the same ethereally lovely woman Dan had first met. He saw her clearly now with a viewpoint that was his own, not dictated by any controller of his thoughts. Now he could see that her nose had a slight bump in it, that she had some lines at her throat, that she was not perfect at all. He loved her even more than he did before.

"Dan," she said, helplessly.

"The trouble is," he continued, looking at her sleepy eyes. "I still can't break the conditioning. When Carson wants me to do something, I still do it. If I try and tell anyone, I get sick. Remembering everything hasn't made any difference."

"So that's why you tried...?" She took his hand and squeezed it. He responded the same way and covered her hand with his other one.

"That's why."

They paused for a few more moments. A loudspeaker in the corridor outside asked for Doctor Hendricks to go to Room 22. It occurred to Dan that he was able to tell Emily, but nobody else. Was there another crack in the conditioning somewhere? She seemed to gather herself for an important question.

"Dan, you know I love you, don't you?"

"Yes. I think I've always known it, but things got in the way the last time we talked."

She smiled with a slightly rueful look. "I'll say they did! We've got to think about how to break this thing, don't we?"

"Do you think there's some way we can?" A wave of hope flushed through him, and his hands tightened on hers.

"I have some ideas, but it means fighting my father. We'll have to destroy him."

"Can you do that?" Somehow, he knew that she could. He was beginning to think that most things were within this woman's capabilities.

"Yes, I can," she said with firmness. "Dan, it will hurt, I can't deny that," she continued. "And I'll pay for it for a long time. But I know what he is and what he's done to people, and even if he's my father, I hate him for that. The world will be a better place without him."

Dan looked at her. Her anger was barely below the surface.

"Tell me about your father," he said. "All I've seen is that well-dressed, bald-headed business executive. Who is he, really?"

She looked at her hands for a few seconds, then raised her eyes to him. "He joined the KGB when he was a major in the Red Army. I've heard stories about his times in small wars. In Angola, he led a troop of soldiers into a native village and killed six hundred people. It was reported that he used his pistol and personally killed over thirty women and their babies."

She was silent for a few moments again. "He was based in Minsk when I was a little girl," she continued. "I know now, though I didn't then, that he was ruthless in searching for anti-Soviet movements. He arrested hundreds of people, and supervised their interrogations. Many of them died in the process. Usually he had no evidence against them, just suspicion."

Dan was motionless, watching her pain as she spoke.

She paused and took a breath. "And now I know that my mother killed herself when she discovered what he was. I was fourteen when that happened. Soon after that, he asked for this assignment in the USA. I didn't know any of that at the time, and I was ready to join the security forces a year later. When I discovered the real story, I told him I wanted no more to do with him. So believe me Dan, destroying my father is no big deal."

He took her hand and stroked it. "I understand," he said.

"But there's another problem we'll have to face if we go that way." She looked away from his face and stared into the corner. He waited. She needed her own time to tell him. Then she looked back into his eyes.

"It may destroy me, too," she whispered.

"Then I don't want to try it." Dan couldn't think of anything that frightened him more, not even the prospect of remaining a murderous puppet of Vincent Carson's.

She shook her head impatiently. "Dan, there's no option! The only people who can help us are the very people I used to think of as enemies. And vice versa."

"The intelligence services?"

"The CIA. There's a specialist group there that can do it."

"The CIA?" The idea did not give him any cause for enthusiasm. "Why would they be able to help?"

She paused a moment to consider her words. "When I left you I had to contact my father. I asked him a few questions, and I don't think he realized just what he was telling me. Remember those old CIA projects I told you about, Project Bluebird, MKultra and the rest?"

"You'd mentioned a few of them. I didn't really believe you."

"You should have done," she said with a small smile. "The details are public knowledge now."

"Are you saying they still exist?" The idea was startling.

She nodded. "They didn't fold up when they were supposed to, despite what they told the President. Carson gave me the KGB reports from his files. There was a specialist group that has kept on researching and experimenting right up to the present, and there are a few American equivalents of you in Russia."

The idea sent a shudder of pain through Dan. It was a hateful thought that other men and women had gone through the same nightmare that he had.

She felt the reaction in him, and understood. "It's a horrible fact, but it gives us the once chance we have," she said urgently. "It means that there's still a project team somewhere, that has the knowledge and resources. But it means confronting them."

"Then no bloody way!" he protested. Like most people, Dan felt no great affection for secret security organizations. But unlike most people, he had direct reasons for his attitude. The idea of putting their lives in the hands of the same sort of people that had corrupted him before was impossible.

"Why don't I just use all that incredible training they gave me in Murmansk?" he said, thinking rapidly through the years of his past.

"For what?" she asked, looking at him with an uncertain expression.

"To kill Carson and that Greshtyenka bitch."

He felt the shudder run through her.

"No Dan!" she said. "Please, no! No more killing, not by you." She raised his hands to her mouth and kissed them softly. "Not by you," she repeated. "How could we ever live together again if you did that?"

He thought through her words. Even though his hatred of Carson and his assistant made a blood lust rise hot in his body, he saw the sense of what she said. How could a marriage survive the fact that he had killed her father? That last idea shook him a little. Just how could they ever live a normal life, either?

She sensed his train of thought. "We have some tough times ahead, Dan."

"Mikhail," he said gently. "Or Misha."

She smiled. "Misha at home. Dan outside."

"I can live with that!" He freed one hand and stroked her cheek. Her eyes closed for a second and she smiled.

"Good," she murmured. "Can you live with me?"

"We seemed to do okay before!"

Her smile faded, she opened her eyes and a wave of sadness shadowed them. "That was before, Misha. There may not be an after, unless we're very lucky."

"How lucky?" He kept stroking her cheek, fascinated by the smoothness of her skin. A small gleam of tears was just visible in her gold-flecked eyes.

"Think, Misha!" she said firmly. "I was a Soviet spy working for an espionage group. And you've killed two people!"

"Yes!" he said, his throat making him flinch with pain. "That's why the idea of going to the same sort of people who put me in this mess scares the hell out of me!"

"I know," she said, nodding gently. "That's why I'm praying that they recognize you had no choice in the matter. But that's exactly why we have to go to the CIA. The people in the project will be the only ones who might understand that."

Under the wave of panic that the idea of returning to the environment he thought he had left behind in Murmansk, he still could see that her words made sense.

"We'll have a bargaining point too," she added. "If I throw them Carson and Greshtyenka, they might leave us alone afterwards."

"Could you do that? To your father?"

"I said it before. I'll pay for it, but I'll do it." She smiled at him. "And when I think of the alternative, it's worth it. After all, I'll get you in exchange."

He tried to laugh, but his throat wasn't having any of that. "All right, I'm sold!" he whispered, and leaned forward to kiss her lips. They were wonderfully sweet, and the taste of salt from the tears was a tiny added flavour.

"Have you got any idea of how to do it?" he asked, leaning back against his pillows.

"Yes, I do. But I have a lot of details to work out first."

"Can we start right away?"

"Not yet." She stood up, the energy seeming to flow into her. "Let's get you out of here first and get ourselves ready. It's going to need time."

"How long?" he said, looking up at her. Despite the fatigue, she stood straight, and the curves of her body affected him even through the weariness and pain of his recovery.

"I've no idea," she said, touching his cheek. "I need to do some research."

"Then I'd better call the office and...."

She put a finger over his lips. The sharp, acrid whiff of freshly applied nail varnish was a tiny dart in his nose. "Shhh," she said. "I've already done that. Told them you were ill and needed a couple of weeks off. I spoke to David and he said it was all okay, they've counted it against your vacation. He could hold the fort for as long as necessary, things are a bit quieter now."

He leaned back against the pillows. The fatigue was catching him again, but he felt safe leaving things in the competent hands of Emily. Then he remembered something.

"Carson wants me to do another job. Probably any moment."

"Yes, I know. It was supposed to be yesterday. One of his senior Vice-Presidents. The man is getting too ambitious, he says."

"My God!" Dan tried to sit up. "We have to stop him!"

"It's okay, it's okay," she said with a smile, pushing him back against the pillows again. "He can't get at you in here, and there's nobody else he can call on. When you're ready to leave, we'll move to another place for a while."

"And then what?" The fatigue was almost overwhelming him, but he still needed to know what she had in her mind.

"Misha, wait. I have to get a few things sorted out first, then I'll tell you."

"Okay," he muttered, his eyes getting heavy. "I'm getting a bit froggy again."

She laughed and kissed him. He fell asleep, feeling very much a prince.

* * *

Another three days passed before he could leave. A tense, though friendly enough meeting took place with a psychiatrist who wanted to explore Dan's past life and the reasons he had tried to kill himself.

"Doctor, you'll have to believe me," said Dan. "The reasons for it have gone. It won't happen again."

"How do you know that?" She was large and solidly built, a comfortable fifty plus, with auburn hair tied neatly in a pale green ribbon behind her neck. She scorned a white coat and wore a dark red dress of almost ankle length. Her office was light, airy, the furniture all Swedish pine and greenery. Dan sat down in a remarkably comfortable cushioned pine armchair and smiled at her across her desk.

"She came back."

She snorted in derision, swinging her chair back and forth on its stand as if shaking her head. "Horseshit, Daniel! Men like you don't overdose because a woman has walked out on them." Her look was direct and disconcerting, seeming to drill through to his private thoughts.

"Why not?" he said with a small smile at her, working hard to retain his composure. He had secrets to maintain, and this professional woman was working at ferreting them out.

"Because you're bright enough to know that no woman can be that critical," she said forcefully, a smile hiding the power of her personality. "And anyway there'll always be another one along eventually!"

She stood up and went to the bookcase to get herself some coffee. She towered over him, and while it was not in any deliberate threatening way, Dan thought that she used the ploy as a subtle persuader.

He laughed at her, digging deep into himself to stay composed and guarded. "Like a bus?" he suggested.

She tried to hide her grin by turning back to the coffee pot as she poured sugar into a large mug with a bright red Canadian Maple Leaf on the side.

"Pretty well!" The rattle of the spoon as she stirred her drink accompanied the words.

"Well, you're probably right, doc," said Dan, turning sideways in his chair to face her. "But it was part of the reason, and the rest I can't tell you."

"Can't or won't?" That direct look at him again. He felt certain she knew he was hiding something.

"Can't." *If only she knew how truthful I'm being,* thought Dan. The truth, if she heard it would startle her and probably receive a derisive laugh of disbelief. She returned to her seat with a swirl of her long dress and took a careful sip, looking closely at him.

"Maybe some hypnotherapy would help," she said thoughtfully. "Whatever you've got in there, it needs to come out."

This was dangerous ground, very dangerous. Dan hid his face in his own coffee mug and tasted the strong aromatic brew. The heat felt good in his throat.

"No way, doc," he said, shaking his head. "You'll have to take my word for it. The situation has changed completely, I know the answer lies inside me, and I'll find it."

She leaned forward on the desk and looked hard at him. "That's always the way, but not everybody sees it. How come you've got it so quickly?"

"I had help." He was still nervous inside. This woman had the capacity to probe, and he was frightened that she might stumble on a question or idea that would trigger a programmed reaction in him. God knows what would happen then. He sipped his coffee, praying she would stop this meeting.

She leaned backward in her chair, and seemed to ponder something, still watching him carefully. "Okay Dan," she said. "Go with God."

"God, doctor? God has no place in this." *Carson, you bastard, that phrase has haunted me for months*, he said to himself, feeling anger building. Now I'll use it for myself, and God help you, instead.

"Why not?" she asked, a curious expression on her face. Dan rushed to correct his mistake.

"Because I'm an atheist, doctor! As I said, the answer is in me, not any outside source."

He stood up and put his coffee mug on her desk, trying to curtail the meeting. She seemed to accept it, and smiled warmly.

"Look after yourself, Dan."

Misha, he said to himself. *Misha Vorosov.* "I will, doctor, believe me."

He waved at her as he walked out, breathing more easily.

He called Emily at her client's office from the pay phone in the corridor and packed his bag. He waited patiently in his room, not risking sitting outside in a public area, reading a Dick Francis novel that she had thoughtfully brought on her last visit. An hour later, she tapped on the door and entered, looking beautiful in a pleated blue skirt and white blouse, but with a beauty that was his to create and see, not the one imposed on his mind. He stood up and they held each other for a few moments.

"Emily James," he said, tasting her name with delight. "How could I ever have thought I could manage without you?"

"Because your mind was all screwed up!" she chuckled, and kissed his cheek.

"Shall we start the process of unscrewing it?" he said, stroking the graceful line of the small of her back and shoulders.

"I think so," she said, her eyes sparkling. "I have the absolutely finest remedy for the first stages of that process!"

"I bet you have!" he laughed. "Let's get the hell out of here and see if you're right!"

She eased away from his clasp, took one hand, leaving him to collect his small bag with the other, and they walked out of the hospital. In the parking lot, she showed him to a blue Grand Marquis. He raised an eyebrow at it.

"Rented," she said briefly, unlocking the car doors. "I've stored both our cars in a lockup in DeKalb, as far away from Carson's territory as seemed reasonable. I've got a phone in here, as well."

Dan climbed into the spacious passenger seat while she walked round to the driver's side, strapped herself in and started the car with a gentle murmur of the V8 engine.

"I didn't want anyone to spot either of our cars, because we're going into hiding for a few days," she said, smiling at him, then reversed out of the parking spot and drove out of the hospital grounds.

"All this spook stuff! It's all new to me," he said, relaxing in the care of her excellent driving.

"You'd better put up with it for a while," she said, sliding away from traffic lights and heading for the

Stevenson expressway to the west. "It's our way to freedom."

"Yes, boss!" he said with a grin, and contentedly watched her as she pulled onto the expressway and accelerated. He dozed for a while too, because when he next looked, they were slowing down outside a small apartment block.

"Where are we?" he said, slightly slurred from sleep.

"Glen Ellyn," she replied, stopping the car in a spot behind the building. "It's a good long way from Carson's haunts, or Greshtyenka's."

They were about thirty miles west of Chicago in a pleasant village. Dan knew it, because a colleague of his had once lived there and he had visited his family on a few occasions.

"A good idea," he said, and suddenly thought of something. "Where do those two live, anyway?"

"Carson's got a house in Evanston," she said, opening her car door. Dan did the same, grasping his bag, and closing the door behind him. "And the skinny bitch lives in a company apartment near Wrigley Field, not all that far from your place."

They walked up to the entrance and Emily extracted a set of keys.

"We might have been followed," Dan said as she opened the front door and held it for him.

"Not a chance," she replied, letting the door swing shut and walking to the elevators.

"Why not? What about his other agents?"

The elevator door opened immediately.

"What other agents?" she asked, pressing the button for the fourth floor. The elevator jerked and began to ascend. The walls were covered with protective cloths as if somebody had recently moved heavy furniture in or out.

"Hasn't he got any?" Dan was fascinated by her reply. Carson had indicated he had a number of people working for him.

Emily shook her head and delicate waves of hair flew around her neck. "Greshtyenka's the only help he's got now that I've quit."

The elevator stopped with a shudder. The car doors opened, and Dan followed her along a gloomy corridor to the last door on the right. She unlocked the door and a dead bolt and walked in ahead of him, again holding the door.

The apartment was a tiny one-bedroom unit. He placed his bag on a chunky imitation leather armchair and prowled round the place, followed by Emily wearing an amused smile. The kitchen was barely large enough for one person to stand in, and a vestigial balcony perched as an afterthought outside the window. Basic furniture sat stolidly in the places it should be. He made his way to the bedroom, picking up his bag on the way. The room was reasonably large, but dingy, with stained wallpaper and mirrors on the closet doors that had lost much of the silver backing. A huge water radiator stood against the wall, and plaster sagged away from one corner of the ceiling. The bed was suspiciously seedy. No telephone provided any outside access. The whole place was unlike anything Dan would have suspected to exist in affluent Glen Ellyn.

It was perfect, he decided.

"Come," she said with a warm smile and led him to the tacky bed. They lay down and cuddled together, badly needing the comfort and ease of communication that close contact had always given them. The mattress was lumpy and squeaked in a way that indicated problems of privacy.

After a time of restoring their closeness, she murmured into his ear. "I was telling you about Carson's workforce."

"That's right!" Dan rolled onto his back, and she snuggled against his shoulder, her right arm across his chest.

"When I first came over here," she began, "he had three other agents who had been trained the same way as you, but not as intensively. You were still on your own, nobody was allowed to contact you because Moscow felt you were the best of the bunch and should be left for major assignments."

The clanging of the level crossing was barely heard as a freight train took its leisurely path through the middle of the village.

"The first one broke apart after he was given his first job, to shoot an air force officer who was test-flying a super-top-secret fighter prototype. He did it, but went totally insane a few days later. He died in hospital about a year later, but had not been able to say anything. The conditioning worked to that extent."

"A partial success, I suppose," muttered Dan. "At least he did one job, the poor bastard."

"The second one was the big disaster," Emily continued, not responding to his angry comment. "She was ordered to set herself up in Washington for a visit by the French President and assassinate him. It was Carson's most ambitious project, and he thought it could be done. Instead, the woman stayed in Houston and went crazy with a rifle. She killed a number of people in a restaurant before the cops shot her."

The next door tenants closed their door behind them, and their voices were a little too audible for comfort. Dan looked forward to being able to return to his own apartment before long. A toilet flushed loudly and the man coughed a smoker's helpless refrain.

Dan thought about the contrast between the mundane sound effects from next door and the dreadful things Emily was saying, and couldn't relate the two. It was all too crazy.

"The last one simply went catatonic one day," Emily said, shifting her position and kissing his neck as she did. "He was in a vegetable state in Kentucky for years. Then Carson financed the legal costs for his so-called "family" to get him taken off life-support and he died a few years ago."

Dan stroked the hair lying on his shoulder and contemplated the pain and despair that Carson had caused. "But he told me that he had a lot of help getting to his current position. Who did it for him?"

"Not Soviet agents, that's for sure," she said firmly. "He used local crooks, took contracts on the bigger jobs, hired prostitutes for a couple of blackmail jobs. If he told you he used his own staff, he was talking through the wrong orifice."

Dan's throat had healed enough to let him chuckle without great discomfort, though the bruising in his chest and stomach still let him know not to overdo the merriment. "Delicately put, Miss James! So what do we do now?"

She put a hand up to his cheek and stroked it gently. "First, we let you get over it for a couple more days. The main thing is not to talk to anybody. That's why I haven't got a phone in here. You mustn't check your answering device at home in case either of them has recorded a trigger phrase. Let me do that, and I'll do it on my cell phone so that nobody could possibly trace it back. Use the cell phone also to call work once a day, but make sure you only speak to David. If he says anyone has asked you to call them, don't do it. Whatever you do, don't risk getting a trigger from either of those two."

"You're the boss!" he said, thinking over her instructions.

She squeaked a small protest from somewhere under his right ear. "It's a joint venture operation, sir!"

"Good!" He tightened his arm around her shoulder. "Incidentally, you said you'd arranged a vacation for me. What have you done about your own job?"

"Same as you," she said, her voice a little muffled. She was stroking his cheek again, and he was fast losing interest in organizational matters. "I'm a freelance, so I've just let the customers know I'm on vacation for a couple of weeks."

"Good planning," he said, smiling at the tatty ceiling, conscious of her warm face in his neck. "If we're supposed to be a couple on vacation..."

"Why, Comrade Vorosov! Do you have something in mind?" He felt her stretch her slim body, and she slung one leg across his hip. The heat in the room seemed to rise a notch.

"Most definitely, Comrade!" he said firmly. "Call it increased comradeship!"

He was right. The squeaky bed caused real problems, but they didn't care at all what the neighbors thought.

* * *

For six boring days they lived the secretive life. Emily did the shopping wearing a wig and horn-rimmed glasses that were enough to cause the casual eye to pass over her. Dan stayed inside except for a short walk round the streets once a day to get some fresh air. He huddled in his heavy sheepskin coat and a ski hat that covered his face. Also once a day, he called David on the cell phone. On the third day, the conversation got a little tense.

"Hey, Dan!" said David, cheerfully. "How's it going?"

"Boring, but no problem," replied Dan, muting the truth a little. "You guys coping without your venerable leader?"

"Staggering through. We miss your autocratic and authoritative style of management, though." Dan detected his friend's suppressed laugh at the other end.

"Not a problem, David," he retorted. "The thumb screws are in the right hand drawer and the polygraph is in the cupboard behind the door. Hanging next to the rhino-tail whip."

"Excellent!" said David. "I'll get them out immediately. Incidentally, a Miss Clements had been calling three or four times a day, absolutely demanding to speak to you."

It sent a little shiver down Dan's spine. Miss Clements was undoubtedly a thin, rat-faced woman with a forty-year-old hair style and the power to put him in hell.

"What did you tell her?" He tried to keep his voice level.

"Just said you were on vacation in Antarctica, and I had no way of contacting you."

"She obviously didn't believe you."

"That's for bloody sure!" David said with obvious feeling. He had picked up many of Dan's English speech patterns in the years they had been friends. "The old bitch is still calling! Who the hell is she?"

"The mother of my seven children," said Dan, somehow summoning a laugh. "Forget it, David. Just keep her away."

"Yes sir, Boss! Take it easy!"

"I will. Remember the thumb screws!"

Dan pressed the "End" button on the phone, trying not to think about Carson and his assistant, Sasha Greshtyenka.

Emily checked the telephone in Dan's apartment several times a day, too, making sure he was not nearby when she did so. Apart from numerous blank messages that were the standard telephone marketers trying to sell him things, she said Greshtyenka had tried twice to leave the "Consider doing something special..." message. Emily reset the system and wiped the messages. Dan felt like a swimmer in Australian waters, knowing the shark was near, sensing the presence and terrified of the moment when the teeth would suddenly take him.

On the evening of the sixth day, they were eating a take-out Chinese meal at the battered, rickety table, drinking a reasonable Californian white wine. Dan was getting a touch of cabin fever and Emily knew it.

"Tomorrow," she said, picking out the last sautéed shrimp from the mixed seafood plate.

Dan drained his wine glass and poured more into both glasses. They were thick, ugly tumblers, standard issue for cheap apartments. He pushed his plate away. "What happens tomorrow?"

"We go and see somebody." She speared a chunk of honey chicken and gnawed at it with fine white teeth.

"Does this somebody know we're coming?" Despite her relaxed attitude, Dan felt his nerves begin to tighten up.

"Hardly!" she said, swallowing the chicken and examining the bowls for any other remnants. "He's heard of me, but he has no idea who I am or what my name is. He'll only know me by the CIA code name they would have allocated. He probably thinks I'm dead or been recalled."

She began to gather up the cardboard boxes in which the take-out dinner had been delivered, and Dan stood up to help her clear away.

"Do you know where to find this guy?"

"Oh yes, I've always known where he worked," she said, dropping the cardboard boxes into the garbage can in the kitchen. "The last couple of days I've been calling around to confirm he's in Chicago this week."

Dan went back to the table and took a mouthful of the wine. The thick glass rattled a little on his teeth. “Emily, I’m scared out of my tiny mind,” he said, admitting it to both of them. He had been trying to stay cool about the whole business, but impending action made him face the truth.

She came round to him, put her arms round his waist and snuggled her face into his neck. “Me too, honey. But if this works out, we’ll be free of the whole mess. There’s no other way that gives us a real chance.”

His arms went round her shoulders, and for a long time they stayed like that, drawing comfort from each other and the chance that whatever faced them in the next few days gave them the possibility of a normal life together. Later, they went to bed and made love in a slow, dreamy way that didn’t cause the neighbors any difficulties but gave them the courage to face the next day.

* * *

They stood by the apartment door. The day was one of those wonderful Illinois November days of bright sunshine, clear, brilliant skies, and intense cold. They would walk to the station and take the commuter train. They looked at each other. The sound of several cars starting up in the frigid outside air provided a backdrop to the small private space they had.

“When we get there,” she said, “we’ll be in a world where the normal rules don’t apply.”

“You mean I’ve been living in a normal world the last six months?”

Her smile was tiny. “Not really. But this will be just as weird. Sometimes it’s silly, too. The protocols and norms of the intelligence world make no sense at all sometimes.”

“You’re trying to tell me something.”

She moved to him and held his arms. Under her woollen hat, her hair covered one eyebrow and her eyes were warm. She had concentrated extra hard on the makeup, and her face was almost cover girl quality. He couldn't resist kissing her forehead, and the hat tickled his nose. The whine of cold transmissions told of the cars leaving the parking lot, their tires crunching on the first fresh snow of the winter.

"Emily," he murmured into the woollen hat. "I know I'm putting my life in your hands and I know you're risking both of us. This is a world you understand and I don't, so if you've got some ideas of what may help, I'll go along with it."

She raised her hands to his face and touched both his cheeks.

"Dan, this is what I'm thinking," she said gently. "We can't risk you saying anything that could ruin the meeting. You might hear some things that will shock you, or scare you, and I need you to stay quiet when that happens."

"So you want to put me under control." It was a statement, not a question, and as much as he hated the idea, it made sense. She nodded, grateful for his understanding.

"We should do it now, too," she said. "Just in case anything happens on the way there and I need us to act fast."

He looked at the time. They had five minutes to get to the station. He smiled at her and she spoke the words.

The building on North Michigan Avenue was one of those narrow, old-fashioned structures that had been moderately well-renovated, but without the style and cost of those edifices further up the "Magnificent Mile." The marble hallway on the ground floor had no lobby, just the space outside the two elevator doors, and they waited with a pair of young women in down coats and sneakers.

"This is where we start the process?" Dan asked as they waited. He had the freedom in his conditioning to ask questions, and this was the first one he felt he wanted to ask.

She nodded, watching the ancient pointer above the elevator bank wind back down as the elevator descended. "This group keeps itself under a low-key cover. It works well."

"How did you find it?" He was curious. He would never have thought of the CIA living in seedy premises like this.

"I didn't. It was told to me a few years ago when one of our people tracked down the man we're going to see."

He shook his head with amusement, despite the tension building within him. "It's like a scene from *The Spy Who Came in from the Cold*," he said.

She chuckled, which helped alleviate his fears. "Highly appropriate, when you look at the weather outside," she said, turning her eyes towards him. "That's exactly what we're doing!"

The elevator took a long time to come down to the ground, and they had undone their coats and let their faces thaw out by the time the old-fashioned wooden doors swung open and the scissor gates folded aside. The two young women walked in ahead of them and stood at the back while the elevator climbed slowly, accompanied by the grinding of ancient mechanisms. Dan and Emily were the first ones out at the fifth floor, and nobody had spoken in the elevator as they rose. Emily pulled open the gate with a crash and took his hand to lead him out. He got a curious look from the two women, and he imagined a whole conversation starting up after they had gone.

The corridor was well lit but dingy. Brown wooden walls, scuffed tile floors, home for small enterprises that spent nothing on frills. Emily stopped by a sign on the wall showing the offices on that floor. Small companies with dull names, attorneys, unidentifiable partnerships and trading companies. She placed her finger under Hobson Communications, Suite 505.

"That's it!" she said softly.

"You were right!" he said, grinning at her. "The ways of spooks are exceedingly weird!"

"It'll get weirder, believe me," she responded, and turned left to walk down the gloomy corridor. He followed obediently.

The door to Suite 505 was heavy oak. She opened it and had to push quite hard to swing it wide enough to let them in. Inside was a small desk and four chairs against the wall. No windows could be seen, and only a strip of neon on the ceiling provided light to the area. A small Tiffany lamp on the receptionist's desk laid a tiny yellow pool on the dull brown surface. A single door led off this miniature lobby. The place seemed empty. Dan looked curiously at Emily, but she appeared completely at ease.

The door on Dan's right opened, and a tall redhead walked in. She looked in her twenties, thought Dan, unable to stop wondering if this receptionist could possibly represent the real nature of the office. The woman gave Emily a bored stare and sat down behind the desk.

Emily took Dan's arm and pointed to a chair. "Misha, take your coat off," she said softly. "Sit down, say nothing."

The redhead watched him carefully as he moved to the rear wall and sat down, then she turned her eyes on Emily. Her smile was limited and her expression disinterested. *What is this place?* thought Dan. He sat still and watched the show.

"Can I help you, Miss?" The redhead's voice was pleasant with clear diction. Dan adjusted his first impression of her. *Perhaps she's brighter than she looks,* thought Dan, already changing his ideas about what the place might be.

"Colonel Allen Markbrite, please," said Emily with a courteous smile at the other woman. She might have been asking for the manager of a supermarket.

"I beg your pardon?" The redhead reached into a drawer of her desk and extracted a copy of *Cosmopolitan*.

"Colonel Markbrite." Emily repeated the name, with just the tiniest edge of impatience.

"You must have the wrong office, Miss. There's nobody of that name here." The woman's expression was uncaring and bored. She picked up the magazine and turned a few pages.

"I have the right office." A crackle of authority entered Emily's voice, and the other woman closed up the magazine and looked up at her. Dan detected a small tension in her attitude.

"I want to talk to Colonel Allen Frazier Markbrite," continued Emily crisply. "United States Marine Corps, attached to the Central Intelligence Agency, Project Parthenon."

Something subtle happened to the receptionist. The dull face became hard, the eyes bright and the posture less slumped. She didn't appear to move, but on his left, Dan heard a faint click from the heavy oak door. Departure was no longer an option. No low-grade receptionist, this one, he decided.

Emily stood straight, a slight smile on her face. She removed her coat to reveal the same blue business suit she had worn the first time Dan had seen her. She hung the coat on a coat stand by the wall, and returned to the desk, still smiling. The tension across the desk almost made the air burn.

"Tell the colonel that Goshawk is here to see him."

Neither woman moved, neither dropped her eyes from the other. Small, wriggly things seemed to move about in Dan's stomach and he felt his breathing become shallow. A crisis was arriving.

The door on Dan's right opened again, and a man stood in the doorway. He was about six feet tall and skinny, wearing grey slacks and business shirt, with a dark red tie pinned down with a gunmetal clasp. His hair was conservatively cut, dark brown, frosted with grey. Light glasses gave him a slightly studious air, but Dan's instincts said that books were not this man's main concern. He looked taut, nervous, and the hard stare he gave Emily was not the look of a supermarket manager expecting a complaint. For the first time, Dan became aware of the meaning behind Emily's warning that he was in a world of which he knew nothing, and whose rules were not those of civilized society.

The man advanced slowly from the doorway, letting the door click shut behind him. He stood about six feet from Emily.

"Goshawk?" he said. His arms were loose by his side, but Dan saw the readiness in him. It was the electric readiness of one trained in unarmed combat. Dan recognized the stance. He also saw considerable respect in the way the man looked at Emily. He gave Dan one swift glance then returned watchful eyes to her.

"I am Galina Sergeyvna Morayeva. I am Goshawk."

There was so much pride in her, thought Dan. He realized he had never thought about her real name.

"It never occurred to me ..." said the unnamed man.

"No."

She looked so magnificent it almost made Dan's heart shake. She looked the other man in the eye as equals of great ability regard each other. Whatever disparaging way in which she had referred to her previous work, thought

Dan, she had been less than truthful. This man was looking at what he knew to be a worthwhile, dangerous opponent. *Galina Sergeyvna Morayeva, who are you, really?* he said to himself. *And how could I ever stop loving you?*

Dan tested his powers of movement and found that he could look round the lobby. He saw the tiny camera in the far corner where it covered the whole area. Undoubtedly with a microphone too, he decided.

"We thought you had gone home." The man was still alert, still watchful, though Dan wondered what he thought Emily could do in this restricted spot with the door locked.

"Operations were cancelled, but I wanted to stay."

"Why?" The word was snapped out like a parade ground order.

"I had a change of heart." Her relaxed stance was a contrast with the wire-taut appearance of the slim man before her.

He nodded, as if he understood the significance of her words and had heard them many times before. "Is that why you are here?"

"Partially."

"Only partially?" He looked at Dan again and seemed to collect his thoughts. "You've been inactive since the Meridan affair?"

"Yes."

Dan watched, eyes moving from side to side as if at some lethal tennis game. He had no idea what they were talking about, but something serious had taken place in the Meridan affair.

"You hurt us pretty badly then," said the man. No anger or bitterness, just recognition of a good play by the other team.

"At the time I thought I was doing my job."

He nodded again and looked at Dan, relaxing a little. "We knew the stuff you were getting, and I knew you must be living somewhere in Chicago," he said, returning his gaze to her. "That's why this office was established. I just never expected to find you were as young as this. And a woman."

"I was well trained," she said, fixing her eyes firmly on his.

"You must have been. You even know your CIA code name."

Emily gave him a tiny smile and appeared to settle back on one foot, her left hip moving out in almost a model's pose. "I liked it," she said, her voice a little more friendly than the clipped, authoritative manner in which she had addressed the receptionist. "Better than something like Piglet!"

The man grinned, suddenly cheerful and his face softened a degree of two, but left the eyes still hard. "We got Piglet years ago!" he said, a smile crossing his face then vanishing into the electric air of the room.

"Piglet was stupid," snapped Emily, a look of disapproval on her face. "He deserved what he got."

The man gave another brief smile and nodded at Dan. "And who's this?" he asked.

"He's the last of the Gemorov team."

"The last?" The man had not moved, but Dan sensed his acutely heightened interest.

"There were only four."

"Four?" This time, the surprise caused him to move from his rigid stance by the doorway. "Good God, we thought you had thirty or forty in the country!" He looked at Dan with renewed interest.

"Four," repeated Emily in a flat tone.

"And the others?"

"All dead."

He jerked his head in Dan's direction. "How about this one? Is he a working model?"

Working model? said Dan to himself in irritation. Being described as some sort of household appliance was insulting.

"It nearly worked perfectly with him," said Emily, giving Dan a small smile, as if telling him to ignore the rudeness.

The man looked thoughtfully at Dan the way he would look at a car he might buy. "He completed missions?" he asked, still studying him.

"He did."

"And never knew?" Dan could hear the fascination in the other's voice.

"Not till later. Then it began to break down."

A small pause ran round the room as four people reviewed the information that had been revealed.

"He's under control now?" asked the colonel, for Dan assumed this was Colonel Markbrite.

"Yes, he is." Emily's voice was flat, expressionless.

The colonel moved toward Dan, bent down and stared into his eyes. Dan looked back, unable to speak because Emily had ordered him not to. Close up, the colonel's skin was quite lined, though his eyes were hard and intelligent, a light blue colour without warmth. He smelled of Old Spice aftershave and hair spray. He straightened and turned back to her.

"So why are you here, Goshawk?"

She stared at him.

So much strength in her, thought Dan.

Markbrite grinned in sheer admiration. "Wanna negotiate?" he said, folding his arms and leaning one hip against the desk. The Tiffany lamp threw a huge shadow of him on the rear wall.

She nodded, her face without expression as if she was already discussing terms of a settlement.

"Then let's go to my office," said Markbrite cheerfully. "Sergeant?"

He stood up, and moved to the door behind him. A small click indicated that the receptionist had released a security catch. *A marine corps sergeant?* thought Dan. She had to be somebody special, and she had played the game well. He looked at the tall redhead with increased interest, and she gave him a small smile of understanding.

"Misha, follow us." Emily's voice was firm.

Dan stood up and walked behind her into whatever faced them.

The colonel led the way into a small conference room with six chairs around a circular table. The walls were a light brown colour, baby-shit brown as Dan thought of it. The carpet was a basic grey broadloom. A single window permitted a meagre ration of light. The room smelled military.

The colonel took a seat at the table and waved at the other two to do the same. Emily nodded at Dan and they sat down, Emily directly across the table from the colonel, Dan to her left. An appropriately lethal-looking cactus plant sat in the middle of the table. The three of them looked at each other, but the colonel now seemed more interested in Dan.

"Has he really completed missions and then forgotten what he did?" The manner was still that of a man asking a salesman about a car's performance.

"Indeed he has, Colonel."

"What sort of missions?"

"Don't be silly, Colonel!" snapped Emily. "Negotiations, remember?" She was smiling pleasantly, and he turned back to her regretfully, leaning back in his seat.

"What do you want, Goshawk?"

She sneered. "I think we can dispense with the silly names, Allen. I am known as Emily James here, and that's how I want to stay. The old stuff, that was over a long time ago."

He grinned, cheerfully. "Sounds good to me, Emily. And him? Does he have a name?"

She looked at Dan, and he received a mute signal.

"I am Dan Bailey." His voice cracked a little. He had not spoken for some time.

"Aha!" said Markbrite with raised eyebrows. "You can talk! I was beginning to wonder. Can you release him at any time?" He turned back to Emily.

"Naturally. But not yet."

He shrugged. "Okay, as you wish. So what do you want of us?"

She leaned forward on the table and moved the cactus away to get a clear view of him. "I want total immunity for Dan for the missions he completed when under control by the leader of this operation," she said clearly and firmly. "I want immunity for myself for the work I did as a foreign agent. And I want your help in deprogramming Dan."

His eyes widened and he leaned back in his chair. "The hell you say! That ain't chickenshit, Emily! That's big time! I don't even know if I can give you all that. What are we going to get in return?"

She sat back, her face cold and blank. "Can we have some coffee?"

He seemed to consider for a moment as if recognizing a bargaining play for time, then stood up. "Sure," he said, moved to the small filing cabinet by the door and picked up the telephone sitting on top of it. In a few moments the door opened, and a man walked in carrying a tray. The powerful build, short hair and hostile eyes said this man was no waiter. He put the coffee cups on the table, left the cream and sugar on the tray in the middle, gave the visitors a searching look and walked out.

For a moment Emily and the colonel busied themselves mixing coffee the way they wanted it. The colonel took sugar and cream, Emily nothing. She nodded at Dan and that gave him the freedom to pour sugar from a paper packet into his cup and stir it. The long enforced period of control was beginning to get stressful, but Dan was unable to say anything.

"Okay, Emily," said the colonel, stirring his cup with a plastic spoon. "Let's have it. What does Uncle Sam get in return for your immunities?"

She took a sip and put the cup back on its saucer carefully. She nudged it away as if deciding to take no more. "In return, I will tell you who is controlling this operation. I will also give you all the details of what he's been doing since his original orders were cancelled."

"Okay. That's a start." Markbrite looked unconvinced, but prepared to keep listening. It looked like another good bargaining ploy, and despite his confinement and the risks that he knew were being taken here, Dan was enjoying watching two masters of the game at play.

"I'll tell you who the other three were," continued Emily. "Though that's just for historical interest."

"Sure." Markbrite looked disinterested, sitting back, his right ankle crossed over his left knee, but the hawk-like attention he was paying spoke otherwise.

"I'll tell you the names of all the other operations that the Russians are still running here without official Moscow sanctions," said Emily, her voice urgent, underlining the value of what she was offering. "I'll tell you what those operations are and where they are, but I won't tell you the names of the agents."

She raised one hand to forestall the protest he was about to make. "Don't expect me to betray my own countrymen, because they themselves don't know they're operating illegally," she said. "You can raise hell with the Russian embassy who can beat the bejesus out of the people and get them stopped. If you know the details I'll give you, they'll have to assume you know everything else and could pick up one hell of a lot of agents."

He sat back again and nodded approval. "Sounds good so far. Anything else?"

"Yes. During the deprogramming of Dan, you'll obviously learn a lot about the techniques we used. It's clear you haven't got anywhere near as we did, so you can catch up fast. Though God knows why you would want to keep following this path."

He steepled his fingers in front of his mouth and looked at her. "What makes you so sure we're so far behind you?"

She looked him firmly in the eye. "Because your attempts to do the same thing in Russia have failed."

"Don't be silly, Emily. We've never tried to do anything like this." Despite the firmness of his tone, Dan could see a flicker of anxiety in the colonel's eyes.

"Really, Allen?" Emily's tone was derisive. "Then how come John Baxter, Fred Merkowitz, Helen Anderson and Dianna Johnston are buried in Russian graveyards?"

As she recited the names, he seemed to curl up with suppressed tension. He slowly moved his crossed leg so that both feet were on the floor and he looked ready to spring at any moment. Emily saw the tension, but continued.

"They blew up when your people gave them their first assignments," she said. "We knew them as Ivan Kozlovski, Leonid Kutaisov, Elena Geskova and Anna Shostakova."

His face seemed frozen. A long pause took place before he spoke again, and Dan could hear the small sounds of the city that found their way through the reinforced glass of the single window.

"Say that again," Markbrite said with ice in his voice.

"You know I don't have to, Allen," replied Emily. Dan could hear the sympathy in her voice. "They were your deep cover moles in Russia, the products of projects MKultra, Cyclops and Parthenon. You never made it. I also know that you were supposed to have discontinued this research when MKultra was scrapped, and the CIA reported to the President that they had done so. Cyclops and Parthenon were never approved by the White House, but you kept on going."

"Jesus Christ, lady! You're well informed!" The impact of her bombshell was still on his face, but he spoke almost with admiration.

"Aren't I though!" She smiled at him with great pleasure.

Despite his shock, Markbrite smiled back, reaching for his coffee. "Always knew you were good, Goshawk!"

"Thank you. What do you say, Colonel?"

"I'll have to refer it to higher authority."

"That's not true, Allen. I know very well you have total authority in this area. You report directly to the Director of the CIA, and he prefers not to know anything at all, because your whole operation is illegal."

The colonel had taken some heavy hits this day, and this was another one. His eyes were wide open and his coffee cup stayed suspended about six inches from his mouth. Then he seemed to come to a decision and replaced the cup on the table.

"Tell me, Emily," he said, his eyes cold. "Tell me why I just shouldn't have you both taken from here and put in the deepest cells we can find, and later shot. You're a Russian agent. He's a killer, I suspect. I could get what I want from you in time."

Finally, Dan saw why Emily had wanted him under control. Had he been able, he would have leapt at the colonel and broken his neck. Somewhere inside of him were the skills to do it, Dan knew that. The colonel seemed to think so too, because he gave Dan a sudden, alarmed glare.

"Allen, you're not the fool that makes you sound." Emily's voice was ice cold. "If I fail to make a series of telephone calls within twenty-four hours, complete documentation of your illegal Operations Cyclops and Parthenon will be sent to every major news agency around the world. So too, will details of six specific and highly questionable operations the CIA is currently running in Israel, South Africa, Australia and Great Britain. You know the ones I mean. What do you think that will do to you, your agency, its director and the President?"

Dan saw the colonel's Adam's apple move sharply.

"Wow!" said Markbrite, subdued.

"That about sums it up," she agreed, and he laughed out loud, the frost gone from him.

"Lady, you're a natural born mule-trader," he said, stood up and walked round the table to her seat. She stood up to meet him and for a moment two old adversaries stared at each other. He stuck his hand out, she took it and they clasped firmly.

"Deal!" he said.

"Deal!" she echoed and they sat down. The atmosphere in the military office eased.

"Will you take Dan out of control now?" Markbrite asked. "I want to see it."

"I will let you go now, Misha," she said, instantly, and Dan felt the drag released from his body. He stretched and stood up, stiffly. He had been under her control for two hours, and a lot of muscles were protesting their captivity.

"Thank you," he said. "Not before time. Where's the toilet?"

To friendly laughter, Dan followed Markbrite's directions to the small, austere bathroom further down the corridor.

When he returned, they were deep in conversation. They broke off when he walked in, and Emily gave him a smile of great warmth that helped to relax his cramped legs and arms. He returned to his seat and sat down, looking at both of them.

The colonel turned to Dan. "Okay, Dan, I need to know some stuff about you and your activities here. What were the missions you carried out?"

"I can't tell you." Dan felt a tiny bolt of pain run from his head to his left arm that signalled possible dangers in this line of conversation.

"Goddam, Emily, I thought we..." Markbrite turned sharply to Emily, his face cold.

She raised a hand and stopped his angry outburst with a gentle smile. "He really can't tell you, Allen," she said in a placating manner. "That's one of the most successful blocks they put into him. But it's not a problem, because I can tell you."

She paused a moment and looked at Dan. He looked back and they talked at length in that brief exchange.

"He killed Kevin Fitzpatrick and Paul Jackson," she said. "Both of them were murdered on the orders of Vincent Carson."

"Vincent Carson? He's the President of the Hanfield Group, isn't he?" Markbrite's voice rose in excitement.

She nodded. Dan could see a tiny vein jumping in her neck. It was the only sign of the dreadful cost of keeping her composure as she betrayed her father.

"Major General Arkady Morayev, KGB," she said, just the slightest tremble in her voice. *Dear sweet Emily*, prayed Dan. *I wish I could help you through this.*

"Morayev? Related?" The colonel's voice was sharp edged with a predatory hunger. Dan could see visions of new horizons open up before him.

"My father."

"Christ on a crutch!" For a moment, it appeared to Dan that Markbrite had lost the dreams of slicing into the spy network with a realization of the price Emily had just paid. *Maybe the colonel has some human emotions, after all,* he thought.

She said nothing and turned her face away toward the window. Dan saw the wetness round her eyes, but he had to let her handle it alone, even though it tore him apart to see her pain.

Markbrite looked at Dan again with increased interest in his eyes. Sympathy for Emily had been submerged under the professional hunter's needs.

"You really can't tell anybody about yourself?" he asked.

Even thinking about it brought on a headache and Dan's hands clenched uncontrollably, cramping painfully.

"Allen, he can't," broke in Emily, returning her attention to the table. Her face was under control again. "Stop pushing, it causes him a lot of pain."

The colonel looked back and forth between them for a few seconds. "We could never get those sort of blocks implanted," he said, finally. He spoke quietly, almost to himself. "We got to the point with the four we sent over there that they really believed they were Russians with all their memories. A couple of field tests we did indicated that they'd perform as we wanted, but the rest was a bit patchy. We never did know what happened to them, only that they vanished."

"You didn't have as long with them as Gemorov did with me," Dan said quietly, a little surprised that he was able to say it. A warning clutch on his heart stopped further words. Markbrite looked interested.

"Something stopped you?"

Dan nodded.

"Jeez." The colonel looked impressed, stared at Dan carefully for a few moments, then seemed to come to a decision. "Okay, people," he said, in almost an affectionate tone. "First thing is to get you out of here to somewhere we can study the situation."

"You mean study me, I take it?" Dan said with an uncomfortable thought that he was about to start a new life as a laboratory specimen. It was an essential price to pay, he knew, but he had no illusions that he would enjoy it.

"That and a lot of other stuff," agreed Markbrite, nodding at him. "We also need to get a lot of information from Emily and find the right person to start deprogramming you."

"Any idea who that would be?" asked Emily. She stood up and slung her handbag over her shoulder as if ready to leave immediately.

Markbrite thought for a few seconds, his steepled fingers touching his mouth and his eyes staring at the table top.

"Harrington would be the obvious choice. He was the main programmer in Cyclops and Parthenon. If he's available, we'll get him."

Emily nodded with a small smile. "Paul Harrington. Doctor of Psychiatry from Johns Hopkins. He came closest of all to the work they were doing in Murmansk."

He smiled with a weary expression, almost of defeat. "Dammit Emily, is there anything you don't know about all this?"

"Not much," she said with a cheerful smile. "We had our people in every one of your teams, starting with Project Bluebird."

"Who?" A feral glare appeared in his eyes. *I don't think I would want to be hunted by this man,* thought Dan.

"Don't be silly, Allen!" mocked Emily. "You don't really believe I'd tell you, do you, even if I knew it?"

"Of course not," he said, the blood lust fading from his eyes and his body relaxing again. "Dumb of me! I wouldn't tell you who were our people in your teams either."

"Of course not. You're a professional." Emily softened the tension further.

"Stupid damned business, wasn't it?" Markbrite surprised Dan with a smile of considerable charm. "We both spent so much blood and sweat chasing each other round the garbage pile!"

"Colonel, if you believe that," laughed Emily, "there's hope for us all yet!"

He joined in her laughter, more relaxed than he had been before. "Emily, you're something else!" He stood up and moved to the phone on the filing cabinet. "Let's get the travel arrangements sorted out."

"To where? Project headquarters on Long Island?"

Markbrite paused before picking up the telephone and looked at her, shaking his head in disbelief. "Where else? As if you didn't know!" He picked up the telephone. "Get me Colonel Harkness at O'Hare," he said when somebody answered. He turned to face the room as he spoke.

"Charlie? Anything going to New York today? You have? Good. I'm sending four with you. They'll be met at the other end."

He pressed the button to disconnect the call, then spoke again into the phone. His tone was more authoritative than the friendly note of the previous conversation.

"Corporal, get the van. My guests are going to O'Hare."

Then he placed the phone back on the hook and walked back to the other two. "Emily, this has been quite an experience, and I'm pleased we could clear things up this way. Maybe when it's all over we can meet again on easier terms." He turned to Dan and grinned with genuine warmth. "Dan, I can't even imagine what you've gone through, and it's not over yet," he said. "The same goes for you. When you get through it all, come back here and we'll drink a few beers."

"I'd like that, Colonel," said Dan, relaxing a little with the signs of humanity in Markbrite.

"And in the meantime," continued Markbrite, "we'll pick up Carson."

"No! Please don't do that." Emily's voice was sharp.

The colonel looked at her with some irritation. "You expect me to leave him alone? He's an ex-KGB General, for Christ's sake! He could be doing all sorts of damage! There's too much risk to this country's security."

Dan shook his head. "No, there's not," he said. "His interests are in business espionage, not political. And he's got no helpers. Until he finds Emily and me, he's going to be panicking, unsure what's going on. It would be better to wait until I'm free of his control, or we'll never know what else he could do."

How strange, thought Dan. He was able to tell Markbrite all that without the block taking effect. Maybe they had just located another minor bug in the program in his head. Were the numbers of bugs increasing as time wore on, or was it the presence of Emily that allowed small gaps in the barriers to giving information?

The colonel was studying Dan. His hostility seemed to have faded. "If I wait, what then?" he asked.

"Then you can take him in your own time," answered Emily.

The colonel turned and raised an eyebrow at Emily. "If you agree that he's helpless at the moment, I'll wait till you get back," he said.

She nodded at him, a sad look in her eyes.

"You've got it," said Markbrite. "I'll wait."

They shook hands in an oddly formal, yet friendly way. The waiter came back in, this time wearing a coat that hid the pistol on his belt.

"Sir? Miss? Will you follow me, please?"

He led them down another staircase and they walked the full five floors to the ground, emerging at the rear of the building. Another young man with the same tough, blank stare was standing by the door of a minivan, and he opened it and waved them in. Emily and Dan sat down together, a soldier in front and one behind, plus one driving. However friendly Colonel Markbrite might be, thought Dan, they were most definitely under a prisoner escort right now. Feeling some trepidation about what they had entered, he reached for her hand and they held tight as they drove the fifty minute run through the dense morning traffic along the Kennedy Expressway to O'Hare Field.

They didn't go anywhere near the normal terminals, but followed the signs for the Air National Guard and didn't stop moving till the van was parked under the nose of an elderly Hercules C-130. One soldier in front, one behind, they were shepherded up the steps of the venerable old craft and escorted to seats just in front of the wing root. Their guards sat themselves a little way from their charges. Behind them were several crates lashed down to the floor. They were the only passengers.

Within minutes, engines started up and fifteen minutes later, they were climbing in beautiful blue skies, heading east. Despite his nervousness about what was ahead of them, Dan slept most of the way into New York, and when the Hercules landed, he had no idea where they were. Certainly not La Guardia, he decided. He walked out onto the steps by the Hercules' nose and looked around. A small building behind them housed a control tower, a medium-sized hangar stood over to his right, and six F-15 fighter aircraft were parked in front of it.

Two large pickup trucks were at the back of the aircraft, taking crates from the loading platform which was lowering them from the inside of the Hercules. Another van met them as they walked down the steps with their escort, and they drove off rapidly, neither soldier being any more conversational than they had been on the way to O'Hare. Half an hour of New York roads, and they pulled on to the Long Island Expressway. Dan assumed they had landed somewhere on the Island at another Air National Guard station.

"Where are we going?" he asked the general population of the minivan. The military types maintained a stony silence.

"Southampton," replied Emily. "The project headquarters were moved there in 1980."

That earned her a disapproving glare from the marine in the front seat, and she smiled sweetly at him. He turned to face the front rapidly before his training let him down. Dan hadn't checked his watch, but he estimated that they had been driving for something under two hours before leaving the Expressway and pulling into a long driveway of a beautiful, elegant mansion.

It was almost like checking into a luxury country hotel. Two porters in white jackets took luggage from the minivan, indicating that the bags were theirs, though neither Emily nor Dan had left with any. Some quick logistics had been completed somewhere along the line. One of the porters pushed a trolley with their bags along a series of corridors and finally opened a door. A large and beautifully decorated room opened up before their eyes.

"Wow!" said Emily. Dan stared at thick grey carpet, cream coloured drapes, peach walls, a bed of truly gargantuan proportions and a luxuriously furnished sitting room with a bay window looking out to the shoreline. They walked into the room and explored their new habitat. There was a fridge stocked with wine and beer, and a cabinet next to it opened to reveal scotch, brandy, vodka and gin with all the needed mixes. Even a bottle of Laphroaig Dan noticed, and wondered how they knew.

The porter dropped the bags on the bed and quietly moved to the door, obviously not expecting to be tipped. He was barely in his twenties, pink-faced and innocent looking. But he had the hard eyes of a man who has seen harsher things than luxury hotels. *Another of Markbrite's wolves in woollen garb?* wondered Dan. It seemed likely.

"Dinner will be at seven, sir," he said in Dan's direction, and closed the door behind him. Emily smiled at the closed door. The departing wolf had not recognized one of his own kind.

"We need a drink!" she said firmly, extracting brandy from the cabinet and poured two healthy slugs into balloon glasses. He took one, touched hers and put his free arm round her waist. "To us!" he said softly.

She reached up and kissed his cheek. "To us," she echoed and sipped the fine liquor. He followed her example with a slightly larger gulp and let it do its magic on his insides. Then he pulled her down to the large settee facing the bay window and put an arm round her shoulders. She snuggled up, and they spent the next couple of hours just dreaming together.

At seven they stood up, stretched a little and walked out of the door. A marine sergeant in full dress uniform was standing a few yards away. His presence sent a small whisper of anxiety through Dan. Were they to be guarded at all times? How different from Murmansk was this to be?

"Which way to the dining room?" he asked.

"One moment please, Sir." The marine lifted the telephone next to him with white-gloved hands and spoke softly, his clear grey eyes watching Dan closely from under his peaked cap. A moment later, the young man who had shown them to the room appeared in the corridor and they followed him. He led them along a corridor, down a curved flight of steps, and they reached a small dining room a single large table, as luxurious as the rest of the mansion. Smells of excellent cuisine reminded them that they had not eaten since early morning.

Dinner was fine. Nothing extraordinary happened. They were left alone to eat, served by silent, fit-looking young men in white jackets, and the food was as good as it smelled.

When they had polished off the Brie and crackers with the last glass of a good California Chardonnay, they stood up, and immediately their guide moved to them. His hard gaze at Emily indicated that perhaps he had now recognized what she was. They returned to their room, watched the news on the large television, enjoyed another small glass of the excellent brandy, and were ready for bed by ten.

Despite the luxury surrounding him, Dan found it hard to put away serious misgivings that he couldn't yet share with Emily. The scenery might be different, the guards wore elegant uniforms, and the accommodation was better than a top class hotel, but he and Emily were still in prison. It was not a regular prison either. If Emily was speaking the truth, the place did not officially exist. The work being done here had no legal sanction. Even worse, both he and Emily were self-confessed saboteurs of a foreign country. What was there to stop Markbrite and his wolves from wringing the last drop of information from them both and then dropping their weighted bodies in the frozen lake outside? An hour passed before he could sleep, by which time, Emily's breathing was deep and regular. He turned over and closed his eyes.

Day one at the Southampton headquarters of the illegal Project Parthenon had passed. By no means could it be called ordinary, but as Dan was to learn, it was the only relatively normal day of the next few weeks.

Chapter 8

Several other people joined them for breakfast in the well-decorated dining room of the mansion house. Two of the men wore the uniforms of the US Air Force, one a major, the other a captain. A middle-aged woman dressed in a smart black business suit and crisp white blouse, two younger men dressed in equivalent male fashion, dark suits, white shirts, subdued ties completed the group. Emily and Dan sat together and ate a light meal. The others sat around the same table and the conversation was deliberately low key. Nobody introduced themselves, but when the woman addressed Emily as Miss James, Dan decided the others' presence was probably connected with their own. The weather, the snow storm of last week, the chances for the Super Bowl contenders, nothing substantial was discussed over the cereals, hash browns and coffee. Dan wondered why the others were here and what was going to happen. For an operation that was supposed to be lacking in Presidential approval, the joint was really jumping, he thought.

As the last coffees were poured, one of the two young men in formal suits addressed them. "Miss James, Mister Bailey, my name is Jack Gregory," he said. "I will meet you outside your room in twenty minutes." He looked about thirty, earnest, perfectly-cut black hair, clear skin and eyes without humor. He reminded Dan of the sales representative at MidWestern who had been so shocked when Dan told him he was replacing their computers.

Dan nodded, and he and Emily returned to their room for a last-minute preparation for what would come. He held her close, his arms round her shoulders, while she snuggled her face into his neck. "Now that it seems to be happening, I have to admit that I'm scared," Dan murmured into her right ear.

"Me too," she said gently. "It's nothing to be ashamed of. We knew this could get tough for you."

"Not just me, I'm worried about you," he said. "Can you give them all the details you promised Markbrite? What if they think they should get stuff you don't have?"

"Dan, that's not the problem," she said. She shifted her arms round his neck and kissed his cheek. "I'm certain I can give them enough to drool over for months. It's you I'm scared for."

He eased her away and looked into the hazel and gold eyes. "Why?"

"Misha," she said, touching his cheek. "Programming you took three years in the tank and over twelve years of intensive conditioning with techniques these people haven't discovered. Clearing all that stuff away is not going to be easy. This guy Harrington, he's good, but he doesn't know everything about how it was done in the first place."

A twinge of fear ran through Dan, and he tried hard to suppress it. He was well aware that without her presence, he would not be able to handle himself with any dignity. She gave him courage. He pulled her head back on his shoulder and stroked the back of her neck. "Will you stay with me while he tries?"

"Just try keeping me away!" Her voice was muffled, and her breath was warm on his chin.

"In that case, I'll be fine!"

"I know you will." Her smile was beautiful, but the anxiety was strong in her eyes as she lifted her head and looked at him again. Jack Gregory's tap on the door came to signal that the process of rebuilding Dan's mind was about to start. Regretfully he took his arms away from her, she gave him a quick kiss, and they walked to the door.

Jack Gregory led them along a series of corridors until Dan felt lost. Finally he opened a door and stood aside to let them in, followed behind and closed it again.

The room was spacious, elegantly done in green and white. There were no windows. A wide settee stood against the wall by the door, four green leather armchairs faced each other around a coffee table in the middle of the room. It looked like a men's club in a fashionable part of town. A table against the far wall held a coffee urn, and a tray filled with glasses and china cups and saucers was next to it. There was also a jug of orange juice and iced water. Dan felt that he had been in this scene many times in his life. Every business conference he had ever attended had a room like this.

"Coffee or drinks, anyone?" Gregory indicated the coffee urn and poured himself a cup, then sat in the settee, saying nothing more. Neither Emily nor Dan took a drink, and they sat stiffly in their armchairs.

Dan recognized how different and yet how like this scene was to the waiting for the old man in the compound building. No guard in smelly military uniform stood sniffing behind him, holding a rifle. Instead, the guard sat at ease on an antique settee, dressed in a Brooks Brothers suit, the shoulder holster only marginally visible. The room was a beautifully decorated place, regency-striped green and white wallpaper and cream carpet, quite unlike the dirty green walls and unpolished wooden floors of the Murmansk training camp. Dan sat in a comfortable armchair facing Emily, instead of alone on a hard wooden chair. Yet he was waiting for the same thing. Somebody was going to come through that door and start to walk through his mind. The Blank Days were about to start again, and Dan was afraid.

The door opened and all of them stood up. The man who came in was nothing like the old man in Murmansk. He looked like a friendly bear. Over six feet in height, he was large in girth, his hair long and untidy. He was, perhaps, in his sixties. His features were generously placed on a broad face, the nose could have provided shelter from the rain, and the mouth was full-lipped, smiling. He was everybody's favourite uncle and Dan couldn't help warming to him. The newcomer smiled at Dan, then addressed himself to Emily.

"Miss James, it is my great delight to meet you. I am Paul Harrington." His voice was strong, the speech educated and slightly old-fashioned in manner. He inspired confidence, and Emily responded to the old world charm.

"Professor Harrington, I've heard a lot about you. Please call me Emily."

He bowed gently. "And I'm Paul. I think we will all be together for quite some time, so I'm glad we can be friends."

He turned to Dan and took his hand. The warmth in his smile was disarming, and Dan felt knots of tension unwind inside him.

"And I know that you are Mikhail Vorosov," said Paul Harrington. "Misha, I cannot tell you how pleased I am to meet you. And fascinated, too, I must admit. I've been hearing about you on and off for some years."

"My pleasure, Paul," said Dan, relaxing even more. "Especially if you can do something about the state of my head." His fear was declining in the face of the man's warmth. This was not like Murmansk at all.

"Then why don't we sit down and start on that very subject?" Harrington said.

He waited for the others to be seated, then shifted one of the armchairs until it directly faced Dan, and moved it closer so their knees were perhaps a foot apart. He sat down, but leaned forward towards Dan.

"Misha, I need to know how the conditioning began."

"I don't think I can tell you."

"Why not?

Dan shook his head, already feeling panic, his hands beginning to cramp up.

Paul watched with interest. "A block?" he asked gently.

Dan nodded, and even giving him that small piece of information caused a yelp of pain as his heart seemed to turn to fire for a split second. Over Paul's shoulder, he saw Emily flinch.

"Paul, please!" she called. "The block is very painful to him."

"Alright, let's try it another way," said Paul, sitting back and turning slightly to look at Emily. "Emily, I assume there's a control trigger and also a command trigger?"

She nodded, the anxiety showing in her face.

"The control trigger, please," he said, turning back to face Dan. She spoke the words and Dan settled back into his seat, the familiar heaviness creeping over his body.

"How extraordinary!" Paul gasped. "That was far quicker than we ever achieved." He leaned forward a little further.

"Now, Misha, tell me how the conditioning began."

Dan tried. He really tried hard. "The old man would..." His heart felt as if it exploded and he jerked forward, clutching his arms round his body.

Emily leaped out of her chair. "Misha, stop!" she cried, wrapping her arms round his shoulders. "Stop trying to tell him! Just think of me, think of us!"

The pain ceased immediately. Dan looked up at her in gratitude, trembling with the aftershock, feeling sweat on his face. She kept her arm around his shoulder. *Dearest Emily,* he thought, *I need you around to keep me safe.*

"Paul, that isn't going to work," she said. Dan could hear the urgency in her. "It's too deep."

Paul was studying Dan with interest. "Obviously," he murmured, putting his chin in his right hand. "I'm sorry, son. They really did a number on you."

Despite the trembling, Dan managed a grin at him. "Hey," he said, his voice shaking. "In this place you get to earn your money the old-fashioned way. You have to work for it!"

"So it seems," replied Paul with a tiny smile. "Coming at the programming behind the shield of the control triggers isn't going to work." He paused in deep thought for a moment or two, then snapped his fingers.

"Okay, Emily back to your seat," he said decisively. "We'll try a different approach. First, take him out of this control."

"I will let you go now, Misha." Her voice was subdued, still frightened by the results of the psychiatrist's first attempt. Harrington looked from her to Dan, clearly fascinated by the effectiveness of the command words. Then he concentrated on Dan.

"Son, we may not have achieved quite the effects your man in Murmansk achieved," he said. "But we had our moments, and I've got a pretty fair idea of the processes he used on you."

"That's what Emily said," croaked Dan, still not quite recovered from the shock of the jagged pain in his chest.

Paul smiled slightly. "What I'm trying to do is identify the source of the control programs," he said. "I'm going to try my own approach to putting you in deep hypnosis, and then go deeper and deeper. The first thing I'll do is just explore your brain to find the location of the programming."

"Can you explain that a bit more?" Dan was intrigued, despite the nervousness. Exploring his brain was a terrifying but weirdly fascinating idea.

"Sure," Paul said with a smile of understanding. "What we've learned over the years is that specific skills and abilities are maintained in different lobes of the brain. Motor skills in one area, languages in another, different memories in others, and so on." He looked around the silent room. "I know that your Soviet teams worked pretty well the same way as we did," he continued. "There were enough double agents and spies in both projects since the fifties, so we know a lot about each others' work."

Emily emitted a small grunt of agreement and Paul looked at her for a second.

"So we know that the programs of your conditioning were placed in one of those lobes," he continued. "And the first problem is to find out which one."

"How can you do that?" Dan's voice was harsh with strain.

"I'll do a sort of expeditionary force." Paul, gave a small smile of sympathy to Dan. "I'll get you to do a number of different things, which will use a lot of different lobes. We know that they will have placed some powerful defences against intrusion into the area where the main instruction programs are situated, and the nearer I get, the more they'll defend against me."

"Defend?" Dan was confused.

"Truly, defend in a real sense," said Paul with a nod. "Your mind is programmed to resist precisely the sort of intrusion we're about to try. If we get near the area where the programming is stored, you'll start to get agitated, maybe angry."

"It makes me sound like a damned computer!" said Dan, trying to laugh and failing.

"In some ways, that's how the mind works. If we get really close to the programs, something else may happen."

"Such as?" Dan's tension level rose sharply.

Paul leaned back from him and sat sideways in the armchair to address all three of them in the room. "When we tried this with our own people," he said, almost in lecturing pose, "most of them reported that they experienced the process of defending against me as a realistic hallucination of some sort of battle. The types of battle varied, mainly it seems, according to the materials they already had available in their minds. It depends what you've been reading, or what you studied in your past, could be anything. It seems the mind picks whatever props it can and makes them the basis of the hallucination, and within your head you fight a battle that seems totally real."

"Can you give us any examples?" asked Emily. She looked scared but fascinated, leaning forward in her armchair and listening intently. Dan felt his breathing quicken.

"Sure!" Paul grinned at some memories. He stood up and walked to the coffee table, pouring himself a cup. "One of our guys was an amateur boxer who used to watch movies of all the great fights in history. He really was an expert, knew just about every round of every fight. When I tried getting into his head, he experienced a complete ten-round bout with Muhammad Ali. When he woke up, he was tired and aching in every limb!"

Paul moved carefully back to his armchair and sat down, balancing his coffee cup on his knee. "Another one was a science fiction freak," he continued. "And in his mind, he joined Captain Jean-Luc Picard on the bridge of the Starship Enterprise and fought a space battle with the

Romulans. Totally realistic, they said. They both came out of their hallucinations quite exhausted."

He took a gulp of the coffee and gestured at Dan. "From your viewpoint, Misha, it could be anything, or it could be nothing. I have no idea exactly how your man in Murmansk planted the defence mechanisms, or how deeply, so I can't forecast what sort of reaction you'll have to my probing. We'll know more after the first session."

"It sounds incredible," said Dan. "Could I get violent?"

"In the real world, here?" Paul looked at the ceiling as he pondered. "That's possible, I suppose, but unlikely," he said after a second or two. "None of our people did. All the time they were fighting their battles, they moved around their chairs a bit and moaned and shouted, but none of them got violent. Anyway, if you do, Jack and I should be able to handle you."

"Okay, then let's get started." Dan was feeling a strange mixture of excitement and fear. Whatever was facing him, he thought, it was time they got into it.

"Good," said Paul. "Sit back son, watch my hand."

Dan relaxed back in the armchair. From the side of his eye he saw that Jack Gregory was watching with interest. Over Harrington's shoulder, Emily still looked worried but determined. Dan gave her a quick smile then concentrated on Paul's hand poised by his right shoulder.

"Watch my finger," said Paul. "I'll be using conventional hypnosis technique to start with. Once you're under I'll be using some other techniques to get you really deep, but you won't be able to remember them."

His finger began to move towards Dan, and Dan watched it carefully. As it reached towards his nose, it appeared to grow in size, then moved up to his forehead. Dan felt his eyes strain to watch it. As it touched him just below the hairline, he felt relaxed and closed his eyes. His senses expanded to explore the room. He could smell the coffee in Paul's cup, even the faint tang of Gregory's after-shave lotion. He sensed Emily watching him, and smelled her perfume, the tiny whiff of roses that her lipstick gave off. He heard minute bubbles from the heat of the coffee-pot warmer, and felt the thick cloth of the armchair under his wrists. *I can open my eyes any time I want to*, he thought lazily... *I just don't want to. This is pleasant, the armchair is extremely comfortable.*

"Okay, Misha, think about going down an escalator." Paul's voice broke the gathering cloud of peacefulness Dan was feeling. His hand was suddenly on Dan's right shoulder, just like the old man with the blue eyes used to do. Dan saw a clear picture of himself standing on the escalator at O'Hare Field, descending to the frenetically coloured lights of the walkway between the terminals. He was alone. *That's strange*, he thought. *Usually the terminal is alive with throngs of people, where are they all...?* He went further down ...

"The further down you get, the deeper into hypnosis you'll be." Paul's voice seemed to be coming from further away than just the length of his arm. "Everything's fine, you're feeling comfortable..." His hand was firm on Dan's shoulder, his voice a deep accompaniment. It's nice and safe, thought Dan. *Comforting, like being a small boy again and Poppa talking gently to Momma while he held me on his knee...* Gradually Paul's voice seemed to fade into the music until everything went perfectly quiet for Dan. He still knew he could open his eyes any time he wanted... the green and white room was still around him... Emily was here... Jack was over there... He heard the sound of the orange juice in Jack's throat... *So Paul isn't going to be able to hypnotize me the way the blue-eyed old man had done*, thought Dan in hazy amusement. *But this seems like a good time to catch up on some sleep, I'm dreadfully tired for some reason ...*

The three watchers in the room watched Dan's head drop onto his chest, and he slumped in the armchair. Paul Harrington took his hand from Dan's shoulder and stood up.

"A moment, please," he said. He walked to the door and opened it. From the corridor, somebody handed him a leather bag. He took it and returned to his seat across from Dan. He opened the bag, extracted a hypodermic and a vial, inserted the needle in the vial and drew a volume of a greenish liquid.

"What's that?" asked Emily, anxiety in her voice.

Paul turned to her, holding the needle carefully upright. "Something we developed," he said with a friendly and reassuring smile. "It augments the subject's receptivity to suggestion. It's quite harmless."

Looking only a little less anxious, Emily sat back in her chair and watched as Paul injected the contents of the hypodermic into the inside of Dan's elbow. Dan jerked a tiny fraction as the needle bit into him, but showed no other effect. Paul sat back, looked at his watch and held Dan's pulse.

Some time has passed, I can't tell how much. I feel as if I have awakened with a sensation of panic. But I don't know where I am... I can't get back to the friendly room... I'm alone and someone is walking around outside, somebody evil, threatening. The silence is stifling, hot and humid... I'm exposed... NO! YOU CAN'T GO IN THERE!!! I have to stop it, fear and loathing rush through my body, I'm sweating heavily... KEEP AWAY! ... Oh God! NO! YOU CAN'T GO THERE.... I'LL KILL YOU!.. blind terror in every atom of me... in the distance the sounds of armies moving... engines roaring.... shouts of frightened men... whistles... where in God's name am I?... and then...

"Blue Squadron, Blue Squadron, scramble, scramble, scramble!" The sirens blast through the quiet tension of the operations room where all twelve of us have been sitting, lying, sprawling around the place, reading, smoking, sleeping. Charlie's voice is loud as he repeats the orders coming over the telephone he had just picked up on the first ring.

The room explodes like a whale breaching. We grab parachutes and run like hell through the light wooden door, out into the open field and the bright, cold sunshine. I sling my chute over my shoulder and race for Zulu Oscar standing third in line, clumsy in my winter-weight flying suit and fur-lined boots. I jump up on the wing, throw the chute into the cockpit and fasten up the Mae West securely before scrambling into the cramped space. My ground-crew corporal climbs up after me and leans over to help me strap on the complex strands of webbing belts that hold the chute to me and then me to the seat of Zulu Oscar. He plugs the helmet radio lead in, wipes the goggles and oxygen mask and hands me the leather headgear. I give him my peaked cap for safe keeping until I return.

"Give 'em hell, Sir," he says in his strong Yorkshire accent and slips off the wing. I hit the switches, prime the pump, press the starter, and the enormous three-bladed propeller groans, kicks, groans again and suddenly spins, the blades becoming a transparent disk reflecting the sun. The huge Merlin engine bellows into mighty defiance as the sixteen supercharged cylinders catch the fire. Immediately I slip the brake, let Zulu Oscar pull forward and turn for the runway, fourth in line behind the Squadron Leader and his wingmen. The Spitfire bumps and sways on its narrow undercarriage as I swing the long, beautiful nose to one side every few yards so that I can see forward to the take-off point.

At the end of the field we line up. David is on my right in Charlie X-Ray, his red beard the one flash of colour in the green and brown camouflage patterns of his Spitfire. I grin cheerfully at him, we mouth our traditional greeting to each other "Beware of the Hun in the sun!" and I snap the oxygen mask over my mouth, the familiar scent of old vomit and fear making me gag as always for the first few seconds. Check the dials, test the magnetos, watch Blue Leader's tail. See the green flare from the control tower... His rudder swings sharply left and right... *go!* Full throttle, trim forward, fight the torque of the immense Merlin, and we are howling along the grass and into the air above Tangmere. Two greens, two reds, the wheels are safely up and locked and Zulu Oscar flies smoothly, eager for the killing to start.

"Steer One Niner Fife, Angels Two Four," says the female voice in my headphones. She sounds sexy that lady, one day I would have to visit the control room at Southern Command and see for myself. Blue Leader opens his throttle, and we follow him out over the Channel, higher and higher into the thin, cold air till the sky above turns a deeper royal blue and the sea is a smooth sheet of grey steel reflecting the sun in a dazzling patch. From twenty-four thousand feet, France is a dirty brown line to the south, but more important is the row of minute specks tracking across the steel carpet. Three of the squadron see them at the same time, and the voices are a gabble in my ears.

"Bandits, Bandits, one o'clock low!"

"Okay fellers, plenty for all of us." Blue Leader's voice is calm and the yellow nose cone of his Spitfire swings a little right to intercept. Tiny adjustments of throttle, rudder and stick as we follow in three flights of Finger-Four formation.

Heinkel 111s, lots of them, tight formation, guns on the nose, on the backs, nasty little Krauts coming to drop bombs on England. Not if we can help it. Two miles to close. Stare high and far into the dark blue sky, search for the Messerschmidts that should be up there as a protective umbrella... but the radar would tell us, and Parke's wings have almost wiped out the invading fighters in the last few months...

"Tally Ho, chaps, good hunting!" That means break away, find your own target.

I slam the throttle forward and the Merlin howls with a lust for blood. We are passing over the lumbering bombers now, the swastikas ugly on the tails and wings. Full right rudder, right bank, kick it over, forward on the column, four hundred knots, unlock the guns. I pick out the rear Heinkel, sight on the gunner, center him on the dot and press the button. Tracers streak out, angle in on the massive fuselage, rake it end to end. The plane jerks, that means the pilot is hit... good, another burst, fire breaks out at the wing root, it begins to turn and lose altitude... let it go... another bloody Hun who won't get home...

Kick round right, pick another one, sight, guns.... Jesus! Zulu Oscar shakes violently, the gun turret of the Heinkel spitting flame at me, hit somewhere, take the bastard out, aim, sight, shoot, four second burst, see the gunner throw his arms up, the glass explode in a red cloud, and I'm past... *pull up, pull up, don't give the nose gunner a chance...* roll inverted, scan the battle from upside down... three of the Heinkels turning north west to Southampton, roll back, turn for them.. rake the bastards with eight machine guns... the wing breaks off one and flies up and past me like an autumn leaf. The Heinkel flicks over and flutters like an enormous stricken gamebird. Haul hard right... wings vertical to the horizon... tighter... tighter... blood draining from my head, sight gets dim.. struggle to hold my head against the force of five gravities... hold it, hold it, back round behind the bombers again... straighten the rudder, vision clears, neck muscles ease from the strain, sight, three seconds shuddering of my guns... SHIT! the damn Jerry explodes... I fly through the debris before I get a chance to turn, something splatters on my windscreen... blood... one of the crew... pull up vertical, hard right rudder as the nose flops back down towards the sea... perfect stall turn... that catches the last pilot napping.. the silly bugger flies right past me, leaves me on his tail... *guns, guns, guns,* five seconds, make bloody certain... he jerks like a stuck pig, smoke bursts from his port engine... got the bastard!... turn hard left, roll right, nothing near.. where the hell is everybody?

My God, I got five.. see the squadron far away swarming on the last two Heinkels like hyenas at the kill.. leave them to it.. check fuel.. something rattling behind me. Go home Dan, little boy has had a busy day. Nose down, straight for Tangmere, last five miles at one thousand feet over the town, line up on the grass strip, pull up the nose, barrel roll, one.. two.. three... enough, don't overdo it. Into the circuit, wheels down, two reds, two greens, all okay, touchdown.. bump, another touchdown.. not so good, Blue Leader likes just one takeoff for each landing... taxi in, switch off... total exhaustion.

I climb out of the Spitfire to the greetings of the entire ground crew. They are cheering, shouting and applauding. My corporal walks up with a huge grin on his face. "Three Sir? Great stuff!"

"Three be buggered, Jim! Got five of the bastards!"

The roaring gets louder and they all rush at me, but somehow it isn't as friendly as it seemed. *What the hell's going on?* They are all over me, I am struggling for breath, they have me pinned down, I throw a couple of them off and kick out in my heavy flying boots. Somebody thumps me hard behind the ears and I lose all interest in the proceedings.

* * *

Dan woke up. He was lying in an enormous double bed, the delicious sensation of a warm female body snuggled against his back.

"Good morning!" murmured Emily, leaning up on one elbow and smiling down at him.

"Good God! Who did that?" He stared at the heavy bruise on her cheek. It was a rich purple with orange and green threads through the main colour. Anger rose in Dan. *How dare anyone...?*

"You did, lover boy!" she managed to smile, though the pain obviously was getting to her. Dan sat up with a jerk and took her arm.

"Me? Emily love, what happened?"

She chuckled, though she was clearly feeling some discomfort. "You should see the other guy! Or should I say guys, plural?"

"What?" His confusion was churning his insides around together with his anger. Seeing Emily hurt was getting to him severely. "Jesus, Emily, tell me what happened!"

"I'd say it was vaguely reminiscent of Custer's Last Stand," she said, touching the bruise on her face. She cocked her head up at the ceiling as if in thought. "Or perhaps the Alamo." She looked back at him, her eyes laughing. "Thermopylae, maybe?"

He shook her shoulders, half in laughter, half frustration. She gave a little gasp of pain and he stopped, guilt-stricken.

"Sorry, sweetheart, I forgot." He curled his legs up and twisted round to sit cross-legged in front of her. "All right, in your own time, tell me the story!"

"Actually," she said, snuggling down against her pillows again, and touching his knee. "I can do better than that. The whole thing was taped, and Paul wants you to see the film after breakfast."

Breakfast? Dan suddenly realized he seemed to have lost a lot of yesterday. "Emily, we went into that room at about ten in the morning," he said. "It couldn't have been more than an hour before he put me under. And now it's..." He reached for his watch on the bedside table. "Seven o'clock in the morning? The next day?"

He put the watch down again and lay down with her. She grunted against his shoulder, apparently undisturbed by the twenty or so hours he seemed to have lost. Dan was desperately hungry.

"Sweetest Emily," he said to the pile of soft brown hair on his right shoulder. "I love you to death and for all eternity, and I lust for your gorgeous body too, but this man is dying of acute starvation. It seems I last ate two scrambled eggs and a kiddy-sized muffin over twenty hours ago. So let us swing our collective butts and go *eat!*"

A muffled giggle warmed his arm. "Well this girl had dinner last night in the company of several dashing young military men. We had roast duck, sautéed potatoes and snow peas followed by an English sherry trifle, accompanied by a delicate vintage French Blanc de Blanc..."

Dan leapt out of the bed, dragged the entire coverings to the floor exposing her in night attire of a tee-shirt. He ignored the sight and her scream of protest.

"Enough, wench! Shower then FOOD!" He hauled her out of the bed and carried her into the bathroom, climbed into the spacious shower stall and turned on the hot water. Giggling like small children, the process of getting up took a lengthy and thoroughly enjoyable forty minutes.

By the time they made it to the dining room, nearly everybody had gone. Just Paul Harrington was left, idly stirring a cup of coffee and reading *Time*. Dan received a wide grin as he walked in with Emily.

"Ah, the return of the warrior!" said Paul, folding the magazine away. "Bloody but unbowed!"

It got an understanding chuckle from Emily, as she led Dan to the food area against the wall. "Let's feed the brute first," she said. "Then we can explain!"

Dan gave her a curious look, almost demanded an explanation immediately, but decided that hunger was a priority problem. He filled up a plate with scrambled eggs, four sausages, three bacon strips and a healthy dollop of hash browns and joined them at the table. A waiter poured coffee into all their cups as they looked in pained disapproval at Dan's plate. Emily's small helping of fresh fruit and a glass of orange juice looked meagre compared to Dan's.

"Well, hell!" he said, defensively. "Whatever it is I did, it was obviously active and a long time ago. A man needs to eat!"

"Active it certainly was!" Paul was in a good mood much like Emily, and only then did Dan see the cut on the older man's neck and the bruise behind his ear. He pointed.

"Me again?" he asked. He felt a wave of anxiety. *What the hell had he been up to?*

Paul nodded. "If we hadn't taped the whole thing, nobody would believe it."

"All right, I'm totally confused and intrigued," said Dan, picking up his knife and fork. "Let me get this lot inside me and then you can show me what the hell it was I did that caused this."

Twenty minutes later, they rose from the table, and Emily and Dan followed Paul who seemed to know his way through the endless corridors to the room they had used yesterday. I wonder how long it will take before I find my way around this place, Dan thought idly. Then Paul opened the door and Dan stopped thinking idle thoughts.

The room was a mess.

The four armchairs were all overturned. The table holding the coffee urn was simply a mass of splinters on the floor, the urn itself in the opposite corner of the room, on its side. An ugly stain across the entire wall and carpet indicated that the urn had completed a trajectory from one side to the other, ejecting coffee as it went. The tray of china cups and saucers was a white splash of ground-up splinters on the floor.

"Oh my!" said Dan.

"What?" Paul was looking oddly at him.

"I said 'Oh my!'" Dan repeated.

"I know you did," Paul replied, a twitch of amusement on his lips. "Somehow those dismally limp words fail to express the magnitude of your deeds."

"You have alternative suggestions?" Any formality Dan might have felt from yesterday had gone, and this small game was somehow essential to feeling at ease with Paul Harrington.

The doctor shook his head, the smile severely repressed and his face solemn. "I don't believe there is any expression that would adequately describe the magnificence of your exploits," he declaimed in majestic tones like an actor playing Hamlet. "I was rather hoping you would enlighten us."

Dan shook his head in defeat. "What the hell happened?" he asked, staring round the shambles.

"We need to show you," said Paul, walking to the door. He pressed a couple of buttons by the light switches that Dan had not noticed before. The lights faded, a section began to descend from the opposite wall revealing a massive television screen. Paul took a remote control box from a slot by the screen and pressed a button. The screen flickered, glowed and a picture of the same room they were inhabiting appeared. They turned the armchairs over to their correct position and moved them so that they could watch the screen.

Paul took up the commentary. “This is where we first tried to get you to tell us about your training.”

On the screen, Emily leapt at Dan, called his name and held his head as he doubled over in pain. Dan watched the pictures, heard Emily ordering him to stop trying to tell Paul anything, and the images on the screen settled back.

“Let’s advance to where I put you under,” said Paul. He pressed a button on the controller, and the picture raced forward, minute figures darting and gesticulating. It slowed again and Dan watched his image on the screen, watched his head droop as Paul touched it with his right hand.

“This is where I began exploring,” continued Paul. “As I explained, I was trying to map out your brain by making you do various things and seeing if any abnormal events took place. I figured that if you got agitated, I was getting close to the program storage area.”

On the screen, Dan was raising his hand, waggling his feet, standing up, sitting down, scratching his arms. It looked rather silly to Dan, watching himself in some embarrassment.

“This went on for five hours,” said Paul after a few minutes of the meaningless activities on the screen.

“How boring!” said Dan, for it really did look completely without any value to him. He was feeling disconcerted, watching his image behave like that.

“Not really,” responded Paul. “It was a bit like cutting through the jungle wondering if something would leap out and eat me at any moment!”

Dan chuckled. Paul's sense of humor was almost English, he thought, delicate and ironic. "So when does something leap out at you with carnivorous intent?" he said, picking his words with care.

"At about three-fifteen," answered Paul, suddenly abstracted and watching the screen carefully. "Wait." He fast-forwarded the film and the three of them sat quietly for a while. Then he returned the speed to normal and the frantically gesturing figures slowed down again. On the screen, Dan was bending over, straightening up, standing, talking. The image of Jack Gregory was slumped on the settee, nearly asleep, Emily could be seen in the foreground of the scene, curled up in her armchair, watching with fascination. It reminded Dan.

"Where's Jack?" he asked, turning to look at the other two.

"Sick leave," chimed in Emily, poker-faced.

"Sick leave?" Dan looked at her.

"Wait!" snapped Paul Harrington. "Things are about to happen."

Dan turned back to the screen. The volume was increased by Paul's control. On the screen, Dan's image was standing rigid, staring at the wall with dreadful intensity. The other three were watching, Emily was uncurling, clearly aware that something was happening. Watching the film, Dan's heart began beating faster. Something critical was going on.

The screen image of Dan let out a high-pitched scream of terrifying volume and intensity. The hatred and violence were something Dan had never heard before and he shivered.

"That's me?" he whispered, horrified, standing up to try and ease his muscles which had become cramped.

"That's you." Paul was subdued. "Dreadful, isn't it?"

"Good grief!" murmured Dan. He watched, riveted, as his image suddenly leapt on Jack Gregory, seized his throat and began pounding his head against the wall. On the screen, Paul and Emily shouted and jumped to his rescue, frantically pulling at Dan, with little effect. Jack collapsed on the settee, unconscious and Dan turned on the other two. Emily tried to move back, but Dan slammed his fist against her cheek and continued the movement to rake Paul across the face.

In the corner of the screen, the door flung open, almost breaking off at the hinges, and three marines in full uniform raced in. Dan's image attacked them before they had time to see what was happening. The first, he grabbed by his neck and belt, lifted him with apparent ease and flung him hard against the wall. As he fell, he seized the coffee pot and threw it at Dan's head, but it sailed over the crowd and brown fluid drenched the wall. Dan rushed the next two, swung a brutal shoe straight into the groin of the closest, and as his head bent over in agony, brought his knee up into his face. The third marine reached massive arms round Dan's shoulders and arms, hauled him back. Somehow Dan spun, reached up both hands and chopped the marine's neck. He yelled, dropped to his knees and Dan kicked his face. But the other two soldiers were up again, they dropped on Dan and began pummelling him hard. Dan seemed to wriggle like an eel, crawled out of the melee and began kicking wildly in every direction.

Then the room was full of uniforms, six, seven, eight men poured in, they simply overwhelmed Dan. The last sight Dan could see of his image on the screen was one of them pulling a truncheon and bopping him scientifically on the back of the head. Finally, the raging figure on the screen collapsed, leaving a lot of men milling around, looking confused and embarrassed.

"They put you in a strait-jacket for a couple of hours," said Paul, switching off the video and standing up to replace the remote control under the screen. "But I made them take it off. You were clearly in defensive mode for a time, and equally clearly out of it when we stopped probing. In fact, you were deeply asleep, and you stayed that way till this morning."

"It's madness," said Dan, still staring at the blank screen. He was breathing almost as hard as he had been back in the combat for real, instead of just watching himself.

"Well put," said Paul with a chuckle, walking to the doorway and switching the screen control button. The screen rose back into the ceiling, breaking Dan's fixed stare at it. "That's roughly what we said! You were obviously well trained in unarmed combat techniques."

"Sergeant Kutchinski," said Dan absent-mindedly, his head still full of the images of the raging typhoon he had been watching.

"He did a pretty good job," said Emily with a smile. Dan smiled back at her, and stretched himself, feeling the bruises and strains in his body.

"I feel terrible about the damage I did to you guys," he said, looking again at the bruise on Emily's face.

"It was unexpected," agreed Paul, rubbing at the cut on his neck.

"No doubt," said Dan. "So what do we do now?"

"Let's start at the beginning, and try and identify what really happened," said Paul, returning to his armchair. "Do you remember being put under hypnosis?"

"Yes, I do," replied Dan, following Paul's example and sitting down alongside him. "Didn't seem too much to it, I could remember everybody in the room, I knew I was still sitting in the armchair. It seemed to me you weren't getting anywhere, so I went to sleep." He looked back at the silent screen. “But then I saw you inject me with something, so it obviously wasn’t that simple.”

Paul nodded. “That’s the usual thing with conventional hypnosis. The subject remains aware of the surroundings and often thinks they’re not under. But as you saw, once we reached that state, I began some more advanced techniques we developed during the project. So, do you remember anything?”

Dan reflected. His mind seemed totally blank. He shook his head at Paul. “Not a damn thing,” he said.

“Hardly surprising,” Paul replied. “Too many blocks in there for normal memories to surface. I think we’ll put you under again and go for it that way.”

“If you say so,” said Dan, trying to appear easy about it.

Paul grinned. “Nothing like the last time, Misha,” he said. “This is just to review the performance. Now, watch my hand.”

The process was like before. Dan watched Paul’s finger move to his forehead, he relaxed, closed his eyes, sensed everybody in the room, heard them with enhanced ears, and felt sleepy.

“Now, Misha,” said Paul’s voice from somewhere in the distance. “What happened when I first put you under?”

“I got sleepy,” murmured Dan. “I was sure you hadn’t been able to put me under, so I fell asleep.”

“And then what?” Paul’s voice was soft, gentle. Dan thought about it and memories began to surface. A sense of fear, panic...

“I remember that I woke up feeling terrified,” he replied. “It was rather like the way I was waking up at home when I had those dreadful flashbacks in the beginning.”

“And what then?”

"Then it got really nasty," Dan continued. "I think I was screaming 'You can't get in there' or something like that."

"That's when we started to get near to the program storage areas and began to trigger the defence mechanisms." Paul sounded smug. "As I thought, your programmer had put some pretty heavy defences in the way. Do you remember any of the action after that?"

Dan thought hard. Ghost images thrust their way past his eyes and he grabbed at them. "An air battle!" he said in excitement. "I think I experienced an air battle. Yes! Dammit, yes! I was flying a Spitfire. I got two Heinkels, then I got three more... good grief!"

Dan snapped his eyes open, the light hypnosis broken. Images flooded into his head, and the whole hallucination returned to him. He remembered every detail. *God!* he thought. *It was exciting!*

"That's right." Paul spoke softly. "First you attacked Jack Gregory, then Emily, then the three marines. What happened after that?"

"I landed, got a great reception, then... oh my God!" Dan began to understand how the hallucination had matched the real events in the room. "The ground crew attacked me and beat the shit out of me!"

"It was a large scale attack by a number of men, and you resisted?"

"That's exactly what it was!"

"See the parallels?" Paul was still speaking softly, but there was a smile on his face.

"Christ! Yes!" Dan could see them exactly. Hitting Jack Gregory had appeared to him like shooting the first Heinkel, Emily had been the second, and so on. Under the excitement of remembering the flying warfare was the dismay at what he had done to the people around him.

"Your mind worked with whatever images it could," said Paul. "Were the details clear?"

"Clear? I was living it!"

"And were any of the faces familiar?"

Dan suddenly saw the red hair and cheerful face of his friend and colleague from work. "One of the other pilots was David," he said with surprise. "He's one of the people at work!"

"A good friend?" asked Paul."

"Very good," Dan replied. "He helped me a lot when these dreams started."

"I'd say you deliberately brought him into the hallucination to help you again," said Paul. "You weren't all that certain that you would win this battle."

"You mean I might see him again if we do this another time?" Dan asked.

"Possibly," replied Paul. "Depends on a lot of factors. But it seems that your reaction exactly conforms to the experiences we had ourselves with our own subjects, except for the degree of physical violence you displayed."

"And that's good?"

"I think so, Dan," replied Harrington. "It means that our two projects followed similar lines. So it's likely that I'm going in the right direction."

"Can you break the conditioning, Paul?" Emily stood up and moved to the psychiatrist. He smiled at her.

"Emily, I can't be certain. But I know now that I'm not wandering in the dark as much as I thought. We can work on it."

"So you think you've made progress?" She was staring anxiously at him, then moved to Dan and touched his arm.

"I believe so," answered Paul. "But let's summarize what happened." He settled back in his armchair as if to deliver a lecture. "The first thing is that we located the program storage area. And there's a hell of a lot of defensive mechanisms to make you try and stop any infiltration of that area. Your mind takes images from things that you've read in the past, and creates a massively realistic hallucination of a battle."

"Realistic?" said Dan. "I'll say it was realistic!"

Paul nodded. "This first battle, you won too easily," he said with a small frown. "I was just starting to try a few counters to the conditioning when you exploded into action. I completely underestimated the power of those defences. I think that if we start to give you a real counter-attack, you'll have to fight a lot harder. And it may take a lot out of you, physically."

"It certainly didn't happen like that, this time," said Dan, considering his words. "I feel a few bruises from the fight with the Marines, but nothing else."

"But I think you will, next time." Paul was adamant. "And remember, too, you slept for nearly sixteen hours after that exercise, so it took more out of you than you might have realized."

He paused in thought for a few moments. "Misha," he continued, "I think you should rest up a couple of days, then we'll start again. You expended a lot of energy in that fight, even though you won so easily. Later on, it may get worse. Anyway, now that I know roughly where the program area is, we can home straight in and see what happens. But a couple of precautions."

Dan nodded. It was obvious. "Tie me down?"

"That's one thing. But the main problem is this." Paul was suddenly deadly serious. "We can't break down your mental conditioning without first breaking through the defences in your mind. The conditioning is making you fight a furious battle within a hallucination to prevent that break-through. And those defences are extraordinary. Far more effective than anything I was able to implant in our own subjects."

Dan felt cold. “Can you break them?”

“I think so,” replied Paul. “Eventually. But I’m afraid you’re going to suffer a lot in the process.”

“Why?” asked Dan. “What can this do to me?”

“Just look at what the situation is,” answered Paul. “If I am to break down the conditioning, that means you will have to lose a fight within your hallucination. Right now, you’re powerfully conditioned not to lose, in fact you’ll fight like hell to defeat me.”

“I see the problem,” said Dan, feeling the snakes of fear writhing in his guts. “I have to lose in my hallucination in order for you to win.”

“Exactly,” agreed Paul. “With our own people, it was okay simply to lose. We were able to break the conditioning that way. But your man was much more advanced than we were. You’re programmed to fight to the death.”

“Then that’s what you have to do, Paul. You have to fight me to the death.”

“I know.” Paul’s anxiety was strong in his face. “It means we will only destroy the conditioning when you let yourself die in the battle. But I have no idea what could happen if you die within such a powerfully realistic hallucination.”

“I’ll survive.”

“I truly hope so.”

“You think there’s some doubt about that?” Dan tried to smile at Paul, but his lips were frozen. He looked at Emily, and she was staring wide-eyed at Harrington with her hands held in front of her mouth.

“I don’t know,” said Paul. “But if we assume that you’ll live physically, there may be serious damage, psychologically.”

“Paul, I have faith in you. Whatever you do to me, it can’t leave me in a worse state than I’m in at the moment.”

The room was silent.

"Kill or cure, Paul," said Dan. "That's the way it has to be."

"We'll do the best we can," said Paul Harrington. "Meanwhile, we'll continue in a couple of days after you have a thorough physical. This is going to be rough."

Dan reached for Emily's hand. "I've got good support," he said.

Chapter 9

The room was quiet now, the damage repaired, the wall washed clean. The smashed cups and saucers had been replaced, the coffee urn was back on the table by the wall. The carpet had been shampooed, the blood rinsed out of the rich cream-coloured pile. Jack Gregory was sitting on the settee again, the plaster over his nose, the bruises on his throat covered by a soft silk scarf. He seemed to bear Dan no ill-will for the damage. Part of the job description, he said.

Paul Harrington was again sitting before Dan, leaning forward, their knees almost touching. Emily was curled up on the armchair behind Paul and to his left, anxious, frightened, hopeful.

Only Dan was different this time. He was seated not in the soft armchair but in a heavy wooden seat with solid arms and back. The marine major who had found it said it was antique English, very valuable. Dan's chest was secured to the seat back by a heavy leather strap, another one circled his waist. His forearms were pinioned firmly to the wooden arms of the chair by more leather straps borrowed from the resident Marines. Foam rubber strips protected his arms from the hard leather, Paul's suggestion. The scene was disturbingly like the electric chair at an execution.

Dan was frightened, he was excited. He remembered the amazing exhilaration of the aerial combat, how like real life was the sensation of the swooping attack on the bombers, the shudder of eight machine guns, the glory of the kill. He wanted to repeat the experience, and yet he saw Paul's argument that if he won a battle, they would have failed to win the war. Dan was defending the fortress of his mind on the orders of a blue-eyed old man he had not seen in nearly twenty years and who might be dead by now, and he had to lose if he was ever to regain his human soul. *I don't know what it will feel like to lose,* he thought. *Can I actually lose? If I do, will I die? Will I live but be a vegetable?* Paul would not hide from him the fact that such a result was possible.

So Dan was frightened and excited. The battle to come in his mind might take the same form as the fight over the Channel, or it might be something quite different. Or it might be nothing at all. Paul could not promise anything.

But Paul had found the location in Dan's mind where the old man's instructions were hidden, by a simple process of walking through the jungle until something attacked him. He had asked Dan lots of questions that first day, made him perform a series of physical movements, took him through old memories, made him do mental exercises and watched for hostile reactions. Over a period of several hours, he had mapped Dan's brain and found the forbidden zone. Now another Paul Harrington expeditionary force would advance on that area and see what they could see.

Dan was frightened. He was excited.

"Let's do it!" he said. Paul held his fingers by his shoulder, reached forward to Dan's forehead and sent him back down the escalator at O'Hare until the music stopped and the silence blanketed him.

I am standing at the foot of the hills on a dusty plain, the morning sun shining over my right shoulder and making the rocks and stones bright with a clean freshness that I will soon destroy. Trollkiller is in my right hand, the weight of the blade resting on the ground, my fingers clasping the grooved handle under the jewelled hilt. I am wearing a simple leather jerkin and trousers, strong boots up to my knees. The trolls have sharp teeth and I have felt them to my cost in other battles.

My father's knife, Skaarborg is in its sheath on my belt, the single ruby that balances it, a dull, warm glow in the morning sun. Skaarborg was his father's knife before him, Odin willing, it will be my son's after me. I hear the small song of hunger and glee that it sings to me. Before we leave this place, that ruby will be bright like the sun itself with the life force that it will drink. The blade has drunk the souls of many trolls, and my sword Trollkiller has sent many more to whatever pit they go when they die. The Halls of Hel will receive more today and Skaarborg will drink their lives to satiation.

The trolls slink into the town after dark or in the last moments of evening. They come when the shadows are long and the goblins of the night begin to dance in the moonbeams. They kill our animals and leave the ripped, bloodied corpses by our doorways. Huge chunks of the bodies are missing, eaten by the fangs of the trolls. We hear their giggles and squabbles as they fight over the food, and the tearing sounds of the meat being ripped from the bone. Later, when the sun has risen to cleanse the night of the murders, the blood is daubed over our doors and windows, runs along the streets and stains our feet as we walk.

When they can, the trolls take our children or old ones, and days later we find their bones in the streets, tooth marks ground into the surface. Sometimes we hear the screams of the victims echoing in the canyons and gullies of the hill region. The people will send hunting parties into the hills to seek revenge, but they never can. Sometimes the hunters do not return, and the widows weep again in

Ynnisvail and Llannisgan, and the other towns of the north.

When the killings get too much for them to stand, the people send for me. Once they called for my father. One day they will call for my son. I am Stengwulf, Killer of Trolls.

I raise Trollkiller's long blade high and let out a long, harsh, wordless yell as challenge. It echoes back and forth, rings off the ancient rocks and into the caves, and climbs like a hawk to the summit of the trolls' territory. Then silence again. They hear me. I know they hear me as they have heard me before. I let Trollkiller's point rest on the ground again. He will have work to do soon enough.

The first dark heads appear behind the rocks high up on the hill. Soon they are a horde, no longer bothering to hide, staring down at me, the whispers and chuckles dribbling like sand down the hill towards me.

"Oh Man, stupid Man, why do you come? Soon we will dine well on your flesh!"

I roar back at them.

"I am Stengwulf, Killer of Trolls! My father killed you, I kill you, my son will kill you! Come, filth, come and die, let Skaarborg drink your black blood, let Trollkiller send you back to Hel!"

There is consternation on the hillside. I hear the whispers of my name, hear their fear, and I wait. Skaarborg's song grows louder at my belt, and I feel the red ruby pulse with excitement and hunger. Trollkiller's blade begins to tremble, ready for his work to begin. We three have been here before, many times.

The whispers in the caves grow to a rumble as the trolls build their anger above their fear. The first stones are thrown and I ignore them. Bigger ones soar lazily through the air, and I have time to move aside and let them crash into the dust at my feet. Rumbles grow to screams of rage, and dark masses emerge from the rocks. There must be fifty, a hundred of them, they begin to descend, ugly creatures, crouching together drawing courage from their numbers, shrieking their hatred and fear at me, shaking their fists with the rocks in them. They get nearer and now I see them more clearly.

Perhaps the tallest ones are four feet tall, but wide, squat, heavy. They are dark-skinned, their hair is a matted, greasy pile like rotting straw, their faces covered with yellow fungus. Pointed, jagged teeth tell of the eating of raw meat, hands like talons with nails to rip and tear the flesh. Tiny slit eyes of underground dwellers, why do they face the light of Odin's clean world?

They smell, Great Thor do they smell! They are within a few feet now, growling in fear and rage and hunger. Trollkiller's blade rises without orders from me. He is eager for the killing to start. I reach for Skaarborg on my belt with my left hand and show him to the trolls. They hear his song of blood lust and fall back a little, pause and then they rush.

The first sweep takes off the heads of four of them, and small bodies collapse, black blood seeping into the dust, evil heads staring sightlessly at me. The black horde falls back in shock. A wail of fear and rage starts somewhere in the middle of them and grows into a fearful, shrieking chorus. Then they come again, and Trollkiller is busy. I hack, cut and stab, the sword slices arms, legs and heads into the ground, the knife catches throats and hearts.

For a brief few seconds, they fall back again and surround me at a safe distance of a few feet. I crouch, staring at them. Trollkiller is alive in my right hand, humming with happiness, black blood dripping from the entire length of the tempered steel and over my hand. Skaarborg glows with energy in my left, the light of the ruby making second shadows in the dust. There is much killing still to do.

"Misha, you can be hurt," says a small voice in my ear. I shake my head, what witchcraft is this? I scream at the black monsters.

"Come back, Filth! Do you fear Stengwulf? Would you dine on my flesh? Come and eat, little friends, join in Trollkiller's feast, share your blood with Skaarborg!"

Small teeth seize onto my legs, claws rip at my arms and I stab downwards without looking. The teeth and claws let go but I feel the flesh rip. I spin, turn, slice with every move. *Never stop for a second, never pause to think,* my father had said. *Keep moving, keep slashing, keep killing.* Teeth and claws on my arm, slam the troll against a rock, see the crushed body fall to meet the others, slash backhanded into the mob and let Trollkiller eat his fill.

I scream a shout of pure exhilaration, there is no pain, no fatigue, just the task of the Gods to rid the world of these trolls. *Come Thor, lend me your hammer to help in your work! Great Odin, throw your bolts from Asgard, join me!*

Soon the ground is a charnel house, the dust has become bloody mud, my boots with the heavy studded soles keep my footing for me. At last the trolls retreat, howling in dismay and grief, their numbers a fraction of the original horde.

I stand straight, my blood mixing with the black stains of the trolls on my clothes and arms, my breathing like the giant steam geysers of the northern islands. Black ooze drips off the blades of Skaarborg and Trollkiller, they have done their work well today. I turn and walk to the stream to wash my blades, lean over the water...

Instead of my own face, I stare into the eyes of Paul Harrington.

* * *

Harrington was frightened, awed. He looked weary as if he had travelled far or worked long hours. And in his face too, there was sadness. As Dan's gaze cleared from the confusion of returning to the real world, the two men looked deep into each other's eyes the way two boxers do when they have fought each other to a standstill.

Dan looked behind Harrington to Emily. Her hands were placed over her cheeks and mouth, her eyes were wide, she seemed in shock. Then Dan felt the pain in his arms and legs. He looked down at his left arm where the troll... the shirt sleeve was a gory stretch of blood, and more was seeping into the white cloth as he watched. The tear in the flesh was hurting like hell.. *how in God's name did that happen?* he thought in bewilderment. Without damage to the shirt? He had been strapped securely in the antique chair and the straps were still in place. Who had been attacking him? And how?

His attention focused on his right leg. Above the knee, more blood was seeping, ruining the light blue cotton jeans he had been wearing. The stinging pain told of more torn skin, but as with the shirt, the cloth was untouched.

"This is beyond a joke," Dan muttered to himself, struggling to understand, to think of a rational explanation. Somebody had been taking the opportunity of his immobility to inflict damage, or... the alternative simply was not tolerable. But how could anyone have done this?

"Dan? Misha? Talk to me." Paul was hesitant, he seemed confused.

"Which would you like?" said Dan, trying to stay light-hearted, because anything was better than looking at horrible possibilities.

Paul and Emily both sighed as if they had been holding their breath for long minutes.

"Misha!" squeaked Emily and jumped from her armchair and put her arms round Dan, kissing his cheeks, his forehead, his eyes. "I was so frightened!" she whispered, and Dan felt the wetness of her tears. Paul was more pragmatic and began loosening the straps and throwing the leather belts off him. Both were babbling, but whether their incoherence was their fault or Dan's increasingly stultifying fatigue, Dan couldn't begin to guess.

As the straps fell away from his chest, he fell forward, only caught by Paul's beefy arms before he slipped off the chair. Paul pushed him back upright, and his head bumped the high wooden back of the chair with a dull clunk.

"Paul, what's happened to me?" Dan tried to say, but neither Paul nor Emily understood the incoherent moan that came out of him. The pain in his arm and leg was the only thing that seemed clear to him, and Dan could see heavy blood stains on the sleeves of Paul's shirt where the psychiatrist had held Dan as he fell.

He tried to stand up and nearly collapsed on the carpet, only restrained again by Paul's massive arms. Paul swung him around to the armchair and lowered him into it. Dan was feeling weaker than a new-born kitten and he was breathing in small, shallow gasps. He was still clinging to Emily's hand, though he felt she could have blown his grasp away with a light breath.

"Can I have a drink?" Dan had to force the words out, syllable by reluctant syllable. Paul was back with an orange juice in seconds. Dan needed Emily's help to raise his head to drink it, and the juice soaked into his body cells like water into dust. Dan pointed for more, it was easier than speaking.

The door swung open and two men pushed in a hospital cart. They positioned it by the armchair, but Dan had no recollection of them lifting him onto it.

* * *

Three days. Three days of delirium, pain, cramped muscles, dreadful thirst. Three days, while Dan lay in the sick ward of the mansion house, tubes in his arms, never alone for a second as an army of nurses and doctors worked to bring him back to a living condition. He had lost fifteen pounds in the six hours he was under hypnosis, much of it moisture, and the tubes into his arms fed nutrients into his system to replace it.

Three days, while they sewed thirty-two stitches into his arm and leg and tried to avoid the terrifying question of how he got the wounds. Sometimes, he awoke to see a blurred image of Emily sitting by him. She didn't always see him open his eyes because she was reading, or writing, or watching the small colour television in the corner. She was there, and that was enough to quieten the panic in him.

On the fourth day, Dan opened his eyes to see Paul, watching him with intensity. Dan felt reasonably human, though still weak. He could wriggle his fingers without the cramps he vaguely remembered from earlier awakenings.

"Food," he said, forcing the word out against the reluctance of his throat.

Harrington's lips twitched. "I wish all my patients were so succinct," he said with a gentle smile, standing and moving to the bell by the side of the bed. A moment later, a young woman in nurse's clothing appeared, looked at Dan, nodded at Paul and went out again.

"They'll be bringing something in a few minutes," he said, taking the chair from the opposite wall and sitting by the side of the bed. "The IVs were removed this morning, and you're ready for some proper calories."

"About bloody time." The words were a struggle for Dan to get out.

"Can you remember the hallucination?" Paul was clearly bubbling over with eagerness to find out what Dan had undergone while under hypnosis. Dan thought about it, and images began to crawl back into his numbed, slept-out mind.

"Food first," he mumbled, and Paul nodded, recognizing the need in Dan for some strength.

"Yes, I imagine you need it. It will be a high protein diet for a few days. Steaks, vegetables, liver, and all that sort of stuff. It'll shove up your cholesterol level a few points, but you're young enough to handle that. You should be fine."

Dan smiled weakly, and even that effort drained him a little. Paul touched his shoulder.

The nurse returned with a tray. This time, Dan could see the military ribbons above her coat pocket, and the bars on her shoulders. She was army. She was also as gentle as any nurse could be in the way she fed him the undistinguished mush on the tray. Paul watched the proceedings without a word. When she packed up and left, Dan was already feeling considerably more alive.

"So tell me what happened?" he said, feeling stronger by the second. "Did you film the proceedings again?"

Paul's face went quiet, and the expression of sadness appeared again. "Of course we did," he replied. "And while it was certainly quieter than your last little foray, it was perhaps more frightening."

"Why so?" His expression worried Dan.

"Misha, we're getting into some pretty esoteric grounds here," said Paul, shifting in his chair. "It's a conventional wisdom that the power of the human mind is greater than anyone has ever imagined, but we saw some things with you that I've only read about, and then with considerable cynicism."

His sombre face was not the friendly bear Dan had known the last few days.

"Remember how I said that when you faced a real fight," continued Paul, "it would take more out of you than the Spitfire battle?"

Dan nodded, weakly. "You were dead right!" he croaked.

"More than I realized," Paul said softly.

"How so?"

"Ever heard of stigmata?" he asked.

The change of direction confused Dan, but in his exhausted state, he wasn't able to ponder too deeply about what was going on.

"Supposedly signs of crucifixion that some people claim to get on their hands and feet?" he said, feeling his throat tightening in unexplained anxiety. "Never believed it myself."

Paul nodded. "Nor had I until four days ago," he said with a tiny smile.

"These wounds on my arms and legs?"

He nodded again. "They just appeared while you were sitting there. You'll see the video later today. Blood suddenly began pouring all over your left arm, and then your leg a little later on."

"You think I forced those wounds to support my hallucination?" Dan was having trouble believing that idea, but no other solution had offered itself to him.

"I did some reading up in the library in the last couple of days," said Paul, ignoring the question. "There are some weird examples of this in the past."

"Tell me."

"Generally, these things have been reported in a religious context," Paul said. "Because that has always been the main field in which belief can exert such power over human minds, however irrational the belief might be."

Despite Dan's emotional upheaval and distress, he smiled. "Your agnosticism is showing, Professor Harrington!"

"Not at all," replied Paul, shaking his head to hide the smile. "There are lots of recorded example of spontaneous wounds suddenly erupting on the bodies of the true believers in history," he continued. "Usually, the wounds correspond, as you said, to the wounds that Christ is reported to have suffered on the cross. Holes in the hands and feet, cuts on the side."

"But not always?"

"Not always," he agreed. "Some more modern texts correspond in some ways to your experience. In particular, a couple of cases came up. One was in a French mental hospital in Rouen in the thirties. An inmate of some years had constant delusions of being attacked by a monster. Usually, he responded well to sedatives, but one night, the doctors were called in when he awoke in an almighty screaming fit. The reports said that cuts corresponding to tooth marks appeared on his arms and legs, and one at his throat. In fact, he died later the next day, from shock."

"Good God! Wasn't it publicized?"

Paul shook his head. "No way! The hospital covered up the details, officially stating that the patient's wounds came from an attack by other inmates."

"So how did you get the story?"

"Remember young Misha, what an elder statesman of medicine I am!" he said with a modest smirk. "I used a computer terminal here to access the files at Johns Hopkins. The full history is held on our computer there."

"What an extraordinary story!" said Dan. "Are there any others?"

"There's one in a religious context," Paul nodded. "A young English priest in a missionary in Ghana. He was conducting a mass in Takoradi, and suddenly fell to the ground, with blood erupting all over his gown. The congregation took it as a heavy sign from God and went into a religious frenzy, rather than getting medical help. The autopsy showed deep wounds in the man's side, remarkably like the stab wounds of a spear."

"And no doubt, the whole thing was covered up again?"

"Of course," agreed Paul. "None of the churches likes to have unexplained phenomena occurring, unless they're in the Bible. It got written up as an attack on the priest by marauding tribesmen."

"So you think that beliefs can be so great that the mind will actually cause the body to sustain damage?"

"I certainly think you believed so firmly in the battle you were fighting that your body just had to back up the belief."

"Will the medical profession believe all this?"

Paul shrugged. "A lot of them will deny it, of course. But my thinking is that if the body can cause damage to support beliefs, can the opposite occur, and the body heal itself in the same belief structure?"

Dan stirred, the bandages on his arms and legs feeling scratchy, unable to get a comfortable position after these days in bed. "That's almost unbelievable!" he said.

Paul shrugged, stood up and poured a drink of orange juice for Dan. Dan smiled with appreciation and took a sip.

"It's totally unbelievable!" said Paul, shaking his head. "Or was, until I saw what happened to you. I got the idea you were fighting something or somebody, and you had let out a couple of loud yells that gave some indication of the story. Did you read Norse mythology as a kid?"

"I read everything," said Dan with a small smile. "Not much else to do for a large part of the time in Murmansk, especially in winter. And I'll give them credit, they had a hell of a good library in the compound." The relatively lengthy speech had dried his mouth again and he took another deep gulp from the glass of orange juice.

"That explains Stengwulf," nodded Paul, speaking more to himself than to Dan.

"Huh?" Dan stopped drinking and looked up at him.

"As I said," Paul repeated. "You talked a bit while the hallucinations went on, not always clearly."

"I'd better see the tape." Dan felt considerable urgency to see what had actually taken place.

"You will." Paul looked serious. He paused for a long few seconds, then moved his chair nearer to the bedside and sat down.

"Misha, we've got a problem." His clear eyes looked straight at Dan who felt a small spasm of fear. "The programming is planted incredibly deep," continued Paul. "I've found exactly where it is, and how to get to it, but what I didn't expect to find was the power of the defences they put in place. There's a whole goddamned army in there!"

His face was a mixture of uncertainty and excitement. The academic had found a new area of a problem and was intrigued, despite the problems it was causing.

"Just what is it that you do, when you've located the program?" asked Dan.

"It's relatively simple," replied Paul. "Having got you under, I start trying to counter the belief system they programmed into you. I start with simple statements such as 'You are free to do anything you want', a few specific ones like 'No words or phrases can cause you to be controlled by any person' and so on. Then I get really focused and I try the trigger words followed by denials of their power."

"And what happens?" asked Dan, remembering faint visions of voices coming at him out of the air during the fight against the trolls.

Paul grinned. "You go crazy!" he said.

Dan laughed weakly through the constriction in his throat. "That seems a properly technically-worded statement!"

Paul smiled, seemingly relieved at the calm way Dan seemed to be taking it. But Dan wasn't anywhere nearly as calm as Paul might have thought. Inside, slow despair was crawling through him.

"So what do we do?" Dan hung on the reply.

"It's really up to you," said Harrington. The sadness was returning to his eyes. "I found one weakness in the defences, and I think that when I tried it, you suffered the wounds, but it showed one thing."

"Which is...?"

"Whoever programmed you did an amazing job," said Paul with unwilling admiration. "He seemed to cover all the bases and programmed a response to almost everything I could do. Any time I said something that directly contradicted your programming, you reacted with astonishing hostility. Of course, he would never have realized that everything he did was being passed through to us by our own agents. So I think he missed something."

Dan sensed the excitement, and reacted with a surge of hope for his survival. "What did he miss, Paul?"

"I think he failed to anticipate that somebody might get far enough into the program location to give you additional instructions, rather than try and change existing ones."

"Is that what you did?" The idea made sense to Dan. The logic was similar to the logic behind computer security systems.

"Yes, it is," nodded Paul, looking thoughtful, as if still working at the problem. "What I did while you were fighting the last one, was tell you that you will get hurt. And you did."

"Yes!" croaked Dan. "I remember that! I heard this whispering in my ear, I thought it was witchcraft! Then the troll bit me!"

Paul looked interested. "Trolls, eh? You can remember the details of the battle?"

Dan looked inward and tested his memories. "You haven't had to hypnotize me this time, but I can still recall the hallucination," he said.

Paul looked smug. "The barriers are definitely breaking down," he said. "You think you have all the details in your mind?"

"Too bloody right!" said Dan, shivering with the ugly memory. "Paul, it was so vivid! I was really there, really living it!"

"That shows the depth of the conditioning," Harrington agreed. "What seems logical to me is that I can actually order you to let yourself be hurt rather than simply to lose the fight. I can also tell you that you want to break free. You may keep struggling for a time, but the order will probably sink through because there's no specific instruction to prevent it. But ultimately, the one thing they forgot to consider was that you yourself would want to break free. Whatever I do, it will only work if you deprogram yourself."

"Let's do it! Let's get started!"

"It's not that simple, Misha," he said, waving his hands at Dan as if to stop him from getting up from the bed. "Firstly, you can see what the fights are taking out of you.

The conflicts inside your head are so massive that the breakdown you're facing is far and away greater than any mind should be able to take. Quite honestly, it may kill you if it goes on much longer. Second, I just don't know what it will do to your mind if you lose. We've discussed this before, and I've told you the risks."

There was no debate needed. "Paul, it's a no-brainer. I won't live under the constant fear that somebody will one day use those triggers on me again. Maybe Carson's not the only one who knows them, maybe there's a file somewhere in KGB headquarters in Djerzinski Square. Maybe some other power-hungry lunatic will read it. Not on your bloody life, Paul! It's a simple decision, kill me or cure me."

Harrington stood up with a decisive nod and pressed the bell again. "I'll head to the meeting room and set things up to show you the tape," he said, moving to the door. "Somebody will come and wheel you down there."

He left with a friendly smile and Dan had only a few seconds before a muscular orderly appeared with a wheel chair.

* * *

For all the lack of violent action, the second tape was no less frightening and awe-inspiring than the first. Dan sat with Emily on the settee, hands clasped together while Paul took an armchair and leaned back, almost stretched out, and mused on what they were seeing, or gave specific commentary as it applied. His long legs crossed, his feet occasionally waggled to add emphasis to a point, and his arms waved violently.

"Here's where you went under again," he muttered, more to himself, as his screen image touched the face of the man strapped to the Hepplewhite chair. Dan watched the images as the head of the man in the chair drooped, then straightened again as Paul began the dangerous trip to the centre of Dan's mind. Dan couldn't understand the whole of what Paul was doing, much of it seemed to be disconnected orders and questions to him.

"Misha, move your right foot..."

"Misha, tell me about your mother's apartment in Kharbarovsk..."

"Misha, did you have a pet when you were a child?..."

"Misha, multiply ten by twelve and add sixteen..."

Sometimes the bound man in the chair answered, sometimes he did not. Sometimes the answers were given in a simple straight-forward manner, sometimes they were rambling, disconnected Russian sentences which Dan had trouble following. But each response gave Paul some information, because he ticked off notes on a pad. At one point, the screen image of Dan gave out a long, howling call of such misery, it brought tears to Dan's eyes. It sounded more like a lost puppy than a human being. Paul was apparently satisfied however, because he wrote several lines of notes as if he had discovered something new.

Things changed. Answers and reactions became increasingly agitated, and the bound Misha began to fight the straps. Both the screen images and the living counterparts in the room sat forward with heightened interest.

"Paydirt," said Paul. "Watch this!"

On screen, Paul spoke in excellent Russian to the man in front of him. "Now Misha, you are four years old."

With utter astonishment and delight, Dan watched his face lose the sharp lines of adulthood and fall into the soft curves and unformed features of a child. The eyes seemed bigger, clearer, the skin was suddenly smooth, pink and lovely. A soft exclamation of pleasure fell from Emily and she clutched his hand hard.

"I want one just like him!"

"Wait till later and we'll work on it," he whispered, too fascinated to look away from the screen and the sight of himself at the age of four.

"Hello, little boy. What's your name?" asked Paul gently. The child in the adult body, incongruously bound by leather straps to a heavy chair responded in a clear, high voice, also speaking Russian.

"My name is Misha Vorosov. What's yours?" The child cocked his head to one side and studied Paul in the intent way that children have.

"I am Paul Harrington," answered Paul, speaking softly. "Do you live near here, Misha?"

The child nodded enthusiastically. "My momma and poppa live over there," he said, nodding his head to his left. "In that building with the green roof and the tree in front of it."

Paul looked where the bound man was nodding, but there was only a wall. Dan sat rigid with fascination. He had no recollection of this discussion while he was under Paul's hypnosis.

"It looks like a nice house," said Paul in a confiding way. "Shall I tell you a secret?"

The little boy bit his lip and nodded, eyes glowing with sudden excitement.

"One day, Misha, when you're a really big boy, when you're a grown up, some nasty men will try and tell you some terrible things. One of those things will be that if you ever hear the words 'We are your overseers, we are your legs, oh throne', you will have to do everything that man says. You mustn't believe him, Misha, he'll be lying...."

The change was horrible. The lovely child vanished, and the features changed before the eyes of the watchers like a horror movie showing the metamorphosis of man to wolf. The face grew coarse, the eyes narrowed, the whole body seemed to twist, and became almost a cartoon character of a Sunday morning television hero in a comic strip. The head rose and the face turned up, staring into some distant scene. Then the bound man let out a harsh, powerful yell of intense ferocity that rattled the crockery in the tray.

"I am Stengwulf, Killer of Trolls!"

All of them, the images on the screen and the flesh and blood watchers in the room fell backwards against their seats, blown by the force of that primeval yell. The power was so great that the sound distorted the loudspeakers, which rattled and squawked.

"Dear God in heaven!" whispered Emily. "It's just as bad the second time, even on screen. Imagine what you sounded like at close quarters, sitting in that chair!"

"Impossible," muttered Dan. "I don't believe it now, I sure as hell wouldn't have believed it then!"

The man in the chair was rocking back and forth, muttering. Dan tried to recall what he went through in the hallucinated battle with the trolls, and remembered enough to shiver a little with memories of fear. Images of black blood all over his arms mixing with his own, evil, tiny heads staring at him in hatred as they died, cut from the misshapen bodies by his sweeping blade.

While the man in the chair wrestled with the invisible trolls that attacked him, Paul sat before him and occasionally said something. At one stage, the "now" Paul turned up the volume and the screen image said "Misha, you can be hurt, you can be wounded."

Within a second or two of those words, blood appeared on the sleeve of Dan's image on the screen. It was a massive explosion of crimson that flooded all over the upper half of the arm, then drained down over the elbow and onto the wrists. Seated next to Dan, watching the events play themselves out on the screen, Emily jerked with the shock and moaned slightly, even though she had been expecting it. Dan did the same. It was irrational, horrible, impossible. Paul was muttering to himself and writing rapid notes on his pad.

Another patch of blood appeared on the right trouser leg of the man on the screen, less sudden this time as the cloth was thicker, but it spread rapidly over his knee and down to the ankle. Dan's image continued rocking back and forth in his leather bonds.

"This went on for another half hour," said Paul. "We didn't dare do anything until you opened your eyes and looked at me."

All three of them sat and stared in silence. Paul began talking quietly, Dan was not sure whether to himself or to all of them.

"This is why I got into this business," Paul said quietly, still staring at the screen. "Who ever had any idea of the real power of the human mind? I hated what the project wanted me to do, but I could see the possibilities for curing trauma with the techniques we learned. But we never thought, never had the faintest idea of what we were playing with."

He swung his eyes away from the screen and turned to Emily and Dan where they sat behind him. "Look at that, tell a man he's four years old, and he *is!"* he said urgently, waving his right arm at the screen. "Tell him to defend himself, and it takes eleven trained marines to subdue him. It's just not possible that he has that power in his body, but he finds it. Where does it come from? What haven't we even begun to see in the mind?"

Silence fell for several minutes. Paul subsided back into his seat and looked miles into the distance. Dan continued to hold Emily's hand and thought about the sight of himself with a four-year-old face. On the screen, the man in the chair continued to rock back and forth and mumble. At one point, Dan heard him say more clearly *"die.. die.. die.. die.."* in a low growl and he kept it up for over a minute before falling into restless silence.

Paul switched the tape off and began rewinding it. He stood up and stretched, looking as weary as Dan felt. "Misha, there are some goddamned strange things that happen," he said, walking to the coffee table and pouring himself a glass of orange juice. He took a deep gulp and refilled the glass. "A small woman sees her child trapped under a car and lifts the whole damned car to get him out. Men walk for miles with bullets in their bodies, carrying a buddy out of the battle, and die when they get to help. People find strength that simply cannot be in their bodies, but they find it anyway."

He drank more juice, put the glass back on the table, then walked towards Emily and Dan. "And you are taught to kill and forget," he said, looking down on them, "when the real Mikhail Vorosov is a gentle, kind person who just couldn't do it."

He rubbed his eyes, leaned over and placed his hand on Dan's shoulder, almost as if he was about to put him under hypnosis. "Misha, the strength has to come from somewhere!" he said, looking hard at Dan. Dan could see the worry in his face, and Emily squeezed his hand tighter. "Wherever that is," continued Paul, "you sure as hell pay for it. Look at you! A couple of hours in that chair and a starved kitten could beat the crap out of you. You need two weeks of rest and recovery before we can try again, and God knows what will happen next time. We saw the signs there that it can be beaten. Can you try it again?"

Both of them were looking at Dan. He gazed into Emily's eyes for a few seconds then looked up at Paul. "I said it before, Paul. Kill or cure. There's no middle ground."

Paul stood upright. "Okay, son. So be it," he said, fatigue in his voice. "Two weeks for recuperation, minimum, and I'll be supervising your diet, and we'll be boosting your system with a few additives. Plus exercise, training, a lot of preparation. I have to admit, I totally underestimated your man in Murmansk. I wish I knew who he was."

So do I, thought Dan in a surge of rage. *Then I could kill him. But I might settle for Vincent Carson, whatever I promised Emily. Forgive me, Galina Sergeyvna Moroyeva, but it might be the only way I can find peace.*

* * *

The two weeks became four weeks and they were no vacation. Dan found that even allowing for the after-effects of his battle with the hallucinatory trolls, he was in pretty poor physical condition for a man of thirty-five. Although the stitches healed rapidly, nothing else was impressive about his health.

So a pair of marines took over Dan's life. Corporal James T. Halloran was a beanpole of a man who could bench press over four hundred pounds and had all the warmth and sympathy for Dan that an Egyptian overseer had for the Hebrew slaves making bricks. To Dan's pleasure, he recognised the second as the tall redhead who had met them in the Colonel's office that day in Chicago. Sergeant Alana Denton was a triathlete, and it showed in her fearsome energy and stamina. Each morning, the two led Dan on a run through the woods, and vanished almost immediately. At intervals, they waited for him, breathing easily while Dan staggered up to them, more concerned about a heart attack than anything else, and the marines would flitter off again, hardly leaving any track of their passing.

He ran, swam, did sit-ups, knee bends and generally worked up a foaming lather every day, plus a fuming hatred for his tormentors. They grinned at him, taunted him with calls of "Civilian!" and were far less civil than

Corporal Kutchinski in Murmansk. The two of them were magnificent, and Dan's hatred faded as his breathing recovered and his strength grew.

Meal times were regulated. Dan didn't get the choices that the others got. Rather, he received a special plate with marginally good food and always a glass of peculiarly coloured mush that Paul insisted he swallow. Sympathetic looks from Emily were no compensation.

He also spent two hours a day under deep hypnosis. Just as at Murmansk, the routine developed. Paul sat in front of him, simply touched his forehead, and off he went in his mind down the moving stairway of O'Hare Field until everything went quiet around him. Paul told him he was planting some deep suggestions in Dan's mind that he could be hurt in battle and that he truly wanted to break free. He said the ideas would gradually sink into the program storage area and gently loosen the ferociously powerful grip on Dan's defences that had been planted there so many years ago. Rather like spraying rust-removing mixture into an ancient, seized-up bolt, he said. They both knew that the result could be a complete fracture of the bolt, total breakdown, not an undoing of the grip.

On one occasion, Paul worked on the commitment to the KGB that had been implanted in Dan. Dan had slipped under quickly, the process of imagining the descent down the escalator to the flashing lights of the tunnel at O'Hare Field having become routine. The lights were replaced by a deep, calming blackness, like waking in the middle of the night in the familiarity of one's own bedroom. Paul's voice came from all around, impossible to detect as a single point.

"Who are you, Misha?" he asked.

"I am Mikhail Vorosov," replied Dan. "I am a Russian." He spoke softly, almost as if to himself.

"Yes, you are a Russian," agreed Paul. "But are you also a member of the Committee for State Security?"

"No," said Dan. He was firm about that.

"But you are here to serve your commander, Major General Morayev, are you not?"

Dan felt muscles tense up inside. "That was not my choice," he said. "They took me away from my mother when I was eight. I didn't want to go."

"And how do you feel about it now, Misha?" Paul's voice was gentle.

"Angry. I don't want to do what Carson tells me."

"So why do you, Misha?"

"Things inside my head make me do them. I don't want to."

"So you do not serve the KGB?"

"No, I don't want to."

"Remember this, Misha." The voice was all around him, swirling in the darkness like mist in the breeze. "You were taken away from your mother when you were a child. You had no wish to go and you didn't want to become what they made you. So you have no obligation to do anything Carson tells you."

"Good." Dan's voice sounded to him like a child's. *I trust Paul so much,* he thought. *He will protect me.*

"When you next have to fight somebody, Misha, remember that the fight is for you. You don't have to fight back, because that is only the order of the KGB. Let me come and rescue you, Misha, and everything will be made good."

"I'll try." Even in the friendly dark, Dan began to feel sick.

"Good," said the invisible voice. "When you are free, you can come back to your lovely apartment with Emily and be happy."

"I want to," said Dan. How badly he wanted that.

"Yes, I know. Don't fight back, Misha."

"I'll try," said Dan, then woke up as he vomited all over the carpet and his knees.

"SHIT!" he said.

"Not at all," said Paul. "Merely the on-going struggle. Let's get you cleaned up and give the janitors the unpleasant task of tackling this room again."

"Are we getting anywhere?" asked Dan, standing up on trembling legs.

"We'll see when we have our next deprogramming session," said Harrington with a small smile. "But I think so."

Some of the time, Paul and Dan talked about the life in Murmansk. About the training room with Gemorov; about the language training with Georgii Vilnikov; about the British village with its pub, corner shop and British cars; and about the books Dan had read in his twelve years there. From these, they worked out some possibilities for the next battle scenario.

"I know that you enjoyed the air battle," said Paul. "But that was the result of the powerful defensive capabilities you were given. It was too easy for you."

They were sitting in the music library listening to the St. Matthew Passion. It was a Sunday, so the music was appropriate.

"I truly did," Dan admitted. "I had the feeling of invulnerability, and I'd always had a fascination with the air war of that era."

"The danger might be that you'll try and relive that one," mused Paul. "That sense of invulnerability was certainly implanted in you, and you'd read a great deal about the subject, too."

"It wasn't the same when I fought the trolls," said Dan. "I certainly didn't feel invulnerable, and I got hurt."

"And it has to get a lot worse than that," said Paul. "If I break down the defences, you'll experience it as a loss in a battle. So far, you've fought very physical battles. Assuming that keeps up, losing one means severe physical damage within the hallucination, maybe even subjective death."

"But that's exactly what we have to achieve, isn't it?"

Paul nodded, and his face twisted in anxiety. "It is, Dan, and we don't want to lose you. The trouble is, with the extent of your reading at the camp and since you left, I can't predict what sort of battle you'll fight next time. So we can't prepare anything too specific."

"Anyone's guess, then?"

"As you say, anyone's guess. But we'll get there."

"We have to," said Dan. "I'm not letting those bastards get away with it."

* * *

The mansion house was beautiful, and the ground spacious, but Dan soon found he was as much in a prison as he had been in Murmansk. Guards walked the grounds, dressed in combat greens, all with side arms. As soon as Dan walked outside the house, one marine always attached himself to Dan, leaving a discrete distance between them, but still following wherever Dan went. Only once did Dan walk down to the main gate. There were three men at that point, and they were clearly prepared for Dan's arrival. Dan assumed that the trailing guard behind him had alerted them by radio.

Dan got within ten feet of the gate, but by then, the three marines were lined up, facing him. Their faces were cold and hostile.

"That's as far as you go, Mister Bailey," said one of them. He wore sergeant's stripes. Dan turned and looked at the soldier who had been following him. He was talking into a radio. The message was quite plain. Dan was here as long as Colonel Markbrite cared to keep him. Almost like Murmansk, though this time, Dan had two friends instead of just Georgii Vilnikov. He knew he could never go through with this without Emily. And Paul Harrington was his one chance of returning to a normal life.

He walked back into the house.

Within the house, however, Dan was left alone when not undergoing training or when under Paul's hypnosis. He had days to himself, because Emily was paying her portion of the deal, and being interrogated by CIA agents on her life as a Soviet operative.

On one day, Dan was simply walking around the mansion house, exploring the building while Emily was in one of her own sessions with Markbrite's people. He checked out the music room and the library, played some solo games on the pool table, and found out that several personal computers were installed in one study. But when he tried to access the Internet, he found it blocked. No emails, in or out, it appeared.

By this stage, nobody bothered to accompany him within the building as a guide. He walked along a lengthy corridor, admiring the collection of modern art on the walls, when he heard Paul's voice coming from a partially open door. He stopped to listen.

"There is no doubt that the Gemorov team in Murmansk achieved more in this field than we did here," Paul was saying. "However, nobody could claim that theirs was an unqualified success, either. In fact, only one subject, Misha Vorosov was brought to the point of operational effectiveness, and as we now know, that effectiveness was not total."

I'll say, Dan smiled to himself, sidling a little closer to the open door. The room was slightly larger than the room used for the deprogramming sessions, and was filled with the military personnel Dan had already seen at the first breakfast, plus a few new faces. Paul Harrington was standing at a podium and had a lap top and projector ready for use with a screen behind him.

"We learned that only four moles were sent over here as legends to work for the KGB operative based in Chicago," he continued. "We have the identity of that man, and he is under close surveillance, but for specific reasons, his arrest is to be delayed for a while."

Because I want the bastard! said Dan to himself, feeling a flush of rage pass through his body. *How I look forward to the moment when I can face Carson without the fear of what his words can do to me!* For a second or two, he thought about the idea. It seemed a great way to end the business, he thought, having a final confrontation with Carson when the triggers had been made harmless. He resolved to ask Colonel Markbrite if that could be arranged. He turned back to Paul.

"... under the name of Virginia Page was sent to South Carolina. She had been in training in the Gemorov team for five years, and she was sixteen when she was brought into the USA. The original Virginia Page of Dallas had died of leukaemia when she was five, and the KGB was highly skilled in obtaining genuine papers for their legends in such cases. She was, apparently, born Tamara Makashkova in Minsk."

Tamara! gasped Dan inside himself. *My God, I remember Tamara!* He got a memory of a slender girl two years older than he was, with a strong, face, not pretty, but personable, a ready humor and sense of fun. She sat next to him on some of those dreadful days when Gemorov sat the children in his torture chambers. The sound of her weeping from the pain of the earphones and Gemorov's cane made little Misha rage with helpless fury at what was being done to them. Tamara was being taught to be an American from Dallas, and she was forced to watch endless pictures of that city, its parks and streets until she was as familiar with them as Misha was with pictures of Manchester. She vanished when Misha was fourteen.

"... was given her first assignment five years ago, after living in the USA for over twelve years. Apparently she had not suffered quite as badly as Misha did when first exposed to the trigger phrase...."

I'm glad about that, Tamara, thought Dan. *I would not want anyone to go through that. Except Carson.*

"This operative believed that she would perform as required," Paul was saying to his attentive audience. "However, she did not station herself in Washington to assassinate the French President as instructed, but retreated to an office building in Houston and fired on several civilians two days before the president arrived, and she was killed by the local police. We shall never know if she simply went out of control, or decided to commit suicide in a particularly awful manner, or a combination of the two. Note that Misha also tried to kill himself, but in a more private manner."

Oh poor Tamara! thought Dan. *What ghastly things they did to us!* He swallowed a sour taste of bile as he remembered the dark, intense eyes of the girl she had been at thirteen and fourteen. She never spoke of her family, but she cared for little Misha when sometimes he broke down and wept for his mother before he had learned not to. *Damn you, Carson!* said Dan to himself. *You'll pay for all of us.*

"... named George Richmond, originally Peotr Zamorov, was conditioned to believe he was from Baton Rouge, and arrived in the USA twenty years ago." Paul consulted notes on his podium, turned a page and continued. "He was activated by the KGB five years later, soon after the Virginia Page episode."

Peotr Zamorov? That name meant nothing to Dan. He decided to listen to all of this, and slid in through the door. He walked softly to the rear of the line of chairs and sat down. In the lights from the podium, Paul did not appear to see him.

"... but was even less successful. It seems he responded badly to the first exposure to the trigger phrase but was still assigned his first task. We have no idea what that task was, because he broke apart completely before fulfilling it. The medical records show that George simply collapsed in a supermarket in Baton Rouge and died a year later without regaining consciousness."

"Did his insurance records lead anywhere?" The question came from an air force officer just two rows in front of Dan. Paul shaded his eyes to look at the man, and in doing so, saw Dan sitting there. For a second or two, he seemed to pause and consider, then answered the question.

"Nowhere," he said. "George had been working as an engineer with a small firm, and had been covered in the normal way."

The officer leaned back and folded his arms.

"The last died a few years ago," continued Paul. "Viktor Gruzhba came over here eighteen years ago as Terry Watson and was activated successfully eight years later. He was responsible for the killing of Colonel Simon Carstairs, USAF..."

He was interrupted by a loud "Oh Jesus!" from one of the pilots. Paul looked at him over the lights.

"You knew Colonel Carstairs, Captain?"

"He was my uncle, sir."

A shocked murmur ran round the room.

"I am most terribly sorry, Captain. I had no idea."

The silence was intense for a few moments.

"Viktor Gruzhba was in a persistent vegetative state in a hospital in Bowling Green, Kentucky," continued Paul into the emptiness. "It happened without warning a week after the assassination, and he never recovered consciousness. With the knowledge we now have, we have traced the payments made on behalf of his so-called family for legal efforts to have him removed from life support. They lead back to the KGB operative whose identity we already know."

Paul stood upright from the leaning stance he had taken against the podium.

"As you know from your own experiences, being ordered to commit an act that you would personally find reprehensible sets up conflict within the mind. The conflict depends upon the degree of conditioning given the subject. If the subject can be made to forget the act, the conflict is deeply suppressed, but not entirely so. It seems that the human mind forgets nothing at all, and however deeply the memory is pushed down, it is still present." He walked away from the podium, put his hands in his pockets, and continued.

"In the case of Misha Vorosov, the conditioning was by far the deepest. Gemorov had him for over twelve years from the age of eight, and subjected him to three years of long sessions in the sensory deprivation tank, more than any other of his subjects. There is no doubt that Misha has committed at least two killings on the orders of his operative. For a lengthy period of time, he appeared to have truly forgotten the fact of those killings. But, despite all the heavy conditioning, the memories somehow floated back from the subconscious level to the conscious. He is fighting the demons in his mind now, and I assure you, his personal hell is greater than I can tell you."

He hunched his shoulders and moved around the floor. Dan began to feel his throat tighten up with tension, mixed with some self pity. *Don't start crying, Vorosov,* he said to himself, and concentrated hard on what Paul was saying.

"It is equally obvious to me as I work on his deconditioning, that he desperately wishes to break free. His hatred of what was done to him and the philosophies behind those acts is intense and genuine. Shortly, I will begin to tell you about how we are conducting the deconditioning, and what we are learning from it. Meanwhile..." he said, stopping and turning to the front of the room, "Misha, will you stand up, please?"

Damn you Paul, said Dan to himself, but stood up anyway. Paul turned up the lights from his podium, and ten or eleven faces rotated to stare at him. Expressions were mixed, ranging from deep interest to strong hostility. *I should have expected the latter,* he told himself, trying to stay calm. Most of the people here were military personnel, trained to consider the one-time Soviet Union as the most likely potential enemy. Dan was certainly, by any measure, a Soviet agent in their midst, regardless of what he wanted for himself or how he thought of himself. He tried to look back calmly.

"Does anyone have any questions for Misha?" Paul asked.

What are you trying to do to me, Paul? Dan raged inside. But as he thought about it, Paul's action was logical. If Dan appeared to these people as a human being with serious problems to overcome, they would be less inclined to think of him as the enemy.

"Yes, I do!"

It was the air force captain whose uncle had been killed by one of Misha's classmates from Murmansk.

Oh hell, thought Dan. *This could be rough.* "Yes, sir?" he said. The officer was younger than Dan by about five years, but some humbleness was appropriate just now.

"Do you think of yourself as Misha Vorosov, or Dan Bailey?" asked the captain.

"Yes!" Dan replied, straight-faced. A murmur of amusement ran around the room. Paul was watching him carefully. Others in the room were watching without obvious expression.

"That answer is actually quite genuine," Dan continued. "The two persona seem to co-exist quite successfully in my mind, and I can think of myself as one, just as easily as the other. While I can accept that many of my memories as a child are the result of the conditioning, especially those of my English parents, I still have genuinely loving memories of them. And yet I remember my Russian mother, and feel sad about her..."

He stopped, tears were threatening his composure, though for which parental memory he could not tell. His answer had been true. The nearer listeners saw what was happening to him, and he could see some of the hostility fade.

"And how do you feel about the killings, now?" One of the woman naval officers had risen to her feet and faced him directly. She was a tall, slender woman with a thin, intelligent face. There was no warmth in her expression.

"Let me ask you this," said Dan, after reflecting for a second or two. "Supposing you were driving home, taking every care you could, with a passenger in the seat next to you. The passenger is a man, much bigger and stronger than you." Dan looked around the room. They were all watching him intently. "As you approach a pedestrian crossing, the passenger goes berserk, stamps on your right foot and accelerates the car, grabs the steering wheel and takes you into a crowd of people waiting to cross. You kill three of them. It's not your fault, you had absolutely no control at all. How do you feel?"

The young woman stared at Dan for a moment then nodded. "I see," she murmured. "I'd feel terribly helpless but still guilty."

"That's a fraction of how I feel. I've been getting memories of the killings only many days, even weeks after committing them, and the memories vary in vividness. But I know that I have killed two men. I may discover one day that I have killed more than those two, and I'm terrified of that possibility."

Dan paused again for another survey of the room. Complete silence ruled, and some of the faces that had been hostile were now looking more interested.

"Remember that I tried to kill myself, once I had realized that Car..." Dan stopped short. "That my operative had plans for me to kill somebody else. I would have succeeded if Emily had not returned to the apartment, and it was a close call, even then. Please believe me, it's no joy to have these memories, and one day, I may recruit Doctor Harrington to try and do something about them."

The silence continued around the room, but was broken by another of the pilots, a major, looking in his late thirties. He stood up and turned to Dan, his expression still harsh.

"Do you consider yourself a Russian now?" he asked.

"I refer you to the earlier question of my identity," Dan replied. "I know that I am a Russian by birth. But at the same time, I have no difficulty thinking of myself as an Englishman, which I was for many years."

"So is your loyalty to the communists or to us?" the major snapped.

"I understand the basis of your question," said Dan, feeling nervous at the officer's hostility and trying to placate it. "But Russian did not equal communist during the days of the Soviet Union," he continued. "I feel I am a Russian, just as the many Russian immigrants to the USA feel that they are Russians. But that does not mean that they were ever communists, in fact, quite the reverse. I detest everything that was done in the name of communism, especially to me. The presence here of Emily and me surely shows that we opposed the regime that once ran the Soviet Union."

The major sat down again, but Dan could not see if the answer had satisfied him or not. He was beginning to feel shaky inside, whether from the weakness of the deconditioning battles, or his emotions, he could not tell, but Paul saw it.

"Ladies and gentlemen, that's enough of the questions. Let's take a short break, and then we'll get onto the actual techniques being used to break Misha out of the trap."

Dan walked out of the room before anyone could ask him any more questions.

One evening, Dan sat in Paul's room and shared a bottle of heavy, rich burgundy wine.

"What are all these other people doing here?" he asked. "It's obviously something to do with me, judging by their presence at your lecture the other day, but what?"

"Partially, Misha, partially," Paul answered, sipping carefully at the red wine. "The older woman is Doctor Hilary Connors, she was my partner for much of the recent project work. She's here to monitor our attempts to deprogram you. She's also talking to Emily about her KGB experiences."

"And all those military types? What's their function?"

"Ongoing work. One of the key tasks of Project Parthenon was to put blocks into the minds of pilots or other military personnel so they could not be successfully interrogated if captured by the enemy."

"Did they have a choice in the matter?" Dan felt hostility rise in him at the idea that Paul had been doing what the old man in Murmansk had done.

"Yes, they did," Paul replied, noticing Dan's reaction. "The guys were all volunteer subjects last year. They had all been given a small assignment of different types then we tried putting some memory blanks into them to make them forget what they'd done. They're back here for testing to see if they can remember the assignments, but we're keeping them informed on your deprogramming as well."

"How's it going?" Dan was fascinated and appalled at the same time. Paul held his right hand palm down and rocked it gently side to side.

"It varies," he said. "Some of the guys are completely blank on their memories of the assignments, one or two have the overlaid memories we tried to implant over the top of the assignments. Two of them are getting back their memories of the time and events."

"Have you got anything out of our exercises to improve the techniques?" Dan's distress was still high, and he felt a small tremble of anger.

"God, yes!" Paul said, and refilled his glass. The sound of the wine pouring from the bottle was a pleasant distraction for Dan. "Even though we knew what the guy in Murmansk had been doing, we couldn't be certain of all the details. I'm getting a lot of good stuff out of this."

"All to be used to screw up peoples' minds?"

Paul looked sad.

"I'd hoped you thought better of me, Misha," he said. "Yes, I'll use this to improve the insulation we can put into the heads of people on dangerous missions. That can actually help to save their lives too, remember, though I doubt we'll run any missions in Russia again. Or anywhere else for that matter. But I'm also going to develop some therapies for mental illness."

"How?" Dan was still feeling hostile and suspicious, though he recognized his own lack of objectivity.

"Well, think of this, for example," said Paul. "Suppose I get a woman patient with serious problems resulting from, say, a childhood of being battered and abused by her parents, maybe raped by her father. If I can isolate those memories, maybe replace them with more pleasant memories that seem genuine, who knows what I can achieve!"

Dan thought about it. The idea had possibilities, it appeared to him. *Just look at how good I feel about my implanted memories of childhood in England with Les and Freda,* he thought. *Regardless of the knowledge now that it was all artificial, and that I could also remember my real childhood in Kharbarovsk.*

"Okay!" he smiled. "Keep it going, Doc!"

"Splendid! Let me refill your glass, Misha."

Some of the time, as much as was left, he spent with Emily. They took walks along the tracks Dan had to run in less leisurely moments, always aware of the agents walking behind them, played music in the library where a sophisticated stereo system was installed, or sat together and read books. A lot of the time, they just lay together on the king-sized bed in their room and held each other as close as they could, horribly conscious of the possibility that time could be running out for them.

Not that her life was any less stressful than Dan's. Her days were as intense as his were, but in a different way.

"We use a different room," she told him one evening after dinner, lying comfortably against his right shoulder on their king-sized bed. They had extracted the bottle of brandy from the drinks cabinet, and were making significant dents in the volume. “It’s small, but the obvious feature is the video camera on one wall. I’m being watched, but they won’t tell me by whom.”

“Who’s doing the interrogation?” He felt worried and angry, though the bargain had always been clear that Emily would give as much information about KGB operations as she could.

“That older woman who was here the first evening, and alternating pairs of two other military people,” said Emily. “Her name’s Hilary Connors, she’s a CIA heavy of some sort, though she’s also a shrink. She worked with Paul on the Cyclops and Parthenon projects, so she knows all about you. Speaks excellent Russian, and she’s astounding in what she knows already about some of the KGB activities.”

“Do they treat you all right, though?” Dan was prepared to go to war if they were hurting Emily. She nodded, and took a sip of the fine brandy.

“Oh yes! That’s not the problem at all. All very friendly, plenty of civilized creature comforts. It’s just the pounding of constant repetitions of the same questions.”

“Trying to catch the inconsistencies?”

“Sure! Standard interrogation techniques. And long hours to make me tired and more prone to giving myself away.”

“How long?” He looked down at the beautiful, calm face against his shoulder and wondered how he could ever have been fully alive before she appeared.

“We start at seven in the morning most days, and go on without a real break till ten at night.”

“Hell!”

“It is!” she agreed with a small grimace. “It’s harrowing. But think how much worse it would be if I was really trying to hide anything.”

"At least they leave you alone while Paul works on me," said Dan, sniffing his brandy. The fumes caressed his nose.

She laughed softly. "I told them that was part of the deal. If they tried working on me while you were in one of the deconditioning sessions, I would clam up completely. They got the point."

"You have that ability for gentle persuasion, Madam!" he laughed.

"In that case, can I persuade you to pour me another drink?" Her smile was gentle, and her eyes glowed. Dan reached for the bottle on the table by the bed, and watched the brandy chuckle softly into her balloon glass.

She touched the crystal to Dan's. "I am beginning to believe that we have a future, dear Misha," she murmured.

"To our future!" he responded, and they drank together. Dan was less confident than Emily. He could still feel the enormous barriers to freedom in his mind.

"At least we seem to be sleeping very well here," said Dan. "I haven't woken up once during the night ever since we've been here."

"It's true," she said thoughtfully. "And the odd thing is, I don't think I remember a single night of dreaming, either. Normally I remember my dreams quite well."

Dan lay back against his pillows, thinking. "You know," he said. "It's the same with me. Nearly two months, and I can't remember a single dream."

"We must just be too weary," she said, and sipped her glass. Dan nodded in agreement.

"I wish I could dream about us going back to our jobs and leading a normal life," he said, the wonderful brandy soaking down to his inner self.

"Why can't we?" she asked softly.

"I'm not even sure I have a job to go back to," he replied. "Jobs at that level aren't too easy to find, either.

There's a small matter of my mortgage, and food, and things like that!"

She laughed, a low delicious laugh that had always had the power to melt his worst moods.

"We don't have a problem," she murmured.

"We don't?" he echoed. "Why not? You can probably go back to your free-lancing, but that's not going to keep us in Veuve Cliquot at the rate we were used to!"

"I may not want to work at all," she chuckled, obviously teasing him. He was intrigued and amused. She was holding something from him.

"All right, dear lady, what's the secret?" he said, touching her cheek. "Have we won the lottery while we've been away?"

"Much better than that!"

"Better? What could be better?" He tucked an arm around her waist and nuzzled the side of her neck.

"You'd better watch it, Vorosov, or I'll get too distracted to tell you!" she whispered.

"All right! Hands off! Please do tell me!"

"Consider the requirements of a security operation in a foreign country," she said, shifting away from him a little. "What would one major need be?"

Dan considered the question.

"Supplies, communications, support personnel," he said, thinking aloud. "Quite an expensive.... oh, oh!" Suddenly he got the point. "You have an expense account stashed away somewhere?"

"Indeed I do," she said happily. "I liberated it from Carson's control while we were in Glen Ellyn, and it's nicely spread around a few banks and other institutions."

"And just how much did you liberate?" he asked, responding to her happy mood with a smile.

"Thirty-two million," she said.

Little else of coherence was said that evening.

Jack Gregory talked briefly to Dan at one point, just after breakfast while Dan was dressing for the first run of the day. He said somebody had been to see Dan's boss, the president of MidWestern and told him that Dan would be working for the government on a matter of national security for another few weeks. The agent had invoked the law about holding jobs open for reservists called up for duty, and the agent reported that the president had been fairly relaxed about it all. Dan seriously doubted he would ever be back in his office on Monroe Street, but crossed his fingers secretly and hoped. He had liked that life.

Another horribly fascinating conversation took place with Gregory, a day or two later.

"We've cleared the air on the killings," said Jack, as they sat in the armchairs in the music room one evening.

"You have?" Dan said in astonishment. "How?"

"A man called Bob Peterson was arrested in Des Moines a few weeks ago," said Jack, and took a deep swallow of his beer. "He'd killed a cop in Galesburg during a robbery, and he had a pretty lurid record before that. He agreed to solve all our problems most conveniently."

"Can you tell me about it?"

Jack shook his head. "Not all of it," he said. "Let's just say he'll admit to the murders, and give the police some details that were never released publicly as proof of his involvement."

Dan was astonished. "You arranged that?"

Jack nodded, not meeting Dan's eyes.

"But what's in it for him?" asked Dan.

"We'll arrange a fund for his sister to go to college," replied the CIA agent. "He agreed to that."

"But what if some other evidence comes up, or the guy gets an answer wrong during questioning?" Dan was worried. The scheme seemed full of holes.

"Don't worry," said Jack. "Other arrangements have already been made."

"What arrangements?"

"He won't live long enough to come to trial," replied the agent. He looked calmly at Dan. "You can be sure of that."

The coldness from that conversation never quite vanished from Dan's mind.

Chapter 10

The weeks elapsed and Dan was back in the antique chair, imprisoned securely with leather straps. Paul sat in front of him, their knees almost touching, Emily behind Paul and to one side of him, Jack Gregory reclined as usual on the couch. The smell of percolating coffee seemed stronger than normal this morning to Dan and the eye of the video camera stared impassively at him through the small square hole in the wall above the coffee table.

"Okay?" asked Paul.

"Let's party," said Dan, and Paul reached forward and touched his forehead.

My horse blew through his nostrils, and that was the first sound to break the frigid dawn. We had been here for two hours, arriving in the deep velvet blackness and taking a position about a hundred yards from the cave. We had been motionless the whole time. Apart from our short periods of quick meals and to sleep briefly, this was the only time we had stopped since leaving the king's court two weeks before.

"This is a quest that I would ask only my bravest knight to undertake," the king had said to me. "My enemies are everywhere, and I ask you to go forth and destroy the biggest of them."

"I am your loyal knight," I said.

"Then seek out Grimalkin," said the king. "And kill her!"

I studied my king, controlling the wave of fear. He was tall and thin, his face had the texture of an old lizard and his eyes were perpetually as cold as the glaciers of the far northern lands. He carried his staff of office and was not above using it to strike those who angered him.

"I am your overseer, your legs, oh throne," I said.

"Go then," he replied, and waved his staff in dismissal.

I bowed, and backed from his presence.

The sun had nudged a reluctant arc of light above the jagged line of the mountains behind us a few minutes before, and now two monstrously elongated shadows stretched before us, across the dusty, rock-strewn plain, almost to the cave mouth. David, my squire, sat on his horse behind me and to my left as a good squire should, carrying my mace and my axe. I pulled gently on the reins and my horse backed slowly till I was level with him. A slight jingling of the mouthpiece and stirrups rang lightly in the air, and both horses whinnied gently at each other. Everywhere else was silent, not the squeak of a mouse, the call of a bird or the rustle of a squirrel searching the trees. The animals knew better than to loiter anywhere within sight of the Grimalkin's cave.

I reached a hand over, encased in chain mail, and my squire put the axe handle into it. I hung the weapon with the gleaming edges of the two blades onto the buckle of my saddle and reached once more. This time the mace with its heavy bulbous head and short, evil spikes was passed over to be hung away for possible use. My right hand stayed firmly clasping the moulded grip of the lance. The heavy two-handed sword swung from my belt on my left.

"Now move away, boy," I said gently. "This is not your fight."

"Sir," he began to protest, but I cut him off with a short wave.

"Grimalkin is a knight's battle, David, not for some stripling with his nose still snotty and his sword unbloodied."

He smiled slightly, his eyes amused over his neatly trimmed red beard, for he had proved his worth to me in the past, and the blood of the king's enemies had indeed stained his sword in my company. I knew that David believed he should accompany me into battle against the beast, as he had before against other foes, but he was a squire of a king's knight and knew not to disobey. He pulled his horse round and they moved slowly towards the sun and the shelter of the large rocks. I listened to the sounds of his retreat, the metallic jingling of his bridle and the muffled thuds of his charger's hooves on the dust, and wished I could call him back. He had been my squire and my friend for some years. If I failed this task, he would at least sing of my valour in the king's court when he returned.

The sounds of bridle and hooves vanished into the distance, leaving me feeling dreadfully alone. I began to move gently towards the cave. The black opening echoed evil, the smell of musk and rotting flesh reached me even here. A small shiver rippled down the neck of my steed, but he was battle trained. Together we had faced the might of the northern barbarians and trampled many of them into the cold mud. We had withstood the massive onslaught by the armour of Sir Guy de Balfour's armies at Monmouth, and he had carried me bleeding and barely alive from the bloodbath at Peterborough.

Grimalkin would frighten him as that evil beast of hell terrified all who had the misfortune to meet her, but he would not falter.

Our approach must have warned the monster even as she slept, for a heart-stopping snarl rumbled from the black opening. It was a warning.

"Come no closer!"

I ignored it, as I ignored the freezing sensation in my limbs under the heavy armour. A king's knight could show no fear. I kicked my stirrups gently against the heavy protective cloth that hung around the sides of my horse, and we continued moving slowly towards the cave. Only a tiny jingling of the bridle accompanied our progress, but it was enough. The snarl was repeated, much louder. The evil hiss which followed it was like that of a monstrous snake staring down at a mouse. My heart pounded a little faster, and my chain-mailed hands grew damp. I lowered the lance so that the needle point aimed directly at the black cave.

In the shadows, something moved, blackness within blackness, storm clouds in a night sky, wings of ravens in the dark woods, felt rather than seen. The snarl had subsided to an angry undertone that rumbled out into the morning air, made the dust move by the horse's feet and lightly shook the air between us. The stench of rotting offal made me gag slightly. Then she appeared.

A massive, evil head stared out of the blackness, little else but huge eyes and a phalanx of teeth from which drooled stalactites of foam. Framing the gateway of the teeth were shoulders two yards wide, heavy black coat shining in the rays that reached over the mountains and struck her. Two front legs were pillars of muscle the height of a man atop claws of a predatory bird, stained with the blood of old kills. The body tapered back from the monstrous killing mouth and claws, beautiful in its unholy way, down to back legs, lighter but still powerful enough, with claws that could disembowel an ox with one sweep. The haunches were bent like a hunting cat's to let the creature crouch close to the dust while the long, thin tail twitched with suppressed rage in the darkness of the cave mouth.

The most dreadful sights of all were the two other heads, human heads, on long, serpent necks growing from the monstrous black shoulders. They grinned at me, sharp teeth gleaming, blood still staining the gums from their last meal, eager for the killing to start. They weaved from side to side, crossing over the rolling black hillocks of the creature's back, and all the time they stared at me, laughing in anticipation of the feast.

Needing no order from me, the horse thundered into its charge immediately. I sighted the lance on the point where the left neck joined the shoulder and denied the fear that welled up within me. Grimalkin crouched, the middle head snarling, the mouth open to reveal rows and rows of teeth stretching backward. At full tilt I pounded towards the hideous sight, we closed, and at the last moment, she moved and the lance slid off the rolling, oily muscles under the sleek thick fur over the shoulders. We hit with murderous force, two tons of warhorse and armoured knight, my lance swung outwards, struck the cave side and splintered.

The cat screamed, a human howl of pain and fury and reared back, talons hissing as they lashed at the air between us. I snatched the two-bladed axe from its hook as the head on my right launched a strike at me like a cobra. I swung and caught the top of the neck at the join with the man-like head. Green blood spurted, the head screeched and stared at me with the painful, furious eyes of a man. I swung again and the dreadful thing dropped to the ground, leaving the neck waving in confusion and agony, pouring green ochre over the smooth black coat of Grimalkin and over me.

I had not been able to watch the other two heads while I fought. The nightmare of drooling teeth fell forwards from its initial move back and closed with a scream of rage on my horse's shoulder like a bear trap, narrowly missing my left leg. My horse collapsed under the weight and the shock, bellowing with pain and fear, and I was sent sprawling backwards, out into the sunlight, the axe falling from my green-slimed hand. The remaining human head streaked out in another cobra-like strike and seized on the horse's neck, tearing a massive chunk of flesh and blood. Both sets of eyes glared furiously at me as they ate, blood running in floods from their mouths.

The fear had been suppressed while I battled but now began to rise up in me. I reached for my sword and pulled it from the scabbard, both hands clenched on the handle. As long as a man, but perfectly balanced, I had sent many enemies to their maker with the finely sharpened blade. I held it before me, trying to ignore the trembling and shock from the loss of my steed. I began to walk forward, steeling myself to close the gap between us. I advanced carefully, kicking away bones of other victims that had strayed too close.

The remaining human head resumed its bloody grin at me, the beast's jaws spat out bone and gristle, and the huge black shape launched itself at me in one unearthly bound that nothing created by God could have made. I held the sword point out, the creature landed straight on it, slamming me to the floor and then immediately leaping up again. The sword had done nothing, it had slid like the lance off the impossibly smooth and thick black fur of this Devil's creature, and in turning had broken my wrist.

The human head smiled and spoke in a gentle, hissing tone. Its eyes were deep blue, the hair was long and untidy, the skin was of an old man, it almost looked kindly, a friendly bear.

"Now Sir Knight, we feed again!"

I howled with rage and terror and swung my sword at the cruel talons of the foot nearest to me. With a jar that sent sheets of pain through my broken wrist, the blade hit the evil, blood-stained claw and sliced through it. The claw was snatched back, but with the speed of a hunting cat, the other one whipped from the side and struck me on the ribs, sending me sprawling hard against the rocks at the side of the cave, my sword flying from my hand.

The terror overwhelmed me. I turned, running from the cave as fast as my armour would let me, dreading the expected strike from one or both heads on my back. Tears of shame destroyed my vision. I knew not where I was running, but simply flung myself forward, anyway there was to escape the dreadful death that waited behind me. I stumbled on rocks, ran into boulders, but I ran, my breath in painful, tortured whoops of strain.

God knows how far I ran, but at some stage I was no longer on the dusty flatness before Grimalkin's cave. I was in woodland, the smell of salt told of the sea nearby, and I was cold. But far worse was my shame. I had run from the battle and betrayed my king. Trembling with weariness and cold, I unstrapped the leather bonds that held the breastplate, trying not to moan with the agony of my broken wrist. I let the heavy sheet of beaten iron drop into the grass, removed the leg covers, the back plate and finally took the helmet from my shoulders. I looked one more time at the proud iron, the blue plume so jaunty on the top, the gleaming visor.

"I am your knight no longer, my king," I said. I dropped the helmet to the ground, turned my back and walked away.

The cold began to drain my stamina immediately. I trudged through the bleak forest towards the sound of the sea and eventually reached a stony beach by the side of the grey, icy waters. I turned west and began to walk, looking for shelter. I looked to my right and saw shadows in the woods, soldiers of the king! They must already be looking for me, aware of my shameful betrayal, ready to capture me and bring me for punishment before my lord. I ran, crouching to try and hide behind the miserably stunted grass and bushes that followed the shoreline. I heard a shout, taken up by others, the soldiers converged on my location, calling their comrades to witness my degradation.

It was useless, soldiers cut off my escape routes in all directions. I stood upright, slumped in weariness and despair, shivering heavily, praying now for the sword cut that would give me peace. One of the men, a large, grey-haired sergeant-at-arms walked up to me. I stared at the familiar, grizzled face.

"Hello, Misha," he said softly.

The freezing air shimmered a little as if a wave of warmth had passed through, and the scene before me shifted. Instead of armoured soldiers, I saw troops in jungle greens, their swords became radio antennae. The icy grey sea and bleak shoreline did not change.

"What are you doing in my dream, Paul?" mumbled Dan, lips stiff with cold.

"Dream's over, son," Paul touched Dan's shivering arm. "I think we're getting somewhere."

"Well, that's okay then," Dan muttered, took the heavy sheepskin coat Paul pushed at him and began to follow the older man to the line of camouflaged marines waiting by the truck on the roadside.

* * *

"The colonel's going to be mad," said Dan, surveying the shattered remnants of the antique chair.

"I think I can handle the colonel." Emily smiled gently. "He's had a lot more out of us for the price of a chair than he ever imagined. Anyway, I'll just give him my best fluttered eyelashes and he'll melt away."

"Seems a reasonable forecast." Paul was looking a lot more confident than the last time they had returned to the green and white room for a review of the hypnosis session.

Two weeks had passed since Dan's recapture in the woods by the sea, and he was still in a wheelchair. He had climbed into the truck unassisted that day, and then collapsed with alarming rapidity, to Paul's dismay. For the mile or so back to the mansion, Paul was keeping him alive by mouth-to-mouth breathing, and given a radio advance warning, the well-equipped medical unit in the mansion house met the truck as it screeched to a halt by the front door.

Three days had passed before Dan was out of the coma. Yet again, Emily had been faced with a lengthy vigil by his bedside, uncertain if he would come out of it, or if he did, what his mental state would be. The strain showed in her shadowed eyes and hollow cheeks, in the occasional brittleness of her voice, and the ease with which tears would come.

Dan was able to recall every detail of the horrible battle with the Grimalkin, especially the instant at which the human head had spoken to him, and he had described them to Paul while tape-recording the story. A secretary had later transcribed the tape and they had read the description several times since.

"I leaned over you at one point," admitted Paul. "You stared up at me in such blind terror, it was horrible to see. That's when you smashed the chair and erupted out of the room, running into chairs, tables, breaking the door off its hinges. I'll never know how you broke the chair, or got out of the building and past the marine guards, but you were a mile down the road before we found you. You must have drawn on some incredibly deep resources and burned them up like a jet fighter using its after-burners."

"I ran from the cat in blind panic," nodded Dan, vividly remembering the rocks and boulders in his way and how he had stumbled over them. The plaster over his sprained right wrist was itchy. He had probably damaged it in one of the collisions with furniture.

"Interesting mixture of images, that hallucination," said Paul, thoughtfully. "Normally, the knight in armour bit would have suggested a dragon as the monster. Or perhaps something of Mordred from the Arthurian legends. The cat, I have a suspicion came out of a science fiction story. Possibly a Heinlein novel, my senile memory tells me. Quite fascinating."

"Quite horrible," Dan agreed with a shiver. "Did we get anywhere with that bloodthirsty little episode?"

"I haven't been able to check everything yet, but I'm pretty certain we did," said Paul. "The images you used were highly informative. The king as you described him sounded like Gemorov in Murmansk."

"So he did!" said Dan thoughtfully. "I remember him now, it really was Gemorov! So I assume that his orders to go and kill Grimalkin were my way of seeing my mission here as attacking the United States?"

"Without a doubt," agreed Paul. "Remember also, that the words you used to accept your mission from the king were the words of the trigger phrase that places you under control."

"Of course!" said Dan, understanding more of what was going on with every second. "I wondered why I had used such a strange phrase!"

"Then when you ran in such fear and panic, that showed your desire to break free of the conditioning, and also an awareness that you could lose the fight. I suggest also, that the way you took off the armour and resigned your status as a knight was a symbol of your wish to give up the Russian loyalty. Or at least, the loyalty to the KGB."

"That's absolutely right!" said Dan, nodding his head vigorously. "I knew I was breaking away from a strong tie at that point. It's amazing the way my mind interprets these thoughts as images this way!"

"You're certainly getting more detailed hallucinations than our people got when we tried the same thing," agreed Paul. "I think that's actually a help to the deprogramming process too, because the emotions are running so much higher."

"You think so? I do hope that's right!" said Dan with deeper feeling than he realized. A memory flew into his mind. "David was there again," he said, remembering the red-haired squire who was so offended that he had been dismissed from the battle.

"Of course," replied Paul. "In the second battle, you sustained damage. You called up some help again for this one."

"But I wouldn't let him fight," Dan objected. "He was my squire, and I sent him away before the fight started."

"Interesting," said Paul with a thoughtful stare out of the window. "Moral support only, perhaps. And an awareness that you really did have to do this thing alone."

Dan felt confused. "Does that mean progress or not?" he asked.

"Compare the damage you sustained to the almost superhuman feeling of invulnerability that you had in the first battle, and the progress is obvious," said Paul with confidence. "I was hoping we could do a trial of the conditioning now. How are you feeling?"

"Still weak, but otherwise no ill effects," Dan answered, running a quick mental check on his body parts. He stood up and stretched. Everything was in place, the weakness was no longer the nightmarish feeling of dragging himself through thick mud, but it was still enough to prevent a return to the physical exercises. "I think I'd like to try," he said.

"Misha, please be certain before you risk anything." The dark shadows around Emily's eyes showed her tension. He reached for her hand.

"Why don't you do the test?" he said to her with a smile. "I'll feel a lot easier."

She looked up at Paul. "Could we have done anything that would change the effects of the trigger phrases?" she asked.

He shrugged. "I honestly couldn't say, but it's highly unlikely, I would think. I'm pretty confident that what we did was to ease the force of the existing instruction set."

He paused and looked closely at Dan for a second or two.

"I doubt we've wiped the triggers out completely," he said. "Because Misha ran away rather than be destroyed by his nightmare. But he was badly hurt, he certainly lost the battle, something must have given."

"We're not going to find out if we stand around and talk," Dan broke in. "Emily, let's just try the control trigger."

She looked again at Paul.

He nodded. "You should sit down first, just in case," he suggested.

Dan took the armchair, Emily knelt at his feet and took his hands. He smiled at her. "We have to try sometime," he said. "The worst that could have happened is that nothing's changed. So let's give it a whirl! You never know your luck!"

Paul stayed standing behind the armchair and placed one hand on Dan's shoulder. His touch was reassuring, thought Dan.

"Okay?" asked Emily, clearly worried.

"Okay," Dan nodded, trying to feed her encouragement from his own confidence.

"Misha, listen to me," she whispered in Russian. "We are your overseers, we are your legs, oh throne."

The room was silent. Dan looked at her, then at Paul. Both were watching him with intensity. He felt something, almost a return of some of the weakness, but not the heaviness of previous experience.

"Emily I want you to give him a simple order," said Paul from behind Dan. "Then Misha, I want you to try and disobey."

She nodded at him, and looked firmly into Dan's eyes. "Misha, you are to stay sitting in the chair without moving."

Dan looked hard into her beautiful gold-flecked eyes, then down at his hands in his lap. *Lift up,* he said to himself. *Lift up and touch her.* He strained hard, his arms were sticking to the cloth of his jeans. He clenched his fist and put every atom of strength into it. Slowly, painfully slowly, excruciating millimetre by millimetre, his right arm raised itself and began to move towards her. She watched, fascinated, her jaw dropped as Dan stared into her eyes and continued to drive his arm up the vertical cliff edge of the twelve inches to her face. His fist unclenched, it got easier... he touched her cheek.

"Misha!" she shouted and flung her arms around Dan's head. Paul let out a loud yell and applauded as if he had just heard the greatest operatic solo in the world.

Dan laughed out loud. "Now watch!" he grunted, still breathing hard from the labour. He concentrated again, then began to lean forward. He felt as if a mighty wind was blowing him back in his chair, but he kept pushing. He leaned forward over his knees, let his weight fall onto his feet and began to push hard down. *Dear God,* he thought. It was like climbing the face of the Matterhorn in an ice storm, every inch of movement was bought at a fearful price.

But he did it.

He stood up.

And she had ordered him to stay seated.

"Carson, you're screwed!" Dan muttered to himself, feeling as if he had won the lottery. Such triumph in such a little act!

"I'll be..." Paul was staring with wide open eyes, a grin of such delight on his face that Dan had to smile back.

"Probably," he said, and collapsed back in the chair.

"I will let you go now, Misha," said Emily, the words falling out of her mouth in the rush. Dan felt no immediate change. So he tried again, and in reality, standing up again was not all that much easier than the last time, under control or not. Perhaps some of the struggle had been against his jelly-like weakness as much as against the hypnotic conditioning, he thought.

"You know what, I think we're there!" he laughed.

Paul shook his head. "Not yet. But we've obviously broken the grip of it. There's no way we could try the punishment trigger yet, but we're clearly getting somewhere."

Dan was holding Emily close and the warmth of her was the greatest medicine a man could have. "One more session," he said confidently, admiring the perfect skin of Emily's ears and neck. "Just one! We'll kill it."

Paul nodded. "Yes, we probably will. But you have to be even better prepared than last time. This has to be the last one. I don't think you'll survive any more."

The shudder that Dan felt pass through Emily reminded him that they had a long way to go yet. He stroked her neck and kissed her forehead.

"I won't have to," he said, more confidently than he felt.

* * *

Despite the training and the obvious progress, Dan and Emily still knew what the risk was. When they finally went into the last deconditioning session, Dan could come out of the room on a stretcher, dead or in a comatose state. Even worse, he could be a drooling basket case, his mind totally destroyed by the conflicting demands placed on it. In a quiet, personal session with Paul and Emily two weeks earlier, Dan had written precise instructions and had them witnessed by them both. In the worst case, death of the mind without death of the body, no medical efforts were to be applied to keep the body alive.

A shadow had hung over them for an hour or so after signing that piece of paper, but eventually they had forced it away in the light and laughter of a spirited evening of boat races, mess rugby and general rowdiness that is common in an officers' mess when the majority of the people are young, fit and forceful.

Since taking up residence at the mansion, several others had also moved in for whatever purposes of their own. They never discussed their projects during the dinners or evening entertainments, but the population of Southampton Headquarters now consisted of four air force pilots in their late twenties and early thirties, two civilian psychiatrists who may or may not have been associated with Paul's work on Dan, two naval women lieutenants and two army psychologists, one male, one female. These were the members of the audience that had listened to Paul's lecture, and whom Dan had also addressed. The air force captain whose uncle had been assassinated by another of Gemorov's Murmansk trainees had eased his hostility to Dan after Paul had demonstrated in the most effective manner possible, just how it was done.

The captain had been one of the experimental subjects who had volunteered to receive some of Paul's conditioning as part of project Parthenon. Paul had muttered some words to him, and immediately, the pilot had stripped down to his shorts and run outside in the sub-zero temperatures, returning twenty minutes later shivering and confused.

He stood in the lounge room, and was released from his conditioning by another word from Paul. He stared around the room in dismay. "What happened?" he demanded, hurriedly dressing himself again.

"You've been for a run through the woods," said Paul.

"I've what?" The captain was disbelieving. It took ten minutes to convince him of the fact, and he went silent and retreated to the bar on his own. He approached Dan later that evening as he stood with Emily and the naval lieutenant who had asked him in Paul's lecture how he had felt about the killings. Her name was Ursula Kendrick, and she and Emily had hit it off immediately, despite the initial wariness between two one-time military adversaries. The three of them were standing together, discussing some of the mental trauma of the deconditioning process, when Captain Peter Carstairs approached them.

"Dan," he said. He was a heavy-set man, about Dan's own height, with almost black hair and thick eyebrows that met over his nose.

"I have to apologize," Carstairs said firmly.

"No you don't," said Dan. "You can see now how impossible it was for that poor bastard not to kill your uncle. That's why he broke apart."

The pilot clasped Dan's arm for a second, and walked away.

Add to the military group a few hard-faced, cool young men of Special Services, the fairly complete medical and nursing staff, and the mixture had possibilities. So the young, mixed and very fit crowd in the mess each evening was perfectly capable of providing its own entertainment. The therapy for Emily and Dan was wonderful. They partied every night, well past the hour at which Paul would excuse himself with a small self-deprecating grin and go to bed. It was the only real relief from the unrelenting pressure on both of them, and the constant menace of the fact that they were still in prison.

Another month was needed before the medical staff would approve the final combat session. Dan had sustained almost no physical damage in the fight with the cat, so he had little to heal other than a slightly sprained wrist, and he was back in shape quicker than after the battle with the trolls, but Paul was merciless. Dan could have been in training for a world heavyweight contest or an Olympic pentathlon the way Paul forced his fitness program. Dan returned to the daily murderous sessions with the beanpole Corporal Halloran and the whirlwind energy of Sergeant Alana Denton, and this time he was more capable of staying near enough to them to reply to their cutting calls of "Civilian!" with equally insulting gasps of "Squareheads!" When they finally decided on the day for what Dan knew would be the final episode in the deprogramming of his mind, he was in better physical condition than he had ever been in his life.

On the morning of the final day, the tension was as high as in a marine unit preparing to invade enemy shores. Dan walked down the lengthy corridors with Emily, Paul and Jack Gregory in attendance as his handlers, feeling incredibly fit, the lightest he had been since he was in the Birmingham University track and field team over twelve years ago... Dan had to pause and check his recollections and dates for that one, yes it was a genuine memory, not an implanted one... and he was both uplifted and frightened at the prospect of the coming showdown.

He walked hand in hand with Emily, both of them aware of small trembles running through their bodies. Occasionally, Paul Harrington muttered something to himself, his face strained with concentration. Neither Dan nor Emily asked him what he was saying. It was clearly something private.

Jack Gregory opened the door and they entered, took their usual places. Jack first poured himself a coffee and sat on the settee. Paul and Emily took orange juice, Emily curled up in one armchair, Paul moved the other one around to face Dan.

They had spent many hours debating the issue of tethering Dan. That they had to was not the issue. Dan had proved his capacity for violence under hypnotic command three times now, and nobody wanted a repeat. In the end, they had settled on a simple enough solution, the strait-jacket that the marines had used on Dan after the first incredible conflict when eleven of them had been needed to subdue him. Despite his horror at the idea of being so harshly confined, Dan accepted the need for it, and he stood erect while Paul fitted the white canvas garment around him, fighting off the mild panic as his arms were folded and the straps tightened behind his back.

"Would you scratch my nose, please?" he begged Emily as he was lowered into the armchair and she chuckled gently as she obliged, completing the operation with a kiss.

"You can't go into battle with lipstick on your nose," complained Paul, and Dan had to submit to the indignity of having his face cleaned like a little boy. Both Paul and Emily tried unsuccessfully to hide their smiles while this process went on. It was a useful way of covering up the undercurrent of fear that was running high in the room.

Dan's feet were strapped together, and one of the large leather belts was used to wrap all the way round him and the armchair.

Dan took a last look around the room. Jack was stretched out, his coffee cup resting on the floor beside him. Emily was in her usual relaxed curled-up position, and Paul was sitting upright in front of him. The coffee urn was steaming gently on the table, the neat array of cups, saucers, glasses and jugs looking so ordinary in a room that had witnessed some extraordinary events. Outside the door, a few rattles and bangs indicated that the medical team had taken up station. They would come in once Dan was under, and be ready immediately if he ran into difficulties. The tiny gleam of the camera lens behind the small square hole in the wall above the coffee urn was the only sign that the video camera was working.

Emily uncurled and got up, walking softly in her bare feet to Dan. She put her hands on his cheeks and looked intently at him. Her eyes had just a suspicion of tears in them, but Dan was mainly conscious of her perfume, her soft hair and the flawless skin. She kissed him, and returned to her seat. Dan smiled, but both of them knew that their small embrace might just be the last one they would ever have.

It was kill or cure. That's what they had all agreed, that's what Dan had told Paul. *Kill me or cure me.*

He nodded at Paul, struggling to control the wave of fear that came over him. The pain and damage of the last two battles were too fresh in his mind to let him believe that he could come out of this session any way but in severe pain and distress.

"Time for me to see that damned escalator at O'Hare, I believe, Professor Harrington."

Paul's eyes were serious, and Dan knew he was a little scared too. Dan had come too close to death the last time.

"Okay, son," he murmured. "Let's get the bastards."

The rains had finally eased. Six days of continual flooding had swollen the Broad River until its name was a mockery of itself, made the hills soggy, and depressed our morale terribly. The twelve days of Christmas had been miserable for everyone this year, but who could have a happy Yuletide so far from home and in such dreadful conditions? The news of Saratoga had depressed our spirits, for it had been a terrible defeat, and now Tarleton had marched us here through wet roads, moonless nights and muddied fields, and we were exhausted. For eight hours, we had tramped our way through drizzling cold rain that had never eased to anything less than a wet mist, and at times had thundered down on our heads as if the rivers had been lifted from their beds and carried over us.

At ten, we had made camp, and reveille had blown at two this morning. We struggled to wake up from our broken sleep, unable to get proper rest in the cold and the damp. I had lain on my cloak and found that the rains had soaked the ground until it was a quagmire. Anytime I had rolled over to try a more comfortable spot, the water had followed me like a pet dog and snuggled into my boots, my jacket and my trousers with cold affection.

The camp fires had been miserable and pathetic, barely holding their own against the overnight drizzle. The few lucky ones who had been able to find a spot to lie within sight of the flames said they had felt nothing, and instead had spent more time trying to keep the tiny glow alive than they had resting. As the trumpets blew, we cursed and swore, hauled on our soaking red tunics that had not been dry now for weeks and made a hasty breaking of the fast with sodden biscuits and a quick gulp of rainwater collected in our eating irons before moving out at three. At least something could be said for the perpetual downpour. We had fresh water to drink, something that had been rarely true through this damned campaign.

God damn the rebels! I muttered to myself as I tried to strap the powder casket to my belt and adjusted the blade of the bayonet. My legs were chaffed red raw from the forced march in the miserable wet, my back ached from the fifty pounds of powder, balls and supplies I carried. The musket had developed a vicious life of its own over the long night, and my arms were creaking in protest.

Yes, damn them! They could have this godforsaken land as far as I was concerned. Why in heaven's name did King George want to keep it? We muttered, grunted, groaned and protested as foot soldiers have done since time began, hoisted our packs and muskets, checked the flints, the powder and the spikes, gave the bayonets a final touch with the sandstone and reluctantly shuffled into line under the harassment of the sergeants. Even those perpetual tormentors of men, the non-commissioned officers were struggling to lift their voices into the outraged scream of fury that was the trade mark of a man with stripes on his arm.

Up by the ridge we heard the shots, the squealing of horses and the shouts. A murmur of excitement ran through the lines. Our dragoons had already made contact with some of Morgan's men, it sounded like. May God be with them and smite those damned rebels to the dirt. Then I could go home to the hills of Cheshire, the good ales of Lancashire, back to my mother, back to the land where I grew up. I prayed that it would happen soon, the agony of this war was breaking my soul like twigs under a cartwheel, and I could not survive much longer, I knew.

As the sun stuck its head up to have a look at what the night had left, our spirits rose. I stood upright and looked at the sight. To my right, the long lines of the British Redcoats stood bright and magnificent, distance hiding the wet gloom. Over to my left stood the Loyalists in their green. The splendour of the massed armies of the king would have made the blood of any Englishman stir with pride.

Our scouts had been sent out as the skies lightened into a dull, sodden grey, and now they were riding back. Their news flashed like wildfire up and down the lines. Morgan's Continental Army has fewer men than us, report the scouts, said the man on my right, and I passed the news on, my spirits lifting. They have none of those excellent, small three-pounder guns, grasshoppers as we call them, said the second wave of rumour, while we had two of them and enough powder and shot to blast them all to hell. The murmurs of confidence and hope that we will live out the day spread through the green and red lines, and men stood straighter and watched the action on the hill with brighter eyes.

The sergeants and officers kept us moving with screams and yells of rage, threats of punishment worse than any American rebel can visit upon us, and accusations of the deficiencies of our ancestors that they have honed on lines of men over the years. Our boots squelching in the mud, we dragged our fatigued bodies towards the hill, and by seven, with the sun clearly above the horizon, we saw the enemy at last.

We were only four hundred yards away, and we could see clearly the advance pickets of Morgan's men half way up the hillside, mixed in with the oaks and the chestnuts that caught the weak wintry gleams of the January sun. Atop the ridge, the main force of his Continentals watched us as we settled in. They have the high ground, I thought with a twinge of worry. I must remember that a man tends to shoot high when shooting uphill. Aim at his knees to hit his heart, said the sergeant. I look around in the lightening of day, and see just miserable soaked fields, weakling trees and the vast, dull, sullen spread of the river. The scouts told us the area was called the Cowpatch. It seemed a poor name to give to another British victory which all of us were certain would be ours by lunchtime. Despite Saratoga, how could these raggedy rebels believe they could stand up to the might of the British Empire?

Lieutenant Colonel Banastre Tarleton was watching from his command post on the hill three miles away. "The brass always kept themselves safe," I muttered and hitched my musket nervously. I never saw the man, nor any of his high command, except when the enemy was far away and valuable sleeping or eating time was wasted by another of those damned parades.

I heard the toot of the trumpet and saw the dragoons moving out again on a second sortie. A murmur ran through the lines and a few muted cheers. Good, let the young gentlemen risk their backsides for the king instead of us! The men sat proudly on their horses, flags hung miserably down the masts, clinging to the staff instead of flying bravely, but no matter, they were the King's colours. The dragoons were advancing on the picket lines up the hill, a trumpet rang out in the still, sodden air, and then they charged. God be with thee, boys! We were cheering aloud now, expecting those poorly armed and half- trained country yokels of the rebel army to fall back and run before our king's dragoons.

Something's wrong! They weren't running! My God, they dropped fifteen of our men out of the saddle on the first volley! It was a slaughter, red coats were falling into the mud and rotting leaves, horses were screaming and milling around, trampling on wounded men, the remaining horsemen have turned and fled... dear God, a whole squadron of men almost wiped out! Many men were praying around me, their mumbles a low drone like a far away migration of bees.

The drums began tapping behind us. The calls echoed down the line as the sergeants took command. Their voices were calm, controlled. Did those men know no fear?

"Fix bayonets, men! Advance in line!"

We straightened our shoulders, right hands reached behind our backs and took out the bayonets, snapped them in place on the muskets and we moved forward, muskets at the port arms. The fear ran down my back, made my breathing faster, squirmed in my guts. I looked at my old friend David, two ranks behind me, and tried to smile. His face was white, under the red beard, but he waved his hand and somehow summoned his regular grin that could light up the night. Oh Lord, if I fall this day, take my soul in peace...

All of us, the green lines of Loyalists, the red lines of British started that awesome tramping advance that would put the fear of God into any man's army. The popping of muskets began among the trees on the hill, small puffs of smoke rippled, and the first men fell among us. Some screamed as they fell, others just gave out a choked sob, some said nothing but fell dead instantly. They were the lucky ones. No matter, fill the gap, move up, stride over the writhing bodies, keep the line moving, we are the King's Light Infantry...

My ears were shattered by the explosion that darkened the sky to my right with the eruption of the wet soil as a shell landed but a few yards away. A strangled scream was hauled through the dead throat of the man on my right, his head and right arm had gone, the blood sprayed out and soaked into the ground as the corpse collapsed almost as if trying to catch the blood before it vanished. Another man fell in silence on my left and tangled up my feet so that I nearly stumbled to the mud. More men from the lines behind me rushed forward and filled the spaces. God, we were magnificent! Despite the soul-crushing fear, the pride burst from me, and I yelled a loud wordless challenge at the rebels on the hill.

Dimly I heard the trumpet calling the bayonet charge, and we began to move faster. The rebels were dropping back! We had them! Hurrah for King George, hurrah for Tarleton! The Dragoons were moving to the right to attack Morgan's wing, the wild skirling of the Highlanders' pipes began as the Scots started their advance too, the excitement built up in us all. The stink of gunpowder mingled with the smell of fear and the sodden wool of our tunics. Victory by lunch be damned! We'll have it by ten!

On the right, Morgan sent out his own cavalry. Damn, they have stopped the dragoons! But never fear, the Highlanders have moved now, their pipes the sound of death to the enemy. We kept running forward, bayonets in the attack position...

"The Rebs are dropping back up the hill!" howled the leading troops. "We have them scared and running!" The shouts rose to a fury, we were eager now for the killing to start. Never mind the pain of running up the side of the ridge, let me at them! Give me a rebel to bayonet!

But... what is this?... they've turned, the rebs have turned! They were firing straight at us from the hip, men were screaming, the rebs were running back at us, their bayonets lunging... oh my God, their cavalry has joined in! Full tilt down the ridge they came, the hooves of their horses sounding a drumming from Hell, the sun shining off the blades of their sabres and lances, men were turning, running, howling in fear. Even the Highlanders threw down their muskets, they were calling for mercy... God! The dragoons have fled the field... out of the smoke, men appeared, dirty men, without uniforms, they yelled wildly, their bayonets in front.. the sharp points!.. dear God I am lost, what will...

* * *

Shadows. Sometimes an unintelligible whispering. Much pain. Occasionally I feel gentle hands cleaning me. I don't know where I am. Blackness again.

* * *

Arms and legs have no feeling. Are they even there? Is this finally my worst nightmare? Once, I had read of a man who came back from the trenches of Ypres without arms, legs, sight or hearing. What must he have suffered before he was mercifully allowed to die? Was I now like that man? Where am I, anyway? Tears well up in my eyes which may have no more sight in them. Blackness again.

* * *

Burning, searing pain attacks my side, lesser agony chews at my legs as if the trolls were feeding again. Who said you could only feel pain in one place at a time? How wrong can anyone be, I felt it everywhere. Surely I still have my legs if I can feel so much pain in them? But Douglas Bader had said he felt pain in his legs all his life, despite losing both of them in his early twenties. Had he been flying with me when I shot down the Heinkels near Tangmere? Don't be silly, Misha, that was just a dream. Only shadows in the cool dark. Is this all I will ever see again? So much pain... I welcome the blackness with gratitude.

* * *

Hours later... days? Why not years? I just don't know. Somebody is wiping down my chest with a wet cloth... my arms too? Pray that I really can feel the dampness on my arms... somewhere near the lower ribs the careful hands take extra care, wipe around bandages where the steel point of the rebel's bayonet caused my scream of... but that was just a dream too, Misha, your mind is going... But they had to sew up the trolls' bites on my legs.... Misha, this way lies madness. Return to the cool dark, it's safer.

* * *

Later. Much later. Feel the tubes sticking into my arms. The dryness in my throat. Try to say something, ask if my arms and legs are still there... a sudden rush of whispering in the shadows, like the trolls on the hillside... Somebody leans over me, a darker shadow... *Grimalkin! Oh God, the cat!* Try and struggle, arms and legs won't move, dear God, I have lost them, tears of grief... tiny prick on my skin and the shadows darken into peace.

* * *

The room is curtained to keep the light out. Small scouts of brightness evade the blocks and explore the cool white walls with insolent disregard. Flowers on the table near the door. If I move my head a tiniest fraction, I see the tubes leading somewhere unknown from my right arm... my arm! I have my arm! Try and look left, almost terrified to see, but my left one is truly there too! I cannot look down, I seem to be nearly flat on my back, but I feel a lot more certain that my legs will be there when I can look. Hell, it was only a dream... but the stitches for Stengwulf's injuries, the dressings on my stomach... what else has happened to me?

I gasp with remembered pain of the bayonet ripping aside flesh, the dreadful, unbearable agony of the steel in my guts, the frightened yet exhilarated face of the boy in front of me, holding his musket while I stare with shock into his eyes, then sink to my knees as the sounds of battle around me fade...

A flurry of movement off to one side, flash of white coat, small buzzer sounds, I don't understand any of this. There is a man leaning over me, I don't know him... he is saying something firmly to somebody else... the flash of white again and it expands to become a nurse who moves to the door and opens it, closing it behind her.

The man opens his mouth and says something completely unintelligible. I look at him, wondering what the fuss is all about....

"... hear me? Misha, can you hear me? Blink your eyes if you can hear me."

Why is he speaking English? No wonder it took a while for me to understand him. I blink my eyes and he seems to breathe a sigh of relief.

"Drink," I say. I am parched.

"Peach?" he echoes, bewildered. Of course, English, silly Misha!

"Drink," I say again, this time so he will understand. I speak English? How come I speak English? Oh, of course, Murmansk. It all seems clear now. Murmansk, Gemorov, England, Carson, Emily... *Emily!*

And she's there. How did she appear so quickly? Maybe I was back in the shadows for a while. But she's here now, holding my hand, putting a plastic beaker to my mouth, so wonderful to drink something again... everything is fine. Carson, I have unfinished business with you... but the blackness embraces me again with familiarity and stops that idea for a while.

Only for a while.

* * *

"I find it especially interesting that you selected a role in a battle where you knew you were going to lose. If you were going to be true to historical facts, that is."

They were sitting in the music room in the basement of the mansion. The lovely tones of Bach's Fourth Brandenburg were rolling from the huge speakers, though the volume was fairly low. Captain Carstairs, the air force pilot who lost his uncle to one of Dan's colleagues was sitting in another corner, his arm round the shoulder of Ursula, the navy psychologist. In her pleated skirt and white sweater, she looked more like a cheerleader from the local high school than a thirty-year-old military Ph.D. who had asked Dan about his reactions to the killings. They seemed to be enjoying themselves, she was holding the hand draped on her shoulder and resting her head against the side of his neck. Occasional laughter from both of them floated across to Dan. *Great inter-service co-operation,* Dan thought in gentle amusement.

Paul was leaning against the mantle piece of the large fireplace that contained a small log fire, despite the excellent central heating that warmed the beautiful mansion against the bleakness of February on Long Island. He wore an ancient grey cardigan and a red plaid shirt tucked loosely into the most faded blue jeans Dan had ever seen. On his feet was a pair of bear-feet slippers, complete with toes and claws. He was inordinately proud of those slippers, which, he said, his granddaughter had given him for Christmas.

Emily and Dan sat on either side of the fire place on embroidered cushioned stools, a matched pair which the original owner of the house, apparently a retired owner of a chain of butcher shops, had bought on a trip to Istanbul before World War Two. Emily cradled a crystal glass of scotch and looked, Dan thought, positively edible in close-fitting red ski pants and yellow sweater. She saw him looking at her and smiled warmly. He treated his eyes for a second then looked up again at Paul,

"You think I had already decided to lose the last fight?" asked Dan. "That would mean you had already deprogrammed me, effectively. Does that mean the last battle was unnecessary?" He had a brandy snifter of global shape and size, and periodically lowered his nose to inhale the wisps of fine cognac.

He had spent three weeks in the hospital bed, unable to care for himself, before the doctor would let him out. Even then, he had to move around in the wheelchair for another two weeks until he was able to stand, trembling, shaky, but on his own feet. He had missed Christmas and the New Year, though Emily had crept into his hospital room with a bottle of champagne and two tulip glasses a few minutes before midnight. They had toasted the new year the way Dan had wanted to since meeting Emily the previous spring in Chicago, a glass of bubbly and his lady in his arms. She had cuddled him a few moments more, then left him, his eyes closing almost before she was out of the room.

"No, no! You had to go through it," said Paul, firmly. "I think you had decided to lose all right, but you still needed to experience the trauma of dying for the conditioning to break down finally. The whole process was done in stages."

"It was?" queried Dan. "I thought we just banged away until I finally gave in mentally?" He took another sip of the ambrosia in his glass and let it slide down his insides, soothing some of the pain and stress away. Memories of the horrors of warfare were still making him wake up most nights - the first interrupted nights he had experienced since arriving. He had no idea from where he had picked up the historically accurate details of that battle, but in researching the history books since, in the mansion's library, he had discovered to his fascination that he had the details almost as if he had been there.

"Of course, stages!" said Paul. "If you had tried that last exercise at the beginning, I'm quite certain it would have killed you literally as well as in your hallucination!"

He bent over the fire and poked at the logs with a long brass poker. Sparks flew straight out at him, and he flinched, then repeated the exercise until flames started climbing up the chimney. He hung the brass piece on its stand and stood up.

"The first essential stage was to accept that you were not invulnerable as your programming had taught you, but could be hurt. That happened with amazing effect during the second battle, the one against the trolls, and it was an essential step. It prepared your mind for eventual death."

Emily rose from her seat and moved over to Dan, kneeling against his left knee and taking one hand. The possibilities of Dan's death had been a constant ghost at the dinner table for some weeks now, and they both needed each other for reassurance now that the crisis was over. He squeezed her hand, needing the contact just as much as she did.

"The other interesting indicator throughout the battles," Paul suddenly broke in with a fresh thought, "was the thing we discussed before, how you had your friend from work, David, appear in three of them. I think that showed a clinging to something familiar in your American life that you wanted to retain and help you."

Dan recalled how David's friendly, almost handsome face had provided something for him to hang on to as danger approached.

"But not in the battle with the trolls?" he said. "Why would that be?"

Paul shrugged. "Impossible to say," he answered. "But maybe as we discussed, after the easy victory of the first battle in the Spitfire, you told yourself you didn't need help."

Dan thought about it for a few moments, but was unable to come to any better conclusion. He was pleased that David had helped him in at least three of the battles. He wondered if he could ever tell him about his contribution to Dan's life.

"In running away from the cat in the third battle," Paul continued. "You showed your desire to abandon the Murmansk conditioning and left your mind wide open for the break." He had refilled his brandy balloon in the short pause, and was swirling it around under his nose. "When you dropped your armour and symbolically abandoned your knighthood, you obviously made the emotional break with any remaining loyalty to Gemorov, the KGB and Murmansk. So for your final action, I think you deliberately chose a path that would lead to your destruction as a Russian agent. We can't yet be certain that all the conditioning is broken, however. Remember, we haven't tried the punishment trigger yet."

The physical damage was severe. Just as Dan had created the troll's teeth wounds in his arm and leg in his conviction of what was happening, he had experienced and created quite intensive stomach wounds, nowhere as terrible as a true bayonet would have caused, but enough to require surgery and considerable convalescence. The scars on his leg and arm would eventually fade away, those on his body might never go. It was mid-February before he was able to abandon the wheel chair and take a few short walks outside in the razor sharp winds and sub-zero cold. Snow had been light this year, but enough had fallen for the cross-country ski enthusiasts to follow the trails. Dan had watched from the bay windows with envy and some barely concealed jealousy as Emily had trekked out in the company of the military officers who still seemed to occupy the old house.

He pulled his thoughts back to Paul's last words and shivered at the thought of the punishment trigger. It had to be the last test, and he was hardly confident about it. Emily had said that there was no way of cutting the effect, once the words had been spoken. If the pain still occurred, Dan would have to see the whole thing through to the end unless some alternative could be found. No physical damage was caused by it, at least as far as she knew. Dan felt less confident than he would admit about the extent of her knowledge on the subject.

"I know," he said to Paul, looking down at Emily's beautiful hand held in his own. "Sometime soon we have to. I have business in Chicago." Emily looked up at him at those words. Her expression was sad, but resigned. At some stage, her father had to be thrown to the wolves, and she understood that.

Dan was still uncertain just what he wanted to do about Carson. *Major General Arkady Morayev, you and I have to do some heavy talking,* he thought. He had passed a request to the colonel that he could have some time alone with Carson before the colonel arrested him. He wanted a few moments to humiliate Carson and show him how his plans had failed. Jack Gregory had promised him ten minutes alone with Carson before the colonel's men came in for the arrest. Jack said that Colonel Markbrite had agreed to it. Just leave Carson alive for the arrest to take place, he added. Of course, Dan had agreed, but when he thought about that condition in his private moments, he wondered if he really could go along with it.

The Brandenburg came to an end, and the only sound in the room was the crackle of the wood fire and the murmuring of the couple on the other side of the room.

"But we sure broke the main conditioning!" Paul was looking smug. Dan laughed at the sight of the big, bear-like man in the silly slippers and happy grin on his face. In many ways, he had taken the place of the father that the Murmansk dream-master had planted in Dan's mind, but was as real as any childhood memory. At thirty-five, Dan was not past needing a real-life father figure, and besides, he and Emily needed a grandfather for the kids.

"That we did!" agreed Dan. And they had, too. One memorable morning a few days ago, they had taken their accustomed places in the room of green and white. To underscore the importance of the tests, Colonel Markbrite had flown in. Judging by his appearance he had flown overnight for many hours, whether from an assignment in the Far East, or a vacation in Hawaii, he wouldn't say. His clean new uniform and fresh shave failed to cover up the fatigue in his eyes and the slumped shoulders of extreme jet lag.

"It's great to see you, Dan," he said with apparent sincerity, and shook his hand. Dan gripped the hand with enthusiasm, feeling a considerable debt to the man.

"I'm truly glad you could be here for this exercise, Colonel," he said.

"I hope it works," said Markbrite with a brief smile. "Probably almost as much as you do!"

Dan had no trouble believing that. He watched the colonel make the rounds of greetings with the others, thinking that he probably had risked a chunk of his career on the deal with Dan and Emily. The colonel's meeting with Emily was a curious mix of affection and reserve as he tried to see her as a colleague rather than the enemy she had been for so many years. His handshake with Paul was polite, but with no obvious affection. Dan put it down to Paul's hatred for what the Parthenon project had been. With Jack Gregory, the meeting was between senior officer and subordinate, courteous but distant.

Then they got down to business. Jack and the colonel stood by the doorway, Emily knelt at Dan's knees and took his hand as she had done before, and Paul stood behind him.

The first test was a repeat of the previous one. Emily uttered the control trigger, and the room went silent.

"Misha, you are to remain in your chair until I tell you to stand up," said Emily with a firm tone.

Dan looked at her, trying to measure what, if anything was happening inside his head. Feeling ghosts of thin fingers trying to hold him back, he stood up and walked round the room, his delight growing by the second. He bent down and pulled Emily to her feet, seizing her in a bear-hug. He felt like a man who had lost the use of his legs and found it again.

"I think it works!" he announced to the silent men standing around the room.

"Careful, Misha!" said Paul. "Let's not jump the gun. You may have an inbuilt acceptance of Emily's faith in you. Another voice may have a different effect."

Dan's delight took a plunge in cold water, and he stared anxiously at the psychiatrist.

"Let me try," said Paul, and Dan nodded, feeling a crawling worm of panic in his gut.

"Misha, listen to me," said Paul in Russian. "We are your overseers, we are your legs, oh throne."

The ghosts had died. Dan felt nothing.

"Walk twice round the room, Misha," said Paul. "And pour a glass of water over your head."

Dan grinned happily at him. "No way!" he said. "I had enough of being wet in that last battle I went through!"

"Good," said Paul, his face still serious. "One more try with a new voice. Colonel?"

The colonel surprised Dan with excellent Moscow-accented Russian as he repeated the control trigger. Nothing had an effect. Dan felt the surge of hope beginning to expand his chest, and looked at Emily with a broad grin. She smiled back, but a tinge of uncertainty shadowed her face.

"Second stage, Misha. All right with you?"

Paul was exhibiting a professional air of examination. He obviously wanted the tests to be thorough before he claimed a victory.

With tension in the air, Paul uttered the second command phrase that should have prepared Dan to receive instructions for a mission. Dan felt a slight jolt as Paul spoke the words and he was truly frightened as Paul opened up a sheet of a set of prepared instructions.

"Misha, this is what you will do," said Harrington, and looked down at the paper. "You are to dress for the outdoors immediately, walk out into the grounds and conduct a single-handed attack on the marine guard-house by the main gate."

Dan had been told that the marines had been prepared for the fact that such an attack might take place, and had increased the usual squad of four to a group of ten. All of them remembered the acute embarrassment of his last encounter with them, and Dan was worried that some paybacks might occur.

Dan stayed looking calmly at the others in the room, then went to the coffee urn and poured a cup of coffee, sat down in one of the armchairs and grinned at Paul. "What," he said, "go out in this weather, Harrington? You have to be joking!"

The room was a riot. Dan carefully put down the coffee cup before he was assailed by all of them, slapping him on the back, cheering and jumping up and down in unison. They must have looked amazingly silly for a crowd of adults, Dan thought. He finally got free of the mob to give Paul a hug of sheer delight. The doctor had taken chains from Dan that no man in history had ever borne before, and Dan owed him his life. Finally, he was able to get to Emily, and they simply stayed in the middle of the room holding each other close while her tears of happiness made his shoulder soggy.

Sometime later in the day, Dan felt a curious wave of dizziness go through him, a sudden urge to get his sheepskin coat and go outdoors. Adrenaline flooded into him in preparation for action, muscles cramped a little then eased as the dizziness passed. He looked up to see Paul watching him intently.

"A minor relapse?" Paul questioned. Dan nodded, trying to subdue the cramps and tell himself it was merely a reaction to the excitement.

"It passed," he said, forcing himself to be completely calm.

"To be expected, I suppose," Paul said diffidently, as if the matter was unimportant. But Dan saw him look quickly across at Markbrite who had been watching him intently ever since they had left the green room.

"Maybe." Dan was trembling a little, glad that Emily was not near enough to share the worry.

He noticed that a couple of marines stayed close with him the rest of the day, and the guard in the corridor outside their room was tripled overnight in case the orders took effect in his mind. Dan monitored his own internal tension until he realized that nothing would happen. Nothing did happen that was of interest to the marine guards, while what happened in their bed was of enormous interest to Emily and Dan, but that was another matter entirely.

That was a week ago.

* * *

"Final test, guys."

Paul's voice was edgy from the tension, while Dan felt oddly calm about the whole thing. Paul had decided that if the test failed and the punishment trigger still caused intense pain, he would simply knock Dan out with a needle full of some substance and let him sleep it off.

The hypodermic was in his hands now as he leaned forward to Dan. No straps this time, but otherwise the scene was as before. Colonel Markbrite sat in the fourth armchair in the room, Jack Gregory this time sat upright, but was still in his normal position on the settee. Emily sat on the arm of Dan's chair, a hand on his shoulder, ready to try and hold him if the pain hit.

"If this works, you'll be completely free, and I'll be out of a job!" Paul grinned at Dan.

Dan swallowed. At last, some fear was getting to him. His throat felt tight, and knots of panic ground painfully in his stomach. He felt warning twinges of the pain that he might soon be feeling at full volume. He couldn't respond to Paul's joke.

"Let's do it," he said, trying hard to keep the tremble he was feeling in his body out of his voice.

Paul looked at him with a doctor's stare. He was still concerned that Dan's physical strength was below par, and that any possible effects of the trigger might do more damage, but he had accepted Dan's need to discover the success or otherwise of the last few weeks. After all, Dan had told him, the rest of his life depended on it. Paul took a deep breath, adjusted his hold on the hypodermic needle and leaned forward a little closer.

"Misha, listen to me," he said, and then spoke the words by Yevtoshenko that had been corrupted into a trigger phrase to cause such pain.

Dan looked at him, aware of the dead silence in the room. He could sense Emily's warm presence on his left side, and her perfume touched him gently. A tiny twinge went running behind his right eye and down to his neck, then died. He tried moving his hands, then his feet, and had no difficulty with either. He realized he had been holding his breath and let it out with a gasp.

"Nothing," he said, barely whispering, so frightened was he of the pain that for a second he thought was about to strike so deep into him.

Paul leaned even closer until his eyes filled Dan's view. He stared deep into Dan as if trying to look directly into his brain. "You're sure?" he murmured so softly that nobody else could have heard him.

Dan's heart was beating like a jungle drum, and he felt the pulse on his forehead keeping time. His breathing was ragged, but now with relief, no longer fear.

"I'm sure."

"In that case," said Paul, leaning back with a broad smile, "Colonel, I'm unemployed!"

The only sound was a long drawn-out breath from Markbrite. A lot must have been riding on this project for him, thought Dan. A small sob came from above him, and Emily swung down from the arm of the chair neatly into his lap.

"Has it really happened?" she whispered into his right ear. "Dan, my love, are we really done with this thing?"

"It's done!" Dan said joyously, kissed her cheek, wiped two small tears from her eyes, gave her a hug, then they both stood up. The congratulations from Paul, Jack Gregory and Markbrite were more restrained than the last time, but the happiness and relief in the room were almost tangible. Dan turned to Allen Markbrite, while keeping his right arm firmly round Emily's waist. He didn't ever want to let go.

"Colonel, time to get back to Chicago, I think?"

"Indeed so, Dan." The fatigue in Markbrite's eyes had vanished, and he seemed to be standing upright without the jet-lagged slump he had carried when he first walked in. "We all have a date with General Morayev."

Dan felt Emily's hand in his gave a hard squeeze. This was still a dreadful final act she had to see, the destruction of her father. Whatever she thought of him, it was going to be painful.

"Ladies and gentlemen, it is time to pack our bags and leave." Jack Gregory made the announcement as if he was a host on a cruise ship about to reach port and everybody broke from their positions around the room and began to drift to the door.

"Paul, which way are you going?" Emily asked and they both turned to him.

"My car is here," said Harrington. "I'll drive down to Washington. There's work to be done at the university, and these few weeks have given me incredible insights into some new therapies I want to work on. I'll see you both again?"

They both grinned at him. Dan knew that tears were not far away for any of them. "If you're not at the wedding, we'll come gunning for you!" he said. "We want you to give Emily away."

Paul put a hand on each of their shoulders. "I wouldn't miss it for the world," he said. "Just don't do it when the Redskins are playing at home! And even if you do, I'll still come!"

Emily gave him a hug, he and Dan shook hands once more and they parted. Dan and Emily went back to their room to pack, still not completely certain that they would be able to leave. But two hours later they were in a limousine heading for La Guardia and a standard commercial flight to O'Hare.

They spoke little on the flight. Dan revelled in his new freedom, knowing he had broken off the shackles that the KGB had placed on him so many years ago. They held hands, ordered a couple of drinks from a smiling stewardess who seemed to think they were a honeymoon couple, and read the papers to see what had been happening in the world while they had lived in the artificial universe of Project Parthenon headquarters.

At O'Hare they took another limousine home to Dan's apartment. It had been nearly five months since Dan had last been there, and they both felt a little nervous as he opened the door. But nothing had changed.

Dan took the bags into the bedroom, adjusted the heat, walked back into the kitchen, opened the fridge and to his delight, found a bottle of Veuve Cliquot ready chilled for them. The cork popped with gusto, and he poured the golden chains of bubbles into two tall tulip glasses, watching the display with the delight of a blind man who has been given eyes. Everything was so new and exhilarating in his freshly discovered world.

"Miss Morayeva?" he called.

"By the phone," she answered. "Misha, you'd better come here."

He carried the glasses into the lounge where she was standing by the answering system attached to the telephone. The green light was winking slowly. Messages were waiting for them.

"I've been checking our messages from the mansion every few days," said Emily. "Greshtyenka has called several times over the last few weeks, and getting increasingly panicky about getting no reply."

"When did you check last?" asked Dan.

"Four days ago," she replied. "So there shouldn't be too many messages here. I don't know if Greshtyenka's called since the last time I checked."

"Would you like to guess?" he asked, handing her a glass.

"I'll bet she's on there," Emily answered, looking nervous. "I know you've been deprogrammed, but just in case, I'm petrified that it might still work if one of those two speaks to you."

"Then we'd better try it and see, while you're here to countermand anything they might do," he said with determination and pressed the "play" button. The tape rewound while they watched it almost spellbound. It clicked and began to play.

Silence... beep. Another foiled marketer bit the dust. Silence... beep. Yet again. Then a male voice, a wondrously familiar voice. "Dan, when you get back, give me a call at home." *I will, David, I promise,* thought Dan. Silence... beep. Strike three against the telephone marketers. Beep... "Mister Bailey, your condominium fees are overdue. Please call me as soon as possible."

"Oh damn!" A shocked gasp came from Emily. "The one thing I forgot! I'd paid two months in advance, never thought it would take this long."

Silence... beep.

It was there.

"Misha, listen to me. Consider doing something special for the Party. You will come to Mister Carson's office at eight o'clock tomorrow morning."

That same thin voice. Dan stared at the whirling tape, conscious of Emily's frightened eyes on him.

Silence ... beep. Another determined salesperson. Beep... "Misha, listen to me. Consider doing something special for the Party. You *will* come to Mister Carson's office at eight o'clock tomorrow morning." The sharp edge of anxiety was clearly defined in her voice.

"Greshtyenka," said Dan. "You can go to Hell!"

Then they drank their toast in one of the best champagnes in the world and went to bed, laughing like kids playing hooky on the first beautiful day of spring.

Chapter 11

Stepping along the icebound sidewalks of Madison Street watching his breath swirl in the breezes of the Windy City; walking up the few steps to the lobby of the glass tower, remembering the first time he had ever made this trip, how nervously he had approached the start of the nightmare; remembering the second time, raging inside at his serfdom to Carson's feudal control over him; this was the third time, and Dan felt different.

Two young men walked with him, a pace or two behind. They had given him no names, no handshake when the Colonel pointed them out to Dan. Fraternal twins, similar height and build, the same expressionless, cloned features, minor differences only in hair colour, ear shape, a yellow paisley-pattern tie on one, a red and black striped tie on the other. They wore identical dark blue suits and scorned the use of winter coats.

"Ten minutes, right?" The colonel had looked hard at Dan from the seat in the rear of the limousine in which the four of them had travelled the short distance from the Michigan Avenue offices. "At least leave us enough to take back in a single bag, okay?"

That passed for humor with the colonel, Dan decided, and gave an appropriate smile.

"Ten minutes, and he can walk out under his own steam, Colonel," he responded then he climbed out onto the sidewalk with his two escorts, the limousine remaining in a position that with any other license plate would have received a parking ticket and the attention of Chicago's finest.

Dan paused in the cavernous lobby to thaw out his face, the chill having struck even in the thirty or forty yards from the warmth of the limousine. He unbuttoned the heavy sheepskin, and let the warmth cover him. For all his calmness, Dan felt uncertain, even frightened. The next few minutes could bring catastrophe.

The crowd was thinning as the hour passed nine in the morning. Most of the workers were in their places, though some still scurried from the newspaper shop and the coffee bar, carrying brown paper bags with their regular coffee, two sugars and a Danish to eat with the reading of the *Chicago Tribune*. Two young men stood by the expanse of glass protecting them from the cold, looking outward as they killed the last few minutes before an appointed hour. They wore extra-well polished shoes, and freshly-pressed dark suits with new shirts. Dan wished them well in their forthcoming job interviews, imagining that they were nervous and excited, much as he was, but for different reasons.

He led the way across the black and white chequered tiles of the lobby, past the security desk where the uniformed guards cast cold, suspicious eyes first on him, then on his escorts. Dan watched in amusement as they obviously made a professional recognition of the two men with him, but said nothing. Their conversation after they had gone would make interesting listening, he thought.

They reached the elevators and waited for the first one to come. Two other people, one a middle-aged man in a black wool coat, the other a messenger from one of the parcel delivery firms stood with them, but something menacing in the presence of Dan's group must have warned them, for they stood aside to let them into the elevator and declined to join them. As the doors closed between them, Dan smiled politely at the man in the black wool coat, and he looked away, confused and nervous. Dan Bailey, what has happened to you in the last few months? he wondered. It was not just the silent musclemen with him, he knew. Something in him was giving people cause to think, and perhaps avoid him.

As they ascended to the Hanfield Group office he almost laughed at the picture reflecting back from the shiny metal doors of the elevator. He stood in the front, dressed casually in blue jeans and a sweater under his heavy sheepskin coat, flanked by two obvious bodyguards in dark suits, white shirts and formal ties. All they needed were dark glasses. Al Capone couldn't have done it better. Dan wished he could have a photograph of the scene. After today, he would probably return to a conventional world. He hoped so. Nervous tension began to gnaw at him, and he shifted the coat on his shoulders. His escorts said nothing.

At the thirty-second floor he walked straight past the beautiful receptionist at her desk and hung his coat in the closet by the kitchen, then ignored her and began to walk down to the corridor.

She leapt to her feet. "Excuse me!" she called, starting to move out of her enclosure and follow him. "Sir!..."

One of the young men blocked her way, took a wallet out of his breast pocket and flashed it at her. She said nothing, helplessly holding her hands to her cheeks, staring transfixed at the wallet. She subsided back to her desk as Dan continued his walk alone.

It seemed to take hours, that short stretch from the lobby to the corner office. Dan was aware of every step, of the feel of the carpet under his shoes, of the slight odour of cleaning fluid, of the gleam of polish on the doors of the other offices. He could hear his breath rasping in his nostrils and the pulse beating in his neck. His throat was dry, and he paused to drink from the water cooler on his left. With a powerful sense of *déjà vu,* he saw that one office was again occupied by three young men with anxiety all over their faces as they studied a computer terminal. He wondered if it was the same problem they had faced back in the summer.

The door to Carson's office was closed. Dan heard a murmur of voices behind it. He paused for a few seconds with his hand on the heavy brass handle, took a deep breath, then opened the heavy door. Inside, three men, two women, Carson and the thin figure of Sasha Greshtyenka sat around a polished table.

Dan recognized two of the other men. One of them was a political figure in the state's government, a tall, white-haired man of enormous photogenic qualities and reputedly the morals and business ethics of a sewer rat. The other man was an eminent banker who featured often in news events, current affairs television programs and high society activities. The third man Dan did not know, nor either of the two women, both dressed in smartly-cut dark suits. Seven sets of eyes turned on Dan in varying degrees of surprise. He closed the door behind himself and leaned his right shoulder on it, folding his arms.

"Good morning, ladies and gentlemen," he smiled to the group at large. "The meeting is, unfortunately, cancelled." *Good stuff, Misha,* he said to himself, *that sounded nice and authoritative.* Just as well, because he had been trying to calm his nerves for the last hour or so.

The political figure turned a noble profile to Dan to look at Carson. "Vincent, what the hell is ..." he started, his voice nothing like the carefully controlled baritone he used for public speaking. He fell silent as he saw the expression on Carson's face. He looked closely at Greshtyenka and saw something in her that made him turn back to Dan with expectancy in his eyes.

"Vincent?" said Dan, and smiled broadly. "Maybe you should all be reintroduced? Ladies and gentlemen, may I present to you your host this morning, Major General Arkady Morayev, Red Army and one-time KGB?"

A cackle of amusement broke from the banker, but the rest of the room was silent. The banker looked round at everyone, the smile fading from his lips as he twisted around finally to stare at Dan. Dan was dangerously close to hysteria, and he swallowed, wondering what was wrong with him. The banker gave him a last look and turned to Carson who broke the silence.

"All right everybody," said Carson, his voice subdued, not looking at Dan. "I'll clear this matter up, and my secretary will call you to reschedule. It would be better if we finish up now while I attend to this regrettable interruption."

The room stirred as everyone rose to their feet and gathered papers into briefcases. The banker replaced his jacket from the back of his chair, looking at Dan as he did. Nobody spoke, except for a few muttered words between the white-haired politician and one of the women, who nodded and scrawled a quick note on her papers.

Dan watched the small activities, struggling to maintain his control. The politician carried only a paper-thin document bag made of what looked like crocodile skin and he had no papers to transfer to it from the gleaming white surface of the table. The small buzz of activity finished, the visitors filed toward the door. Dan opened it courteously for them to leave, and they filed past him, either staring curiously, or averting their eyes firmly. Finally, Dan closed the door behind the last one, one of the elegant young women, who passed in a small cloud of Chanel Number 5. Just for the hell of it, Dan winked at her as she passed, and she dropped her eyes in confusion. Dan remembered with a sharp sense of worry that Paul had warned him that in this situation, knowing that he was free of Carson's control, he might experience the light-heartedness of the end of school term, or the finish of the last exam paper, and might be a little light-headed. With that recollection came complete self control.

Dan looked at Carson and the woman. They both stared back at him and broke into speech together, so rushed were they.

"Misha, listen to me," they said in unison. "We are your overseers, we are your legs, oh throne."

Dan looked back at them and stood motionless. A small smile broke out on Carson's face and Greshtyenka seemed to slump a little in relief.

"Sit down, Misha," said Carson, waving at the chair across from his desk. He walked round to his seat and sat down, watching Dan as he did the same. Carson's confidence seemed fully restored. Greshtyenka came round to his side and moved a chair next to him, sitting down with her hands neatly in her lap. He looked briefly at her in irritation, then turned back to Dan.

"Misha, where have you been hiding from us?"

"In New York," Dan replied, his voice toneless.

Carson paused a moment, considering the import of Dan's words. "That was disobedient of you." His voice was perfectly calm. "You set my plans back considerably. What were you doing in New York?"

"Trying to break free of you."

Carson smiled, totally at ease now. "How foolish, Misha!" he said, as if chiding Dan for buying an unfashionable car or suit. "The conditioning is far too deeply implanted for you to break it. You would need expert help, and the only people who could give it would rather kill you. Not that they could do anything, anyway. Our expertise in these matters is far ahead of the Americans."

Dan said nothing. Greshtyenka was studying him with interest, the traces of alarm still in her eyes. She fidgeted with the gold band round her wrist, and when she saw Dan look at her, swung her gaze to Carson.

"And where exactly in New York were you?" asked Carson, his voice friendly and interested, like an uncle asking a favourite nephew how he had spent his vacation.

"Southampton, on Long Island," Dan answered tonelessly.

That got to him. "Southampton? At the CIA's Parthenon headquarters?" Carson's composure was clearly disrupted and the friendly uncle pose vanished. He had evidently not expected anything like that.

"Was Emily with you?" he asked. Dan could see the sudden strain on the flat, peasant face. He wondered if Carson's anxiety regarding Emily was from the loss of his primary assistant or from the betrayal by his daughter.

"Yes, she was," Dan replied. "She took me there." He could feel his breathing trying to accelerate, and forced control over himself. The final crisis was yet to come.

A shadow passed over Carson's face, leaving a heavy frown. "We shall have to deal with her separately. Disloyalty is a serious crime." He paused for a few seconds staring at his hands in thought, clearly not enjoying the images going through his mind.

"And so, back to you, Misha!" He lifted his eyes to Dan and smiled. The pleasant uncle had returned. "Obviously the CIA psychiatrists were not able to do anything for you, though you must have thought they had, by the way you walked in here!" He turned his face to the woman to share his joke and was rewarded by a glowing smile from the thin lips that were coloured an unsightly pink shade.

His smug joke over, Carson returned to business. "I have need of your professional skills again, Misha," he said, the remnant of the smile still on his face. "When we are done here, Sasha will take you to her office and brief you. The assignment will be carried out tonight. But before you go, we do have one unpleasant duty that must be performed."

Dan looked at him without expression. A crawling worry wriggled in his bowels. He could not forget the horrors Carson had visited on him the first time Dan had sat in this chair. He began to wish he had not opted for this course of bravado. What if things went wrong?

"You have to be punished, Misha," Carson said with a frown. "I will not condone your pathetic attempts at treachery to Russia and to me."

A gleam was appearing in his eyes, and in Greshtyenka's face a look of pleasurable anticipation had replaced the prim coolness that she had displayed until now.

"Please, Comrade General," she said. "Let me. He has been rude to me so much. I owe him this and he deserves it."

It was the longest speech Dan had ever heard from her, except when she had briefed him over the phone for his missions. He didn't like the voice. It was sharp, a whining voice better suited to complaining than praising.

Carson looked at her, considered for a moment, and then with some reluctance, nodded, looking disappointed. But on Greshtyenka's face a smile of delight had flowered. She turned to look at Dan, paused for a second to get maximum pleasure from the moment then opened her mouth.

"Misha, listen to me," she said, and took another few seconds to extract even more happiness from the experience. Dan turned his head to her as she expected. She spoke the punishment trigger and sat back to watch with pleased expectation.

Dan looked calmly back at her and saw the sudden doubt grow into horror. He let a slow, ragged breath flow from his lungs, realizing that he had been holding it for some moments. He turned his eyes to Carson, who pushed his chair back as if to move away from a sudden threat, staring wide-eyed at Dan.

"Sorry, children," said Dan with a small smile. He was feeling exhilarated as the test came and went. "I don't think I want to play that game anymore."

The office was silent. The three of them looked at each other, and Dan began to hear the sounds of the woman's tortured breathing gradually becoming little whimpers.

"You see," he said gently. "You were wrong. The people who could help me were happy to do so. And they did an excellent job, as you can obviously detect. And while we were working on that project, Emily was ensuring that your colleagues in the KGB were shutting up shop everywhere else."

Like a malfunctioning robot, Carson poured himself a glass of water from a carafe on his desk. As he drank, Dan could hear the rattle of the glass against his teeth.

"I'm sorry to disappoint you," Dan continued. "But I have a game of my own I'd like to try out on you both."

The two of them stared back at Dan, who smiled cheerfully, totally relaxed now that the crisis had come and gone. *The KGB controls were truly dead,* he exulted.

"Remember when you told me what a wonderful thing it was that nobody from home knew you were here?" Dan continued pleasantly. Carson didn't move a muscle, simply kept staring at Dan.

"I'm afraid that it's going to work against you, General," said Dan. "If the Russians knew about you, they'd demand your return, and we'd have to comply. But they don't. So we don't have to do anything. And all through the last few weeks, the one thing I was dreaming about was coming in here and killing you both."

Carson choked as he tried to say something, cleared his throat then spoke in a strangled whisper. "You can't do that! All I have to do is call for help right now. The police will arrest you immediately! You couldn't get ten feet from here!"

"Don't be silly, General," said Dan with a smile. "The CIA knows all about you, obviously. Your daughter made quite certain of that. They'll be very happy to take you away from here, and that's the last the world will ever hear of you. You'll vanish into the darkest pit we can find. You might want to ask yourself why your receptionist saw all your visitors leave well ahead of time, saw me come down here without checking with her, and hasn't tried to contact you."

Carson's face went white, and several swallows tried to work their way down his throat. A low keening sound began from the woman. They had both got the message.

"That's right, General," said Dan, exhilaration beginning to be replaced by a cold rage at the two people before him. He had never had any intention of carrying out his threat on these two, he had simply wanted a moment of triumph over them. But as his fury grew, he started to have small doubts about what his actions might be in the next few minutes. "I have a couple of men at the desk," he continued. "They have instructions to leave me alone with you, and then come in for the bodies afterward. They have no interest in holding a couple of Russian agents for the rest of their lives. The people in Southampton made that quite clear to me. Everything will be much easier this way."

"Misha, please," said Carson. His voice was high pitched. "I was only serving the Soviet Union! It was never personal, please Misha, you have to believe me... My God, Misha, you can't..."

"God, Vincent? God has no place in this," said Dan. With that, the anger in him died a little. He had not realized the extent to which that arrogant phrase from Carson had bothered him for so long, and the chance to throw it back at his tormentor was too good to miss. Silence reigned in the room for a few seconds, as Carson seemed to gather himself, looked sideways at Greshtyenka and took a deep breath. Dan felt the tension level rise.

Carson leaned forward, elbows on the surface and looked at Dan. Sudden menace appeared in his voice. "This is all very plausible, Misha, but just how do you plan to kill us both?"

Dan felt doubts erupt. What other weapons did Carson have? What had he forgotten when he planned this exploit?

"You know my training, General," Dan replied, fighting to keep control of his voice. "Don't you believe I can kill you here and now without working up a sweat?"

Carson sneered, and Dan felt a wave of panic. This was not going according to plan. He saw a twitch in Greshtyenka, and her eyes flashed briefly to Carson's lap. Carson put his hands below the desk and stood up. He had a nine-millimetre automatic in his right hand, and it began to move toward Dan.

Sergeant Kutchinski's Murmansk training took over without Dan's conscious effort. Dan threw himself sideways out of the chair, rolled against the wall beside Carson's desk, and straightened his legs, flying like a spear straight at Carson. One hand chopped hard down on Carson's right wrist, and Carson screamed as the bone snapped. The pistol flew in an arc, struck one of the paintings on the wall and fell to the floor.

Like a cobra striking, Greshtyenka went for the gun.

Dan followed her, even faster, grabbed her round the neck as she reached for the weapon and threw her backward, directly into Carson's chest. Both of them collapsed, winded, but the woman rose to her knees first.

Dan's rage boiled over. He swung his right arm and delivered a full blooded blow with the flat of his hand to the left side of her face. She was flung against the wall, her head struck with a dull thud, and she stared, glassy-eyed, and barely conscious.

Carson was on his knees, about to try and stand, and Dan's rage was still thundering through him like the lava eruption of a volcano. He seized Carson by the front of his shirt, hauled him upright and released him, ignoring the man's screech of pain from his shattered wrist. Carson's eyes were wide, terrified. Dan felt a wave of intense hatred flood through his body and a deep desire to kill. With a massive sensation of emotional release, he straightened his fingers and was about to drive a killing blow through Carson's face. At the last moment, something stopped him. The scream of blood lust in his head died, to be replaced by simple anger at the man before him.

Dan slammed a fist into Carson's gut and as he doubled up with a groan, Dan hit him hard on the side of the head. Carson collapsed against his desk and Dan saw movement against the wall. He turned, saw Greshtyenka again reach for the gun, and he was a shade too late. She grabbed it, pointed it, and as she fired, Dan threw himself sideways.

The explosion of the gun was horrific. The glasses and teapot on the table rattled, the windows seemed to shake, and Dan's ears rang. A long, ugly groove appeared in the side of Carson's black desk. The woman screamed harshly, her face a dreadful mask of hatred. She followed Dan's movements with the gun, trying to get a bead on him again.

The door flung open, and Dan's escorts raced in, guns drawn.

"What the hell?..." shouted one, and saw the terrible sight of Greshtyenka, the gun still in her hand, pointing it in the man's general direction. His reflexes took over, and a second explosion filled the room. It took the woman in the chest, and blood splattered over the two paintings on the wall. She was dead instantly, her body sliding to the carpet. She twitched just once then subsided. The thin torso was almost demolished, a horrible mess of blood, body tissue and charred bits of her woollen dress.

The two men stood breathing hard, staring round the room. Carson was still immobile, but was returning to consciousness, emitting harsh groans of pain.

"Colonel Markbrite is going to be mad at you, Mister Bailey," said the second agent. "I don't think this was what he expected." The one who had fired the shot was moving to the body of the woman with care. He kicked the gun away from the outstretched dead hand, then picked it up. The stink of explosive was overwhelming, mixing with the raw scent of blood.

Dan shrugged, his breathing slowly returning to normal and his ears regaining their function.

"I doubt it," he said. "I promised him he'd get Carson in one piece. So take him. The woman is of no value to him."

"Are you coming with us, sir?" the agent asked.

Sir? *That was interesting,* thought Dan. He had done something to earn their respect, he gathered. He shook his head. "Tell the colonel I'll call in tomorrow," he said. "I think we've completed our contract, and I want to go back to work in a normal manner."

The tiniest smile broke the stony features of the young man. "I'll tell him, sir," he said. He pulled a tiny radio from his breast pocket and spoke briefly into it. Both of them tucked their guns away again, and the other one gestured at Carson who had regained a semblance of awareness. Carson followed him, holding his broken wrist with his other hand, and they walked out of the office. Dan watched him leave, struggling to understand his emotions. Triumph, mixed with sadness, he thought. But he also felt anger at himself. This episode had been grandstanding, he realized. It had been unnecessary. Still, he thought, those heavy blows to both Carson and Greshtyenka had burned away much of the hatred within him.

The remaining agent looked at Dan. "A crew will be here soon to take care of..." He gestured at the shrunken shape on the carpet. "I think you should leave, sir."

Dan took a last look round the room. So much of his life had happened here. He had died, he had been reborn. He had suffered and been revenged. Dan never wanted to see the damned place again. He decided some improvements were still appropriate. Under the curious gaze of the agent, he walked to the blinds and opened them to the full glare of the bright winter sun over the lake. He stepped over the shrunken body of Greshtyenka and went to each of the blood-splattered battle scene paintings in turn, lifted them off their hooks and rested them on the floor, turning them face to the wall.

"That's a lot better," he said, and walked out.

In the lobby the scene was like a major road accident. Everybody had heard the gunshots and the floor was crowded. The silence was extraordinary as the employees of the Hanfield Group watched their president being led away, head bowed. At the moment when the silence was greatest, the door to the elevator opened and Colonel Markbrite walked out into the lobby.

He stopped short as if astounded, staring at Vincent Carson. His gaze turned to Dan, and Dan was astonished to see an expression of fury cross the colonel's face.

Baffled, he watched Markbrite exchange a few muttered words with his agent. The younger man kept hold of Carson's arm while he replied to his boss, shaking his head at the colonel's questions.

Confused by Markbrite's anger, Dan walked to the closet to collect his sheepskin coat, and the crowds parted in front of him like the Red Sea before Moses, a zone of silence surrounding him while the pressure of hundreds of eyes almost made his skin crawl. Somebody must have called the police on hearing the shots, because there were four uniforms in the lobby also. One of them advanced on the colonel and his agent escorting Carson. A swift check on identity badges and the officer moved back, speaking softly into his radio.

Dan stood back, and let the colonel and the agent take their prisoner into the elevator alone. He could not have faced the ride down with them. He received a final stare of frustrated rage from Markbrite as the elevator door closed.

The crowd gradually dissipated until Dan stood alone in the lobby with the receptionist. Her face was white, but with her immaculate make-up, detecting her degree of shock was not easy.

"I think you had better call all your senior vice-presidents together," Dan said gently to her. "You have some urgent business to clear up."

She didn't move other than to give a tiny nod, and Dan walked to the elevators for his final departure from the offices of the Hanfield Group. He didn't stop trembling until he was on the ground level.

Chapter 12

Heatwave time in Chicago again, and Dan had moved chairs and table out to the balcony, and they were relaxing with beers in their hands, looking over the park.

Paul Harrington was wearing a bright red shirt decorated with a picture of the galaxy. Just below the breast pocket was an arrow pointing to a celestial speck. Below that was the legend "You are here." His blue jeans were as faded as the pair Dan had last seen him wearing.

Emily was stretched out in one of the chairs, dressed in white shorts and a yellow halter top, highly distracting to both men. Dan felt that his own shorts and blue shirt were quite dull beside both of them.

"Definitely the life!" said Paul, taking a deep pull at his beer mug.

"The company helps," smiled Emily. "We're really glad you could come over for the weekend."

"Well, the timing was good," said Paul, gasping a little from the beer. "I've been doing some amazing research at Hopkins the last few weeks, and we've begun to develop therapies we could never have dreamed of last year. We have you to thank for that, Misha. So the University of Chicago wanted me to join in a conference on mental health and tell them about it. Without mentioning your name of course."

He took another mouthful and sighed happily.

"I've also been doing some more work for Markbrite, just cleaning up the notes on your deprogramming, and I got some information you might like."

"On my father?" Emily leaned forward, tension showing in the lines of her arms and body.

Paul nodded.

They had heard nothing since the day of Dan's last confrontation with Carson, and the silence was the sole source of tension in the marriage. Not that Emily blamed Dan for the way in which he had hit back at Carson. She had listened carefully as Dan had told her how close he had come to administering a killing blow to the General, and how something had stopped him at the last moment. The violent death of Greshtyenka had no impact on her, other than to give her a sense of relief, and she understood the need for Dan's confrontation with Carson. She had no love for her father, quite the opposite, but enough emotional connection existed that she wanted to know what had happened. It was important to both of them that Dan had not been the instrument of Carson's death.

"Markbrite finally told me what happened to him," said Harrington. "He's approved my telling you. Not that I particularly cared whether he approved or not. You have to know."

"Paul, what happened?" Emily's face showed her strain.

"They kept him here in Chicago for a few days after you handed him over to them last March," said Harrington. "There was some debate about trying him for murder, but they felt they could never make that one stick. Too complicated, and too public, especially after the effort to get the other guy to confess to the killings that Carson had made you do."

Dan sat back and buried his face in his own beer mug. The pain of those dreadful events would never truly fade, however he tried to tell himself that he could not have prevented them. He had been totally under somebody else's control and no more to blame than the gun and the knife he had used to kill the men. The pain was still raw, and sometimes he woke at night to find himself weeping. Emily touched his shoulder and he smiled at her, grateful for the understanding.

"That course of action was out," continued Paul. "Finally, our guys notified the Russian authorities that we had him. That caused a riot! They had no idea of his presence in the country at all!"

"That figures," chimed in Emily. "The whole project had always been highly restricted. Few people knew about the Murmansk camp, even fewer knew about the Gemorov project. When they closed it down, it was part of a general budget cut and change of political directions with Gorbachev. We just got lost in the shuffle."

"That's right," nodded Paul. "Imagine the reaction when we told them about it! Coming on top of the damage you had already done by giving Markbrite details of all the other unauthorized KGB projects going on here, we had them eating out of our hand! It was a sort of mass Russian collective guilt trip!"

He poured a considerable portion of beer down his throat and took another deep breath.

"Please, Paul, what happened then?" Emily was almost pleading. Harrington looked into his beer mug and seemed to be considering something. With a small tremor of worry, Dan thought that Paul was building up to unpleasant information.

"After weeks of negotiations, we agreed to exchange the General for some of our people still held over there," Paul continued. "About two months ago, one of Markbrite's teams of cool young men escorted him to Kennedy, put him on an Aeroflot plane going non-stop to Moscow and waved him a cheerful goodbye. I could almost feel sorry for him, having to endure eight hours of

Aeroflot in-flight service, but after what he had done to Misha, I didn't."

The little joke didn't seem funny, somehow. Dan felt that Paul was under too much strain. Something unpleasant was imminent.

"Have you heard anything else since?" Emily's anxiety was intense. Paul nodded, and now his face was white with strain. Dan felt muscles tensing, almost as if physical action was about to be needed. *Don't be a fool*, he said to himself, and tried to relax.

"We've heard that he was arrested on arrival in Moscow," said Paul. "I understand that there will be no trial, not in public anyway. Too embarrassing for the Russian administration."

A moment of silence echoed round the balcony, broken only by the sounds of birds in the park and the hum of the ever-present traffic several floors below. The shouts of children playing in the park were a backdrop to the scene.

Emily stood up and walked into the sitting room, her face frozen. Dan stood to follow her, but she waved him back to his chair. He realized that she needed a few moment's privacy to make her own final farewells to her father. Dan had no illusions about Carson's fate. For all the recent changes in Russia, Major General Arkady Morayev was still a likely candidate for a bullet in the back of the head following a brief and private trial.

Five minutes later, Emily returned, carrying a fresh glass of champagne, and took her seat. Her face was calm and she seemed self-controlled.

"I take it," she said, "that Colonel Markbrite has completed his analyses of all the information I gave him? I hope he doesn't want any more."

"No, the colonel has other plans for you both," replied Paul. He put his tankard of beer down by the side of his chair and looked at Dan, then at Emily. His face was deadly serious and something in his expression sent Dan's insides churning with fear. Emily saw it too, and sat up.

"Paul?" she said, hesitantly.

Harrington stared hard at her, and swallowed, as if preparing himself for something, and his eyes were cold, no longer the friendly bear who had saved Dan. Just as Dan recognized where he had seen this before, just as he was leaping up from his chair, just as he was preparing to slam his heavy beer mug on Harrington's greying head, the psychiatrist spoke.

"Telemachus Code Zebra-5709," he said, and old, familiar bonds fell about Dan and pushed him back into his chair. Next to him, he heard the crash as Emily's glass fell to the floor of the balcony and shattered on the concrete. It had happened to her, too.

With a flood of despair, Dan stared at Paul. Like a prisoner released from years of jail only to be arrested again after a few days, he felt panic, rage, sickness, all at the same time. He thought how Emily must be feeling, to experience this for the first time, and wished he'd had time to attack Paul before he had spoken.

"Do you think we would let two highly conditioned operatives like you go unattached?" said Paul. Dan could not speak, and assumed Emily was similarly frozen.

"After we had learned so much about you," continued Paul. "How your conditioning was achieved and how to use it, do you think we would waste a resource like you, Misha?"

He looked hard into Dan's eyes and seemed satisfied that his control over him was total. "And you, Galina Sergeyvna," he said, switching his attention to Emily. "How could we let a gold mine of information walk away from us, without wishing to be certain that we could call on you again?" He watched both of them for several seconds before speaking further.

"It was easy with you, Misha," he said with a small smile, and almost, for just a moment, he was Paul, the friendly bear, the man who had stood next to Emily at their wedding. "When I had you under control during the private sessions, while I was certainly planting the mechanisms to let you break free of Moscow's control, I was planting a few triggers of my own." He turned his eyes to Emily.

"And with you, my dear, it was less easy, but still possible. Every night you slept, we took over both of you. Nerve gas when you were asleep, then several hours of intensive conditioning under deep hypnotic control."

A moment of intense silence covered the balcony, and the sounds of the city beneath sounded muffled, a thousand miles away, heard through a poor telephone line. Dan remembered how he and Emily had commented on how well they seemed to be sleeping at the mansion house, despite the tension and stress they were undergoing. Now he understood why.

Emily broke the silence. "There's something I don't understand," she said. Her voice was harsh, grating, whether through anger or fear, Dan couldn't detect.

Paul looked at her and smiled as if discussing events with a favourite niece. "And what's that, my dear?" he asked.

"The CIA had never been able to develop this sort of control before," she rasped. "You said that yourself. And I know about the failures of your previous attempts." She paused, breathing hard, as if the words had been a severe effort. A small line of sweat was on her forehead.

"So how come," she continued, "you've suddenly developed the skills to put me under control like this after three months?"

Dan had been wondering the same thing. It raised the abilities of Markbrite's team to frightening levels of possibility.

Paul Harrington grinned at them with real pride. "You always were a very bright woman, Emily," he said. "And you're quite right, we could never have done this without help."

A crawling sense of desperation made Dan shiver. Help? Only one person in the world could have helped Harrington do what he had done.

"His name is Anton Voltzec," said Paul, and took a drink of his beer. "He was the chief psychiatrist in Murmansk, a Czech who had worked many years with the KGB. Dan knows him very well, of course." Paul looked at Dan with a friendly smile. "Anton has been with us for a couple of years, now."

The old man with the startling blue eyes! The man who had tortured Dan with the sensory deprivation tanks for the three years of the Blank Days. The Murmansk operation must have worked hard these last few years, thought Dan, feeling sick with fear. They had reduced the twelve year process of conditioning to only three months. What in the world could stop them now? One thing puzzled him. He tried to speak, found his throat tight like twisted rope, and swallowed. This time he was able to force some words through the constriction.

"If Voltzec is with you now," he asked, "why bother breaking the conditioning in me? Why not just use the old triggers?"

Harrington smiled with admiration. "An excellent question, Misha," he said. "The trouble is that several people in Murmansk and in Moscow know about those triggers, just as you anticipated. We had to clean them out and replace the old triggers with our own controls so that nobody else could use you except us."

The answer settled Dan's curiosity, but jangled his nerves even more.

Harrington stood up, taking his beer mug with him and towered over the other two. His presence had gone from being the protective, bulky old man, to a menacing, overwhelming threat.

"This control is tighter than the one imposed on you by the old trigger," he said. "You cannot move, until I tell you, and you will obey all commands to the letter. So now, Misha, tell me your thoughts."

Dan felt his tongue loosening, and fought for control over his insides that threatened to explode sickness over him, the way it had when Carson had first thrown his net over his soul.

"Is this official policy, *Doctor* Harrington?" he said. "Or is it just something you and the colonel have cooked up between you?"

Paul smiled a cold smile of satisfaction. "How very formal, Misha!" he said. "How could it be official? The whole Parthenon Project never existed! That was just a CIA slush fund that the President and Congress knew nothing about. Not even the CIA rulers knew about it, and we've closed the whole thing down, anyway. The house on Long Island has been vacated. The people there have been returned to their units under secrecy oaths that they naturally cannot ever break. No, it's just a private operation between the colonel and me. We have some thoughts about using your specialist skills."

Dan knew better than to argue. Memories of the punishment trigger that Vincent Carson had been able to use to burn his brain were still too close to risk Paul Harrington having devised another one. Dull hopelessness washed through him like polluted water. To have escaped and been captured again. What further agonies waited for Emily and him now?

"And so what do you plan, *Doctor?*" He snarled the last word, hatred his only weapon against a man he had trusted so deeply.

"We meet with the colonel in an hour," said Harrington, unmoved by Dan's tone. "We will drive into the city, we three, and visit the same offices where you first met him. On this beautiful Sunday afternoon, we will have the place to ourselves, and we can discuss our future plans. So, Misha, Galina, please rise and follow me."

With the familiar sensation of being a puppet controlled by invisible cords, Dan rose to his feet. As Emily did the same, he was able to see her face and their eyes met for a few seconds. Her face was white, her jaws were clamped tight so that Dan could see the muscles grinding, and her eyes raged bitterly but silently.

"Find your car keys, Misha," said Paul. "You will drive us to the office."

Dan walked to his study and located his keys on the desk next to his computer. Paul walked to the front door and opened it, and Emily and Dan followed him out, letting it close behind them. They stopped behind Harrington at the elevator while he pushed the button.

They stood silently until the elevator arrived, and the door opened. Paul ushered in the two of them, followed them in like a nurse shepherding two small charges and pushed the button to close the door. They descended to the garage in the basement and exited into the musty, stuffy air, smelling of oil, tires and garbage.

"Your vehicle, Misha?" asked Paul, and Dan led them to the white Lincoln Town Car that he had purchased only a few weeks ago with some of the millions of dollars that Emily had liberated from Vincent Carson. He unlocked the doors and waited for the other two to climb in. He sat behind the wheel, Emily took the rear and Paul the front passenger seat. Until Harrington spoke, Dan sat motionless in the grey leather luxury, not even putting the key in the ignition.

"We will drive to the colonel's office," said Harrington. "And enter the building from the rear where there is a private parking spot."

Obediently, Dan started the Lincoln, reversed out of the parking spot and headed out to the gate. The electric device on his sun visor opened the automatic door and they emerged into the bright sun. Dan headed east to Lake Shore Drive, joined the heavy traffic heading past the beaches and parks and turned off on Michigan Avenue. The drive took place in perfect silence, no tourist comments on the beauty of Lake Michigan or the city's skyline in front of them. When he could, Dan looked sideways at Paul who seemed relaxed in his leather seat, like an elderly uncle being shown the sights of Chicago by his favourite relatives.

The Magnificent Mile was crowded as always by the shoppers, the sightseers, and the curious. Dan took a long time crawling south, occasionally held up by the horse-drawn tourist carriages, and the cars trying to turn right through a mob of pedestrians crossing the road. They crossed the Michigan Avenue bridge at Wacker Drive, and Paul finally spoke again.

"Turn right here," he said as they passed the elderly building that housed the colonel's office. Dan followed his instructions, turned right once again, and stopped behind the building, the Lincoln's nose against the dirty red brick wall. The last time Dan had seen the spot was eight months ago when they had left the office to drive to O'Hare and begin the deconditioning of his mind. Old garbage cans stood along the wall, and a few newspapers skittered around in small circles as the breeze caught them. There was nobody else around.

At a gesture from Paul, they climbed out of the car, and waited by the dirty, lime-green door through which they had once exited to drive to the airport. Paul took a white plastic card from his pocket and inserted it in a slot. The door buzzed softly and clicked open. Inside, the stairwell was equally dirty, smelling of old cabbages and dust. They climbed the five floors, and by the time they had reached the top, Paul was breathing heavily and sweating. Dan had no sympathy for him at all. Outside the door to the main floor, Harrington used the plastic card again with similar results, and they found themselves in the office where Dan and Emily had met with the colonel some eight months ago.

"In the conference room, Misha, Galina," said Paul, and they obeyed. He followed them in, waved them to chairs and sat down at the same round table they had used before for the negotiations with Colonel Markbrite. *How odd,* thought Dan. *I'm in exactly the same state of helplessness as when I did this before.* Only now, there seemed no way out of the situation. The helper had turned on them and become the jailer.

A minute later, the colonel walked in. He was dressed the same way as when Dan had first met him. Sharply creased trousers, military cut shirt with long sleeves. The same after-shave smell drifted in Dan's direction. This time, however, he didn't wear a tie. It was his concession to the lovely summer Sunday afternoon, perhaps.

"Ah Dan!" he said. "And Emily! How lovely to see you both!" He smiled cheerfully, but his eyes were steel cold. "They are both under control, Doctor?" he asked, his eyes not leaving Dan. Perhaps he remembered the way Dan had damaged a number of his Marines, and was not yet confident that the new controls were functional.

"Firmly, Colonel," replied Harrington, the satisfaction evident in his voice. "They cannot move without permission."

The colonel didn't reply, but took a seat at the table. "I truly regret having to take control over you again," he said with no evident sincerity. "It was too good an opportunity to miss," he continued, almost apologetically. "Here we were, years of effort gone down the drain, our techniques working only partially, and along comes a perfectly conditioned specimen like you, Dan."

Dan looked silently at him. He could sense Emily, still motionless and silent by his side, and feel the rage blasting from her. Markbrite gave her an uncertain glance, evidently also sensing the fury.

"You had all the pathways built into your mind," said Harrington, taking over the discussion. "All the mechanisms were in place. All I had to do was break down the original trigger phrases and replace them with our own. Not that it was such a simple task, as well you know," he added with a self-deprecating smile. "And I did manage to fill in some of the loopholes that your man in Murmansk had overlooked."

Harrington was not in Dan's direct line of vision, so Dan could only try and radiate his contempt and rage at him. The man he had come to love like the dream of his English father who had never existed had betrayed them both. There would be more killing before this was over, Dan promised himself.

The colonel sat back in his chair. "We have only one task for you," he said. "When it's over, you can go your own ways again."

Yeah, right, Colonel, thought Dan. *Like we did when we left Long Island, our contracted agreements fulfilled. We will talk further on this matter, Colonel Markbrite, US Marine Corps on attachment to the CIA.* Dan wondered how far this went. Was it an official CIA gambit, or were these two playing some power game of their own? He tended to believe that Harrington had been telling the truth when he said it was only between the colonel and himself.

"We want you to kill somebody," said Markbrite.

Dan felt ice in his body. He knew that he would do whatever he was commanded. The sensation of control was even tighter than that experienced under Vincent Carson, and he was completely without a choice.

"The country is at risk," said Markbrite. "The end of the recent wars in the Middle East has given the liberals too much freedom to cut back our armed forces. We cannot let this lunacy continue. Soon we will be unable to meet any foreign threat."

Dan looked at him, unable to speak. He sensed what Markbrite was leading toward.

"So we are going to get you to assassinate the Vice-President," continued the colonel. "He's too dangerous to America anyway, with his crazy progressive taxation views, so getting rid of him will serve two purposes."

"And if you kill the Vice-President, and we let it out that the killer was a Russian agent, then the anti-peace backlash will translate into guaranteed defence spending increases," said Harrington.

Dan was still unable to speak, but he knew he was dead. The plan was excellent. Of course he would only do one job. Markbrite would place him at the location with a pistol, ensure he had access to the Vice-President, and then when he had done his job, the colonel would make sure he would also die under a hail of bullets. Even if Dan failed, the plan would work. Eventually, Markbrite would reveal Dan's Russian history, and that would be enough to guarantee increased tensions and defence spending. The absence of a communist threat was playing hell with the psyches of today's old Cold War Warriors. Dan was a perfect tool.

"Do you have any questions before I brief you, Dan?" asked Markbrite. He looked calm, almost disinterested, as if Dan was about to be sent on some minor military exercise.

"Just one, Colonel," said Dan without any tone to his voice. "If I'm such an asset, why did you let me go in and face Carson? I could have been damaged."

The colonel smiled without amusement. "You didn't do your job there, Dan," he said. "We knew from our Murmansk connection that your unarmed combat training was top class. I wanted you to kill them both. Having to send General Morayev back to Russia was risky. He might have known about Project Parthenon, and I didn't want the Russians to know we've kept this up. So as part of your reconditioning during your stay on Long Island, we implanted in you the wish to confront Carson, and you were given instructions to kill both the general and his assistant when you went to see them."

His stare turned to Paul Harrington, who looked uncomfortable, then back to Dan. "Somehow, you managed to stop yourself, Misha," he continued. "I do hope that Harrington's work was not defective."

Dan remembered how he had so nearly killed Carson, but pulled back at the last second. So that was the reason for the desire to visit Carson, and the sudden flood of killing rage! Harrington's implanted instructions!

"However," continued the colonel. "We took care of the matter ourselves. After we had drained Morayev dry, we disposed of him."

Dan sensed the shock flow through Emily in the seat next to him. He looked at Harrington. "So all that about seeing the general off to Moscow was garbage, was it

Paul?" he said. "You and Markbrite had already killed him?"

Harrington said nothing, and looked impassively at his hands.

The colonel looked at his watch. "Any more questions?"

"I have a few," said Emily. Her voice was dry, unused for the last hour.

The colonel turned to her in surprise. "Harrington," he said, anxiety showing on his face. "I thought you said they'd not be able to speak without permission? What else is suspect in your work?"

Harrington's voice was calm as he answered. "She didn't have the established mental pathways the way Vorosov did," he said. "It made it a tougher task to condition her. Obviously we missed something."

The colonel glared at him for a second or two, then turned back to Emily. "Yes, Emily," he said with a pleasant smile. "What can we tell you?"

"Are we here alone?" she asked.

"Naturally," replied the colonel. "We cannot have anyone else involved."

"And does anyone else know the codes you used to control us?"

The colonel shook his head, a slightly puzzled expression on his face. "No," he said. "We could not risk the controls being available to others."

"What about Anton Voltzec?" persisted Emily.

"Not even Anton," replied Markbrite. "He gave us the techniques, but is not involved in the project."

"So nobody else knows about this at all?" she continued, her voice easing a little and confidence returning. "This is strictly a Markbrite-Harrington game, is it?"

"Yes, it is," replied the colonel, and Dan saw the sudden alarm in his face. Markbrite started to rise to his feet, but he was too late. A lifetime too late.

Emily had stood up a fraction before him, and simply leaped across the table. She landed on her feet next to Markbrite and Dan saw him adopt a defensive posture, but it had no chance. Her left foot flew up in an arc and caught him squarely in the jaw. He started to collapse, but she hadn't finished.

One straight-fingered jab caught him in the point where his rib cage joined, and Dan heard bones crack. The side of her hand flashed at his neck and struck it solidly and more bones broke. The colonel was probably dead before he reached the floor.

She stood rigid for a second or two then relaxed, a long sigh slowly escaping from her lungs. She looked at Dan, and smiled. *I was never that good,* said Dan to himself in complete confusion. *Even after several years of training in Murmansk, learning the best that Sergeant Kutchinski could give me, I was nowhere near that good.*

Emily turned to Paul Harrington. The psychiatrist was still sitting in his chair, not having moved a muscle in the two or three seconds that the murderous performance had taken.

"Release him, Paul," she said. Her voice was calm, unflustered. He stared at her, then at the colonel's body on the floor. A tiny twitch shook the body, then subsided. Paul looked back at her, and his breath was gasping worse than when he had reached the fifth floor of the stairwell.

"Release him, Paul," she said again.

His face was white. "Then you'll kill me!" he stuttered. Saliva was falling onto his shirt front.

"I won't hurt you, Paul, I promise," she said with a sweet smile. "But release him."

He looked once more at her, great fear in his eyes, but he must have believed her for he turned his face to Dan.

"Ulysses Code Thunder-3365," he said, the tremble in his voice distorting the words. It still worked however, and Dan felt the ropes fall away, just as when Carson had released him.

"Thank you, Paul," said Emily, and her right hand flashed out again, the edge meeting his neck like a cobra strike. Harrington collapsed back in his chair. He was dead.

"As I said, Paul," murmured Emily. "It didn't hurt."

She walked round the table to Dan, and he stood up. They wrapped their arms around each other. Dan could feel the steel-hawser tension in Emily's body, and the beginnings of violent trembling.

"How?" he said, struggling to speak, not looking at the body of Paul Harrington who had been almost his adopted father a few hours ago.

"I had defences programmed in me as well," she whispered into his shoulder. "There was always the chance that this sort of thing could happen. And it was Voltzec who did it, because he's the best in the world at these tools. He put something like a computer virus-killer into me. Ever since Paul put us under, I've been feeling the program working, testing out the controls, blocking them off, cancelling them." Her voice was beginning to shake, and Dan could sense the tears close by.

"Can we get away with this?" he asked, looking at the scene. The colonel's body was half hidden by the table, but Paul was slumped in his chair right in front of him, his eyes still open with the shock.

"Yes, absolutely," she said. "Nobody else is involved. I'll explain in the car. Let's get going."

"We're out of here," he said, and released her. They walked out of the office and descended the smelly stairs.

At the bottom, Dan cautiously opened the door, saw nobody outside, and they walked into the sunshine again. He hurriedly unlocked the car, Emily took the passenger side and they drove cautiously into the crowds on Michigan Avenue.

As they pulled onto Lake Shore drive, Dan began to breathe more easily.

"Emily?" he said, as the Lincoln eased itself gently into top gear.

"Yes, Misha?" She turned her head and smiled at him. She had been rubbing the edge of her right hand, and Dan could see the slight bruising starting to show.

"Don't ever let me get on the wrong side of you," he said. "That was frightening."

She nodded, a sad look on her face. "You could never cause that reaction in me," she said, and touched his right cheek. "I pray we never need it again."

They drove on, the Lincoln flowing in elegant silence, turned off the Drive at Belmont and headed west for a couple of blocks. Traffic was heavy on this lovely Sunday.

"I still have contacts," she said as the car stopped at the traffic lights. "I found out that Markbrite had gone rogue."

"Rogue?" Dan turned to look at her.

She nodded. "The whole Parthenon thing was not supposed to be what Markbrite had made it. He had taken CIA slush funds and set it up himself, ostensibly to develop mental blocks to enemy interrogation. But he disobeyed orders by continuing to work on creating agents like you. The last venture with us was totally unsanctioned, and the colonel and Harrington had gone out on their own. So the CIA was trying to stop him."

"The way you did just now?"

"They had assigned several groups to find him and terminate him," she said. "Each group will think one of the others did it, and nobody will want to ask questions."

Dan eased the car forward as the lights changed. "But what about Voltzec?" he asked.

"He can't know about us, either," she replied. "Remember, he put the defences in me. If he'd been involved and knew I was being worked on by Harrington, he'd have known it wouldn't work with me. So he can't be part of this exercise, and he doesn't know what the trigger words will be."

"So we're safe," he said, praying that she was correct.

"Not entirely," she said, her voice calm. "We'll always have to worry that somebody will call us with a new trigger."

"I know," Dan replied, and tried to suppress the fear.

www.ingramcontent.com/pod-product-compliance
Lightning Source LLC
LaVergne TN
LVHW020658110826
845149LV00012B/2039

* 9 7 8 0 9 9 2 3 4 2 2 0 3 *